W9-AOM-614

Also by Harold Courlander

NOVELS

The Master of the Forge
The Mesa of Flowers
The Bordeaux Narrative
The Caballero
The Big Old World of Richard Creeks

NONFICTION

The Drum and the Hoe: Life and Lore of the Haitian People
Negro Folk Music, U.S.A.
Haiti Singing
The Fourth World of the Hopis
Tales of Yoruba Gods and Heroes
The Heart of the Ngoni
A Treasury of African Folklore
A Treasury of Afro-American Folklore
Big Falling Snow
Hopi Voices

FOLKTALES AND ORAL LITERATURE

People of the Short Blue Corn: Tales and Legends of the Hopi Indians
The Crest and the Hide and Other African Stories of Heroes, Chiefs, Bards, Hunters, Sorcerers and Common People
Kantchil's Lime Pit
The Hat-Shaking Dance and Other Ashanti Tales from Ghana
Terrapin's Pot of Sense
The King's Drum and Other African Stories
The Tiger's Whisker and Other Tales from Asia and the Pacific
The Cow-Tail Switch and Other West African Stories *(with George Herzog)*
The Piece of Fire and Other Haitian Tales
The Fire on the Mountain and Other Ethiopian Stories *(with Wolf Leslau)*
Uncle Bouqui of Haiti
Olode the Hunter and Other Tales from Nigeria

THE AFRICAN

HAROLD COURLANDER

HENRY HOLT AND COMPANY
New York

In Memory of
Maurice Serle Kaplan
1908–1951

Henry Holt and Company, Inc.
Publishers since 1866
115 West 18th Street
New York, New York 10011

Published in Canada by Fitzhenry & Whiteside Ltd.,
91 Granton Drive, Richmond Hill, Ontario L4B 2N5.

Library of Congress Cataloging-in-Publication Data
Courlander, Harold.
The African/Harold Courlander.
p. cm.
1. Slaves—United States—Fiction. 2. Afro-American men—Fiction.
PS3505.0885A69 1993
813'.52—dc20 93-13923
CIP

ISBN 0-8050-3000-X (An Owl Book: pbk.)

Henry Holt books are available for special promotions and
premiums. For details contact: Director, Special Markets.

First published in hardcover
by Crown Publishers, Inc., in 1967.

First Owl Book Edition—1993

Printed in the United States of America
All first editions are printed on acid-free paper. ∞

10 9 8 7 6 5 4 3 2 1
(pbk.)

Preface to the New Edition

Try to recall one of those sad mid-nineteenth-century photographs of a Negro family huddled in front of a slave cabin, looking unsmilingly at the glass-plate camera documenting the scene for posterity. It was really not so long ago. My father was born in 1866, only a year after the Civil War, which produced the Emancipation Proclamation. His parents lived when those photographs were taken. Some of us during our lifetime may have seen obituaries or feature articles about recently deceased or still living persons born into slavery. Even in the 1940s, Blacks in the Georgia coastal islands remembered and spoke of the first generation Africans who had lived among them. One man from the Western Sudan region who could speak and write in Arabic left behind an Islamic religious document that he had written down from memory. While engaged in research in Cuba in 1941, I myself met an aged Kimbisa man who had made the Atlantic slave crossing when he was young, and he could still speak fluently in his native Bantu language.

I have often pondered the trauma these unwilling transatlantic voyagers suffered in being completely cut off from their own cultures. Endless forced labor without esteem from anyone, with no prospect of release, and with frequent harsh treatment, was enough to bear. But being totally removed from the values, traditions, and support systems of their homelands and villages placed additional burdens on them. In their villages they had teachings to serve them in their everyday lives and wise men to guide them in solving crucial problems; age and social groupings to integrate them into community life and define their roles in their tribes, villages, and families; and religious beliefs to give them a sense of relationship to the world around them and to the unseen but living forces of the universe.

For all this they were offered, in exchange, a world that was totally foreign, where their deeply absorbed values could do little for them at all. In fact, their values were quite irrelevant and generally worthless in their new surroundings. Many of the new arrivals contrived to adapt as a means of survival, but there were also those who clung desperately to the ways and teachings of their homelands. In times of crisis—and slavery itself was of course a prolonged crisis—they must have reached back often to the learned but slowly dimming meanings of earlier days for help. This is one of the central elements in the story of Hwesuhunu, the Fon boy who is the protagonist of this narrative.

The African was written in the mid-sixties, by which time I had been deeply immersed in the study of African, Caribbean, and African-American cultures. It was not "researched" in the usual sense—everything was "up there" waiting for me to use it. When the idea came to me that there should be a story such as this one, I reflected quite a while on what form it should take. I had never read a novel about enslaved Africans that encompassed what I had to say, and therefore had no models. But one morning I just sat down at my typewriter and began. Another writer will understand me if I say the narrative seemed to write itself, and I simply went along with it as a companion wherever it led. By the time the book was finished I had the feeling that Hwesuhunu (later called Wes) was a real person who had shared himself and his life with me.

Harold Courlander, 1993

SOME WORDS, AFRICAN AND OTHER, APPEARING IN THIS TALE

Abomey, capital of the old Kingdom of Dahomey.

Adanzan, king of Dahomey at the end of the eighteenth and beginning of the nineteenth centuries.

coffle, a slave caravan.

dokpwe, a Dahomean communal work society.

dokpwegan, chief of the dokpwe.

Fa, a system of divining among Dahomeans, and the name of a cult built around this concept. It is said among Dahomeans that the fortunes of an individual conform to the writings of Mawu, one of the original deities. Thus, Fa is equivalent to fate.

Fon, a Dahomean or Dahomeans; language of the people of old Dahomey.

Legba, a Dahomean deity, messenger between humans and gods, considered to be the spirit of whim, disorder and accident.

Lisa, one of the original Dahomean deities, believed by some to be an aspect of Mawu.

Mawu, one of the original Dahomean deities.

Muskogee, one of the Creek tribes of southeastern United States.

Nago, sometimes Anago, a subgroup of the Yoruba people and near neighbors of the Fon people.

Ogoun, Dahomean deity of iron, the forge and warriors.

orisha, term used among the Nago people to designate the spirits or gods. Same as vodoun among the Fon.

Shango, a Dahomean deity identified with fire and lightning.

Tsoyaha, an Indian tribe of southeastern United States, also known as Yuchi.

vodoun, a term used among the Fon people to designate the deities.

THE
◎◎◎ AFRICAN

◎◎◎ PART 1

The Voyage

HWESUHUNU HEARD a distant cock crowing before the eye of day opened. He lay looking at the straw roof above his head, still partly in the dream he was leaving behind. A cock in the village answered the distant challenge. It was the same as always. The distant cock said, "The eye of day is opening," and a cock in the village replied, "It is opening, it is opening."

Hwesuhunu thought: "Today my brothers and I will make arrows, and I will teach them how to stalk antelope." His mind drifted, he was almost back in the dream. He was riding a horse through the tall grass. The horse's face reminded him a little of Senu, the old priest who tended the Legba shrine at the gate of the village. They were talking together about the rain that had not come, and the horse priest pointed to a cloud of smoke on the horizon, where the brush was on fire. Somehow they were then standing at the river's edge throwing water on the burning trees, and the horse had changed into a Hausa trader who was saying, "This is not the way it is done in my country." Then the village cock crowed out again, "It is opening, it is opening," and Hwesuhunu's dream drained off into the night where it lived.

He was truly awake now, and he sat up on his mat trying to think why this day had a special character. He saw his brothers lying motionless, still entangled in the night world he had just left. From the next room he heard his father's voice. He smelled smoke from his mother's fire. And as the parts of the day world came together for him, Hwesuhunu sprang to his feet. Now he remembered. This was the morning he was to go to the fields and work with his father's dokpwe. Today he would be a man doing a man's work. He looked again at his four brothers still asleep on their mats as he tied his cloth through his legs. He was aware that there was more distance between his brothers and himself than there had been yesterday. They were still boys, while he could not appear in public without his loins covered. "Heee!" he called out. "It is time! Get up! Eat! The dokpwe is clearing the fields this morning." The brothers rolled over, rubbed their eyes. "Heee! Let us wash, let us eat. It is time."

They went out of the house, they put water on their faces. They sat on the ground before the house, and their mother brought food in a calabash. They ate. Their father, Sosu, came out with his bush knife and watched them. To Hwesuhunu he said: "Is this the man who will cut in the forest without a bush knife?" Hwesuhunu arose and ran back to the boys' room. He was ashamed to have forgotten. Next to his sleeping mat, where he had carefully placed it, was the new bush knife his father had given him. He picked it up and carried it loosely, casually, in his hand, just as the drum signal came riding in on the sweet smelling morning air. It said, "Dok-pwe! Dok-pwe! Dok-pwe!" Then it said, "We are meeting! We are meeting! We are meeting!" Then: "Praise the king who deserves praise! But plant corn with your dokpwe!"

Sosu, his father, stood up, saying, "Corn does not come from the sky. Let us go." Hwesuhunu fell in step behind him. And behind Hwesuhunu, his four young brothers carrying calabashes full of water. As they went down the trail that descended from the high ground, Hwesuhunu watched his father's long, easy stride, and he stretched his own legs so that he stepped wherever his father left a footprint. As the trail went into a palm grove, the sound of the drum became faint. When they emerged it sounded loud and near. Another trail angled out of the tall grass and met with Sosu's trail. There, his bush knife in hand, Agosa, the dokpwegan, chief of the dokpwe, was waiting. They greeted each other, then went on together.

As the trail lifted over a rise in the ground, there suddenly before them were the other workers. Badja the drummer stood at the foot of the trail, beating out "Dokpwe! Dokpwe!" Some were sitting on their heels talking. A few were honing their knives with stones. Four men were laughing at the story of a gay exploit. The air was full of sound—of metal, of voices, and drumbeats. Hwesuhunu was glad. He stood with his weight on one leg, casually, ignoring his brothers. He picked up a stone and sharpened his new blade which needed no sharpening. Dokpwegan Agosa clapped his hands three times, and the drum echoed the beats. He held up his fly switch, saying, "Our shadows are long, our work is great; let us begin; they who make the gunpowder win the battles."

The men went straggling toward a field overgrown with trees and brush. There they formed two groups, one on the east, one on the west. Agosa flourished his fly switch. The men began to sing as they slashed at the brush with their knives. One group sang: "If you want a large fish, give something to the stream." And the other: "Their legs go fast, but their feet are on slippery clay." Badja beat out the work signals, and the knives rose and fell to the drum's compelling voice. The dokpwegan sat on a fallen tree to judge the competition. As the brush fell it was gathered and placed on a fire. To the sound of cutting, shouting, laughing and drumming there were added the smell of heavy smoke, the rising of sparks and the gentle falling of dead ashes. Hwesuhunu worked with sweat on his body and sweetness in his veins. Today, at last, he was truly a man.

From time to time Sosu glanced covertly at Hwesuhunu, seeing a man clothed in the slight body of a boy. Hwesuhunu's dark skin glistened and his keen-edged knife glinted in the sun. At first his strokes were too rapid. When he became aware of it he slowed his pace, for it was a discourtesy to his fellow workers to exceed them. Also he understood that the woodcutting would go on and on; when one goes on a long journey he does not run as though fleeing from a leopard. Once or twice the eyes of the dokpwegan rested briefly on Hwesuhunu. He thought: "The boy is small, his arms are thin. But he bends his back, there is spirit in his bush knife. He will grow, and his body will be nourished by work for the village. Today the dokpwe is richer by one soul. As old men fail and fall away, new ones come to take their places. The dokpwe lives forever."

As for Sosu, when he glanced at his son, observing without seeming to, he saw himself passing from boyhood into manhood. Even now Hwesuhunu resembled Sosu. Men had commented on it. There was an intentness about his eyes, a looking at things that could not be touched by the hand. "In time," Sosu thought, "he will have a beard like mine. Already one can see the fine hair on his face when the light falls on it. But he does not laugh as readily as other boys. He meditates long on things. He is serious. He wishes to take the clothes off the words he hears. Perhaps there is a sorrow in him. Perhaps he communes with the Old Ones."

It was late, and the eye of day was closing. In the village the dokpwe was finishing the evening meal provided by the family whose field had been cleared of brush. Sosu arose to take care of things that had to be done at the Sagbata shrine, of which he was a priest. Hwesuhunu went with him. He said, "Is not Sagbata the greatest of the vodouns? I thought so. But my friend says it is Hevioso that is the most powerful."

His father answered, "No one can say who is the greatest. Each vodoun has his own powers. As they say, Mawu gives comfort at night, Lisa rules the day. As it is with men, no single vodoun is supreme over the others. Legba, the seventh child of Mawu and Lisa, was the least of them all. There was no domain left to place in his charge, so he was made the messenger. It is he who carries words between men and vodouns, as though he were the servant of a chief. But Legba is yet the most powerful of all, for it is said: 'Words are sharper than the point of a spear.' Even so, Legba is not equal to Fa, our destiny. Legba is unpredictable. His character is compounded of whim. Like rain, he comes or goes when he pleases. He carries a message or forgets it. If a traveler asks him the direction to Abomey, he may point to Cotonou. He may despise a girl and make love to her grandmother. He deceives, he jokes, he tricks—whatever his mood advises him. He is powerful, but he is not dependable. His substance is the substance of accident. Thus we invoke Legba for good fortune. We placate his anger, so that he will not make mischief. But Fa, our destiny, we do not placate. Fa is immutable. Legba is not always ready to listen; thus, for us, he is not so great as Fa. As it is said: 'The small man who is with the dokpwe at hoeing time, he is strong for us; the large man who is not there, for us he is weak.' "

They arrived at the shrine. Sosu entered, taking up his sacred rattle and his bell from the clay altar. He spoke in the tongue of the vodouns, and asked Sagbata's favor for the shrine and those who attended it. He poured a libation of water from a gourd, and made a small design in flour on the hard packed floor. When he was finished he came out, and with Hwesuhunu he returned to the village. Agosa, the chief of the dokpwe, was telling stories. The men of the dokpwe sat in a circle around him. The women and children sat behind. Agosa's reddish face shone in the firelight. As Hwesuhunu and his father took their places, Agosa turned suddenly and pointed his fly switch at Hwesuhunu. "Heee! Here is our newest member. Let him answer the question. Is he not called 'Thing-of-the-Sea?' The sea is greatly wise, so let Hwesuhunu give the answer. If one is in trouble, does he go for help to his father-in-law, to his diviner, or to his friend? This is the question. Let us hear what you say."

Hwesuhunu replied, "To his father-in-law."

From the back of the crowd came the voice of one of his brothers: "He has no father-in-law. He is only a little boy."

Laughter mounted the night air. Hwesuhunu shrank back, thinking, "I will catch him and put hot peppers in his mouth!"

Agosa spun around on his heel and pointed his fly switch at a man whose laughter was loud. "You, brother of the dokpwe, Bosu, what do you say? If you are in trouble do you go to your father-in-law, or to the diviner, or your friend?"

Bosu answered, "I go to the diviner. He reads the palm seeds for me. Thus I know what to do."

Agosa brought his hands together sharply. "This thing we are talking about, we must understand its meaning. So listen to the story of the hunter. Three men needed his labor. His father-in-law said, 'I need you to work in my field tomorrow.' His diviner said to him, 'You, I need your help in my field tomorrow.' And his friend said, 'You, my friend, my field needs hoeing; come and help me tomorrow.' The hunter went away. He said to himself: 'How can I work in three fields at one time? I must decide.' He took his gun. He went hunting. He saw an antelope in the tall grass. He fired his gun—*ka!* The antelope fell. The hunter did not go to it. He left it there.

"He went to his father-in-law. He said, 'I went hunting. Something moved in the bush. I fired—*ka!* I killed it. It was a man. What shall I do?' His father-in-law said, 'You killed a man in the field? The king will hear of it. There will be great trouble.' The hunter said, 'Father-in-law, hide me. I am afraid of the king's soldiers.' The father-in-law said, 'Go away. You will bring trouble on me. I want to hear no more of this affair.' The hunter went away. He went to his diviner. He told the diviner he had killed a man in the bush. 'Help me. Read my fate in the palm seeds. Tell me what to do.' The diviner said, 'Is this affair mine? When you come to hear of your Fa, you bring me a goat. I cast the seeds. I read your fate. But this killing of a man has nothing to do with me. The king's soldiers will come. Do not bring trouble on me. Go away.' The hunter went then to his friend. He said, 'I am in great difficulty. I went hunting. By accident I shot a man. He lies out there dead in the bush. I need help.' The friend said, 'Let us go and bury him.' The friend took his hoe and they went to the edge of the bush. He dug a grave. When he had finished, he said, 'Let us bring the dead man here.' The hunter said, 'No, I don't want to go after the man I killed.'

"The friend went alone. He looked. There was no dead man there. It was a dead antelope. He brought it back, saying, 'You killed no man. You killed an antelope. Why did you send me?' The hunter said, 'Three men asked me to work in their fields on the same day. I can work in only one. My father-in-law asked, my diviner asked, my friend asked. I wanted to know to which of the three men I should give my labor. The diviner and my father-in-law told me to go away; they said my trouble would bring trouble on them. My friend, he did not ask this and that. He merely took his hoe and went out to the bush. I shall work with him.' Thus it is," Agosa said, "that when one is in trouble he goes first of all to his friend for help."

Once again it was morning, and Hwesuhunu heard the cocks crowing. He arose and adjusted his loincloth. His brothers slept on. He called to them, "Heee! Our shadows are long, our work is great; let us begin." His brothers rolled over and rubbed their eyes.

Still lying on his back, one of them said, "Listen to Hwesuhunu! He is only twelve years old, but already he thinks he is the chief of the dokpwe!"

Another said, "Look at the way he wraps his cloth, as though he had something worth covering!"

Hwesuhunu held his dignity. "You too will be members of the dokpwe. Do not make fun of it."

One of them said, "You promised to make arrows with us and take us hunting."

"Yes, we shall do that when the fields are cleared," Hwesuhunu said. "Bring your spears with you, and when you do not have to carry water you can go after hares."

He took his bush knife and went out. He sat with his father and ate. When they heard the dokpwe drum in the distance they departed, Sosu in front, then Hwesuhunu, then his four small brothers with calabashes full of water on their heads; sometimes the water sloshed out of the calabashes and ran down their faces. They went out to the field where the brush was to be cleared. It was the field of Senu, the priest of the Legba shrine at the village gate. When Hwesuhunu saw him, he remembered his dream of the horse with the face that resembled old Senu's. He pondered on its meaning. The horse . . . Senu, the caretaker of the Legba image . . . Legba, the messenger. Perhaps it was a message from the vodouns. He remembered the brush fire. Danger, perhaps. He would ask Sosu about all this.

Hwesuhunu's part of the dokpwe took the eastern end of the field. With the first strokes of their knives they began singing: "Work, work, life is work; but working together is like a feast." From the other end of the field came another song: "Many hands move, one stomach is filled; the dokpwe is like one person." The brush was piled on the fires. Smoke hung over the field. Hwesuhunu's brothers sat in the shade at the edge of the field. When someone called for water, they brought it, and poured from a calabash into a small gourd.

Hwesuhunu was thirsty, but he was embarrassed to call his brothers. He was turning the problem over in his mind when a faint call, sharp and commanding, pierced through the sounds of woodcutting. The moving knives became motionless; soft laughing became brittle and broke in the middle; and all heads turned toward the village, tense, striving to hear. The harsh cry of a crow sounded overhead. The noise of crickets swelled in the silence. The men waited. And then the alarm came again, a woman's sustained high-pitched trill. The men were suddenly running up the trail that led to the village. A hoarse throat that only a moment before had been full of laughing barked out sharply, "Get your weapons!"

But they never reached the village. Where the trail passed through a small stream at the edge of a cluster of banana trees, the troops of King Adanzan awaited them with pointed guns and spears. Other warriors swarmed out of the tall grass behind them. Shots were fired. Agosa raised his fly switch in the air, then fell pierced with a spear. Another man ran toward the banana grove pursued by soldiers. He was caught, slashed, beaten and dragged back. The affair was ended. The men of the dokpwe were crowded tightly within a ring of shouting soldiers and feinting weapons. Hwesuhunu, pressed between larger bodies, could see nothing. He could hear this man and that saying, "What have we done? We are Adanzan's children." Or again, "Are we malefactors? Have we stolen? Have we conspired? Why are we treated in this fashion?"

One by one, the men were brought out of the ring. One by one, wooden collars were put around their necks and fastened with iron pins. Each collar was linked to the next by a chain. And soon the slave convoy was moving on the road to Abomey. Hwesuhunu's collar bore on him heavily. It was made for a man, and it slipped loosely back and forth on his thin neck. When one chain tugged a little, the collar slipped backward; when the other tugged, it slipped forward. It began to eat at the skin over his collarbone.

The coffle was kept moving till nightfall. They camped at the edge of a river, where the captives had water and received a few grains of rice. They slept with the collars still on their necks. Before sunrise they were moving again. On the third day they reached King Adanzan's slave stockade on the edge of the city of Abomey. Their collars were removed, and they were herded roughly through the gate. Hwesuhunu threw himself on the ground and pressed his face to the hard-packed earth, taking no notice of the blood that oozed from his flayed shoulders. He closed his eyes with the certainty that this horror would fade away, and that he would find himself once more in his father's house and smell the smoke of his mother's fire. But the voices of aggrieved men came to his ears, some angry, some resigned, and all near the edge of exhaustion. And at last, because he had had so little experience at being a man, tears began to flow and fall on the hard earth which he hugged in his misery.

Even when his heart had no more tears to spend, Hwesuhunu lay without moving. For him it was neither night nor day. Only a few days before, he had been given all the world had to give him—manhood. And now he was even less than a child. He felt a hand on the back of his head. There was only one hand like it in all Dahomey. He knew before opening his eyes that his father was there, sitting on his heels beside him. Hwesuhunu brushed the dust and wetness from his face.

"I had a dream," he said. "There was a fire burning in the brush, and we couldn't put it out. I meant to tell you."

"The fault is not in us," Sosu said. "It is a saying that 'When the mighty are hungry, they eat.' " He wiped the drying blood from Hwesuhunu's shoulders.

"It is also said," Hwesuhunu answered, "that no creature eats its own kind. We are not Sobo people. We are not

Anago. We are not Mahi. We are Fon. We are of the same blood as Adanzan. You yourself have said it."

Sosu turned his head away. "In time, Adanzan will find his destiny, as we shall find ours also. The mysteries of Fa unfold one by one, and it is only at the other end of life that we know truly what was marked out for us."

The men of the dokpwe came and found Sosu. "What is the news of the village?" they asked. "What became of the women and children?" Sosu did not know.

Hwesuhunu said, "My four brothers, they hid in the bush. I saw with my eyes."

The men went elsewhere to ask their questions. Little by little it came to be known that most of those who had been in the village had escaped into the fields, but some women had been taken.

The days came and the nights came. Each day more captives were thrust through the gate, until the sweat and stench of the stockade rose up and hung like a cloud over the city of Abomey. The stockade itself, one could learn to endure it. By the time a week had passed, Hwesuhunu had explored along the great fence and found cracks through which he could see something of the outside world. On one side he could see men hoeing King Adanzan's fields. He could see women planting. The stockade lay between the fields and the city, and Hwesuhunu noticed that in going to Abomey from the fields the workers took a long curving trail that skirted the slave camp. Even where the trail came closest to the stockade, no one looked directly at it; they averted their eyes, as though the slave pens were not really there. On the other side of the enclosure Hwesuhunu located a crack which revealed the city of Abomey itself, and distantly he could hear the voices of vendors in the great marketplace. On a third side, near the gate, he could see the encampment of Adanzan's soldiers. Among them was a boy no older than Hwesuhunu. He tried to speak with him. The boy sauntered to the wall, and through the crack Hwesuhunu asked, "Are you one who lives in Abomey?"

The boy answered, "Yes, I am from Abomey. You, where are you from?"

"My village is Yabo," Hwesuhunu said. "What are they going to do with us?"

The boy replied, "All these people, the King is sending them to Cotonou."

"Where is Cotonou?" Hwesuhunu asked.

"I have never been there," the boy said. "It is on the edge of the sea where the great ships come in."

Their conversation ended then, because one of the soldiers from the encampment came and slapped the boy's ears, making him run.

One night a commotion broke out on the far side of the compound. There was angry shouting, followed by gunfire. The word was passed rapidly from mouth to mouth in the darkness: Two Mahi men had tried to tunnel their way under the pilings to freedom. They were caught as they came out of the hole; they were killed by musket balls and their bodies mutilated by spears, and afterward their corpses were stuffed back into the compound through the hole, and the hole was filled with rocks. Other Mahi prisoners dug graves for them near the wall and buried them. They sat all night singing a wake.

The next night a new song was born among the Fon captives. It began quietly in the mouth of a single singer. Someone found sticks and beat out drum rhythms on a dead tree limb. More voices joined the singing. The men began to dance, stamp, and clap their hands in the darkness. The din became great. And for the first time within the compound a torch was mysteriously lighted. No one could say where the fire had come from. But the torch burned, and a dancing crowd pressed around it. The song, having been created, was now the property of all:

The frog fills himself with air,
And thinks he is a water buffalo.
Yet he does not eat his friends.
A personage made great by Fa
Has become bloated with power
And destroys those who feed him.
The cottonwood rises above the forest,
It says it sees to the end of the world,
But in the ground its roots are rotten.

As the commotion grew, torches appeared at the top of the stockade walls. Muskets were fired into the air, but the dancing and singing went on. The Mahi people joined; the Anago joined; the Sobo joined; the Hausa joined. When the drummers tired, other drummers took their place. It was as though frenzy and madness had entered through the gate. Some men were mounted by their vodouns. They staggered and fell in jerking spasms, and were carried off and left lying by the walls. The compound was an agony of sound and motion. Six hundred men melted together in a wild departure from the world of King Adanzan and his soldiers. When at last morning came, the captives were exhausted and spent, and the earthen floor of the slave stockade was covered with them.

It was not quite the end. Adanzan's nephew, chief of the slaving operations, appeared at the wall. He was excited. He ordered the soldiers to bring out the man who had given birth to the song that had desecrated the house of Adanzan. They became agitated in the manner of their chief. They entered the gate, jabbing with their spears and firing their muskets. And when at last they went out, they dragged a man with them. They held him by the feet, and his body left a trail in the dust. The gate slammed closed. A little later a pole was raised over the eastern wall of the stockade. Impaled on its sharpened top was the head of Senu, the aged priest of the Legba shrine. It remained there until the day the huge slave consignment began its march to the sea.

The men were brought out a few at a time and wooden yokes placed around their necks. Hwesuhunu stayed close by his father's side, but as he passed through the gate he was seized and pulled one way, while his father was pulled another. They were separated. The men sat on the ground in the full glare of the sun. Hwesuhunu saw the women and girls being brought from another compound a little distance away. He heard the girls crying as they received their yokes. Then began the long walk. The king's soldiers stood aside. The slave drovers took command. In the front of the long procession was a drummer. Following him, astride a white horse covered with shining and tinkling trappings, came the king's nephew, the royal slave agent. A servant walking alongside the horse held a large, red, tasseled umbrella over the rider's head. The drumming announced to the countryside: "This is the convoy of King Adanzan." The procession moved southward. There was crying and wailing among the women. The drovers rode back and forth, using rope whips to keep the captives walking at a fast pace. Ordinary travelers on the road to Cotonou scattered into the fields or hid in the brush when they heard the drum and saw the coffle coming. For it was known that captives died on the march, and that the slave drovers often took replacements wherever they could catch them. Whenever the procession passed a village, that village would be empty. Though smoke might sift through the straw roofs, and though cattle still could be seen in the fields, there were no people there.

The coffle stopped at streams so the captives could drink, but there was no food until they camped for the night. Then each person received as much rice as he could hold in one hand. The king's nephew slept in a tent. The drovers slept in turns around a fire. Those on guard patrolled with spears. The captives lay on the bare ground, their wooden yokes still in place. Some slept, some could not. Those who were awake conversed and sent messages back and forth from one end of the caravan to the other.

A question was passed from mouth to mouth, "Is it true that we are going to Badagry?" After a time an answer came back, "No, a guard was overheard to say Cotonou." Many of the questions were about people: "Has anyone seen Azizan from Hwebo?" "I, Ayo, am here; you Agbo, are you here also?" "I, Ku, from the village of Dumu, I am ill. Tell my wife, Aso, and see if she is well." Sometimes the messages were addressed to the world, and no answers were required. "Dinku from Jenna was captured, his brothers were slain. Dinku from Jenna was about to be married. They burned his house and drove off his cattle. They dispersed his village. Dinku is among you." Hwesuhunu heard, he passed the messages on. And at last there was word from his father. "I, Sosu, am here. Where is Hwesuhunu?" He replied, "Hwesuhunu is here." After that, though the yoke on his neck was a living fire and though the mosquitoes tortured his body, Hwesuhunu slept a little.

Sometimes there was singing to ease the pain of the yokes and to blot out thoughts of the final destination. The songs were bitter: "King Adanzan's warriors came, they made war on the Anago. They won the battle, they took the Anago as slaves. But you, people of Dahomey, your king has also chosen you for slaves. You also are degraded. Therefore, who is great, and who is nothing?"

Hwesuhunu's body ached with the need of more food and more sleep. He no longer saw the hills and fields. He saw only the moving bodies in front of him, and thought only of the necessity of keeping his own body in motion. Sometimes, though his legs kept moving, his mind slipped away into the soft darkness. When he awoke from these spurts of sleep he was frightened. What if he had fallen? Already two men, because they had fallen, had been taken from their yokes, speared, and thrown into the brush. The days and nights merged into an ocean of exhaustion and despair. At last, two weeks after leaving Abomey, King Adanzan's slave caravan arrived in Cotonou. The yokes were removed, and the prisoners were herded through the gate of the stockade. Thus ended the long march from Abomey.

It was dark in the belly of the ship, but Hwesuhunu had grown accustomed to the gloom. A cut-glass eye set into the deck overhead captured stray beams of daylight and sent them palely down to the upper tier, where Hwesuhunu and an unknown number of others lay, fastened to their places by leg-irons. It was possible to discern the vague forms of the men who lay on either side of him. He thought sometimes that he could even see their faces, though he knew them better by the sound of their voices. The ship was already four days at sea, as he knew from the cycle of light that came through the cut-glass eye.

Those days were not days as Hwesuhunu had once known them. There were no cocks crowing, no sound of crickets and tree toads, no smell of the morning fire, no feel of wet dew on the feet, no laughing sounds, no distant echo of bush knives or hoes, no human calls from one hill to another. There were instead an endless creaking of timbers, movements of the ship which caused saliva to flow and sickness to come, heat, and the evil smell of sweat and human offal. The time between one day and another seemed longer than Hwesuhunu had already been alive. The deck above their heads was so low that a full-grown man could not sit up. Hwesuhunu, because he was smaller, could sit if he bent his head and rested his chin on his chest. But there, just under the deck, the stench was worst. It hung in the air with no place to escape. Hwesuhunu wondered how conversation could go on when the world had stopped. In the blackness he slipped easily from awareness into dreams, and often he hovered between the one and the other. Sometimes he thought of the weeks spent in the stockade in Cotonou. There, once again, he had been able to be with his father;

hope had filled his body again; it was possible to believe all was not lost. He had asked Sosu, "What shall we do?"

"Above all, let us live," Sosu had answered. "Our destiny is to be alive. There is plenty of time to be among the dead. If we have not grown to be strong men when we go to join the family ancestors, why, we shall be boys forever, for once we arrive there all growing stops. If there is grief ahead for us, let us remember that nothing happens that is not designed by Fa. Every man is equipped to deal with his own destiny. We were made so. Otherwise, there could be no Fa. Some day we shall return when death overtakes us, for our ancestors live here. So let us not hurry to die. It is best to work with the dokpwe, but if that is not possible, we shall work elsewhere, because life is work."

Hwesuhunu asked, "Where will they take us?"

"It is said, a place across the sea. What it will be like, who can say? For until now, none have come back to tell us. But each man's destiny is different. As for you, are you not named Hwesuhunu, Thing-of-the-Sea? The sea is your Fa. Fa is greater than King Adanzan. It is greater than Dahomey. One cannot dispute with it. It is the pattern of life. The grain in the fields, the game in the bush and the rivers that flow, they are the substance of Fa."

Hwesuhunu was troubled. He said, "Are evil things also Fa? Was it fate that caused Adanzan to treat us this way? If so, can it be said that Adanzan is evil?"

"Had he chosen another way, that too would have been Fa," Sosu answered. "His Fa is in his character. It is a saying among us: 'When the king's mind is troubled, many people suffer.' "

And Hwesuhunu remembered also the day when the ship arrived in Cotonou to take them away. A cannon was fired from the ship three times as a signal. Adanzan's agent went out in a small boat to discuss the matter. Strange-looking men came ashore from the ship to examine the captives from a platform at the top of the stockade.

The next morning the loading began. Hwesuhunu and his father were separated. Because Hwesuhunu was one of the last to be sent out in the small boats, he was placed in the highest tier, just below the deck. Later, he passed the message: "Hwesuhunu is here. Where is Sosu?" But there was no reply. Again he asked, and when the question had been relayed by every mouth, and had descended to the bottom tier, an answer came back: "Sosu, father of Hwesuhunu, he did not come aboard the ship. He is not here." Once more, as he had done in the stockade at Abomey, Hwesuhunu cried. But this time it was a little different. Then he had cried for his degradation and his misery. This time he cried for the fate of his father. Thus, though his body was that of a boy, Hwesuhunu had acquired the spirit of a man.

The suffering was the same, but his relationship to it changed. He assumed the power to absorb what was thrust upon him against his volition, and to forge it and temper it into the magic weapon of himself. He accepted the chafing of the leg-iron as though it were rice, and his presence on the slave ship as though he had chosen it. He did not think of it in so many words, but it came to him that his tears for his father were the last he would ever shed.

The man next to him on his right was of the Nago people, but he spoke the language of the Fon also, and so he and Hwesuhunu could converse easily. Neither had seen the other in the light. Hwesuhunu created an image of him out of his voice, an image of a strong and fearless hunter. The man did not speak of the hardness of the planks or of the foul darkness around them. He spoke instead of his village at the edge of a forest, of his son who had been killed by a leopard.

"Since that day," he said, "I have been known by all leopards as their enemy. If there are leopards where we are going, let them beware, for Dokumi is coming." And when they knew each other better, Dokumi said, "In time of danger stay close to me, my juju will protect you." The man on

Hwesuhunu's left spoke little, except to talk to himself. Hwesuhunu imagined him to be old with gray hair and few teeth. He addressed him as "Uncle," but Uncle never made direct conversation. If Hwesuhunu asked a question or voiced a politeness, there was no response. Yet once he heard the old man saying in his ear, "Hwesuhunu—it is a good name. You have a strong fetish." When Hwesuhunu answered, the old man seemed not to hear.

It was on their seventh day at sea that the captives were taken out of the ship's belly and brought to the deck for exercise and cleansing. Hwesuhunu's legs were weak. They seemed to belong to another person who was not there. The slaves came up in chains of ten. In his chain Hwesuhunu was the tenth, after Dokumi the Nago. The sunlight was blinding after so much darkness, and it pained their eyes. Each chain of slaves was made to jog back and forth on the deck. Then they were given pails with ropes attached, so they could bail water from the sea and wash themselves. When they finished, the next chain was brought up from below.

The first in the next chain was the old man who talked to himself. He was just as Hwesuhunu imagined—a grayed grandfather, whose teeth were nearly gone. As this group approached the bailing pails, Grandfather, encumbered by his leg chain, flung himself over the deck rail, pulling a second man after him. The others in the chain clutched at ropes to prevent themselves from following. The two that went over the side hung upside down, Grandfather just above the white-capped waves. The ship's crew hauled them back, making ugly gestures and voicing angry words. When they had Grandfather back on deck, the crewmen struck him several times. Though the captives did not understand the words, the meaning was clear.

Going back into the ship's belly was almost unbearable after a few moments of cool sea air, warm sun, and things to be seen with the eyes. The stench below deck was sickening. Grandfather lay without moving now. The other men of his chain berated him for nearly dragging them into the ocean. He did not answer them. He no longer even talked to himself. A few days after, Hwesuhunu became aware that the space next to him was empty. He listened attentively and knew that Grandfather suddenly was not there. He moved his hand until it touched the body. Then he turned the other way, saying to Dokumi, "Old Grandfather is dead." When the food bearer came they called his attention to the stilled body. He held up his lantern and peered into Old Grandfather's face. But it was the next day before some of the crew came and dragged the body out. Dokumi said, "You see, they could not prevent him."

Friendship and understanding grew between Hwesuhunu and Dokumi. One day, after they had been speaking of their villages, Dokumi reached out a closed hand, saying, "Here, take this thing. Hide it safely in your cloth. Do not lose it."

Hwesuhunu took it, a small smooth object which he couldn't see in the blackness. "What is it?" he asked.

"It is a wari nut," Dokumi said. "It is a thing from our land. Keep it with you. It will help you remember. It will be your juju. If things go hard with you sometimes, it may help you. I picked it from a bush on the road to Cotonou. I thought, 'If I am sent away from my country, I will have something to help me remember it. I took two nuts. One is enough for me. You, take this one. It will be your friend.' "

Hwesuhunu tied it into his loincloth. He was grateful because it was a gift. A small thing, a wari nut. At home it was useful for nothing, except to make beads, or perhaps strikers for calabash rattles. Here it was a big thing, a thing one person could give another. But how could it be a friend? He wondered about it. Once when he awoke with a feeling of terrifying loneliness he felt the nut in his cloth. He remembered that Dokumi had given it. A sensation of gratitude swept over him. He was grateful for Dokumi's presence. Whenever he touched the wari nut it seemed to say, "I am the nut given by Dokumi." And he understood how this small thing could be a comfort. He wanted to give something in return to bind their friendship. There was nothing to give. Why hadn't he, also, thought to pick up something on the road to Cotonou? A seed pod perhaps . . . a handful of earth . . . a leaf . . . anything. No, he had been too concerned with his tiredness and his pain. And now what was there to give his friend? He thought about it a long while.

Then, at last, it came to him. He said, "Dokumi . . . do you hear me, Dokumi? I have something for you. It is a small thing. It is the only thing I have to give you."

Dokumi reached out a hand.

"No, I can't give it to you in your hand, your hand will not hold it. It is a word."

Dokumi replied, "Give it then, I will receive it with thanks."

Hwesuhunu said, "The only thing I have for you, Dokumi, is my secret name. I am called Alihonu, He-Who-Is-Born-on-the-Road. Thus I was called at birth. This secret name was given by my father and mother. My four brothers do not know it. But you know it. I entrust you with it."

Dokumi said, "Hwesuhunu, I have heard. I have received it. I will keep it as a trust."

To the damp sick foulness in the belly of the ship there came to be added another torture—lice. At first there were just a few, but between one day and the next they turned into a plague. They were everywhere. Every sweating body, every plank swarmed with them. They crawled on the skin, bit, crawled, and bit again. They worked their way into the hair and the body crevices. They crawled on the face and drank at the corners of the eyes. It was a new agony, one which made life before its advent seem almost pleasant. But it was a tangible enemy, and thus it provided a purpose. The hands lay poised waiting for the sensation on the skin. If the fingers caught the predator, it was killed between the fingernails.

Then one waited for the next. And the next. One heard the endless sound of scratching, exclamations, epithets, curses. And after the lice came the rats. In the beginning there had been an occasional one scampering along the planks. Emboldened, attracted by the foulness, encouraged by the immobility of the bodies, they now were everywhere, nibbling at toes, biting fingers, sometimes peering into human faces.

Dokumi, the hunter, played a game. He spat a little saliva on the planks at a carefully selected place. He waited, eyes fixed on the spot, nerves tense, as though he were in the bush with the leopards. Then, hearing rather than seeing a rat poised to drink at the spittle, perhaps sensing even more than hearing, Dokumi moved. His hand shot forward with the speed of a spring snare and closed around the rat's neck. If the hold was right, his fingers tightened, the animal struggled, then became still. If the hold was wrong, the rat bit him and escaped.

The face of the enemy had changed. First it had been Adanzan's slavers; then the drovers; then the ship that had swallowed them, and the crew which manned it; and now, at last, predators that one understood—rats and lice. Even though they could not be seen in the blackness, still they had the character of rats and lice; one knew how they lived, what they sought, and how they died.

Down in the lower tier two women died of ratbites; another's arm was swollen so she could not move it. Reports traveled from mouth to mouth. Nothing occurred that was not known throughout the hold. It was almost like the marketplace at Abomey. There were facts. There were rumors. There was a continuing discussion of their destination. It came to be said that the ship was taking them to Brazil. There was an argument then. Another opinion was that they were going to a place called Guadeloupe. The argument became heated as it traveled back and forth in the blackness.

It was only stilled when an aged Yoruba man gave his opinion: "Some say this, some say that. Who knows where it will be? Does it matter what kind of a name a place has? It is not a journey to attend the festival of a chief. When we came aboard the ship did anyone ask us, 'You, people, where are you going?' Did they ask us, 'Are you well? Are your gardens prospering?' They take us where they wish, and we no longer have gardens. Wherever they take us, we shall work in the fields. Are those fields ours? No. Therefore, it does not matter where they are. If we do not like it where we find ourselves will we go elsewhere? No. Let us be done with the argument. The name of the place does not matter."

Humor sometimes intruded in the midst of despair, as though the vital force of life refused to lie inert with them on the planks. There were stories about heroes and, on occasion, a riddle. Because some men did not understand others, the stories sometimes were repeated in translation. When the tale was finished on the first tier it was retold on the second. One night—or was it day?—a man put forward a riddle known in every Fon village: "Water standing up." The answer was known to every child—"A stalk of cane." But those who knew refrained from answering, leaving the ignorant to ponder on it. The reply, when it came, was triumphant: "A penis!" The laughter rose like a wave. It splashed and gurgled like the sea in all directions.

A day came when the slaves were again brought up to the deck. Once more there was the stabbing glare of the sun and the water, and the ecstasy as the skin was washed clean of the stale foulness of the hold. A chain of women came out of the darkness. Some of them fell on the deck and refused to go forward or backward. They lay screaming, invoking, calling on their unseen protectors to witness their misery and degradation. They had to be forced to the bailing pails. A little later, a chain of Ibibio ascended. They moved purposively to the rail and began to climb over it. Crewmen ran forward with sticks in their hands. They beat the Ibibio and tried to hold them, but in a moment it was over. The

Ibibio went plunging into the sea, dragging a crewman with them. There were excited shouts from above. A sail was furled, and the ship swept around in a wide arc, circling the place where the men had gone overboard, but of the slaves and crewman nothing at all was seen.

Dokumi observed the horror in Hwesuhunu's eyes. He said, "They have chosen it to be that way. They have considered it carefully. They are Ibibio. Ibibio are impatient. They prefer to be with the ancestors. They cannot wait. Ibibio are that way."

The Captain and the officers were agitated. The Captain spoke angrily. Muskets appeared among the crew, and the captives were herded tightly together. The Captain came to speak to them. Beside him was a crewman with a dark skin like their own. As the Captain spoke, the dark-skinned crewman translated into something that was not Nago or Fon, but a mixture that the prisoners nevertheless seemed to understand. And after a few minutes their eyes were only on the dark man, and the Captain faded into the background. The dark man gesticulated, moved one way and another. This they understood. He said:

"You, you people, listen. These are the words of Captain Brook, he is the chief of this vessel. Here on this ship, Captain Brook is the headman. He is equal to a king in Dahomey or Whydah. What he says here is the law. This ship is his nation. You, you people, listen. Captain Brook, he is sorry some people have died in the sleeping place down below. He is angry, though, that the Ibibio jumped in the water. He says the crew will shoot their muskets if any more people try to make trouble. The muskets are good ones. The powder burns. The bullets fly straight. Make no more trouble.

"You, you people, listen. The ship has sailed far. The distance ahead is less than the distance behind. Captain Brook, he says if there is no trouble among you, you can be on deck every day except in bad weather. One hour, two hours every day, forty people at one time. You breathe good air, make yourselves clean, grow strong. Those with sores, the Captain will give them medicine. Clean the sleeping places below with brooms and water, do not foul the planks any more. Use the pails here on deck and empty them. If you make no trouble, this is the way it will be for the rest of the voyage. If there is trouble, you will be punished. You cannot go and hide in the bush. When the voyage is over, your feet will be again on the earth. Again you will eat and sleep as you did before. All will be well. Do not make any more trouble. The Captain says this."

When he was through speaking, the translator stood in tall dignity as though the words had been his own. A voice came out of the crowd, saying, "You, who have spoken, what kind of man are you?"

The translator said, "Me, I am a Gola man. I am Mister Sam."

A voice came back, "I too am a Gola man. Among the Gola there is no such name as Mister Sam. The Gola do not wear clothes like you wear. If you are Gola, what is your Gola name?"

The translator said, "My Gola name is Sangara. The Captain, he is chief of this country. He is my friend. He gave me the name of Sam. Therefore, that is my name. You, when you address me, call me Mister Sam."

Another voice came out of the crowd: "You, Mister Sam, your words are empty. You are only a drum on which the Captain plays. When he beats, you make a sound."

Strained faces relaxed. There was laughter. Mr. Sam became agitated. He gesticulated. He spoke rapidly in Gola.

Someone called out, "What is Mister Sam saying?"

Another voice answered, "It is nothing. It is just the sound of spittle falling on the drum."

Again there was laughter. Now the Captain spoke again, and the crowd fell silent. Mr. Sam translated: "Captain Brook says let there be no trouble, and he will be like your father. If there is trouble, *kao! kao!* the muskets will speak! If there is trouble, you will stay down below in the stink."

But the crowd was not yet quite finished. A voice said, "You, Mister Sam, are you a free man or a slave?"

Mister Sam again became agitated. "You, be quiet! The Captain is my friend. I work for him. You, who are you? Where is the chief that is your friend when you are far from your village?"

Then they stopped heckling Mister Sam. It was true. Where was the chief that would be their friend?

Now, as the days followed one on the other, heart began to grow in the captives once more. For a few hours between dawn and sundown they were allowed to depart from the region of rats, lice, darkness and perpetual foulness. Even the task of scrubbing down the sleeping planks became an activity which justified existence. Because work and sound were inseparable, there was singing in the hold. New songs came into being, about the march to Cotonou, about the slave ship, even about Mister Sam:

Little parrot,
Your feathers are beautiful.
Little parrot,
Your feathers are beautiful.
You make the kwiku bird look shabby,
But your words are only spittle on the drum.

Each day when they ascended to the deck the first mate examined their bodies. If a man had a bad sore or a swelling, he was motioned aside, and later the Captain treated him. He put ointment on the festering irritations caused by the dirty planks or by ratbites. If a captive's skin looked gray and flaky, the Captain rubbed oil on it. If a man's flesh had withered and shrunk, he was given a tonic. But the Captain's medicine was not good for all things. One man's leg became swollen and gangrenous. There was nothing that could be done except to amputate it, but this was not done because a slave with one leg was worthless. The man died and was thrown into the sea. There were other deaths, sometimes two in a single day.

Captain Brook was often on deck to survey his human cargo. He watched the Africans silently, seeming to brood on what he saw. His eyes would fix on a man coming through the hatch, follow him to the wash pails, and see him douse his skin with water as though to wash away not only the stench but even the memory of the hold below. He heard the voices calling back and forth, and laughter sometimes, and he also saw the helpless hunted look in the faces of some and the mute hostility in others. He could not help but wonder how this man or that woman had come to the slave market in Cotonou, and what kind of crime had been committed to merit their presence there. For he had heard it said that most of the captives were either criminals or prisoners of war who might have been killed except that slavery offered a profitable alternative. He tried to visualize how these Africans would be behaving were they free people in the town of Lagos or Harcourt.

He caught sight of a man and a boy emerging together from the hold into the bright sunlight. The man was lithe and muscular. He moved with the ease of one who has great reserves of strength. From the three parallel scars on each cheek the Captain knew him to be a Nago. The boy was thin, perhaps even thinner, the Captain thought, than when he had been taken captive. Though he was dark, his skin did not have the deep purplish tint of the Nago, and there were no tribal marks on his face. It came to the Captain, with a sense of surprise, that the boy, also, was examining people, watching their faces for what he might read there. Once, for a moment, the boy's eyes met his own. The Captain read and the boy read. Then the boy turned his face away. Another day the Captain again saw the man and boy come on deck together, and it was clear to him that they were friends.

One morning at airing time Hwesuhunu and Dokumi

were motioned to the side by a crewman. The Captain came later and put ointment on their sores. He called Mr. Sam to translate for him, and spoke to Hwesuhunu. "Where are you from? What is your name?"

"I am Hwesuhunu. I come from Dahomey."

"What are you doing here? You are very young."

"I am a man. I worked with my father's dokpwe."

"You are too young to have committed a serious crime."

Dokumi interrupted: "Those who committed the crime are not here."

Mister Sam said, "You, be silent, you were not spoken to."

But the Captain said, "What did the man have to say?"

Mr. Sam repeated Dokumi's words. The Captain said: "What crime do you mean?"

Dokumi said, "The crime of the gluttonous Adanzan, king of Dahomey, he who took slaves from his own kind and sold them to foreigners. In the country of the white people, does the king capture his own kind and send them away as slaves?"

The Captain's eyes narrowed. "Are you one of Adanzan's people?"

"I am a Nago. Hwesuhunu, this boy, he is Fon. We are not of the same nation, but we are related. Our color is dark. We can speak to each other. Our spirits, we call them differently. The Nago call them orisha, the Fon call them vodoun. We grow yams and hunt antelope. Among ourselves we sometimes quarrel. But when we have seen the white strangers and their curious way of life we understand that the Fon and the Nago and the Mahi are of the same family. So it is one thing for Adanzan to capture us for his service. It is another thing to send us away from our own land, to sell us to strangers that care nothing for the things we value greatly. So, I say, Adanzan, he is the criminal. He is not here. It is not for small people like us to exact justice from kings. They find their justice when they are conquered by other kings or when, at last, they die and go to face their ancestors."

It was not evident whether Mister Sam conveyed to the Captain exactly what Dokumi had said. The Captain did not respond. After he had put ointment on their sores, he sent them to join the others.

Hwesuhunu said, "He is a good man. He gives us medicine."

Dokumi answered, "He is evil, like Adanzan. He cares for our sores only because a sick captive is worth little, while a healthy captive is worth much."

He was silent for a while. He looked at Hwesuhunu thoughtfully. "You still believe that it was worse for Adanzan to take you for a slave than to take the Nago and the Mahi and the Hausa? Why was it worse? Adanzan sent his army to get Nago slaves to sell to the whites. His army was boastful. It was too sure of itself. It thought, 'We are the breed of Dahomey. The enemy will throw away their spears and muskets when they see us. When they hear the name Adanzan they will fall on the ground and cry.' It was not this way. The Nago did not flee. They took their weapons. They put on their war caps. They took their shields. They went out to meet the Dahomeans. They surprised them. They fought. The Nago killed many. Adanzan's soldiers fled. They took only a few captives. They brought us back to Abomey, saying, 'Adanzan, we are victorious. Here are the slaves you asked for.' Adanzan was angry. He said, 'I sent you for many hundred. How many did you bring?' They said, 'Sir, we have brought thirteen.' The king said, 'If Dahomey has become so weak and cowardly, then let Dahomey bleed.'

"He instructed the captain of the army this way: 'There are three days. By the third day, let there be four hundred slaves in my stockade.' The king's soldiers went out. They caught Mahi and Hausa, they caught Fanti traders on the roads. Whoever walked alone, they took him. They took women and girls returning from the market. And still there were not many hundred. They said, 'Did not the king tell us to let Dahomey bleed?' They went out to the villages and caught the men and women they needed. So, here we are together on the ship that takes us to some strange country, treated like people cursed by their ancestors. You were taken from your village. I was taken from mine. What is the difference?"

Hwesuhunu replied, "It is the same. I didn't see it until now." He looked out over the sea, searching hungrily for the sight of land, but there was no land, only the endlessness of the water. The greatness of the ocean came upon him, and with it he felt sharply what he had only understood before. He said: "I think I shall never go back to Dahomey."

Dokumi said, "Perhaps no one here will return. Yet each day we shall have a message from our country. The sun rises in Africa, and whenever we see it we shall remember the place of its daily birth."

Now that they were spending part of each day on the open deck, Hwesuhunu recognized some men and women that he had known before the day of the slave raid. There was Dosu, the hunter, who had lived in a nearby village. On his left cheek and extending down his neck to his shoulder were three parallel scars where a leopard's claws had dug deeply into his flesh. His color was copperish red, and the pale white scars stood out lividly. Hwesuhunu approached him, saying, "You, Uncle Dosu, I have seen you at the festivals. I am Hwesuhunu, eldest son of Sosu."

The man looked solemnly at Hwesuhunu, saying, "You, nephew, I don't recognize you, but your father, Sosu, I know him. I saw him in the stockade at Cotonou. He is my friend."

Hwesuhunu spoke of the slave raids on the villages, but Dosu looked off in the distance, and was silent. Hwesuhunu saw Dosu each day on the deck, and spent time sitting near him. Sometimes Hwesuhunu spoke, but Dosu was taciturn. He listened, but his conversation was made of small gestures, slight movements of his proud head, and silence. Hwesuhunu referred one day to the necklace of leopards' claws that hung around Dosu's neck, saying, "Uncle, are these claws the medicine that protect you in the hunt?"

Dosu said, "No, they are not my medicine. My medicine is in this bag on my arm. The claws, they are in memory of the leopards I have taken. My vodoun is Sebo, the leopard spirit. The claws proclaim to creatures of the bush to beware, because the essence of Sebo is within me."

Hwesuhunu said, "I, I have no medicine. But I have this." He took from his cloth the wari nut which Dokumi had given him in the darkness of the hold, and showed it to Dosu. "This nut, I shall keep it. And some day I shall plant it. Thus, Dahomey will be alive and grow wherever I am." He spoke of Dokumi, his Nago friend, pointing him out in the crowd. Dosu nodded. "I knew him for a hunter by the way he walks. I will speak with him." In this way Dosu and Dokumi became friends.

The hunters were together often. While Dosu spoke little to others, with Dokumi his talk came freely, though often his words were bitter. When he heard the sound of laughing among the captives his veins swelled with anger. "Look," he said, "they smile, they laugh. What is the matter? Everything is taken away. They are chained. They are degraded. They are beaten. They are made to live with the rats. Then they are given something no bigger than a cowry, a small spoonful of sunlight. They are grateful. They are happy. They are saying, 'Whenever has life been so good as this?' "

Dokumi answered: "They have more than a cowry shell left. They have life in their bodies. Their laughing, it is good. They will not throw themselves into the sea like the Ibibio. They will meet their destiny this way. Don't you remember that a slave in ancient times became the king of Fidah and founded a dynasty? Who can say what destiny holds in store for Hwesuhunu? Each man has his fate to meet. He carries it within him, as it was planned. If the captives laugh, that is not bad. Laughter has within it the fluid of life. Let us remember the tale of King Da. It is said that Da was conquered by King Tacoudonou, and Tacoudonou ordered that Da's head be cut off. Da smiled when his head was cut from his shoulders, and in time Tacoudonou was driven out of his mind because the smile would not depart from Da's face."

Dosu replied: "Perhaps it is so. Perhaps it is their Fa to forget. But the hunter is not allowed to forget. All his senses must be burning. He must hear what the farmer cannot hear. He must smell what others cannot smell. His sinews must always be taut as a bowstring. His eyes must pierce the darkness. When he hunts in the forest where the forces dwell, he must himself become a force. Thus it is with the hunter. His Fa is different. Old Grandfather, he who tried to throw himself into the sea and failed, he whose soul departed thereafter, he had left his Fa behind in Dahomey. But I, my Fa burns within me. The laughing is scorched and dies in my throat. I am Dosu, who hunts antelope and leopards. The claw marks on my face are the writing of Fa. What is being done to us, I cannot accept it."

Dokumi said: "I, also, am I not a hunter? I too have gone alone into the forest. I too have killed many leopards. But are we now in the forest? Where is a living tree? Where is the grass? The sounds we hear, are they the sounds of the creatures of the bush? And where are the weapons? There is no spear, there is no musket. Did you not say that when a hunter goes where the forces dwell he himself must become a force? Let us become such forces. We are without weapons. But let each man become, himself, a weapon. Let each man become, himself, a shield. Let each man become, himself, a juju. In the forest one day I lost my spear. Because I had no spear, the leopards understood I was helpless. And one of them came and confronted me. In his eyes I saw the words, 'You, Dokumi, you are helpless. I will destroy you now, because you have killed many of my kind.'

"But I stood and spoke to the leopard with my eyes. I said: 'You, leopard, you are wrong. Because it is not my spear that is Dokumi the hunter, the hunter lies inside me. Should you attack me and wound me, even should I die, still you would not have destroyed the hunter. The hunter lives forever. The hunter is like a bolt of lightning, which comes with a roar and is gone. Because it is silent thereafter, is it therefore dead? No, it comes again and again. You, leopard, your Fa is written. Never can you destroy the hunter.' I spoke thus with my eyes. And the leopard turned and disappeared into the forest darkness. So it is with these people whose laughter disturbs you. Lacking weapons and shields, they become weapons and shields. Does not a spear glisten in the sunlight? Therefore men laugh in the sunlight."

Often they spoke this way, but the bitter fire in Dosu did not cool. Dokumi, when he watched the crewmen of the ship at work, when he watched the surge of the sea, when he listened to the crack of canvas and the creak of straining timbers, he seemed to be taking these things inside him, placing them a certain way, like corn in a granary. Dosu, he also observed everything, and took it in, but for him the sights and sounds were as fuel for his fire.

One morning as he and Dokumi and Hwesuhunu sat together on the deck Dosu said, "There are fifteen white men in the crew. There are two hundred of us, forty on deck at one time. Only a few of them carry muskets. Should we not make a plan?"

Dokumi answered, "Yes, it is so. But it is not time yet to plan. Let us say it is like this: We fall on them and kill them. We take the muskets. We are masters of the ship. What then? Can we handle a ship such as this? And if we learn to handle such a ship, what then? This is a great sea. Where is Dahomey to be found? If we become lost, the food and water will soon be gone. No. This is not the way. We must stalk them like the elephant. We follow. We watch. We stay downwind. We wait."

"This is wrong," Dosu said. "Once we have arrived where we are going, the time will be past. Once we have set foot on land, we cannot again return. Who has ever heard of a man who left Cotonou in a slave ship and returned to tell of his adventure? No one returns. Thus we cannot wait."

Hwesuhunu asked, "What kind of country are we going to? Perhaps there is bush country there to which we can escape."

Dokumi said, "It is true. We must know something about the country where we are going."

Dosu said bitterly, "The country where we are going is full of slaves who waited to see it."

"And the sea, the impatient Ibibio are in it. Let us get information. Let us speak with the Gola man. Let us ponder on things."

When the time was right, Dokumi spoke to Sangara. He said, "You, countryman, Mr. Sam, you have traveled to the end of the sea. What is on the other side?"

Sangara said, "Many things, many countries. The white men, like us, they are of many nations, they speak different languages. Sometimes, like us, they fight. The British fight the French, and the Spanish fight the British. Their ships meet at sea, there are battles. The big guns roar, there is fire and death. Their armies meet on land, their muskets spit, *kao! kao! kao!* Also there are the Americans. They have a large country on the other side of the water. It spreads from sunrise to sunset. To go across it is like walking from Douala to Mali. They too have great ships on the sea, taking cargoes, bringing slaves."

Dokumi said, "In these countries, have many slaves escaped?"

Sangara said: "No, not many, only a few. There is no place to go. Well, one place only, an island named St. Domingue. There the black ones revolted and drove out the French masters. But St. Domingue is an island lost in the sea. Elsewhere it is the land of the white men. The slave, he is dark.

Wherever he is seen it is known that he is a slave. If he runs, they catch him again. They whip him. Perhaps they kill him. You, when you go there, do not be a great man. They will beat the skin from your body."

"And you, Mr. Sam," Dokumi said, "you have seen all this?"

"I have seen it," Sangara said.

"When the ship was at Cotonou, why didn't you escape and go to your own village?" Dokumi asked.

Sangara laughed. "My village? In my village I was already a slave. When the Hausa trader came, I was sold to him. Then I was sold again. I was sold many times. I was placed on this ship. But the Captain took me to work for him. He did not send me ashore with the others in Jamaica. I am a member of the crew. Why should I go back to what I came from?"

Dokumi asked, "If the Captain wishes, can he not sell you to another?"

"The Captain is my friend," Sangara said. "He will not sell me."

Dokumi said, "Is it not a sad thing for you to work with these foreigners that take your countrymen into slavery?"

Sangara became angry. "Do you not know me? I am Sangara the Gola. I have been a slave among the Hausa, the Senufo, the Bobo. I have been nothing but a slave until now. If there are Hausa here on this ship, shall my tears fall? If there is a Bobo here, shall I cry? You, from your cheek marks I see you are a Nago. Had I not had good fortune, I would surely one day have been a slave of the Nago. Here I belong to the Captain, and he is my friend. It is not bad. It is the best life I can remember. And who knows? Perhaps on this deck I may some day see one of the masters who bought me and sold me. Is there anything better in life? And these people here, are they my countrymen? I have no countrymen."

But each day Dokumi and Hwesuhunu greeted Sangara, and after a while they were able to get much information from him about places to which they might be going. Yet there was little comfort in it. Nothing he told them provided any answers. For Hwesuhunu, Sangara's descriptions of Jamaica and Trinidad only aroused anxiety and gloom. And he thought often of his father and mother and his brothers, and his insides felt heavy as though he were filled with stones.

As for Dokumi and Dosu, though they were friends, they quarreled.

"You," Dosu said, "it is said you are a hunter. But aren't you like the man watching the corn grow so his wife can grind it into meal? You converse with Mister Sam, who knows nothing and wants to know nothing, waiting for him to say a magic word. You yourself said, 'Every man must be a weapon.' What kind of weapon are you, then? A spear carved in the headman's door?"

After a while Dokumi said, "Let us speak gently to one another. We are friends. Let us remember the story of the two hunters who quarreled. Each went separately into the bush to hunt. They met in the bush. One said, 'You, hunter, go elsewhere. Was I not here first?' The other said, 'It was I who was here first. You, go away, hunt elsewhere in the bush.' They struggled. They fell into a pit dug to catch game. They considered what had happened. They helped each other out of the pit. They quarreled no more. They were friends. They hunted together. Thus came the proverb: 'Two hunters quarreled in the bush, they fell into the pit.' Dosu, let us be friends together."

The quarreling passed. But Dosu was greatly silent.

Some of the captives were put to work at special jobs on the ship. Sangara went among them asking for a blacksmith, and someone pointed out Doumé, the Nago ironworker. Doumé was taken forward and shown what work was to be done. There were carpenter's tools to be repaired and new links to be made for a chain. Quiet and passive though he had been only a few moments before, Doumé became suddenly assertive and self-confident. He demanded of Sangara a hammer, tongs, and a forge.

"You," Doumé said in a tone of disgust, "how does a man shape iron without a forge?"

Sangara said, "The Captain has instructed you in this."

Doumé said, "Tell the Captain to bring me a basket made of smoke and I can shape iron without a forge."

Sangara found the Captain and brought him back. Again Doumé demanded a forge. The Captain said, "We have no forge. You'll have to make one. Sam will get you what you need."

So Doumé sent Sangara for this and that. He sat in the shade, ordering Sangara about as though he were an apprentice ironworker. Sangara brought pieces of iron plate, two great iron kettles, and miscellaneous hardware. Out of these things Doumé fashioned a crude forge, raised six inches above the deck. He made a bellows out of sailcloth, and when the fire was at last alive, he demanded someone to operate the bellows. Sangara went off and came back with Hwesuhunu. Doumé instructed Hwesuhunu what to do. When the deck beneath the forge began to scorch, Doumé ordered Sangara to spill water on it. He forged the chain links and repaired the tools. Then Sangara brought broken iron pots to be patched, locks and musket parts to be fixed. And four days later, when Doumé was sent to rejoin the others, his mood of resignation to fate had been left at the forge.

He sat with Dokumi and Hwesuhunu, and after a while he spoke, "While I worked at the iron my orisha, Ogoun, came into my head. Thus, my arms became strong, and the fire hot. Ogoun said, 'Do not forget me. I am the orisha of the forge and also the protector of warriors. I brought the forge to man so that he would learn to make spears and knives. Thus, all hunters need me too. Without me the warrior and the hunter would go out to kill only with clubs and sharpened sticks.' "

Doumé reached into his waistcloth and brought out two pieces of shaped metal. One was a small knife blade without a handle. The other was an iron key. He gave the key to Dokumi, saying, "I saw the key used to lock the chains down below. I looked many times. I remembered. I made this. Keep it. Perhaps it will be useful." The knife blade he put back in his waistcloth. "This is the symbol of my orisha. It is iron, it is a weapon. It is the substance of Ogoun. Therefore I shall wear it."

Dokumi said, "I am a hunter. Ogoun is my orisha also. Therefore I shall wear this iron key to remind Ogoun of my presence." And he placed it carefully in his waistcloth along with the wari nut he had found on the road to Cotonou.

That night, down in the belly of the ship, Hwesuhunu said to Dokumi, "I have thought about what Dosu said. Is he not right in saying that once we have been taken ashore the hole will have been filled? Is not the crossroads of our fate here on the sea? We are many, they are few. What if we were to capture them and take their muskets and powder? Could we not force the Captain to take us back?"

"I too have thought this," Dokumi said. "I have also counted forty-one days since we left Cotonou. There is not enough water or food for such a trip. Should we go somewhere for water or food, the word would spread that we had captured the ship. Other ships would pursue us. And what if the Captain took us not to Dahomey but to a country of white people? And if we returned to Cotonou, would we not be seized and placed once again in the stockade? This way we would begin the dance all over. Our trouble is that we know nothing about sailing a large ship on this endless sea. Yet, I have considered these things. A time will come when the answer will be given."

"Is not this the domain of Agbé, Lord-of-the-Sea?" Hwesuhunu said. "Perhaps it is Agbé who will reveal the answer."

The winds that had been blowing steadily from the northeast fell off. When the slaves came to the deck that morning they saw a red sun rising behind a wall of mist that hid the horizon. The waves subsided into swells. The ship's crew was busy with the sails, furling and resetting. The water became choppy, and turned from blue to green. A new wind came from the southwest, gusty, angry. The sails snapped, the timbers creaked, the ship heeled. The red sun faded. Running ahead of the rising wind, the waves mounted and towered. When they struck, the ship shuddered. It seemed to stop its forward motion momentarily; then, recovering from the blow, it plunged, digging its bow into other waves which came from another direction. A lashing, stinging rain swept across the deck.

The ship's mate came with Sangara, leaning into the gale, half blinded, water pouring down their faces. Sangara motioned to the captives where they huddled and shouted: "Down! Go down!" The Africans shoved their way through the hatch, jostling, bruising each other, and found their way to their places in the darkness. The canvas lashed over the hatch billowed and snapped. The sound of the rain on the deck and the creaking of timbers merged with the roar of the hurricane wind. The vessel heeled heavily, rolled, pitched, and trembled.

Though the captives in the hold were unshackled, they lay in their places and clung to the naked planks. At first there was merely fear; then came sickness, and the spreading odor of vomit. Hwesuhunu's stomach contracted, there was choking in his throat, and a painful disgorging of half-digested food. The cut-glass eye in the deck above gave no hint of daylight. It was like the world of the accursed dead, those who had incurred the enmity of Hevioso, struck down by lightning, buried in isolation, and doomed to an eternity of darkness and agony.

There was the sensation of tilting over and over, waiting for the movement to end, but no end. One movement of the ship gave way suddenly to another. There was no rhythm to which the body could adjust. A roll began, the ship heeled, the motion was interrupted by the blow of a wave striking broadside. The ship seemed to drop into a void, and before the senses had become accustomed there was a thrust upward, another thundering blow of massed angry water, another pitch. Nothing was completed. It was an endless agitation that tormented the surprised body and drove from the mind everything but awareness of epic destructive force.

Hwesuhunu tried to summon up a vision of sunshine on the deck, a picture of his village, a scene of the dokpwe at work, but nothing came. There was no room in him for anything but the sensations of storm, uncontrollable and meaningless motion, and the futility of trying to contend with the rage and fury of Agbé, ruler of the ocean. Slowly, imperceptibly, a dullness came over him. His body seemed drugged. Still clinging to the planks with his fingers, he felt his mind slip away. He slept.

When he awoke, nothing had changed. The sounds were the same. The wild movement of the world continued. But the sickness had left him and his head was again clear. He seemed to have dreamed. He recalled his father saying, "Are you not Hwesuhunu, Thing-of-the-Sea? Your Fa is in you. Hug your destiny closely." He sat up, and felt the dripping of water from above.

He leaned close to Dokumi, saying, "My sickness has passed. And you?"

"I am well."

"Whenever has anyone before seen such a storm as this?"

Dokumi answered, "Yes, it is truly a mighty thing."

The canvas over the hatch was torn away, revealing a faint reflection from a flickering lantern. Sangara and a white crewman descended the ladder shakily, water pouring off their oilskin jackets. Sangara held the lantern forward and moved along the tier, as though searching. He shouted to be heard above the roar of wind. "Where is Doumé the ironworker?" When he found him he spoke rapidly, gave Doumé an oilskin jacket he carried under his arm. Doumé arose from the planks, put on the jacket, and ascended the ladder with Sangara and the white crewman. The canvas cover went back over the hatch, and again there was total darkness. The news was passed from mouth to ear until it was known in the furthest reaches of the hold: "A white crewman has been washed overboard. They took Doumé above to replace him."

Later, no one knew if it was day or night, three crewmen descended into the hold. One of them held tightly to a dripping musket. The other two began replacing the shackles and the chains. The captives protested, but they were silenced by the guard with the musket. Someone called out, "Why are we shackled again? We have done nothing." But the crewmen understood nothing of what was said, and if the protests were loud, the man with the musket pointed it threateningly. When it was done, the crewmen left. Someone said, "If this vessel sinks, we will join the Ibibio." The time for food and water came, but nothing was provided. About the food, many did not care. But after the vomiting there was great thirst, and later, when Sangara came down again with his lantern, they asked for water.

"Water, I cannot bring it now," Sangara said. "We cannot get to the water casks on deck until the storm subsides." They protested their shackles, and Sangara answered, "In the storm the captives are always shackled. Else they might take advantage and make trouble."

Someone said, "You are a Gola. You are our countryman. This is misery for us. What if the ship goes down? We will die. Help us. Remove the shackles."

Sangara answered: "This is the way it is done. Captain Brook, he understands these things. It is he who decides. The shackles make no difference. If the ship should sink, where would you go? Are you going to swim to Dahomey?" He moved along the tier, holding his lantern aloft, until he found what he was looking for. "You," he said to a Hausa, "come with me." He took off the man's shackles.

"Has another white man been swept into the sea?" they asked.

"No," Sangara answered. "He has broken his arm."

Dosu the Dahomean said, "Take off my shackles. Take me up. I have studied how the work is done."

Sangara answered, "You, do you think I do not know you? There is a fire burning in you. You will make trouble. Stay here where you are." And he took the Hausa away with him.

"The Gola, there is a serpent eating in his belly," Dosu said. "In his country he was a slave, but here he considers himself as counselor to the king. The tree lizard imagines himself a crocodile. Before I leave this ship I will surely hang his head on the mast."

The ship creaked and groaned in the wild blackness. Water was sloshing through the lower level. At last Dokumi asked, "Who is the person at the end, where the chain is fastened?"

The answer came back: "Koba the Nago."

Dokumi took from his waistcloth the key forged by Doumé. He held it in his hand, and called on the orisha Ogoun: "You of the Red Cloth, listen! You, patron of the forge, hear me. You of Oyo whose substance is iron; you who guide the hand of the hunter; you who give the spear point its temper, the fire its heat, and the warrior his courage, guide this iron key in the lock. The chains which hold us, they are iron, and all iron is yours. This key, it was forged by Doumé, your child. I who hold it am also your child. We have given you the blood of bulls. We have brought lodestones to your shrine. Guide this key for us."

He then passed the key, saying, "This is for Koba." The key went from hand to hand until Koba received it. He could not sit up to reach the lock near his feet, but he lay on his side and bent at the hips until the lock and key touched.

All heads were turned in his direction. The minutes passed. And the word came back to Dokumi that the key was too large, it would not turn.

Dokumi said, "Let him continue. Ogoun will help him." And again he closed his eyes and sang. More time passed. Then the word came: "The key has turned!" The chain was pulled loose and the fetters removed. Koba slid from his place and felt his way to the next lock, and another chain was loosened. When at last all the fetters were off, the key was brought to Dokumi. He placed it once more in his waistcloth. As it touched Dokumi's skin, Ogoun came into his head. He called out strange words in the darkness. His muscles tensed. He became rigid. His eyes turned inward. In a few minutes it was over.

The people on the lower level struggled out of their watery beds and surged upward. But there was not room for all. Some moved toward the ladder. Just as they reached it, the canvas was wrenched from the hatch, and Sangara and another crewman began to descend. Hands reached up and pulled them into the hold. The crewmen shouted, but their words were muffled and lost in the roar of the wind overhead. In a few minutes they rolled silently and limply in the thin wash of seawater.

Dosu, the hunter, picked up the musket the white crewman had carried. What followed came simply, naturally, as though it had been carefully planned. It was the crystallization of fantasies on which they had dwelled for weeks while lying in the dark foulness. Dokumi went up first, then Dosu, and after them the other men. On the open deck the driving rain stung their bodies. They were exposed now to the full rage of the wind and sea, and they clung to ropes and rails to keep from being swept away. They moved slowly, clambering through a tangle of fallen spars and ropes, able to see little in the gray of the storm. Guided by a pale lantern that flickered like a faint and distant star, they groped toward the quarterdeck. Out of the half-light there emerged the figure of a crewman desperately hacking at fallen tackle with an ax. His moment of surprise was short. Hands clutched at him from all directions, and he went hurtling over the side without having said a word, lost to sight before he struck the seething water.

Hwesuhunu gripped his way from rope to rope, shivering in the wetness. He sought the form of Dokumi, but could not find him. He saw only vague shapes moving toward the flickering light on the quarterdeck. They went up the ladder. At the top was the sodden figure of the first mate. In the shock of recognition he stood frozen for an instant, then turned and ran toward a door that he never reached. They struck him down, dragged him to the rail, and threw him over at the moment a mountainous wave struck broadside. The water received the living body of the mate and hurled it back. Hwesuhunu was carried in a cascade to the deck below into a tangle of spars and ropes. When he arrived again at the top of the ladder, bruised and bleeding, the mate had been disposed of for the second time. Several Africans were missing. Those who were left swarmed toward the helmsman. He saw them only at the last minute. He let go of the wheel and backed away, peering blindly into the rain for somewhere to go. They caught him and dragged him to the rail, leaving the wheel spinning crazily.

Another group groped its way to the Captain's cabin, and jerked the door open. He was sitting at his desk, working over a map in the pale lamplight. When Dosu stepped across the doorsill, Captain Brook reached for a pistol on his bunk. Dosu's musket went off, and the Captain fell off his chair.

The Africans explored all the openings. They went through the cabins, the galley, the crew's quarters. And when it seemed there were no more of the enemy to seek out, they stayed in such places of shelter as they found. Sangara was dragged up from the hold, bleeding, swollen, and sodden. They put him at the wheel, and slowly the vessel swung around and began to move bow foremost ahead of the thrust of the wind and waves.

When morning came, the storm was not yet blown out, but the wind had diminished and the rain had begun to thin. It was possible to see ahead of the bow from the helm and to verify what the senses had told them in the darkness—that the ship was listing heavily to the side where the mainmast had fallen. When the vessel rolled the mast dipped into the water; and when it rolled back the mast hung dripping and ugly a few feet above the whitecapped waves. Sangara was now resting in the galley, and Doumé, the ironworker, full of Sangara's instructions, stood tensely gripping the wheel, staring into a meaningless chaos of wind and water that stretched out ahead. Many of the Africans slept, curled up in the cabins and the crew's quarters, exhausted by what they had expended of themselves the afternoon before. Some of them were gone, swept away in the fury of Agbé's wrath, but who they were would be known only when the storm was at last gone, and the eye of day fully opened.

Still, Agbé was not finished with them. The vessel did not seem to be moving rapidly. It seemed to resist the force pressing from behind, while dipping heavily into the deep troughs which followed the larger waves. And yet when the splintering shock came, when the prow jerked up out of the water and the seams burst, one knew that the forward movement which had ended so suddenly had been rapid. Those on their feet were thrown sprawling and skidding onto the wet deck, and the last remaining mast broke halfway up and toppled over the side. The prow slowly raised itself still higher, then slid down with a coarse grating sound. The vessel swung around slowly under the pressure of the wind, and in a few moments it was broadside upon the invisible reef.

There was no longer any running before the wind. The waves struck against a tortured vessel which had no place to go, which could only respond by grinding itself to death against unseen rocks. The hold began to flood, and those Africans who had stayed below for shelter emerged through the hatch to be submerged by waves that washed across the deck.

Hwesuhunu, huddled behind a piece of sail, abandoned his sanctuary and sought to make his way to the quarterdeck. He had almost reached the ladder through a jungle of debris when he was crushed under the weight of a great surge of water. He no longer felt the planks under his feet. He sensed that he was turning over and over, spinning in darkness, swallowed by Agbé's sea. Watery hands tugged him downward and pressed the air from his lungs. An agony of blackness and nothingness. His awareness slipped away, stretching thinner and thinner, and when it seemed that the thin strand would snap and disappear, he found himself gulping air at the crest of another breaking wave. Again water washed over him, again the sensation of being turned, twisted and crushed in a mountain of heavy liquid blackness. Then, somehow, he was at the surface once more clinging to flotsam, clinging with a desperate fear of descending again into the fearsome depths. He was alone in a world made of nothing but turbulence, water and wind. He lost all feeling of time, but came to be aware that the wind was dying. Above his head he saw stars in the black sky, and thus came to understand that it was night. His body was cold and numb, and now he held only loosely, carelessly, to the splintered wood which kept him afloat. His eyes closed. He felt a dull heaviness steal upon him. Sleep, the one you never see coming, whose older brother is death, took him.

When his eyes opened again he had difficulty in relating himself to the world around him. He was suffused with overpowering indolence. Before him stretched a wide plain strewn with large boulders. He stared listlessly, wondering what place this could be, this desert without trees or grass. After a while the huge boulders shrank into pebbles, and it came to him that what he was looking at was the gravelly earth against which his face was pressed. He saw a hand lying limply beside him, and when it moved a little he was amused. Slowly understanding came that the hand was his, and that if he chose he could raise it to brush the sand from his lips. But he did not try. He felt the sun warming his body. He closed his eyes again, expecting to fall away into the hammock of sleep, but sleep, having departed, would not return. He began to be aware of sounds. There was a hum of voices in the background, familiar words that he had heard somewhere, and the call of birds. For an instant he believed that he was on the river bank near his village and that the wind carried to his ears the hum of the marketplace. But there was still another sound, a pulsing that was part roar and part hiss, that he did not know. He sat up, and saw a long stretch of beach and the surf washing over it and then draining away. Nearby was a cluster of familiar faces and bodies, men and women whom he had last seen on the ship of nightmares.

Someone called to him: "You, nephew, are you well?"

He said, "I am well." Then his eyes took in a wider panorama, and he saw other groups scattered along the beach. He arose unsteadily and began to walk.

A woman stopped him, saying, "You, small one, your vodoun has taken care of you." She brushed the sand from his face with her hand.

He said, "Mother, where are we?"

She answered, "Who knows? Agbé has thrown us out of the sea. Some have come out, some have remained."

His mind tried to put things in their place. "Have you seen Dokumi the Nago?"

She turned her head, signifying no. She took him by the hand to the water's edge, and there she washed the dirt from a gash on his neck and shoulder.

"Mother, I must look for Dokumi," he said. He walked along the beach, scanning faces and figures as he went. There, in one group, was Doumé the ironworker. There, sitting alone, was Dosu the hunter. Beyond was a man wading into the water to retrieve a floating body. Hwesuhunu went with him. They dragged the body onto the sand, and looked down into the bearded face of Koba the Nago. They brushed the sand from his lips and left him lying there. Other people too were combing the beach, gazing seaward toward splintered wreckage. Hwesuhunu saw two women being brought ashore from the fragment of a mast that had carried them in. Friends greeted each other, saying, "Are you well?" There were more bodies along the beach, some still awash in the water.

The sun rode high. And people began to move into the dense grove back of the beach for shade. They found palm trees, broke open coconuts to drink the milk, returning again and again to scan the sea. As the sun began to fall toward the west the scattered clusters of people moved closer together. The purposelessness began to fall away. They shared their knowledge of who had survived and who had been lost. When it was dark they slept.

Before the stars had faded in the morning light, Hwesuhunu was awakened by Dosu the hunter. They left the beach and went through the trees seeking game. They killed ground lizards with sticks, and on the way back they found wild avocado trees laden with fruit. They gave what they had found to the women, who divided it for the others, and another team went out to get more. Things were beginning to fall together. They knew that of those cast up alive there were thirty-three, twenty-six men and seven women. They talked of where they were and what they would do.

When there was a question, eyes turned to Doumé the ironworker. "We are of different tribes," Doumé said. "We bear different marks upon our skins. But as of today we are one village. We are many heads with a single stomach. Those who have died in the sea, they are of our own family. Let us remember. Let no one say it was the Nago who captured the ship. Let no one say it was the Fon. Let no one say it was the Mahi. It was the village. Of our village few are left. Of our village some remain to be buried. Let us prepare them, so that when they join the ancestors they can say, 'The village respected us. They washed our bodies. They mourned.' Let us do this."

The bodies were carried from where they lay along the water's edge and laid out for the women to care for. Hwesuhunu looked again, thinking that perhaps he would see the face of Dokumi, but Dokumi was not there, and he had final knowledge that he would not see his friend again. Eleven graves were dug among the trees and lined with leaves and grass. The women gave out mourning cries and threw dust on their shoulders and breasts. Doumé the ironworker said: "Is there any among us here in this strange land who is a priest of a shrine? Is there among us one to whom has been given special understanding by the orishas and vodouns? Is there a man here who has crossed Azaka Médé, the stream of the dead, and returned?" No one came forward. "I, my father was a babalao in the service of Chango and Ogoun," Doumé went on. "Therefore it falls upon me to invoke the good will of the orishas, and to see that our dead countrymen are sent properly on their way."

Hwesuhunu spoke, saying, "Uncle, my father, Sosu, is an elder priest of the family of Sagbata. I have been with him often at the shrine."

There were disparaging remarks. Someone said, "He is only a boy, what can he know?"

But when at last Doumé answered, he said, "Though a body be small, yet those who enter it and speak through its mouth are powerful. Let us not offend the vodoun who has chosen him. You, Hwesuhunu, will be my other hand."

He sent Hwesuhunu among the trees to find a dry seed pod for a rattle. And when it had been found, the service for the dead began. They sat in a circle around the corpses, with Doumé and Hwesuhunu in the center. Doumé shook the dry seed pod, and began: "Ogoun, Shango, Sobo, Balisai, Loko, Adja, Dadal, listen to your children, ago-é!"

Hwesuhunu added: "Listen, also, Legba, Nananbouclou, Mawu, Lisa, Hevioso, Agbé, Damballa, Ayida, Mivèvou, Alovi! Listen, Spirit of Twins, and the dead who went before us, ago-é!"

Doumé, waving a green branch over the bodies with one hand, shaking his rattle with the other, his eyes half-closed, said: "You, our orishas and vodouns, hear our misery. We were many, now we are few. We were taken from our villages and our country. We were marched to the sea, driven with guns and whips. We were taken to a strange place, we do not know where we are. Many died in the storm, and we have not found them. But these who lie here, for whom we invoke your strength and kindness, they must be buried. As they died in the sea, they will be buried near the sea. Eleven innocent countrymen are to be placed in their graves. We do not know what villages some of them came from. We do not know the names of their ancestors who reside in the land of the dead. But they were our friends in this time of evil and misery. Somewhere their mothers cry for them. Their wives or their husbands carry grief in their hearts. In their villages these men and women are remembered.

"There is Agili, from Abomey; he is dead. There is Doki, a Mahi; he is dead. There is Dogwé, from the Amine people; he is dead. There is Koba, a Nago from my country; he is dead. There is young Dosilu, a Fon; she has been in the world only a short time; she is dead. There is Adjaku, the Fon; he is dead. There is Bo, from Allada; he is dead. There is Malosi, the Fon woman; she is dead. There is Kama, the Ibibio; he is dead. There is Iridisu, the Hausa; he is dead. Their families are not here. Therefore, we speak for their families. Have pity on these good people. And you, ancestors, be kind. Do not forget the suffering here in the land of the living. Leave the brothers and sisters, fathers and mothers, wives and children of these people at peace. Do not torment them. Do not make demands they cannot fulfill."

Doumé shook his rattle and waved his green branch over the bodies. "You, our friends, when you see our parents and our grandparents, tell them how it is with us. If they can aid us, encourage them to do so. Do not forget us. We shall not forget you. Ago-é! Ago-vi! Ago-tchi!"

The men arose to carry the bodies to the burial place. The women remained where they were, crying out words of grief and throwing dust on themselves. Two men began to beat sticks against a piece of hollow driftwood, and to the sound of this drumming the bodies were laid in their shallow graves, covered with grass and leaves, and then with sand, until the mounds were finished. The drummers changed their beat. A circle formed. The dancing began. Voices rose in a song of the Fon villages. But it did not last. One by one dancers dropped away, drained and exhausted by the long march to Cotonou, imprisonment, and the struggle to survive the sea.

While Doumé fashioned a fire bow and shelters were being constructed near the beach, Dosu, Hwesuhunu, and another Fon, Kana, began an expedition into the countryside. At first they followed the irregular shore line, which revealed little except occasional broken beams and planks which had washed onto the sand. Where a small brook emptied into the ocean they went inland, through stands of wild palms. Though they could see little through the dense foliage, they were aware of the lift of the land. Where at last the trees thinned out, they could see a sloping grassy plain before them. Then, once more, the ground dipped into a lush green valley. Beyond it was a row of high hills, and beyond them, in the far distance, a tree-covered mountain soared skyward. They stared silently, until Hwesuhunu said, "What can lie beyond this mountain?" And Kana answered, quoting a proverb: "Beyond the mountains are mountains."

Dosu's eyes moved in a restless search for game trails or the marks of animals. He examined the earth for tracks and sought bits of fur caught in the bark of trees, but he found nothing. "In a country like this," he said, "there should be the marks of boars, leopards and antelopes, yet there is nothing but the trails left by birds in the sky." They saw small ground lizards among the rocks, and once, for a brief moment, they saw an iguana, then he was gone. They sat down to rest. Dosu said, "I smell the smoke of fires. Somewhere men are burning brush." Hwesuhunu could smell nothing. Kana said, "Yes, I smell it." Hwesuhunu tried again, and this time he believed he detected something that was not the odor of sunwashed air. Dosu said, "Let us go to the crest of the small hill." They arose and climbed, and from the top they could see cleared fields in the valley. Thin strands of smoke stretched upward from burning woodpiles. They heard faint human voices, exclamations, laughter, the sound of hoes on hard earth, a bush knife hacking into green wood. And as their eyes became accustomed, they saw small human figures working in one of the fields.

They walked silently, skirting small groves of hardwood and bamboo, and near the field they crawled into the tall grass from where they watched the men working with hoes. "Their skin is like ours," Hwesuhunu said, "they must be countrymen."

Dosu said, "They wear clothes like the white men."

And after a while Kana said, "They have no weapons. Let us go forward and talk."

They arose from their place and walked across the field. The fieldworkers stopped hoeing. Some of them became agitated and ran to the far side of the clearing. Two remained, an old one with a gray beard, and one lacking a foot who leaned on a crutch made of a green branch. Dosu, Kana and Hwesuhunu stopped within speaking distance.

Dosu said, "We are Fon. You, countrymen, let us talk."

The two workers spoke hurriedly together. The bearded

one said to Dosu, "I understand you a little. I am from Whydah. My friend, the crippled one, he does not understand. Where do you come from? Who owns you?"

"We are three men of Dahomey," Kana said. "No one owns us. We are free Fon. Our ship was wrecked. We came ashore here. Many died, a few are left."

The bearded one said, "They will catch you. They will put you to work in the fields."

Dosu asked, "Who are the 'they' who will catch us? And you, you men, what are you doing here?"

The bearded one answered, "We were captured, we were sold, we were brought here. Among us there is no single nation. I am Yoruba, my friend is Bafiote, and the others over there, they are of all kinds. Some of them were born here." Then the crippled one spoke, and the bearded one translated. "My friend asks how things are in his country."

Dosu answered, "We do not know, we have not been there. Our own country is sick. The king takes his own kind and sells them. Who is the ruler here?"

The bearded one said: "The ruler is he who owns the slaves. The white man, he rules. The dark man, he sweats. This country is called St. Lucia. The whites, they war on each other. They are of different nations, like the Fon and the Nago and the Ibo. They fight. Those who rule here now are called the French. A few years ago, their enemies, the British, ruled. We were brought from a place called Guadeloupe. That is our story. My friend, he is called Sabo. His foot was crushed on the ship that brought him. The flesh rotted. The doctor cut the foot off. Me, I was paid for heavily. Sabo, because he was crippled, he was not much wanted; he was paid for lightly. But you, you men of Dahomey, there is no place for you to go. This land is surrounded by water. You will be taken."

Dosu replied, "You, Uncle, whose name I haven't heard, come back with us. Bring your friend Sabo. Bring those others there, who fled from the sight of three free Fon. Join our village by the sea. Let the white men till their own fields."

"Before I came here I was known as Yalodé," the bearded one answered. "Now I am called Jean Labarbe. I was captured too long ago. Now I am too old. Sabo, he is crippled. They would catch us, they would beat us, they would kill us."

Dosu said, "Uncle, give us something. A gun perhaps. We are hungry. We must hunt meat." The old man answered: "Spears, there are none. Guns, the white men have them. Wild meat, there is little. Here is a bush knife. It is yours. I will say I lost it. They will beat me. But perhaps they will not beat too hard, because I am old. If we can find anything for you, we will bring it. We will leave it by the large rock at the edge of the field. Do not get caught. The whites call you bossal. That means the wild ones, like animals in the bush. They will tame you or they will kill you. Go away. Take your people up on that mountain. Others have run away and gone there. Some were caught and brought back. They were beaten, they were shot. But a few never came back. Maybe they died. Maybe they are still there. Who knows?"

The crippled man, Sabo, spoke again, and the bearded one translated for him. "He says that if you ever meet one of his countrymen, ask how things are among the Bafiote."

Kana answered, "We will do it."

Dosu said, "Uncle, you have given us something. If you are beaten for it, may the blows be light. May your years be many, and may you live to make corpses of the hyenas who claim to be your masters. May their crops wither, may their women and cattle dry up, and may they hobble around on one foot like Sabo. That is all." And Dosu, Hwesuhunu and Kana went back into the tall grass from which they had come.

It was Hwesuhunu's task to come every second day to see if something had been left at the rock near the field. The first time there was nothing, but that day he saw the white master riding his horse among the slaves in the field. He lay a long while in the grass, watching the scene before him. The master, dressed in white and wearing a large straw hat, spoke excitedly, riding back and forth, gesticulating with the riding whip he held in his hand. Some of the slaves had red kerchiefs bound around their heads; others were bareheaded. The master seemed to be urging the men to hurry. But there was nothing more to be learned, and Hwesuhunu crept away to report what he had seen.

The second time also there was nothing to be found at the rock. But on his third trip Hwesuhunu found a small iron pot, a broken bush knife and four musket balls. Another day there was a little gunpowder wrapped in a leaf, and some broken bits of iron. Still another time Hwesuhunu found a length of rope, some pieces of cloth and two broken gun flints. Back near the coastal shelters, Doumé had constructed a forge, powered by bellows made of iguana skins. There he forged the iron scraps into knives and spear points, hammering them between stones until they were shaped. By now there were six knives in the village and two spears.

It was the stolen musket that brought the supplies to an end. On one of his trips, Hwesuhunu found the musket by the rock, wrapped in straw. Thereafter there was nothing at all, and for three days the workers did not appear in the field. Then one day when Hwesuhunu crept through the grass to the rock he found Jean Labarbe, the bearded one, waiting for him. The bearded one said, "They discovered that the musket is gone. The punishments were great. Five men were whipped. One young one, he was hanged in front of the slave quarters. If a pot disappears they say it is because the slaves can't help stealing. When a gun disappears they are frightened. Now we can't bring anything. Two of the men who were whipped, they will run away when they are released from their irons. They will join your village. They know this land. They know the mountain. They will show you the way."

Hwesuhunu said: "Uncle, I will deliver the message. The village thanks you." And he sought for something more to say. As though he had thought of it before and had planned it, he took the wari nut from his waistcloth, the nut given to him in the darkness of the slave ship. "We have nothing to give in return. We came naked from the ocean. I have brought only one thing from our country across the water. This nut, it was given to me by my good friend Dokumi the Nago. He died in the storm. Perhaps this nut is a small thing to anyone else. For me it is a big thing because it was Dokumi's, and also because it grew in our own earth. Uncle, take it. Perhaps there is the spirit of a vodoun in it."

Jean Labarbe took the nut in his hand. He looked at it as though it were of great value. Then he placed it in a small leather bag which hung around his neck. "You, who have only begun to be a man, you have given greatly. You say your friend was a Nago. The Nago are cousins to the Yoruba. Therefore, Dokumi is my countryman. We shall hold a death service for him and ask the orishas to see him safely on his way. This nut, it is not a small thing. It shall be planted. It will sprout. It will grow into a bush. There will be more nuts. They shall remind us of where we came from."

Several days later the runaways came to the village. There were not two but three—two men and a woman. They brought with them two hoes, cloth and an ax. And there began some discussions about abandoning the beach village and retiring into the hills. The three escapees had been born in captivity. They spoke a mélange of words part African and part French. They conveyed a sense of urgency about leaving the ocean shore. But Doumé was not ready. From the heavy hoe blades which had just arrived he had to make spear points.

And there were other reasons. He was awaiting a sign from Ogoun, the orisha of iron. Three days later no sign had come. But there was something else. Someone had seen white soldiers with guns patrolling the shore on the far side of an arm of land that jutted into the sea. The runaways from the plantation became agitated. They spoke rapidly, urging everyone to go into the hills. Doumé said, "Not yet." Two men were sent out to keep a watch on the soldiers. That night there was a service to the vodouns of the Fon, the orishas of the Nago and the spirits of other nations from which the people came.

Doumé stood by a tree with his ritual seed pod in his hand. He sang a song of the Nagos, calling on the deities to be attentive. Then Hwesuhunu, remembering how it was done in the shrines of his village, took up the song and addressed it to the vodouns of Dahomey. The drummers beat on hollow driftwood logs, and a tight circle of dancers moved around the tree as Doumé marked time with his rattle, his chin on his chest, perspiration dripping from his forehead. A woman went forward and wiped the sweat from his face with her headcloth. The dancers turned, dipped, pirouetted as the drum rhythm commanded. A girl stepped to the center of the circle and sang a song of greeting to the vodoun Sebo, the Leopard, and the dancers took up the song. The nearly naked bodies glistened with sweat. One of the women gave a wild call, staggered, lurched, fell upon the ground and lay quivering. The vodoun Sebo had arrived among them. The drumming became more agitated. Other vodouns and orishas arrived, entering into the heads of the dancers. Those who were mounted by the spirits were led outside the dance court to lie quietly and recover.

There was then a song for Ogoun, the spirit of iron, and Doumé traced designs on the earth with the end of his seed pod, reciting an invocation. And Ogoun came from Whydah, descended the trunk of the central tree and entered into Doumé's head. Doumé's eyes were open, yet he appeared to see nothing. He trembled, grew rigid, and flung himself about violently. While the drums signaled a salute to Ogoun, Doumé moved toward the fire. With an unflinching hand he took from it a piece of glowing iron and brandished it like a sword. He danced in the coals, kicking the embers in all directions. When at last he was spent, they helped him to a grassy place to lie down. The orisha Ogoun had departed, but he had given the sign that wherever his children were he would watch over them. The dancing came to an end. Doumé said: "We will go into the mountains when the daylight comes."

Before they left they tore down their temporary shelters and threw the debris into the sea. They buried the ashes from the fires in the sand. And afterward, carrying their few crude possessions, the Africans began their journey into the mountains. The two men from the plantation led them in a course that seemed directionless, first west, then south, then a little to the east. Usually when there was a choice between a hard way and an easy way, the guides chose the hard way. They swung in a wide arc to avoid settlements which lay between them and the mountains. They pressed through large stands of hardwood. And several times when it seemed they were beginning the ascent, the ground dropped away before them into wooded valleys. They found wild fruit sometimes and stopped to eat, and to ease their thirst they drank the milk of wild coconuts.

It was already late in the day when the real ascent began. When darkness came they camped. Doumé lighted a fire with his fire bow. They sat around it and talked. They told stories. They even laughed. There was an incongruous sense of well-being. For the first time since they were driven into the slave compounds, they felt as though they were not merely inconsequential victims of malevolence and chance. They had a sense of self-reliance, of the power to make decisions, limited though those decisions might be. A feeling of community that had eluded them in the slave ship was born. Whatever this life was worth, wherever the road led, it was a common experience that they shared. They were hardly aware now that they had come from different nations. They borrowed from each other's speech, and a song sung by one person became the property of all. If they spoke at all of their homelands they tended less to refer to Whydah, or Allada, or Dahomey, saying instead Guinea, a word which vaguely took in a wide stretch of the continent. While they were camped there that first night, Hwesuhunu contrived a crude musical instrument, a sansa, out of a coconut shell and fine strips of bamboo. The strips were tied to the shell with grass, and when they were plucked they gave out musical tones. He sang in a low voice to the accompaniment of his sansa, and a quietness fell over the gathering:

In Guinea, there our friends are.
In Guinea, there our ancestors lived.
In Guinea there are fields of corn.
In Guinea, there the sun rises.
In Guinea the sun goes down.
In Guinea things begin and end.

Another man took the sansa and sang a song of his own. Whoever wanted to sing did so. After the singing was over, Hwesuhunu said, "When we have arrived where we are going, I shall make a good sansa." One of the older men said, "Never in my life have I ever heard a better sansa than this one. Never before has a sansa made such deep music."

They slept in the leaves and grass, tortured by mosquitoes. Morning came and they continued the ascent. Where they climbed there were no trails. They sometimes had to use their knives to cut their way through dense vegetation. Several times they reached impassable places and had to go back and find another way. By the time the sun hung directly overhead they stood on the crest of the first and lowest range. Looking back they could see the miniature contours of the coast and, beyond the coast, the great glistening sea. Beyond the arm of land that jutted into the sea were seemingly motionless tiny white sails. Though they could not see past the mountains, they could sense that the country was really an island, that if one stood on one of the two high peaks he would be able to see water in all directions. In one of the green valleys below were cultivated fields and plantation buildings.

Dosu said, "Let us camp here for now. If we go higher the game will be scarce. Let us hunt and find meat."

But the two men from the plantation protested. "There is no meat in this region. There are wild fowl in the valley ahead. We can hunt there."

And so they went on, descending from the first range into the valley. There they camped. Those who had spear points made shafts for them, and hunting parties went out in several directions. The women took the hoes and went to dig roots. Hwesuhunu was in Dosu's party which numbered four men in all. They found no birds, but in a gully they came upon two iguanas. Dosu speared one, but the other escaped. Once they flushed a large ratlike creature out of the brush, but they could not catch it.

Dosu said, "There are no trails here. There is no game. What kind of a country is this?"

"I have been thinking," Hwesuhunu said. "This is not game country. If we were near the sea, we could fish and catch turtles."

Dosu said irritably, "We are not near the sea. Every step we take carries us farther away from the sea. Why do you speak of fish and turtles?"

Hwesuhunu said, "Because I am thinking. I also thought another thing. The white men have cattle. That is the place to hunt."

Dosu looked at Hwesuhunu with surprise. "Your father speaks with your mouth. Let us make our village first and put roofs on our houses. The women shall gather fruit. And we shall go down to the plantation for our meat."

They retraced their way toward the camp. Once they flushed a covey of large birds. They threw spears and stones, but they killed nothing. They arrived in the camp with only their one iguana. Another hunting party also came back with an iguana. The third caught nothing at all. So the ascent was resumed, and by nightfall they were halfway up the second range. They slept again, and by the next afternoon they stood in a small green place surrounded by high hills covered with pines. It was decided that they would build their village here, near where cold water trickled from an outcropping of rock.

The houses were built in a circle. Poles were set in the ground, and crosspoles tied to them with tough vines. When the roof poles were in place, they were covered with bundles of grass. All the houses were roofed first, to provide shade, and then the grass walls were made. When the work was done, there was a celebration with dancing and storytelling.

That night Hwesuhunu saw his friend Dosu smile. Dosu's eyes followed a young woman dancer named Konsi. If she looked his way, his lips parted and his white teeth glistened. She looked elsewhere then so purposively that he took it for an answer and smiled again. When there was a chance to talk he said, "You, girl, are you looking for a hunter?"

She answered as though offended. "If you are a hunter, why is there no meat here?"

He said, "Meat there is."

"Is lizard what the hunter calls meat? Bring us antelope, bring us wild pig, bring us buffalo, then we shall have something to eat."

He taunted her, saying, "One does not run to hunt at the suggestion of a woman."

They were parted by the action of the dance, but Dosu continued to watch her, while she turned her glances elsewhere.

When the dancing was over, the storytelling began. In his turn, Dosu went to the center of the circle, sat down and told a tale. "It is said," he began, turning his face toward Konsi briefly, "that a man does not pursue an antelope to please a woman. This is the tale of two hunters who were friends. There was a girl in the village. She was very good to see. Many young men sought to marry her. But she had a condition. She said, 'I will marry only a man who catches a live antelope for me.' Some men tried to catch an antelope, but they could not do it. The two hunters who were friends, they also went to ask for the girl. Her father said, 'She will only accept a man who catches a live antelope.'

"So the two hunters went together into the bush. They flushed an antelope. They pursued. They became weary. One stopped running. He said, 'Shall I let one woman kill me with running?' He sat down and waited for his friend to finish. His friend went on. He caught the antelope. He placed it on his back. He returned to where the first hunter waited. Together they went to the girl's house. The father saw the antelope and sent for the village elders. He said: 'These two young men went to catch a live antelope because my daughter insisted. One gave up. The other pursued and caught the antelope. Each of them wants my daughter. Judge the matter for us.' The elders asked the two to state the case. The first one said: 'We pursued. My friend gave up the running. But I wanted the girl greatly. Therefore I ran till the antelope was exhausted. I have returned with it.' The second hunter said: 'The running went on. My breath, it almost stopped. I said to myself: "When before has a man had to catch an antelope to earn a wife? I will not kill myself because a woman makes such conditions." I stopped, I waited. I did not come back for the girl, but only to accompany my friend.'

"The elders considered. In the end they said: 'You who have captured the antelope, take it, it is yours. But you who gave up the running, you shall have the girl. Your friend, when he wants something, he thinks of nothing else. But you, you reflect on the matter. If we come to discuss things with you, you will be reasonable. You will be our son-in-law. A man does not chase an antelope to please a woman.' "

There were laughing and applause. Dosu glanced at

Konsi. Her face was turned away. She moved from the firelight into the darkness of the trees. When Kana came into the circle to tell a story, Dosu also went out into the darkness of the trees. A few days later Dosu and Konsi began to build a house of their own.

To Hwesuhunu it seemed familiar, as though time, an ocean and a ship of horrors had not come between him and an old life. Dosu's marriage seemed a natural event, even in this unaccustomed place, and the continuity of old ways was reassuring.

But the raid on the plantation for supplies was something new. The wars in Dahomey were understandable. The rules were known to all. But this thing was something that had not happened before. There was nothing equal in it. Those who were half starved, half naked, and almost without weapons were to confront those who had everything. He himself had been the first to speak of it. It had been logical. Yet now it seemed to be a reckless seeking out of the enemy. He was awed by the meaning of the event, for he saw that the Africans had nothing but a temporary sanctuary here in the mountains, that his life and the lives of his friends would be lived out in unending confrontation with those who had the power to take them from their homes and transport them wherever they wished. He saw that if the village failed to act, it would be like a village of wild game, helpless before the hunter. If the raiding party failed, some or all of them would die. And if it succeeded, it could do nothing but cause counter-raids, probably by soldiers with muskets.

There were fourteen men in the raiding party. Ten carried spears, for Doumé had forged more points from the iron hoe blades, three had bush knives, and Hwesuhunu was in charge of Doumé's fire bow. Their single musket remained in the village for safekeeping. One of the party was Kofi, who had fled the plantation and joined them on the beach. They left before the sun rose, camping that night on the range of hills nearest the valley. And the next morning they made their way to the edge of the canefields. There Kofi pointed out where the cattle were pastured and the outbuilding where tools were kept. The raiding party divided into two groups, one headed by Dosu, the other by Kana. Kana's men were to get the cattle, Dosu's the tools.

While they lay hidden in the grass, Hwesuhunu took the fire bow and crept into the sugar field. Once in the tall cane, he ran without fear of being seen. It was an endless field, he thought. Never had anyone seen so much cane. But he came at last to the far side, to a stretch of half-cleared brush. Finding what he needed for a fire, he worked the bow rapidly until wisps of smoke arose where the drill ate its way into a piece of dried wood. He added moss and leaves. And suddenly where there had only been smoke, a yellow flame sprang up. Hwesuhunu piled on dried brush. He carried some of the flame to another place and lighted the dry grass. When he was certain that the fire would hold, he returned through the cane to rejoin Dosu's party. The Africans lay and waited. They could smell the smoke before they could see it. But they kept their eyes on a distant field where they could see men at work. The first note of alarm was a bell that sounded somewhere among the plantation buildings. They saw a horseman ride out to where the slaves were working. Then the horse and rider headed across the valley toward the brush fire that was billowing clouds of smoke into the air. The fieldworkers followed at a run.

Dosu stood up. Both raiding parties moved swiftly. There was no attempt to remain hidden now. Dosu's group raced to the outbuilding where the tools were kept. They found hoes, shovels, adzes, drawknives and a miscellany of cooper's tools. They wrapped them in a canvas and slung them to a pole. With the captured tools the party quickly recrossed the adjoining field and slipped once more into the tall grass. Following Kofi, they headed back into the range from which they had come. On the way they met Kana's party, driving two young bulls and two cows ahead of it. Lashed to poles they carried three small pigs, and one man carried two turkeys whose necks already had been wrung. From the first hill they could see a wide expanse of smoke where the brush had been fired. Then they moved into the trees. The cattle strayed constantly in the timber. Dosu was irritated because Kana's party had not found ropes to leash the bulls.

They camped that night in a clearing. Six men guarded the cattle while the others slept. At dawn they were on their way again. At noon they came to the village. Those who had been left behind greeted them with singing and took over their burdens, which were piled together in the central court. The cattle were tethered. The raiders were fed with fruit and iguana meat. Thus ended the expedition.

The men squatted around the tools that had been brought back and considered what should be done with them. The hoes were set aside for cultivation. A cooper's hammer was given to Doumé to be reforged into an ax. Shovel blades and other bits of iron were placed in a separate pile for reshaping into spears and workknives. Hwesuhunu and Kofi were set to the task of gathering stones and building a new forge. The women and girls went to gather tough grass for braiding into ropes. The drawknife was used for making spearshafts and an ax handle. Dosu led a party out into the countryside to set snares for birds and small game, and when the first dove was captured in a string snare it was regarded as an epic event, an omen that the woods had consented to feed them.

Women went each morning to the small pool below the spring to wash headcloths and some of the few ragged clothes which the villagers possessed. In the evenings men carved small things out of wood—spoons, crude combs and a mortar in which grain could be pulverized, though there was as yet no grain in the village. Two men guided by Kofi went down to one of the plantations and returned with large bundles of maize. And it seemed that in all that was happening the people of the village were finding a way back to a life that was familiar and understood.

From the plantations there was no sign that the presence of the Africans was recognized. Yet always in the background, even in carefree moments, there was the knowledge that somewhere down there the plantation people and the soldiers were talking about the raids and forays for food. And while the making of weapons continued, sentries were set out on all possible approaches to the village. Three weeks later, when it began to seem as if no one would ever follow them into their inhospitable mountain retreat, Kana came running to report the smoke of a campfire on one of the slopes. There was a hurried council of war, and a party of five was designated to reconnoiter. Dosu, Kana, Hwesuhunu, a Nago named Toto and Kofi the plantation runaway took their spears and descended to Kana's outpost, and from there they moved silently and swiftly through a tangle of trees and brush until they came close to the encampment of the strangers. Hwesuhunu, because he was small and agile, was sent forward to get information.

Holding his spear tightly, he slipped through the underbrush, stepping carefully so that there would be no crackling of dry leaves and twigs underfoot. The encampment was farther away than it appeared; even so, Hwesuhunu approached it by an encircling route that brought him to the far side of the small clearing. At first he only heard voices, though he understood nothing of what was being said. Crouching, alternately moving and pausing to listen, he crept forward. When the voices stopped, Hwesuhunu froze, and in the silence he heard the drumming of his heart inside him. When the talking began again he crept into the last underbrush, beyond which he could not go without becoming visible. Through the tangle of leaves and branches he saw six white men lounging on the ground around a fire. He sensed that they felt no urgency, and that they were unaware of his nearness. From where he crouched so tensely a stone could have been thrown into their fire.

Because they were all white and spoke a strange language, and because they all wore similar clothing, Hwesuhunu at first could not distinguish one from another. But little by little he saw that some were older, some younger; that one had a growth of hair above his lips and others didn't; that two were larger and four were smaller; that some did most of the talking and the others spoke only infrequently; that one spoke with great authority and others with none at all. And he saw that each of the men had a musket, either in his hand or lying on the ground beside him. At last, the loud beating of his heart still in his ears, Hwesuhunu moved slowly back the way he had come. Once he stepped on dry leaves that made an incredibly loud sound, and he stood tensely waiting to know whether it had been heard. But there was no sign, and he went on. When he reached his party he reported what he had seen.

Dosu said, "They are six, we are five. But five who are invisible in the forest are the equal of ten. Let us destroy them by surprise."

Kana answered, "Let us say that we are ten, then. But do they not have six muskets?"

Dosu said, "Silent weapons are better. We can take them in our snare when they are climbing and breathless. Let us do it this way."

It was decided. The five Africans took positions in the dense brush along the route of ascent. The waiting was long, and no one spoke. But at last the soldiers arose, stamped out their fire and resumed their climbing. Their voices and the sound of their careless shod feet became louder. First one man's cap could be seen, then another's. The war party leaped out of the brush and attacked. Kana's spear was launched first, embedding itself in the chest of the soldier first in line. Three more spears followed. Toto's glanced off the cheekbone of another soldier, leaving a welling red gash behind. Hwesuhunu's struck a metal buckle and fell, rattling in the stones. Kofi's went too high and landed in a tangle of vines. Dosu did not throw. He ran forward shouting, thrusting and jabbing. Several musket shots were fired.

Two soldiers who had lagged behind turned and ran, sliding and falling on the slippery rocks. Kana and Dosu followed for a short distance and then returned. It was over. Four dead or dying soldiers lay on the ground. The Africans gathered the muskets, the bullets and the powder. They stripped the clothes from the bodies, which they dragged into the shadows. Carrying their booty of war, they returned singing to the village.

That night as they sat around the fire there were stories about battles, heroes and kings. Little by little fatigue closed their eyes. They slept.

The men sat in the shade near the spring. They argued. "Now that we have killed four soldiers, the French will return," Kofi said. "They will bring many men. They will bring many muskets. There will be fighting every day."

Kana said, "We will meet them in the bush, each time at a different place. Out of six soldiers we will kill four. The others will go away."

Dosu said, "No, this is not the way. Let us give them fear. We go down at night, we burn their fields and their houses, we return before the eye of day is open."

Kofi said, "The whites are many. If we kill them all, others will come in ships. The ships are many also."

Dosu stood up. He turned slowly, speaking first to one man, then another. "Our Fa has been made clear. There are two mountain peaks. Shall we run from one peak to another and then back to the first? Shall we run to the other side and then back to this side? Are we playing-pieces on a mancalla board? Shall we wait for the enemy to make the capture? Or shall we take the play? Thus it is. The island is our mancalla board. We cannot retreat beyond the seashore. It is we who must go down, not they who must come up."

"No, it is better for them to come up," Kofi said. "Let them take the climbing. Let us wait for them in the shadows. Perhaps the British will come and drive them away."

"The British, are they not white?" Dosu answered. "The British, do they take slaves or not? What difference is there, then?"

Kana said, "Perhaps if we do not go down they will not come up. If we burn nothing, take nothing, they will say, 'Let the village be where it is, we do not care.' "

Dosu said, "If it is to be like that, it is like being in the stockade at Cotonou. Who can live in so small a place? Because they are there, we must fight them. Who was it who sailed to Dahomey for slaves? It was not I. Who brought us here? It was not I. Wickedness brought us. It is our Fa. Our Fa is here; they are our fate, and we must fight them. There is no other way, except one. You, men, you can go down to the city. You can say to them, 'We are Fon and Nago, we came from our country, we are here, we will be your slaves. Give us hoes to till your fields. Give us carrying pads, we shall carry stones for you. Give us bridles, we are your horses. The women, copulate with them. If you strike us, do so gently. If you wish, sell us to whom you please.' You can do this. If you do not choose this way, what other way is there? We can fight them. We can burn their fields."

Toto said, "Is it better to till a master's field or to die?"

Dosu answered, "Do not all men die?"

Toto said, "I am not afraid to fight. I was there yesterday. My spear was there. It entered the belly of a man. Was the blood on it different from the blood on any other spear? Yet my question is unanswered. You speak this way and that way. When you were taken by Adanzan's soldiers, did you not say differently than now? You did not say, 'All men die.' You said, 'The fight is over. I am a captive. I will march to Cotonou.' "

Dosu said with anger, "My Fa then was plain. My Fa now is plain. Do not press me."

Toto answered, "I do not press. But who knows what our Fa is? Is there a Fa priest among us to read the shells? When a thing happens, we can say that is our Fa. But as for what has not yet happened, who can say what it will be? One hunts elephant in the bush. One approaches. One fires his musket. The elephant is hit. He turns to face the hunter. There is a moment then. What will he do? He will do what is Fa, but in that moment no one can tell what Fa is. The elephant himself does not know. Only when he is doing it does his Fa become clear. He charges the hunter, or he turns and runs with the other elephant. Only then does he understand his Fa. So do not keep saying 'This is my Fa' or 'That is my Fa.' No man knows his Fa before it happens."

Doumé, sewing a bellows for his forge, said, "It is so. No man knows. If he did, he would have to decide nothing in his life. What one has decided upon becomes, in the end, fate. But not in the beginning before it is decided."

Dosu said, "Very well. I decide. Kofi here, he decided. He ran away. I who have not been taken, I would be less than he if I were to take his place. Let us fight the French."

They argued. They turned the matter over many ways.

Then Doumé put his bellows aside and said: "This is the way it will be. If the French come to get us, we will fight them. If we go down to the plantations we will take what is required, but as little as possible. If we take only a little, they will not become so angry as to make war. If we take much, if we burn the houses, that will anger them too much. So if we need meat, we shall take only a pig. If we need corn, we take only what will last a week. If we need iron, we shall take only a little. They will say: 'Those people up there, they are a nuisance, but they don't take too much. Let us be on guard, but leave them alone up there on the mountain.' They will say: 'Some day when we get to it we will go up there after them, but for the present it isn't too bad. Let us await a better time.' Thus things will remain quiet."

The men agreed. Dosu said nothing. He arose and walked away from the gathering.

As it had been agreed, the things taken from the plantations thenceforth were small. Only a little at a time. And as the days went by, no more French soldiers came up the mountain. There began to grow a sense of permanence. Toto, like Dosu, took one of the women for a wife and built a hut of his own.

Seeds were taken from maize and pumpkins brought back from the plantations. They were dried and planted in little pockets of earth on the stony mountain. It was said that when these crops matured there would be a harvest feast. But the shoots that came from the earth attracted wild birds, and the crops were destroyed before they matured. So Kofi and Hwesuhunu were sent on an expedition to bring back more seeds from the valley. At midday they rested in a grove high on the mountainside. There the two of them exchanged confidences and became friends. Hwesuhunu spoke of his brothers, his father and his mother. Kofi told of his life on the plantation and about his father's town of Agogo in the Kingdom of Ashanti.

"I was born here on the island," he said. "But my father was a brass caster near the city of Kumasi. His castings were known everywhere in Ashanti. He was on a journey to Accra to make castings for a great chief when he was taken by the slave raiders. He was bought by the British, and they sold him to a French ship captain. He was brought first to Guadeloupe. There he was bought by the agent for Beauregard. Beauregard is the master of my plantation. My father was made a field hand. My father worked in the fields like a man with no knowledge. What does Beauregard know of beeswax and molds and brass-casting? He knows nothing, only about rum and molasses.

"My father explained to me the art of casting. But for

whom shall I cast? My father died a year ago. My mother, she is not here. She was sent to another island in the north. There was the incident of the stolen musket. For that, my friend André was killed by Beauregard. I was tied to a post and whipped. I said, 'What is here for me that I should stay?' I left, I came with you. There are no Ashanti in the village, but the Fon and the Nago, they are my people. If Beauregard catches me I will be hanged like André. That is his way. He kills, kills. I have one wish. I wish to drown him in a barrel of molasses and send him to France with his own cargo. But there are others too. The other French planters are the same.

"Saintville, he is like Beauregard. His plantation is the next one to the west. Sometimes he is here, sometimes in Guadeloupe. His chief of the slaves is even worse than Beauregard. Beauregard, he has one slave woman in his house. But Saintville's chief of the slaves takes any woman he wants, even in the fields. He is not happy unless he is whipping. When he is angry he withholds food. He has two great dogs. They are tied to the house. He trains them to attack field hands who come near the house. If a slave offends him, he gives the food to the dogs instead. So I came here. My father was a fine craftsman. He was not meant to be a slave."

"Can you cast brass?" Hwesuhunu asked.

"I have never done it. But my father explained it."

"Can we not do it?"

"We can do it. But where is the brass?"

"Is there no brass at the plantation?"

"Yes, there is brass there. Let us think of it."

In the dark of night they found the maize and the pumpkins. And before they returned, Kofi said, "Wait here. Guard the seeds. I will come back." And he slipped away into the darkness. Hwesuhunu waited. He began to wonder if Kofi would return. The stars moved from one side of the sky to the other. But just when the black began to turn gray, Kofi came running through the field. He carried a small parcel wrapped in cloth. They took up the pumpkins and the maize, worked their way through the brush and began the ascent to the village.

The next day Kofi went to find Hwesuhunu. He sat on the ground and unwrapped his bundle. He spread the items on the cloth. There were some small ship's fittings, several broken wall hooks and a small cracked bell. Kofi looked at them silently waiting for Hwesuhunu to speak.

"What are these things?" Hwesuhunu said at last, failing to solve the puzzle.

"We discussed it. Have you forgotten? These things came from Beauregard's place. They are brass."

"Brass?"

"Yes, brass. I am going to cast." He tied the cloth and picked up the bundle. "Let us find beeswax."

When they had found a hive and extricated the wax they went next to dig clay, into which Kofi kneaded cattle dung. He then made a small figure of a man out of wax.

Dosu came to watch. He said, "What are you making?"

"A man."

"What is it for?" Dosu asked.

"It is a man."

"What is to be done with it?"

"Nothing," Kofi replied. "It is a man. Thus my father made castings. I am his son. Therefore, I make this."

Dosu said, "It is a good man. But we don't need it. What we need is bullets for our guns."

When Dosu had gone, Kofi sat thinking. He said, "Very well, I will make bullets. But I will also make this man." He coated the wax figure with the dung and clay, leaving a small opening leading to the wax core. Hammering the bits of brass between stones, he broke them into small fragments which he encased in the clay which held the wax model. Then he set the shapeless wet mold in the sun to dry. After that he made little bullets out of wax, and enclosed them in the same fashion. He did not stop until his brass was exhausted. Several days later when the clay and dung poultices had dried, he called Hwesuhunu, and the two of them carried the molds to Doumé's forge. Kofi placed his mold of a man in the fire first. He let it get heated through, then he removed it to cool.

"This is the way my father did it," Kofi said. "The beeswax melts and disappears." Again he placed the mold in the fire, using Doumé's bellows now to make the fire glow. And when the brass fragments were molten inside, he turned the mold over so that liquid metal ran into the hollow left by the wax, afterward setting it aside to cool. They sat and watched the mold tensely. When at last he could pick it up with his hand, Kofi broke it open. And there, where in the beginning had been a man of wax, there was a man of brass. The two of them, Kofi and Hwesuhunu, ran around the village showing off their work. People exclaimed in surprise. And after all the showing was done, the two of them went back and placed the bullet molds in the fire. In this way it came about that some of the muskets of the African village were loaded with shot made of brass.

The values of life and the will to live asserted themselves in the village. Men made things out of wood, metal and grass. They planted and replanted. They hunted. They fought. They argued. They reasoned. They joked. They remembered their dead companions. They remembered their villages and their ancestors. They married. And though some were Fon, some Nago, and some Mahi, they made out of these things a single village and a common language. Out of disaster they were slowly and instinctively reshaping old things and formulating a new way. But the forces which lurked beyond their mountain could not be held back.

Hwesuhunu was the first to know that the white soldiers were coming. He saw them first only as a glint in the sun far down on the mountainside. Then, for a moment, there were several glints at the same time, reflections from buckles or musket barrels. For a while there was nothing more to be seen. But when the reflections came again, this time from another place, it was clear that the movement was toward the village.

Hwesuhunu waited no longer, but turned to carry the news. Once his spear became entangled in vines and he fell, but he was on his way again without brushing the dirt from his chest and face. He called out the alarm when he was still at a distance. By the time he arrived, the men were already gathering with their weapons. They pressed around him for the news. "There are many," Hwesuhunu said. "I do not know the number. There were six or seven flashes from their weapons. But the nearest was far from the hindmost. Therefore I think there were others between them whose weapons did not reflect. They still have half the mountain to climb."

Doumé the Nago said: "Call the men from the bush. The women, let them take what food they can carry. We shall hide them."

The muskets were brought out and given to the men who knew how to use them. The guns were loaded. The men put small sacks of powder into their waistcloths. The bullets were passed out, one to each man, around and around until they were gone. Each man placed the bullets in his mouth for safekeeping. Hwesuhunu was one of those entrusted with a musket. Every man carried a spear, and those who had muskets carried spears as well. Doumé sent four scouts ahead to keep track of the French party and to report back if there was any change of route. It was then arranged that the Africans would not attack in a group as long as they were using firearms. Instead, they would scatter in the bush along the line of the ascent, fire when they had good targets, then retire into the undergrowth to reload. After that they were to try to move ahead of the French, again fire, again disappear into the underbrush. When their bullets and powder were gone, they were to assemble near the top of the ascent and take positions for a spear attack.

The men went down, and one by one they turned into the dense brush to find sniping stations. Before they had gone far, one of the scouts came up to report that the French party had been sighted. "There are forty, fifty men," he said, "all armed with muskets. They move rapidly. I cannot be sure, but I think there is still another party following." The news was not good. The Africans discussed things. They could not devise a better plan. So Kana was sent with the message that if the French reached the village, everyone was to reassemble at the hiding place selected for the women.

Hwesuhunu's turn came to drop out. He hesitated, seeing that Dosu and Kofi were going further. "I will go with them to the front," he said.

Doumé looked at him with anger. "Are you a man or a boy? Go here, as a man is told."

Hwesuhunu said no more, but turned among the trees into a tangle of dense undergrowth. He searched for a protected place from which he could see the natural trail which the French must follow. He found it. He rested his loaded musket in the fork of a small tree. He waited.

There were no sounds after that but of birds, insects and tree toads. He did not move. So quietly did he stand that a small ground lizard crawled slowly across his naked foot. Once again, as during the plantation raid, the sound of his heart drumming in his body became loud. And involuntarily he suddenly spoke aloud. "I am a man," he said. "I work in my father's dokpwe. I am not a boy, I am a man." Then he silently sang a song to Ogoun, god of war. When he finished, the sound of his heart had diminished, and there was great silence all around. There was no breeze, and the leaves hung limply on the trees. He waited. Time passed, then more time.

At last, muffled and barely audible, there came the report of a single musket. There was a pause, then a fusillade of shots. Once more, silence and a stretch of time. Again a single shot, followed by a fusillade. And so it was repeated time after time, with the shots becoming louder and closer. He thought he heard voices now, and strained his senses.

Yes, there were voices and the scrape of leather boots on stone and gravel. "They are coming," he told himself. This knowledge was followed by an impulse to turn and flee into the bush. But he said, almost aloud, "Am I not a man of my father's dokpwe?" And he sighted his gun, waiting for the advancing party to appear. There they came, all of them on foot, peering forward, turning from side to side as though their eyes could penetrate the dense underbrush. "Which one?" Hwesuhunu asked himself over and over. "Which one?" One man stopped, his searching eyes turning in Hwesuhunu's direction. Hwesuhunu squeezed the trigger. The lock snapped down, the gun fired. There was a small cloud of smoke, through which Hwesuhunu saw the Frenchman stagger backward.

Hwesuhunu turned and fought his way deeper into the tangled vegetation. He heard the fusillade he knew would come and the snapping of rifle balls through the leaves. He went on and maneuvered to seek a new position from which to shoot. Lungs aching, he sped across a clearing. On the far side, where the trees began again, he mounted a tall rock outcropping. At its summit, cradled among the stones, lay Doumé with his gun and spear. He signaled silently with his arm, and Hwesuhunu descended and worked his way to a point well beyond. He reloaded his musket, braced it in a tree fork and waited. He heard Doumé's shot, but the expected fusillade did not come right away. When it did come, it was from another direction, back in the heavy brush.

In time the heads, then the bodies of the advancing French troops became visible. This time Hwesuhunu fired into a group, and saw one of the men clutch at his shoulder. He plunged into the wild brush once more, anticipating the answering shots. But the threat came from elsewhere. He ran almost into the arms of three Frenchmen whose muskets were at firing position. He swerved as the shots were fired, felt a sharp sting in his left side, but kept going until he was lost in the shadows. Where a beam of sunlight pierced through the leaves he looked at the place where a ball had seared his side, and at the ribbon of blood running down his leg. "Now it can be truly said," he thought, "I am a man." He retied his waistcloth to cover the wound, and again, breathing heavily, moved up the mountainside. But there were no more shots. He found Kana waiting, bullets still in his mouth.

"The Frenchmen have scattered," Hwesuhunu said. "They are coming by different trails now. Some of them are in front of us, some behind." He reloaded his gun and sat with Kana, beginning to feel the ache of his sticky wound. No more Frenchmen appeared. After a while they heard a voice calling for the men to assemble near the top of the ascent. Kana relayed the call, and the two of them proceeded toward the village. When they arrived at the rendezvous station, Dosu the hunter was there. So were Kofi and his fellow runaway, Lafrance. Toto the Nago was there. Counting Hwesuhunu and Kana, there were fifteen men in all. Two, including Hwesuhunu, had superficial wounds. They bound their wounds with cloth to stop the bleeding. One by one other men arrived, until there were nineteen.

There was no sign of the others. Doumé did not arrive. They began to question one another: "Where is Doumé? Who has seen Doumé?"

Hwesuhunu said, "I passed Doumé near the ascent. I heard his shot. I heard the French guns speak. That is all."

Kana said, "The enemy has stopped below. They are tired. There is no hurry. Hwesuhunu and I will go for Doumé."

They went down again, this time in a wide arc to avoid meeting any of the enemy who might be patrolling in the underbrush. They came to the rock outcropping where Doumé had last been seen, but he was not there. They searched, moving into the denser vegetation. It was Kana who found Doumé lying on his face in a tangle of vines. When they turned him over his eyes were open but he did not see. A small oozing blue hole marked his forehead. The spirit which was life had gone from him. They carried him to a deep gully, laid him there and covered him with a blanket of leaves. Hwesuhunu had no words. His wound was hurting him now, but it was the knot in his throat that gave him the greatest pain. Had he been only a boy he would have cried.

As for Kana, he said: "This spear, it was beaten out of iron by my friend. This knife, he tempered it with his sweat at the forge. My weapons will remember him."

When they brought back the news about Doumé it was heard in silence. Then Dosu said, "Nine men have not returned. Some are dead, some perhaps only hurt, but they are not here. Let us consider. Let us decide again what to do, those of us who remain. Some will say 'do this,' others will say 'do that,' but whatever we decide now, it is for all. It is said: 'The village has many arms and legs but only one heart.' Let us speak our minds."

"Who knows for certain what the enemy is doing now?" Kana said. "Are they resting? Are they waiting for reinforcements? Are they encircling us? Do they come from the other side of the hill?"

Toto spoke, saying, "I approached their camp. They were drinking coffee. They seemed to be waiting for something."

Kofi said, "I believe they are waiting for dogs to be brought up. The dogs are hunting dogs. They follow the scent of runaway slaves. When everything was quiet I heard a dog baying down below."

"We cannot hide forever," someone said. "Wherever we go they will follow."

Some said this, some said that.

Kana said: "Let us go to them once more before the dogs arrive. Let us creep up on them in the night. When the eye of day opens, let us attack with our spears. These are the spears given to us by Doumé the Nago. Let them strike the enemy silently. When the outcome of this battle is known, then our choice will be clear."

Dosu said, "I am for this thing. We have four muskets left. Let us divide the musket balls among those who have guns."

The men took the musket balls from their mouths and counted. There were eleven balls in all. They were divided.

Dosu said, "Those who have guns, let them remain on the edge of the camp. Let those who have spears go forward. The muskets, let them be fired only if the spear attack goes badly."

In the night they went down to the fringes of the enemy camp and lay among the trees. When the morning sky became gray, those who had spears went forward and began the attack. They did not throw their spears but used them as lances. Four soldiers were dead or dying before the camp was fully awake. Then the firing of guns began, and the spearmen withdrew. From the edges of the camp the African muskets covered their retreat.

It was the last time the Africans attacked. They had lost two more men. Of the original twenty-eight there were now seventeen. From that moment on they were as antelope running before the hunters in the bush. The soldiers trailed them across the mountain. The next day they heard the baying of dogs. It was another march to Cotonou. They sometimes slept while walking. They lost their sense of direction. There was only one objective, to keep moving. Their tongues swelled with thirst, their bodies became weak with hunger.

When on the fifth day of the flight the soldiers and dogs burst upon them from several directions, the Africans were too weary and sick to fight. Some remained sitting or lying on the ground. Dosu stood up and faced the French charge. He made no effort to raise his spear, but they shot him just the same, and he fell without a protest. Others also were fired upon, even though they had submitted. Six in all were dead when the shooting ended. Those who were alive were tied together and herded down the mountain. In two more days they were marched into the town by the sea, where they were thrust without ceremony into a small stone warehouse building without a floor. They sat or lay on the earth, careless now of where they were or what the future held for them.

Hwesuhunu fell into a sleep that was like death. He heard no sounds, dreamed no dreams and did not even sense the earth under him. It was as though his body was not there. When at last he opened his eyes he could not remember where he was. The first sensation he had was a burning in his side, made unbearable when he touched his hand to it. It was only then that he recalled his wound and the bitter defense of the village. He sat up with difficulty, each movement sending sharp stabs of pain through his chest.

As his eyes became accustomed to the dim light of the windowless room, he turned his head and silently identified those who were present. Kana the Fon; Toto the Nago; Kofi the runaway; Konsi, Dosu's wife; Lafrance, the other runaway. All the women were there. But many men were not. Hwesuhunu's eyes frantically sought other faces, faces he knew were not to be seen. Doumé the ironworker . . . Dosu the hunter . . . His mind refused to acknowledge what it knew. But against his desire, he again saw Doumé lying in the gully and Dosu standing up to receive the volley of French musket balls. Still, his mind would not place things in the right order. He also saw his village in Dahomey, and heard Agosa, the chief of the dokpwe, saying, "Our shadows are long, our work is great; let us begin; they who make the gunpowder win the battles." As for the French soldiers who had brought them down the mountain, they wore the faces of King Adanzan's warriors. In time he became conscious of the sound of voices. People were talking to one another.

Kana stood up and approached Hwesuhunu, stepping over motionless sleeping men on the ground. "You, Hwesuhunu," he said, "how does it go?" He looked at Hwesuhunu's side, where the musket ball had cut a furrow. It was festered and swollen. Kana called to Konsi, who came and washed the wound with water from a pail, and bound it with a strip torn from her headcloth. There was nothing else to be done.

The Africans were listless. When the guards opened the door from time to time to check on them, the prisoners hardly bothered to look up. Night came and passed. In the morning Beauregard, the plantation owner, arrived with the soldiers and pointed out his escaped slaves—Kofi, Lafrance and the woman. They were taken out. As he left, Kofi removed a cord which hung around his neck and gave it to Hwesuhunu. Tied to the cord was the brass man they had made together. There were no words. The door was again closed and bolted. Kofi and Lafrance were taken to the central square and hanged. The woman was taken back to the plantation.

Under a large avocado tree in the central square an inquest was held. The Africans were herded to the ceremony under heavy guard. They sat on the ground quietly, showing no interest in the proceedings. A French naval officer sat at a small table, flanked by a clerk and a translator. The translator was of mixed blood. His understanding of Fon and Nago was imperfect, but in his manner there was no acknowledgment that he did not grasp everything that was said, or that much of what he said to the Africans was not comprehensible to them.

The officer began with the question: "You are escaped slaves from the British ship *Mary Dunstan,* which foundered and sank on the reef?" There was no answer.

"They say nothing," the translator said. "They admit the charge."

The officer continued: "You attacked and murdered soldiers of France who were in the process of keeping the peace of St. Lucia?"

The translator repeated, adding threat to his voice, but there was no reply. "They admit the charge," he said.

"You planned and carried out insurrection against France, and conducted raids against the plantations? You stole and otherwise illegally acquired firearms which you employed against the French military?"

The translator said, "They admit."

The officer became impatient. "They have not opened their mouths. So how do they admit?" He pointed to Osamba, the oldest of the men, saying, "You. Stand up and speak. Did you steal muskets? Did you kill French soldiers?"

Osamba stood up slowly. He spoke slowly. He said: "I did not steal the muskets. The muskets were taken in battle. I did not shoot a musket. I do not know how. In my country I was not rich. I owned only a spear. So they would not entrust me with a gun up on the mountain. I had a spear."

"Who was the leader of the rebellion?"

"Our leader was Doumé, the Nago ironworker. He is dead."

"Who was second in command?"

"Dosu, the Fon hunter, he was second. He also is dead."

"Who was next in command?"

"There were no others."

"Don't you know that the penalty for insurrection by slaves is death?"

"No," Osamba said, "I know nothing of the way you do things here."

One at a time the men were called on to stand and answer questions. The same questions over and over again. When it was done, the officer announced: "The hearing is ended. It is entered in the report that a slave uprising has been put down; that the slaves came from a British vessel and are therefore a prize of war; that two male runaways who abetted the uprising have been hanged with the sanction of their owner, M. Leroi Beauregard; that the leader of the insurrection is to be hanged instantly; and that the remainder of the slaves shall be sold at auction, the proceeds to be remitted to the Government of France."

The ceremony was almost ended. There was a discussion among the French which the Africans did not understand. At last Osamba was selected as the leader, the one to be hanged. The rest were herded once more into their dark prison.

The French vessel *Anna-Marie* rode at anchor in the harbor for more than a week. She had on board some sixty fresh slaves from the African coast. Originally they had been destined for French islands of the West Indies, but the successful slave insurrection on St. Domingue had depressed the slave market in the Caribbean. There was a malaise among the planters. Many of them were giving serious thought to following St. Dominguean planters to the mainland with such slaves as they could transport. Where this shipload of Africans was to go, therefore, was not quite decided. The ship's manifest read:

"Taken aboard in July, August and September, anno Domini 1802, at these various ports between Calabar and Senegal, the following Negroes:

At Harcourt, 19 Ibos
At Lagos, 7 Nagos
At Porto Novo and Cotonou, 13 Fons and Mahis
At Lome, 17 Ewes and Coromantees
At Konakry and Dakar, 14 Wolofs."

Accounting for the slaves who had not survived the passage, the ship's log recorded:

"One male Wolof dead of the swelling disease. . . . Two Ibo males and one Ibo female deceased from scurvy. . . . One Nago male fatally injured by a fall from the rigging, where he took refuge after going mad. . . . Two Ewes lost at sea during a storm on the night of October 28–29. . . . One infirm Fon female deceased of unknown causes. . . . One Coromantee and one Fon hanged for inciting the other Negroes to violence, their bodies suspended to the yard arm for eight hours, after which they were put overboard, an example which left the remainder of the cargo docile. . . ."

Slaves on the *Anna-Marie* were offered for sale to the planters on the island, but few slaves were needed there. Beauregard went aboard and bought two males to replace those who had been executed in the public square. Afterward he filed claims on the government for destruction of his property.

The Africans who were captured on the island were of no interest to the residents, it being a common principle never to acquire slaves that had been engaged in rebellion. But when it was at last decided that the *Anna-Marie* would proceed to New Orleans to dispose of its cargo, the officer in command of the St. Lucia garrison offered to sell the prisoners at bargain rates. "Since the *Anna-Marie* has lost a portion of its cargo in passage," he said, "it can replenish from our inventory." But the captain was reluctant. He pointed out that disposal of the shipment would now be difficult because of British harrassment as well as the generally unsettled market. "Nor," he added, "are you likely to accept trade muskets, powder, blades and a few bolts of cloth in exchange." It was then proposed that he take along with him a dozen of the captives on consignment, to be paid for after their sale. This was agreed to, and the captain and his mate came to make a selection. The prisoners were paraded back and forth to determine whether they had any infirmities. Their legs were examined for yaws. Their backs and chests were slapped to see if they coughed. In the end, three females and seven males were chosen. Among them were Kana, Toto, Konsi and Hwesuhunu. They were taken aboard and chained below decks with the Africans who had made the crossing in the *Anna-Marie*. The following day the vessel weighed anchor and set sail for New Orleans.

Below the deck everything was familiar to Hwesuhunu.

The *Anna-Marie* was smaller than the British vessel, and its cargo was smaller, but the feel of it in the darkness was the same. There were the foul smells, the vermin, the heat, the stretching out of time into a thin invisible thread, and the pervading sense of degradation.

Those who had made the crossing in the *Anna-Marie* pressed the newcomers for news of the outside world. What was told by those who had been captured on the island gave no sense of comfort, only a feeling of unavoidable destiny. The listening began with envy that the newcomers had walked in the grass and been free to wage resistance. But it ended with a heaviness. Momentary thoughts of rebellion on shipboard were quickly drowned in the darkness and stench of the hold.

To Hwesuhunu it almost seemed that everything following the shipwreck of the *Mary Dunstan* was fantasy, that the *Anna-Marie* was the original ship on which he had departed from Cotonou. And during the first hours when he lay there silently, feeling the roll of the vessel and listening to the creaking of tackle, he had the illusion that if he spoke, Dokumi the Nago would answer him. Because he knew that it would not really be so, he remained silent. In the darkness he saw the faces of those to whom he had felt close—Dokumi, Dosu, Doumé and all the others. He remembered giving the nut to Jean Labarbe, and receiving the little brass casting from Kofi, child of the Ashanti caster. What was the meaning of this giving which had seemed so important? One gave, another received. There was a moment of warmth and feeling. But the nut was only a nut, and the figurine only metal. Dokumi who had brought the nut from Africa, he was dead. Jean Labarbe who had received it from Hwesuhunu, he was lost on a tiny island engulfed by an endless sea. Kofi, he was gone.

The only thing that was real was the evil darkness inside a ship, awareness of motion, breathing, scratching. What else was there? What else could there be? Nothing. The giving and receiving, they were meaningless. There was no meaning even in Fa. Fa was merely what happened. So there he was, a thing of the sea. There was nothing else. His life in Dahomey, it was only a dream that came back again and again. Hwesuhunu saw it clearly now, and the world and everything in it became empty.

He drifted into sleep. He and his brothers were sitting around the fire in the night. His father was speaking, imparting the wisdom that the old men had gathered from the winds. Sosu's face glowed in the firelight. He said: "What one touches with the hand is not what is real. The flesh of the antelope is not real, for it is hunted and killed, then it disappears forever. But the force of lightning is real. The force that makes iron strong is real. The ancestors, though they cannot be seen, they are real. You, Hwesuhunu, your nut is nothing, but giving it is the substance of life. The meaning of the dokpwe, can it be seen? Can Dahomey be worn around the neck?" And in his dream Hwesuhunu was suddenly touched by the understanding of the Old Ones. "Truly, it is so. The soul that resides in the head, who has ever seen it? The spirit that makes the forest grow, whenever has it been captured? Can the face of Fa be carved into wood?" His father smiled. He said: "It is truly truly so. The breath of life is nowhere to be seen." Hwesuhunu drifted into wakefulness again. He felt his father's presence in the darkness. He reached out his hand, but there was nothing there to be felt. He spoke aloud, saying, "So it shall be. I understand. This is the meaning of things."

And now came a voice that on another ship would have been Dokumi's. It was a young voice. It spoke in Fon:

"You, there, I heard your words. You are my countryman. Where are we going? Where are they taking us? And what shall they do to us when we arrive?"

Hwesuhunu replied: "It does not matter what they do. Our Fa lies within us. They cannot touch it."

The *Anna-Marie* never reached New Orleans. When she was four days at sea out of St. Lucia a British privateer overtook her south of Jamaica, laid a ball across her bow and captured her without resistance. The French crew was removed and a British crew put aboard, after which a new course was set northeast around the island of St. Domingue. Thirteen days later, under a British flag, the *Anna-Marie* sailed with her contraband black cargo into the American port of Savannah and dropped anchor.

◎◎◎ PART 2

The Landfall

THE BLAIR PLANTATION was some eight hundred acres in size. A goodly portion of it was crop land, but on the western side there was a heavy stand of virgin timber, and beyond it the terrain dipped into swampland with huge trees hung with Spanish moss. Through this swamp a slow river called the Muddy meandered on its way to the sea. When the rains were heavy, the Muddy extended its ill-defined banks to encompass the whole swampland. At other times Blair and his foreman, Rousseau, came here hunting deer, turkey and grouse. Farther east, the Muddy fed into a wide but shallow basin ringed with rushes, and wild duck and geese settled down in the open water in the spring. This spread of the river was known as Eel Lake, and here the slaves sometimes set out eel traps made of small kegs.

The plantation house was close to the eastern boundary, where a red clay road separated the estate from the Walker holdings. It was well constructed, but the white paint had been much weathered on the windward side. The slave quarters comprised two separate camps, one a quarter of a mile north of the house, and the other a similar distance to the south. Several small cabins, belonging to neither camp, were huddled back of the barns. These were the quarters of the house slaves or those with specialized tasks. Tom the blacksmith lived in one with his wife and eight children. Ringo the carpenter had another with his family of six.

Hwesuhunu had been placed in the south camp, in a cabin shared by two families. When he was brought in from Savannah with four other newly purchased slaves, he was assigned to the care of Old Ned, and it was Old Ned who was made responsible for his education. "You take this boy and learn him what he has to learn," Rousseau had said. "Learn him how to talk and what he's got to do, and if you don't break him in good, it'll fall on you."

"Oh, yes, I'll do it, I'll break him in good," Old Ned had answered. "You just leave him to me, I'll learn him how to jump. Old Ned will take care of him." And thereafter Hwesuhunu had slept on the board floor of Old Ned's cabin with Old Ned's children, as close to the fireplace as he could get in the cold weather, rolled in a shredded blanket that served both as covering and sleeping pad.

Old Ned had been born on the Blair estate, but he remembered a little Fon, which was his mother's language. And with this residue of the old language, many gestures and, mostly, no other tool but plantation English, he undertook the education of Hwesuhunu. "First thing to learn," Old Ned said, "is to forget all that African talk. Old Master, he don't like it. Overseer, he don't like it neither. Old Master want all his workers to talk English. Second thing, we goin' to get rid of that African name, else Mr. Rousseau goin' to do it for you. What you say it is again?"

It took a while for Hwesuhunu to understand what Old Ned was getting at. When at last he gave his name to Old Ned, Old Ned said: "That's a mouthful, boy. I goin' to say it like it sound to me. I goin' to christen you Wes, and that Hunu part can go for a last name. Wes Hunu, that's what you are from now on. Another thing, you got to know how to cut firewood. So get on out there with the ax and get busy." Although for a long time Old Ned's language was largely wasted on Hwesuhunu, the chores that had to be done were self-evident. In a few months Wes was beginning to speak English as he heard it spoken around him. If he relapsed, as he sometimes did, into Fon, the children made great sport of it by imitating him. Nor did the other new slaves escape this kind of ridicule, even from adults. Working in the field one day, Wes referred to the field hands as a dokpwe. Big Jim, a tall, gangling man in his early twenties, was working just ahead of Wes. He turned and spoke sharply. "This ain't Africa, son, it's Georgia. And these men ain't a what-you-call-it, they's a *gang*. How long it goin' to take you to learn a few things?"

Wes learned fast. He absorbed everything he saw and heard. But he was slow to feel a part of the plantation life. On all sides were countrymen, or people who should have been his countrymen, but there was a gap between them and himself that seemed very wide. Some of them, like Big Jim, knew nothing at all about Abomey or Whydah or Dahomey, and had never heard of King Adanzan. Like Big Jim, some of them seemed to be carefree, boisterous and endlessly given to funny talk. Not everyone was like that, and Wes could better understand the ones who were a little solemn and more reluctant in their movements, the ones who did not smile all the time and whose faces seemed haunted by private thoughts. It was likely, he thought, that they also remembered passing through the slave market of Savannah, or perhaps a place like Cotonou.

It was in Savannah that Wes had understood for the first time the difference between being a captive and a slave. In Adanzan's compound, and even on the vessels that had brought him to this country, he and his company had suffered what defeated warriors anywhere might be called on to suffer. Even in chains he had considered himself merely a captive with an uncertain fate ahead. The door to that fate was Savannah, and there from a captive he was transformed into the thing known as a nigger. The transformation was accomplished in a ceremony whose meaning cut into his mind each day as he awakened and rose up stiffly from the splintered boards that were his bed. The memory of the rite would not fade.

The captives had been scrubbed, oiled and given ragged clothing to cover them. They squatted silently in the shade of an oak grove at the edge of the public square. Thus it must have been, Wes thought, in the days when the king of Dahomey ordered human victims to be killed to placate the royal ancestors. They, too, had been washed and oiled, and thus they had squatted, each awaiting his turn to be taken by the priests to the ritual places where his throat was to be cut and his blood made to drip over the sacrificial altar. Although the ceremony in the square was not a blood sacrifice, it was an act of ultimate degradation. They came as captives of war, and when the ritual was ended they were only livestock. In Dahomey a slave was taken as an act of vengeance, a consequence of anger or policy, or the need or the whim of a king. Vengeance, anger, policy, all these reasons still acknowledged the slaves as men and women.

And so it had seemed to be even to the last wretched day aboard the *Anna-Marie*. It was the ritual of the slave market in Savannah that had changed everything. One by one the Africans had been displayed on a raised platform in the public square. They had been turned, patted, poked and pried. Their mouths had been peered into, their genitals examined, and their skins explored. The buyers had milled around the exhibits looking for flaws and defects, appraising, making offers, joking, arguing, carting their newly purchased properties away in muledrawn wagons as though they were grain from the fields. As one does not look for communication with a goat in the marketplace, so the buyers' eyes never met those of the captives. In the manner of the auctioneer there was nothing of the conqueror, none of the arrogance of the victor over the vanquished. Instead, it was the manner of the blacksmith bargaining over objects he had fashioned in fire and sweat, objects that had no meaning except the form that he chose to give them and the purposes to which they could be put.

No one asked, "Who is this person? What does he know?" For the Africans were not persons, and what they knew was of no interest.

Hwesuhunu remembered Kana standing on the block, looking over the crowd into the distance. He still could see the auctioneer pulling Kana's ragged shirt aside to show the sinews of his chest, prying Kana's lips apart with the butt of his whip to expose the white teeth. If these people did not recognize Kana for what he really was, neither did he recognize them. And when he was sold and led off to the wagon that was to cart him away, he never once turned his face back toward the Africans who remained behind. One by one they went. When Hwesuhunu was motioned to the block in his turn, he remained for a long moment without movement of any kind, as though he had no awareness of the command; no personal interest in the proceedings that were taking place; as though he were not there at all, but in some distant land.

But then he heard Toto the Nago saying: "You, Hwesuhunu, go forward. Do not let them drag you like a bull. Go forward." He arose, walked to the platform and mounted. He heard the voices around him. When someone called out, Hwesuhunu could not keep from looking to see what kind of man wished to purchase his body. His eyes sought faces in the crowd, but they did not return his look. Only once did his eyes meet others. A small Negro boy standing nearby grinned at him. That was all. When Hwesuhunu's shirt was pulled off, there was a brief argument. Someone poked at his still festered side where his wound was slowly healing. There was a momentary stabbing pain, but Hwesuhunu did not respond to it. And at last he was led off by Old Ned and placed in the wagon along with some unhusked corn, sacks of flour, and some freshly cut wood. There he waited until three more Africans, among them Konsi, Dosu's wife, had been bought and loaded.

Old Ned drove the wagon to the Blair plantation, and behind it, on a white horse, rode Rousseau the overseer. Old Ned continually harangued the mules, and though his passengers understood nothing of what he said, it was understood by all of them that it was for their benefit. Their conversation among themselves was broken by long silences. Two of the slaves had been original passengers on the *Anna-Marie*. Like the others, they were gaunt from the long passage. They were Mahis and regarded Hwesuhunu and Konsi only as distant cousins. Occasionally one of them would comment on Old Ned's grandiose manner, or on the white overseer who rode expressionlessly behind them. Old Ned sensed the insults and replied with unneeded lashing at the mules. There was a little bread to soften their hunger during the half day's ride to the plantation, but nothing else. Hwesuhunu watched Konsi eat listlessly. She did not speak at all from the time the trip began to its end. Her eyes seemed to be seeking out the landscape, but there was a deadness in them, and Hwesuhunu knew that she really saw nothing. Konsi's misery somehow made him feel stronger, and he said to her: "Dosu was my friend. When your child comes, therefore, he shall be my nephew." But Konsi did not hear.

At the plantation, the sight of many African faces promised that the world was not to be merely a desert of misery and shame. These people talked, made jokes, worked in the fields together, and often laughed. There were families and children. Though the cabins were roughly made and did not have the sweet odor of freshly made straw roofs, they were shelters nonetheless. And though the wall of language shut him off from much that he heard, he did not believe that this would always be so. From Old Ned he learned several words even on his first night—water, mule, dog and master.

The names of the children in the cabin he absorbed without effort. There was even a conversation of sorts between him and Jess, one of Old Ned's boys, on the night of his arrival. When Jess saw that Hwesuhunu had finished his tin plate of cold rice, he took him on a tour past the dozen cabins that made up the south camp.

Yet what Wes saw and learned during the months that followed revealed that there was much strangeness around him. It was not language, or the fact that so many of these people had been born in this land. More than anything else it was that a familiar system of order and meaning was absent. Big Jim had been right. Men and women working in the fields were not a dokpwe. They had little feeling for accomplishment, and the incentives were not pride and unspoken awareness of common purpose but rather the coldly watchful eyes of Rousseau, the overseer, and the flicking whip of Josh Ibo, the driver. There was no sound of drums to quicken the blood, no air of festival, no sharing of labor with one family and then another, and no words of thanks to those who tilled the fields.

The meaning of work somehow had shrunk to nothing, and a man did not care whether he had achieved much or little. The meaning of work was to get through the day. It was a process of motion, a little faster when the driver approached, a little slower when he had moved on. The laughter that was sometimes heard in the fields was familiar, but often it seemed to be a sound whose soul had been removed. The system of life Wes once had taken for granted had been replaced by another. And when Old Ned instructed his children in their behavior, these systems contrasted greatly. "Watch your manners, boy, in the way you act to the old folks." That was old and understandable, so clear that it hardly need be spoken. "You, boy, if you don't watch out, Master goin' to beat you good, maybe sell you off."

That was the new thing. And it slowly came to Wes Hunu, as it had to others before him, that the trial was not laboring without reward but the melting away of purpose, pride and obligation. There was also an unfamiliar cruelty in the way the new slaves, particularly the Africans, were ridiculed and taunted because of their difficulty with language, or because of the awkward way they went about jobs they had never done before. Among many of the slaves there was not only a readiness to forget Africa, but even a vanity in having been born in Georgia. A man might speak of his father, his mother, even his grandfather, but never of "the ancestors" and hardly ever of the places where the ancestors had grown, lived and died. It was as though there had never been a village in Africa, as though the slave cabins had always stood there in the slave quarters, occupied by the same people who now lived in them.

But there were some familiar things too. There was Samba, the old man who on certain nights made his cabin into a shrine for Shango or Ogoun. In front of the cabin a broken iron pot lay casually on its side, rusted and almost lost in the weeds. Rousseau had several times told Samba to clean up the mess, including the iron pot, and Samba had said: "Yes, Captain, I'll certainly do that. Right away, Captain, I certainly will." But whatever cleaning was done, the pot remained. And over the doorway of the cabin was nailed a rusted horseshoe. "Why, Captain, that's just for good luck. You know how the niggers is, Captain, they like good luck things."

But the bits of iron scrap with which Samba's cabin was adorned were the symbol of Ogoun. In the rafters Samba kept a gourd rattle covered with a network of corn seeds, which Rousseau's sharp eyes had once ferreted out. "You know how the niggers is with music, Captain," Samba had said. "Every once in a while they likes a shindig, and that old rattle can make a real nice tune." About the drum contrived out of a small keg Samba had said: "The important thing about that drum, Captain, is funerals. Every once in a while one of these niggers dies, then we have to march him to the graveyard, and we needs a drum for that." And so in the main plantation house Samba was known as the black old man who loved to decorate his cabin with junk and was always looking for an excuse to have a play-party.

When Wes Hunu heard the drumming and singing for the first time one night, he inquired of Jess about it. Before Jess could answer, Old Ned spoke up in a scolding tone. "You leave that stuff be. That's from the jungle. Samba is doin' the devil's work, and I don't 'tend for none of my family to mess in it."

But afterward, Wes and Jess slipped off to the other end of the camp and peeked through the cracks of Samba's cabin. Ten or a dozen dancers, crowded together in the center of the room, moved around in a circle, their faces dimly reflecting the feeble light of an oil lamp. At one side Samba stood with half-closed eyes, his corn-seed rattle in his hand. Other people, pressing against the walls, were singing. And almost obscured by the moving bodies, a drummer was playing a salute to the orisha Ogoun, accompanied by a small boy beating on a bench with sticks. Samba wore a white cloth around his forehead. His face, fringed by a graying beard, recalled to Wes the features of other men he had seen in another place across the great ocean. For Jess the event was a lark in defiance of his father's strictness and a challenge to the forces of wickedness. For Wes it was a comfort. And in the days that followed, when he saw Samba working in the rice field, making funny talk or placating the driver with far-flung excuses for his ineptitude, he knew that this man had within him a great strength. He recalled the saying: "Wherever a Dahomean stands, there stands Abomey."

One day Wes noted that Konsi wasn't at work in the fields, and he knew that the birth of Dosu's child was near. He asked a woman from the north camp about it. "Oh, yes," she told him, "that pretty little girl is goin' to have a young one 'fore Sunday, I do believe." The following day she had more to report. "Believe Konsi is 'bout to born her child any minute now, and it's goin' to be a boy."

Wes wanted to know how she knew it would be a boy. "She had a dream," the woman said, "and the father of the child came and revealed it. Told her he was sendin' a man-child, and gave her the name to call him by." The baby was born that night. It was a man-child, and Konsi gave it the name Nyawu. When the news came, Old Ned got permission for Wes to visit the north camp. When he got there, Wes found Konsi's cabin full of women coming and going. Some hovered around Konsi and the baby, giving authoritative advice. Others dropped in to admire and praise. Wes touched Konsi's hand. He looked long and silently into Nyawu's face, seeing there the face of his friend Dosu. He was glad, but he was deeply troubled also, recollecting the things that should have been done for Dosu that had not been done. If Dosu had indeed come to Konsi in her sleep, it was a way of reminding her that a proper service for his death had never been held. The matter was much in Wes's mind thereafter. He knew it had to be taken care of somehow, but he was perplexed how to begin.

It came to him at last that Samba was the key to the problem. Hoeing corn in the field one day, he worked his way to Samba's side. Samba looked around. "Mornin', Uncle," Wes said. Samba nodded. He appraised Wes with an occasional sidelong glance. He saw a thin African boy whose flapping shirt sometimes disclosed a pale, badly healed scar. He took note of Wes's feet to measure the size of the man yet to come. "Goin' to be a naturally big man when he's growed," Samba thought. He observed that Wes made his hoe rise and fall in time with his own. "This boy knows how to work," he thought, "his hoe makin' conversation with mine." He noted the serious look on Wes's face, and deduced that there was something yet to come. He waited.

"Uncle," Wes said after a while, "some friends I had, they died." Samba's eyes narrowed. He leaned on his hoe, facing Wes. Wes tried to say something about the long voyage and the desperate weeks on St. Lucia, but it was too much. So he said simply: "Doumé the ironworker, killed by the white folks. His people was Nago. Dokumi the hunter. His people was Nago. Koba was a Nago too. Dosu, he was a Fon like me. Osamba, named like you, Uncle, he was killed by the white people. Many, many dead, Uncle."

Samba looked down on Wes with quiet understanding. He said: "Boy, what you want with me? Can I bring the dead to life?"

Wes answered, turning his head in a gesture of respect: "Uncle, those people never had no proper service for them. Doumé was put in the ground with his spirit still in his head. It got to be set free, Uncle. And the other ones, too, someone has to fix it for them." Wes struggled with language. It was too hard and he stopped.

Samba began to chop at the ground once more with his hoe. "What's that got to do with me, boy?" he said. "Ain't I just an old nigger round here?"

Wes said: "Doumé, he made a service for the ones drowned in the water. No one fix for him. His vodoun has the name Ogoun. That's your spirit too, Uncle, he's from the same people."

Samba stopped chopping at last. He said: "Boy, ain't you sharp, though. Now I ask you, what you figure to give me for a big service for all them friends of yours? Don't you know it costs plenty? And where's a nigger going to get all that stuff?"

Wes said: "I studied on it, Uncle. Goin' to make three good Fon drums for you, one big, one not too big, one small." And so it was arranged.

Wes had little time for the thing he had obligated himself to do. The slaves were awakened at five in the morning by a large bell hung in the center of the camp. At the same moment the bell in the north camp sounded, like an echo in the distance. Josh Ibo, the driver, tolled on the bell rope with seeming glee, calling out: "Come on, all you niggers, don't sleep the day away! This is Josh Ibo talkin'! Cotton needs hoin', horses need feedin', and the black man needs workin'! Come one and all, join the party, loosen up your limbs, uncramp your legs! Time wait for no man, so the Good Book say!"

One by one at first, then more, the slaves came from the cabins, the sleep still in them. Some were pulling on shirts, but others came just as they had slept, in the only clothes they owned. They splashed water in their faces from the pails that stood outside, more to awaken themselves than to wash. Celina the cook appeared with a large pot of rice on her head, followed by a small girl with more rice. The slaves lined up with their tin plates, into which the rice was ladled, and they ate standing up or sitting on the door stoops.

When Josh Ibo called out, "Let's get to it, now, on to the south field," they moved to the outbuilding where the tools were kept, then straggled to the place where the day's work was to be done. Before they reached it, Rousseau appeared on his white horse, riding silently behind the moving column. Thus began the day. At noon several girls brought food, and the slaves ate in the field. If it was the season of heavy work, the homing bell did not ring until seven o'clock in the evening. And after that, most of the field hands—men, women and older children—had little energy left for anything but sitting and talking until it was time to sleep.

The daytime routines had left Wes exhausted. Though he remained gaunt from the long voyage, it had been Rousseau's decision that he didn't need any conditioning. "All he needs is food," Rousseau had said, "and when he's done his stint in the field he'll get hungry and eat. That'll make him fatten up." Wes stayed lean, but as time passed he felt stronger and more capable, and instead of driving him Josh Ibo began to praise him. The first time he received such praise he felt gratitude, but it was drowned in the exchange that followed between Big Jim and the driver.

Without raising his head from his work, Big Jim said: "It sure seem like nothin' in the world makes some niggers more happy than seein' other niggers help Old Master get rich."

Josh Ibo spoke angrily: "You just watch it there, son, or you goin' to feel the tickle of this switch!"

And then Big Jim stood up, looked straight into Josh's face and said: "They is niggers and niggers. But the lowliest of all is the drivers. If you ever touch me with that switch I'll kill you."

Josh said: "Don't give me no insurrection, Big Jim, or I'll turn you over to Rousseau."

And Big Jim answered: "If you do that, boy, Rousseau better whip me till I'm dead, otherwise I goin' to get up and find you and feed you to the hogs."

Thereafter when he was praised, Wes understood it was to shame someone else, and it was only an embarrassment. But he felt glad that he was able to do a man's work and keep pace with the others.

One day when Rousseau was close by, Wes said to him: "Captain, I need a little wood."

Rousseau looked at Wes as though seeing him for the first time. "What for you need wood, boy?"

"Need to make some drums, Captain."

"How come you need drums?" Rousseau said.

"Need it for music, Captain. They ain't a good drum in the camp."

Rousseau said: "What kind of wood you want?"

Wes answered: "One tree. Cut it, chop out the inside, cover one end with coonskin. That's all Captain."

Rousseau thought. His mind seemed elsewhere. He turned his head to see how the work was going. Then he answered: "Go ahead. Get your tree at the marsh. But on your own time, mind you."

So that night Wes took Old Ned's ax and went to the edge of the marsh and found his tree. He cut it down and left it lying there. The next night he went again and cut it into lengths. He brought three pieces back, and every night after that for several weeks he worked at the drums. He shaped them with the ax and smoothed them with a draw-knife Josh lent him from the toolhouse. A time came when they were done, except for mounting the skin heads. Wes made small game snares and set them out in the marsh. Of the first three coons he caught, along with a muskrat, only one was big enough. But eventually he had what he wanted, three good skins. He trimmed them, mounted them, and shaved off the hair with a fragment of glass. And then one night he and Jess carried the drums to Samba's place.

Samba looked them over carefully, then tapped the skin heads gently with his fingers to hear the tones. He said: "Son, you sure got the know of it. Where you ever learn to make drums like that?"

Wes said: "They make drums like this in my village."

Samba said: "Sure glad we got a good drum maker around. Course, that coonskin ain't as good as cowskin. But she got a pretty sound."

After a while Wes said: "Uncle, I kept my part. Now you make the service like you promise."

Samba looked sharply. "What service I say?"

"For my friends. They must have a service."

"I say that?" Samba answered. "Well, if I say so, I do it. But they's a heap to be done. Got to ask Old Master for permission."

The next evening Samba put on his clean shirt and went off to the plantation house, Wes and Jess trailing at a distance. Samba circled around to the kitchen door, where Jennie, the master's cook, greeted him with the air of one a station above.

"Like to speak with Master," Samba said.

"What you want with Master?" Jennie said. "He's too busy to run to the door every time some nigger want to talk."

"Got business with the Master," Samba said. "Talkin' to

you don't do me no good. Don't make me feel better neither."

"Don't you give me that lift eye, Samba. You talkin' to a lady. Old Master ain't here. So go on down to the cabins with the other ones like you."

"If Old Master ain't here," Samba said, "then I 'spect I'll talk to the Captain."

Jennie acted annoyed. But when she came back with Rousseau she busied herself close enough to hear what was being said.

"Evenin', Captain," Samba said. "Mighty sorry to discommode you so much, Captain, but I got a thing to ask you. Want to make arrangements."

"What arrangements?" the overseer said. "What is it this time?"

"It's like this, Captain," Samba said. "The nigger folks down there in the south camp been talkin'. Mighty hard work this month, and they say ain't it nice to make a play-party one of these evenin's. After all the work been done and the tools stacked, o' course, Captain."

"Seem like you got nothin' but play-party on your mind, Samba. Can't have all this whoopin' and hollerin' all the time."

"Where's the harm on it, Captain? It make us niggers happy, and we give you a sight more work just thinkin' 'bout it. Beside that, it keep the black folk out of trouble. You can just feel the trouble risin' like bread dough some nights, and if we has a good shindig, that goin' to quiet us down for a spell. You do that for us, Captain, and we make the hoe squeal good for you. Besides that, I'll come and give your horse a good curry next week."

"Never mind my horse, the stableboy can take care of him."

"Well, then," Samba said, "I'll leave off the horse if you say so. But what about the shindig, Captain?"

"I'll see," Rousseau said. "I'll talk to Mr. Blair about it."

"Well, I sure am glad, Captain," Samba said, shuffling his feet and clenching his straw hat, "you is mighty kind to us field hands."

When he came back to where Wes and Jess were waiting he said: "That's the first part of it. We can hold the service. Captain says he'll see, and that mean yes. You can ask and ask, but all he says is he'll see. Can't hardly bring himself to say yes right off. Don't want to spoil the niggers. Well, next thing we got to have is a rooster. That part of it is for you, son. A white rooster, white all over. No banty one, neither. Ogoun don't like no banty roosters." They walked slowly toward the south camp. Suddenly Samba turned and spoke sharply to Wes. "Where you get the know of this thing?"

Wes said: "I was born to it, Uncle. Where I goin' to find a white rooster?"

"You got to figure that one out for yourself," Samba said.

Just before they reached the cabins, Wes said: "Uncle, why you speak so with the white folk? What I mean. . . ."

And Samba said roughly, his face turned away, "I know what you mean. If you don't know, what's the use of me talkin' to you?"

It was several days before the question of the white rooster was solved. It came from the north camp. The slaves from the two cabin areas were not allowed to visit together except under special circumstances, but they sometimes worked within sight of one another in the fields. Wes Hunu told Konsi one morning about what was being planned and enlisted her aid. The next day she reported that a white rooster was available in the north camp. The owner wanted, in exchange for it, a wooden mortar, which Wes promised to make.

The service was held in an open area back of Samba's cabin one Saturday night. The preparations were simple—a large bonfire, in the center of which stood an iron bar, and benches and chairs set out on the edge of the court.

Samba stood up, his rattle in his hand. The hum of conversation died. "Friends and cousins," Samba said, "this thing tonight is for the dead. Some of us been born here in Georgia, but some come from Africa. Wheresoever we been born, we got kinfolk in the old place and 'mongst the dead. Now you knows that the older a person get, the more respect you got to give him. Why is that? It's because an old man or woman is closer to the dead, that's why. Soon he will be 'mongst the dead. And the dead must be respected as much as the orishas and the vodouns. If you don't do right by them, why they goin' to do right by you? You forget them, and they goin' to forget you too when you in need. That is why we brings a gourd of rice to the grave each year, so the kinfolk knows we don't forget." Samba was interrupted by fervent cries of "Amen." He went on: "This boy Wes Hunu, he made this drum to pay for this meetin'. He bring the rooster. He is only a boy, but he has the know that lots of folks already forget. The dead we remember tonight is many. Let us start with a prayer." He continued: "All you orisha, and Jesus too, we ask for you to look way down here. See all these black folk on this plantation and listen to what they got to say. We know all people has to die, and us live ones ask you for blessing." He turned to Wes, saying: "Call the roll."

Wes stepped to the center of the court, a pitcher of water in his hand. He spoke in Fon. First he called on the vodouns, and each time he called a vodoun's name he poured a little water on the ground. "Legba, carry the word for us, ago-é! Respect to all the vodouns, ago-é! Mawu, the grandfather of all, respect! Ogoun, who lives in this house, and all his kin, respect! Nananbuluku, Sobo, Obatala, Damballa, Hevioso, Azaka, respect!"

Samba interjected in English: "The orishas too. Oya, Orula, Panchagara, Yemaya."

Wes went on: "Vodouns and orishas, we remember you, we serve you. Ancestors of the Fon and the Nago, heed us. You who have gone below the water, listen. Men who lived among us here in this world have been taken away. There was Doumé, he was killed in battle. There was Dosu the hunter, he was killed in battle. There was Dokumi the hunter, he died in the sea. Many have died. There were Kama, Sule, Malosi, Adjaku, Koba, Dosilu, Dogwé, Doki and Agili. There were many."

Samba picked up an earthen pot decorated with ribbons, holding it poised over his head.

"You spirits who lived in the heads of these people," Wes continued, "this is the night for you to leave them. When you are free, remember their families and their friends."

Still holding the earthen jar, Samba began a song for the orisha Ogoun. The drums joined in. The song was taken up by others, and the dancing began. Thirty, forty, then more of the slaves crowded the dance court, moving slowly in a circular path around an invisible center point. Some danced with half-closed eyes, each person alone among many, compelled by the drumming, supplicating with movements of the shoulders, arms aloft, turning, bending, head tilted back. Their faces glistened in the light of the bonfire.

A boy who had been posted as a sentry came running, pushing into the crowd until he found Samba. He spoke urgently. Samba raised his hand, the drums stopped, the dancers became still. "Old Master and Missus is on the way," Samba said. "Hoist up the banjo." Big Jim sat down, picked at his banjo, and sang a square dance call:

Look to the right, look to the left,
Grab the lady you likes best.
Turn around once, turn around twice,
Kiss that lady, ain't she nice?

The intensity of the dance was gone. Older people moved aside as younger ones cavorted through the figures, part interpretation, part burlesque. When Mr. and Mrs. Blair arrived they saw before them a Saturday night slave dance, with Samba smiling and shuffling along with the others. "Mighty welcome to Old Master and Pretty Missus," someone shouted. "You come to join the fun, Mr. Tom?"

Mr. Blair shook his head. "Just came to see what's going on," he said.

"You like to set a spell and look on, Mr. Tom?"

"No," Mr. Blair said, "you all look happy as you are."

"Oh, yes," Samba said, "as happy as niggers can be. We surely is, Mr. Tom."

The square dance went on. After a while Mr. and Mrs. Blair strolled back to the plantation house, Jess lighting their way with a pinewood torch. "Get rid of the banjo," Samba commanded. The banjo disappeared and the drums were pulled out of their hiding place. The atmosphere again became solemn. Samba stood waiting for the feel of the banjo to die away. He spoke in a low voice, holding up the earthen pot once more.

"You spirits in the heads of all them dead people, you done hear what Wes Hunu have to say. Tonight you got to go. They don't need you no more. Go find someone else. You're free, now, free!"

He threw the pot on the ground, shattering it. The drums rolled. A woman began to sing, and the circle dance again took shape. When it was over, Samba addressed the patron of ironworkers and warriors.

"Ogoun, there is a widder of one of them dead folks here, name of Konsi. Husband of this girl is name of Dosu. This man was a hunter, he went in the jungle to hunt for leopards and lions. 'Cause he carry an iron spear, that put him in Ogoun's care." He motioned to Konsi to enter the circle. She came forward, dust on her face as a sign of mourning, and a white cloth around her waist. She sat in a chair prepared for her. "This is the widder of Dosu," Samba said. "She mourn for him."

The white rooster was brought in by Samba's daughter. He took it from her, offered it to the four directions, and cut its throat, letting the blood drip into a small hole in the ground. Samba waved the still fluttering rooster toward Konsi. She sprang from her chair, her limbs jerking in spasms like the wings of the sacrificial rooster. She lurched from side to side. Strange sounds came from her throat. When her spasms ended, Samba placed a lighted pine stick in her hand. She carried it to the place where the rooster had been killed, and stuck it upright in the ground. Two women took her by the arms and guided her from the circle. The singing came to an end, and Samba said in a tired voice: "Ogoun accept. He take Konsi to his protection, the child of Konsi too. The meetin' is finish."

After the service for the dead, the routine of the plantation settled down to its day-to-day sameness. There was no music in the south camp except for Big Jim's banjo sometimes in the evening, though generally everyone was too tired even for this. Twice again in the next several months permission was asked for another shindig, but the requests were turned down. There was something about the service at Samba's that had bothered both Mr. Blair and the overseer. Something Jennie had said to the Missus was responsible. Despite what Old Master himself and the Missus herself had seen and heard, a feeling of distrust was raised. "Them field niggers," Jennie had declared, "they consorting with the devil down there in the south camp. They call on the spirits and speak to the ghosts. It's a shame for Christian folk to see, Missus Eva. It's bad enough they ain't hearken to the word of Jesus. But they wallows deep in sin like hogs in the mire."

Mister Blair was not too concerned about the salvation of souls, nor did he care whether the niggers believed in ghosts; these things were of no interest to him as long as the plantation ran smoothly. But the reappearance of African activities was not good. For one thing it was a focus of slave organization. Proper control of the slaves required that all their actions be directed toward the plantation welfare and away from any common cause of their own. It was for this reason that the newly arrived Africans were always scattered and put out of touch with one another as much as possible, placed under the supervision of those who were plantation born.

On Mr. Blair's request, Rousseau had sent for Samba to get a better picture of the Saturday night affair. "Samba," Rousseau said, "I want the truth, now. What were all them goings on in the south camp last week? I hear it was a spirit meeting."

"Spirit meeting?" Samba said in surprise, "Why, Captain, don't you know that Samba don't mess with things like that? The niggers had a real good whoop and holler, that's the size of it."

"I hear," Rousseau said, "that a chicken was killed down there."

"Chicken? Oh, yes, that white rooster. Well, you know how it is, Captain, when the niggers dance they get hungry, and you got to have a little something to pass around. Just like the white folks. We hear it say that when Old Master has a ball up here the Missus gives all the company something to cheer them up, and we do the same thing down there."

Rousseau looked sharply at Samba's grinning face. "What about the blood business?" he asked. "What about dripping the blood in a hole?"

"Blood? Blood?" Samba said quizzically. "Oh, yes, Captain, in the hole. Well I ask you, don't the blood have to go somewhere? What the niggers goin' to do with the blood? When they kills a chicken they lets the blood go in the ground and then covers it up. Keeps the flies away."

Rousseau got nothing out of Samba or any of the others he questioned. The thing that gave the event more than usual concern was a report about an abortive slave insurrection near the western frontier. Under the leadership of a field hand named Jack Mason, some seventy slaves from two neighboring plantations had broken loose one night, burned barns and crops, killed an overseer and four house servants, and rampaged over a distance of fifteen miles before being trapped in a swamp by militia and a citizens' posse of several hundred men.

Such reports, though they were not frequent, stirred up an unspoken uneasiness among the planters. Supposing it were not seventy but a few hundred? Or a few thousand? Supposing they were able to hold off the militia for a few weeks instead of a few days? The possibility that their numbers would be swelled with runaways from other plantations was always there. And the effect on other slaves, even if they did not join up, could only be harmful. Thus, anything that suggested secret night conclaves among the slaves was disturbing.

But as one day followed another and nothing untoward occurred, Samba's shindig was forgotten, except that no more Saturday night festivities were permitted for a long while. In one thing, Old Master was not wrong. The word of the slave uprising had reached the field hands also, by various routes. Mr. Blair's stableboy reported what he had heard around the house. And in a way that was commonplace for important events, the story had drifted across the country with the wind. A slave in one field, seeing a distant working party in another, whooped out the news in a kind of song:

Well, yooo-hooo-ah-hooo!
Don't you hear me callin' you?
Captain's woman don't like my brother no more,
She got four little orphans in the house,
Yooo-hooo-ah-hooo!
Got seventy more brothers out there,
Down in the dark bottoms somewhere!
Hooo-ah-hooo!

The sounds drifted erratically, south, east, north. Several days later, fifty miles farther on, a field hand straightened up to stretch his back and called:

Yay-hoo, yay-hoo, yay-hoo!
Ain't them children run from old Pharaoh?
Well, them children gone free
'Cause o' that mean old snake in the apple tree!
Yay-hooooo!

The story came in fragments even while the overseers walked or rode among their charges, listening, amused at how little it took to capture their interest.

On the Blair plantation the field hands heard, and at night they talked about it in the cabins. It was ten days later that the last details of the insurrection arrived. Big Jim made up a song about the event, which he sang one night sitting on the stump in front of his cabin:

Well, Jack Mason, he is gone, gone.
Poor boy, he is gone, gone.
All he want is to leave him be,
But his Captain say leave this nigger to me,
And they hang him to the live oak tree,
So now this poor boy is gone, gone.

If the story of Jack Mason's rebellion didn't create tension among the slaves, it did provoke heated discussion. "I don't know what's the matter with the nigger folk no more," Enoch, Big Jim's father, declared. "When I was young they was plenty of black men fight in the war against the British, and after that they was slave rebellion goin' on all the time. Sometimes up in Carolina, sometimes right over in Macon County. It's different now, seem like the black people just decide to set back and take what comes."

"Well, cousin," someone said, "if you been studyin' insurrection, when does the dance begin? If all the niggers used to do what you say, how come we ain't sittin' up there in the Big House and Old Master and Missus ain't down here pickin' collard greens? And how come you ain't up there in

President Jefferson's place and he ain't down here pickin' the banjo?"

"Just the same," Enoch said, "look around you. Just look at all these happy folks. Not a complaint in 'em, 'less they 'bout to get sold off, and then they thinks Mr. Blair such a fine man they don't want to give him up. I see plenty misery round here, but they ain't enough spirit no more. In my young days I run away three times. Second time I run away from my first master, back in seventeen and eighty two, he sold me off. Then I run away from the new master, year of seventeen and eighty seven, and nearly got to North Carolina 'fore they catch me. That time I get near whupped to death."

Old Ned said: "The only thing about it is there's no place to run to. Don't make no difference if you get to Louisiana or Tennessee, they catch you and send you home. Best thing is to please Old Master and ask him can you buy your freedom. Better that way than fight with him."

"Fight?" Enoch said. "Man, I say fight with 'em. If I got no place to get away, I fight with 'em right here. I fought with 'em since the day I was born. How I do this thing? Do it by bein' a no-good, lazy, shiftless, head scratchin' nigger, that's how. If I is slow at the plowin', puts the fence posts in too weak, can't keep up my place in the cotton row, and don't stir the paint too well 'fore it goes on the barn, ain't that war? Now Old Master know it's war, but what can he do? If every black man in Georgia stop tryin' to show he's the *best* thing they is, and just set his mind to bein' a lazy shiftless nigger like the white folks say he is anyhow, the masters would turn 'em all loose and pay 'em five dollars a head to go away. Let me tell you somethin'. The driver tell one man, 'Hurry up, nigger, we got to get all this cotton in by Saturday.' And the nigger breaks his back doin' what the driver say. Then there's another man, all he say is 'Yes, boss,' and he fumble with the cotton boll and mess everything up like a 'rangoutang, and the driver don't get nothin' out of him 'cept misery. Now tell me, which man is more slave than the other? The one who make the master rich or the one who make him poor?"

"What's wrong about that," Old Ned said, "is only one thing. The man who spend his whole life doin' poorly goin' to lose the power to do things rightly. If it somehow happen that every black nigger in Georgia was turn loose tonight, if they tell him, 'Black man, you are free, go on out there and take them forty acres and do somethin' on your own,' why the man that spend his whole life messin' up the cotton don't know how to do it no other way. That cabin of his goin' to fall right on his head."

Enoch said: "What you say got one thing wrong with it, Ned. They *ain't goin'* to turn the black folk loose tonight or tomorrow or the next day neither. They can't see no way to get on in life without us slaves. Old Master's pretty little Miss Jane, now she got to have silk dresses to go to the ball, don't she? And Missus, don't she have to have a big reception for all the gentlemen and ladies? And Old Master, he got to have carriage and horses, and for that he need the niggers, don't he now, to raise his rice and cotton? Why, he could be as poor as the Irish, but long as he got a parcel of slaves he feel like the King of England. Ownin' niggers is the main thing he got in life, and he ain't agoin' to set them free. Niggers got to resign theyself to stay right here, and right here they got to fight the war till they die, and fightin' is the most they goin' to get out of it. This war is call the Hold Back War. Old Master say, 'Go faster, cut that wood, plow that ground, I got to get rich this year 'cause I didn't do so well last time.' And the nigger got to fight him back with the rheumatism. I studied on this since I been a boy. The only thing they is for a black man is to *keep agoin'* and to *hold back.*"

Old Ned shook his head. "Only thing is, you forgot one thing."

"What's that?" Enoch said.

"Him as was baptise by John in the wilderness," Old Ned said. "It ain't fight what counts, but love." A chorus of amens came from the witnesses to the debate. "The big thing ain't what comes here, but what comes later."

"I done hear a heap 'bout your friend Jesus," Enoch said. "Now I goin' to ask you two things. First, which is the color of his skin, white or black?"

"The color don't matter," Old Ned replied. "Ain't he been crucified and resurrected for the whole world?"

"I don't know all the things he done, cause he's your friend and not mine," Enoch said. "As for what color he is, you already told me the answer. Now the second thing is, has this Jesus ever been a slave down here in Georgia? Course he ain't."

Old Ned interrupted. "Ain't I tell you he been crucified?"

"Yes, you tell me that. You say another thing too, that Jesus is the son of God who rule everything. And when Jesus get through crucifyin' Hisself, God take Him and put Him together and bring Him back to life and take Him home. If they kill me here right now, this old nigger slave on the Tom Blair plantation, you mean to say Father God goin' to step down and make me alive and take me home?"

"Yes," Old Ned said, "if you make yourself ready, Jesus goin' to carry you home. That's what it means by home to Jesus."

"What *I* mean," Enoch said, "is do He make me alive in this here world where I want to be and know somethin' about? Or is it some other world with the dead spirits? You already tell me, it's some other place. The way it is around here, the people just aim to please the most they can and figure maybe Old Master give them a little something special come Christmastime. And all Old Master goin' to give them is more of what they already got, till they ain't no more of it. You can't run nowheres, so all you got left is *hold back.*"

Wes felt mired down. There stretched out ahead of him

fifty or sixty years of flat and empty grassland without a tree, a village or a voice to break the desolation. Here were two men. They had lived long. Each of them had spent his life in this country. Each was born with a master and each would die with a master. Neither had a house of his own. Neither had experienced a single moment equal to Wes's few years in his father's village, or even to those proud weeks of meaningful manhood on St. Lucia. These were the elders speaking, counseling the young with their thoughts, portraying the path of life that others would follow. Was there nothing else? Surely this was only a passing thing, this presence in a place where everyone encased in a darker covering was only a mule with a human face. What lay ahead was like that which lay behind them and spread all around them as far as the eye could see. Was life from this place onward a choice between Samba's painful abuse of himself talking to Rousseau, Old Ned's waiting to be taken home by the spirit Jesus, and Enoch's pitiful unnoticed war of *hold back* against Mr. Blair? Wes was deeply afflicted. He carried his sickness with him to the fields and back again to the ragged blanket in which he slept. Big Jim's funny song that he sang sometimes in the evening when the children importuned him only heightened Wes's despair:

My Old Master promise me
That when he die he set me free,
But he live so long till his head got bald
And it seemed to me he wouldn't die at all.

Master's son he say to me,
That when I'm old he'll make me free,
He change his mind when the great day come,
Lose me in a card game to Captain Crumb.

There was nothing comforting in it. Why was it greeted with laughter, even a little jig sometimes? Three choices only? There must be others, Wes thought; perhaps pride in pain, as in a circumcision ritual. No, that had no meaning here. Was there, then, only the action of those seventy men? Insurrection, despite foredoomed failure and execution in the public square? Wes thought of the slave ship and of Sangara the Gola, servant of the captain. He understood Sangara better now. And uninvited, Sangara's words came again into his head: "You, when you go there, do not be a great man. They will beat the skin from your body." Perhaps Sangara was right about all things, despite the way they had ridiculed him.

Perhaps the sea was the answer, Agbé's ocean. After all, was not Hwesuhunu a Thing-of-the-Sea? Was that not his Fa? But how would he find his way to the sea and a place on a ship? For man is but small, and the road is long, and Legba stands at every fork directing travelers into byways and trails that go nowhere. There seemed to be no answers at all, and he tried to comfort himself with the knowledge that everything that had been and that was yet to be revealed was the working of Fa. But the comfort did not come, for he knew that Fa was not the working of the mind, but what a man chose to do, and the choosing yet remained.

Old Ned took note of Wes's quietness and his inner turmoil. "Boy," he said, "you got a long row to hoe. One of these fine days I goin' to ask Old Master let me get you baptise." It was a kindness, Wes knew, but it did not help. Nor did what happened to Big Jim. They were in the field one day, Wes working directly behind Big Jim in the row. Josh Ibo, the driver, had been warned by Rousseau that the niggers were slacking off. "You keep them moving," Rousseau had said, "or I'll put you back in the row and get me another driver who can do it."

Josh had reacted sharply. He marched back and forth in the field haranguing the workers. He cracked his whip at Mollie, who was pregnant and had trouble bending over. He uttered sarcasms for the benefit of Enoch. "What we needs is more pickin' and less hold back," he said. "You quit fumblin' with the bolls, else you get a tickle with this thing." He laid the whip once across the back of a boy who was sitting in the row, dreaming. "Get on, get on!" he shouted as he moved across the field. "This ain't the Great Jubilo, it's pickin' time, so pick, you black niggers, and get on with it!"

Big Jim was working at a steady, unhurried pace. When Josh Ibo approached, Big Jim ignored him. Josh stopped, sizing up Big Jim the way Rousseau sometimes did. He hesitated before speaking, but eventually the words came. "Now look at this black man here," he said so that his voice would carry. "He think he is pickin' berries. Pick one, eat one, take your time, pleasure yourself in the sunshine." Someone down the row laughed, and it stimulated Josh. "Nigger, ain't I told you before? How many times I got to tell you? That little boy behind you pickin' more with one hand than you is with two." Big Jim didn't look up. Neither did Wes. "Man, ain't you hear what I say? Or do I have to stir you up some?" Still Big Jim ignored him. Josh said: "Listen, black man, I give you 'bout two more breaths, and if you ain't movin' I goin' to tickle you." Big Jim began to whistle a tune. His easy, unhurried pace became slower and more measured.

Josh's control broke. He raised his whip and lashed at Jim's back. Big Jim straightened up and struck at Josh's face. He hit him again and Josh fell down. When Josh got to his knees Big Jim caught him by the neck and, holding him that way, brought his forehead down hard on the top of Josh's skull. Josh sagged and went down. When he tried to get up, Jim butted him again. The second blow split the skin on Jim's forehead. Blood began to flow. The third time he brought his forehead down it left a smear of red in Josh's hair. The driver called out only once: "Captain!" Big Jim kept hitting him until he lay without moving on the ground, two front teeth gone, blood trickling from his mouth. Then Big Jim stepped back into the row and resumed his picking.

When Rousseau finally came out on his white horse, the cotton pickers had moved on a hundred feet or more. Rousseau said, first to one man then another: "What happened to the driver?"

"Don't know, Captain," one said. "Never know something happen to him at all."

Another answered: "B'lieve it must be the heat, Captain. One minute Josh standing there, next minute he's lyin' down."

Rousseau asked Wes. Wes shook his head. He almost said, "Don't know, Captain," but his voice froze in his throat. Then Rousseau was looking at Big Jim's bloody forehead. He drew a pistol from his belt. "Nigger, come out of that row and start walking."

Big Jim straightened up and moved across the field toward the barn, Rousseau riding behind him. Without looking back and without a note of pleading, Big Jim said: "Captain, I told him. I told him many a time if he lay that cat-o'-nine-tail on I goin' to kill him. If he ain't dead, I'm sorry for that. The lowliest nigger of all is the one to whup his own kind, and him only a slave like the rest." He said no more.

He was chained in the barn until Rousseau had a chance to talk to Mr. Blair about it. Rousseau recommended fifty lashes in the presence of the rest of the slaves. Mr. Blair thought about it solemnly. Fifty lashes was agreed upon, but privately, in the barn. Mr. Blair had Christian compunctions. The idea of a public punishment distressed him. So Big Jim's arms were tied around a post.

Mr. Blair said a few words to him. "Jim, you've always been a reliable nigger. I don't know what got into you. I could sell you off somewhere. But I'll wait and see. You got the devil in you today. You nearly killed my driver. I paid a lot of money for Josh Ibo. If this ever happens again I'll have to send you away, over in Mississippi Territory somewhere. You got it real good here and don't have the sense to know it. Right now Mr. Rousseau is going to give you fifty lashes, and I hope that will drive the devil out of you."

Rousseau laid on the first stroke, then the second. At the third, Mr. Blair turned his head quickly and left the barn. When Rousseau was through, Big Jim had sagged to his knees, his chest pressing against the post. His back was a tangle of long, angry, half-opened welts, and some blood was trickling down the calf of his leg. When they untied him he lay motionless in the straw. "Now," Rousseau said, "wash that back off with turpentine to keep him from blood poison." When one of the slaves doused turpentine over him, Big Jim shuddered and fainted. He was dragged back to the south camp and left in front of his cabin. For more than a month he was not able to sleep on his back at night, and the touch of his shirt was an agony.

But he had to be at work in the fields with the others each day. Josh Ibo sauntered up and down the rows as usual, but there was a dark gap where his upper front teeth had been. Big Jim worked in the same easy casual way as always, never acknowledging the driver's presence. As for Josh, he didn't seem to notice Jim at all, and although he urged lagging workers on, he did no "tickling" with his whip for a while. Later he began flicking it again, and occasionally he laid it on a bent back, but with restraint and never in the vicinity of Big Jim.

Wes saw that there were gains from the confrontation. But what about Rousseau? From him the beating had to be taken without recourse. There was a final line one could not cross to seek justice. And yet, one day, Big Jim said as though thinking aloud: "That Captain Rousseau, one day I'm goin' to kill him dead." The consequence of such an act, should it ever occur, was evident. There were no roads leading anywhere, either backward to the place where Wes was born or forward to a different state of life.

Nevertheless, in his third year on the Blair plantation Wes began to see a glimmer of a course. He had been sent to the north camp with a wagonload of supplies from the barn. Back of one of the slave cabins was a half finished rowboat made of hewn boards and hand forged iron fittings. He asked Old Ned about it later.

"Why," Old Ned said, "that boat belongs to Amos. It's the second one. He made one last year with Old Master's permission, sold it to a man over in the next county. Got thirty-five dollars for that boat, less the expenses. Amos say he's goin' to buy his freedom with this money. Don't 'spect he goin' to make it though. He's been payin' in for more than ten years now, and he ain't made a dent in it. Master say the cost is one thousand dollars, and Amos already pay him 'bout three hundred.

"I tell Amos he ain't goin' to live long enough to see it out, the money comes too slow. He say he know they ain't much time to live free, but he 'tends to die free anyhow. Doubt he goin' to do it. In all the time I been here, and that's sixty-five years they tell me, I ain't see but one man bought his freedom. The only reason for that one was he lost his leg down at Johnson's sawmill and wasn't no good for a field hand no more. Old Master let him pay in four hundred dollars and gave him a freedom paper for it. I hear tell they's some other men done it too, but not around here. Cross the way, when mamma of Mr. Walker die, she give her cook freedom, but her boy, he's the Old Master over there now, he say the papers is no good and don't let her go. The cook's name is Nancy. When she hear Old Master not goin' to let her go, well, she been waitin' twenty years for that day, and when Old Master say he not goin' to do what the paper say to do, Nancy went out in the rice 'trashin' house and kill herself. So he ain't got her after all that, he done a bad mean thing and got nothin' out of it." Old Ned fell silent, deep in thought about goings on on the Walker plantation.

"There's one thing, though," he said at last, "a man would think, now, wouldn't he, that any Old Master on this whole earth would set his own chillen free? Mister Walker, he take different slave woman sometime when the Missus is away, and he had two boy children from them. They's half white and half black, but they's slaves just like the rest, and he's as hard on 'em as on the black niggers."

They rode the rest of the way to the barn without speaking. As they climbed down from the wagon, Old Ned glanced at Wes and saw the thickening of his jaw and his cheekbones. It came to him with a start that Wes was now bigger than Jess, and there was a stubble on his chin that could not be ignored much longer. Old Ned paused a moment to look at Wes's rounded, muscular arms. "Boy," he said, "you sure changed some in three years, and that's a fact. You must be fifteen years old now, the way I calculates it. One of these days we got to ask Old Master to let you get baptise, 'fore it's too late."

The notice of a death in the north camp, beaten out on a drum, wafted down on the still evening air, partially muffled by a grove of poplar trees above the main plantation house. Late stragglers coming in from the fields stopped to listen. "Someone's dead up there today," a man said. "Wonder who can he be?" The answer was awaiting them when they arrived at the cabins. A boy from the north camp had come with the news that the deceased was Nyawu, Konsi's child. "Poor boy," Celina said, "and him not three-year old yet." Wes ate his rice and fat meat silently, afflicted by sorrow and guilt. He had said, in his own words, "When your child comes, he shall be my nephew," and he had not guarded his nephew from the hostile forces around him.

When he was finished eating he washed and went to the barn to find Rousseau. "Captain," he said, "I must go to the north camp. The little boy that died, he's my nephew."

Rousseau examined Wes as though he were trying to solve a puzzle. "Nephew? I didn't know that girl was your sister."

"No," Wes said, "not my sister. The father of the boy, he was my friend."

"How does that make the young one your nephew?" Rousseau asked. "You're his godfather."

"No, my nephew," Wes insisted, "we call him so."

Rousseau seemed baffled. But as his eyes strayed toward where some men were working around the toolhouse he said: "There's no harm in it, I guess. All the other niggers will be there before the night is out, anyway. But no mischief, you hear?"

"Oh, yes, Captain, I'll do that," Wes said, wondering uncomfortably if he was talking like Samba.

When he arrived, the setting up was already under way. A group of wailing women squatted before the cabin. Konsi sat on a chair to one side, red-eyed but not crying. As the guests arrived they briefly conveyed that they shared her sorrow and then sought to engage her in conversation about ordinary things.

"Ain't it a shame about that nice child," someone said to her, "and only yesterday he seemed so lively. But he won't never have to do no field work for Old Master, it's a fact. Out there today my back was about to break. Seems like the work gets harder every year. You don't notice nothin', then you turn around and old age got you."

Konsi went through the motions of joining in this workaday talk with the women as though nothing had happened. After greeting her and looking inside, the men sat together in a group of their own, laughing or talking loudly without inhibition. Wes came and sat on his heels for a few moments near Konsi's chair. "Evenin', Konsi," he said, and then could say no more. The weight of his unfulfilled obligation to Konsi, and above all to Dosu, was very heavy. He arose and went inside, where Nyawu was laid out on a makeshift bed of wooden boxes. He squatted by the side of the bed, his arms hanging loosely over his knees. "Nyawu," he said in Fon, "my respects to your father, Dosu. Tell him I didn't know you were sick. This is the truth. Tell him how it is here, I live in a different camp, and I only found out about you when I heard the drum." After that he was silent. He remained there throughout the night.

When people came in to look at Nyawu they spoke to him as though he were alive. "Nyawu," a woman said, "you sure looks pretty today in all them Christmas clothes." And another: "This is Aunt Sarah talkin' to you, boy. You seemed mighty poorly yesterday, but tonight you looks fine. Everything is all right now. Be at ease, child." The mourners outside eventually ceased their cries. They entered to say a word to Nyawu, then went out again to exchange news with new arrivals from the south camp.

Celina, the cook from the south camp, stopped in the doorway. "Oh my Lord!" she cried out. "Born in slavery and die in slavery! Nothin' before and nothin' after, 'cept you, Jesus! Take care of this baby!" She wiped her eyes with her apron as Jennie pushed her way past.

"No use callin' on Jesus now," Jennie said firmly. "This child ain't never been baptise."

Celina answered angrily: "That's all us ever hear from you is baptise. You got too much pride you is Christian, but this baby ain't Christian. He ain't old enough to be one thing or another. And careful how you talk in front of him."

Wes spoke up quietly. "This boy Nyawu, he is a Fon."

Jennie said: "He is African all right, that is what's wrong hereabouts."

Celina answered: "What is *wrong* right now is this poor boy *done die*. That's one thing is wrong. Another thing wrong is that they is some wrong people come to the settin' up. Give this child a good word to take on with him, else pass on to the outside."

As Jennie turned to go she said: "Poor child, he ain't been baptise."

And Celina called after her: "No, he ain't. But he done been *born*, ain't he?"

The ritual for Nyawu was hardly anything at all, because he was so young. The funeral began at seven in the morning. Mr. Blair considered it unwise to let bodies go unburied for more than a single night, both for reasons of sanitation and of plantation efficiency. When a death occurred on a Sunday there was no wake at all, and the burial had to be accomplished within a few hours. Nyawu was wrapped in a cotton cloth obtained from the overseer, for which Konsi would have to perform, at a time of Rousseau's choosing, some extra task.

The body was placed on a door removed from Konsi's cabin and carried by four men. A drummer led the procession. Konsi walked behind the body, her face smeared with flour, the only white powder available. After her came the group of mourners, once again wailing loudly, followed by a straggling line of men, women and children from both camps. When the procession came to a fork in the trail, the pallbearers lurched from side to side as though buffeted by an invisible force. Then they moved on, zigzagging for a while, until they reached the burying ground behind a stand of live oak trees. There Nyawu was laid into a shallow grave that had been dug in the night. They mounded up the grave and set a crude cross at the head. When some of Nyawu's possessions were placed there—a whittled doll, a piece of broken mirror and a battered metal cup—Konsi fell screaming to the ground. She was lifted up and supported along the trail back to the cabins. On the way, the drummer played a lively dance beat, and the slow funeral walk turned into a gay carnival-like procession. The burying was done.

Although Wes's guilt in having failed Dosu in some way stayed with him, it slowly slipped into the quiet place where all his old memories were stored. But another thing, a short and passing moment connected with Nyawu's death, refused to be still. It was Celina crying out, "Oh my Lord! Born in slavery and die in slavery!" Those little words spoken for

Nyawu, were they not really spoken for Celina herself, and Old Ned, and Jeff, and everyone else?

Only a few, the Africans, had not been born in slavery. Yet it seemed to Wes that having been born in freedom placed an even greater burden on dying as a captive. Who in this place but the Africans had ever known the opening eye of the African morning; or the equality among men in one's village or in his work society; or the tie between the living and the dead? Back there, where he had come into life, there was an understanding that in all that happened no person stood alone, but was part of a great family, seen and unseen, that at its outer edges reached into distant villages, and in time reached back into the unknowable past.

Here it was as though no one had ancestors at all, and hardly anyone remembered that the forces of wind, lightning, the sea, the forest, water and iron were released or dispensed by the vodouns. To Tom, who made iron tires for the plantation wagons, iron was nothing more than a material that could be forged and shaped. And those who lurched with a corpse at the crossroads remembered only that it was a thing to do and had forgotten the reason—that the vodoun Legba stood there mischievously to send the corpse to the wrong destination.

The woven cloth of many threads that was life was here no more than the ragged shirt that covered a man's back. How little an old and respected African could convey, even less a young one, of what life was like in another place. Indeed, did not those born here at the consent of Mr. Blair reject the fabric of life in embarrassment? The Christian baptism that Old Ned was always talking about, wasn't it only a fragmentary memory of the power of water, twisted and strained to meet the reality that in this land men lived like trees in the ground, destined to die where they sprouted? One could not know his Fa until the end. But Fa presupposed human will. It could not apply to a stone lying in the sun, suffering heat without the capability of decision.

The paths among which one could choose were clearly visible: The pride of being able to endure degradation; the victory of withholding effort where effort was demanded; offering pain in exchange for pain, as between Big Jim and the driver; or special labor and enterprise, conceived in desperation to die free if one could not live free; or retreat into bitter humor, like the song, "My Old Master promise me"; or passive acceptance, seeing yourself as Old Master saw you. All of these paths, it seemed to Hwesuhunu, led only downward. Sometimes as he lay in his blanket at night the alternatives smothered him, and his mind then refused to deal with them at all. But somehow, perhaps in his sleep, knowledge came.

He awoke one morning more lighthearted than he had felt since leaving his village. He carried his knowledge secretly, as a treasure. There were some in the south camp who saw Wes smile for the first time. What Wes knew was that the only solution was the elemental one: escape. Not today, nor tomorrow, but when the time was right. Whether it would be into the bush, or across the sea, or into the sky he was not yet ready to know. But he understood that he had not survived the slave march, the sea voyage, and the war on St. Lucia merely to be carried on a door to the little plot where Mr. Blair generously sanctioned his black field hands to be buried. The task was to refuse to accept what others were seeking to find ways of accepting; to reject the authority that was a denial of life, even though it was clothed in the waistcloth of a king.

There were warm summer nights when the young people slipped away into the darkness of the woods and fields to make love. Often it was only a casual incident in the shadows, bringing escape from the endless routine of labor without meaning. It was the sole act of volition permitted to slaves. The daily hunger of the belly could be answered only with the food dispensed by Mr. Blair's overseer. But in the dark fields there was no intrusion by overseer or driver. There, for short moments, Old Master was defeated. The body and the spirit belonged to the person who wore them.

If there were offspring from these brief unions, there were no complaints from the Big House, for its inhabitants felt themselves fortunate in the increase. A fertile land, fertile animals, and fertile slaves were testimony to the rightness of life. Once children were born, they became Old Master's property, to be dealt with as he wished, but the passion which created them could not be listed in Rousseau's inventories. It belonged exclusively to the creatures who in all other respects were deprived of identity, who were dependent for small mercies on Mr. Blair's policies, principles, moralities and doubts. The restraints which the older people laid upon casual and reckless lovemaking were tempered by confusion and uncertainties. Some, like Old Ned, sought to surround lovemaking and its consequences with the preachings of the prophets. There were others who sought merely to clothe mating with the meaning and purpose it had once possessed.

But that kind of meaning had ceased to exist. For though procreation went on, and though Mr. Blair recognized certain pairings as proper because they were in some way useful, there was no permanence to anything except death; no certainty that whim or caprice in the Big House would not cancel out a slave union without notice by sale or trade of either of the parties. A strange moral compunction reinforced reluctance in the Big House to permit slave marriages by ordained ministers of the faith. For if a planter was truly a Christian, as Mr. Blair presumed himself to be, how could he ever separate those who were joined by the Church? And so the slaves were left to their barnyard mating, deprived of the Christian rites which would have placed a burden on the master's freedom to sell and trade with spiritual calm.

Although the birth of a child generally produced delight

in the slave quarters, there were some who experienced little pleasure in such an event. For here was a new human creature to be trained, harnessed and driven, and whose education, if he were to survive, must be directed toward the achievement of self-contempt. In the north camp there was Aunt Sally, half demented now with age, whose only claim to fulfillment was that she had born many children for Old Master and Old Missus. Once she had clutched with her emaciated hand at Mrs. Blair's sleeve to beg for a few yards of red ribbon: "Oh, pretty Missus! I make plenty babies for you! Sixteen I had, pretty Missus, and ten alive and workin' in the fields! Oh, pretty Missus, give me some of that red ribbon like you wearin' for dress up my ugly head!"

There was still another by the name of Yunnuh who saw in the creation of life only disaster and sacrilege. "How can a woman put somethin' she love out into this miserable world?" she said. Sometimes she added the thought that slavery would be totally ended, as though by a thunderbolt, if only the black folk refused to procreate for their masters. "Don't give them the next generation," Yunnuh said, "and in twenty years Old Master be livin' in a cabin just like mine, and when it time to carry him to the buryin' ground on a door, they won't even be nobody to carry it." Yunnuh herself had produced no children, and in the Big House she was believed to be sterile. But among the slaves it was known that she had found ways to prevent her children from being born.

Nevertheless, procreation went on, the inescapable consequence of mating, brief or sustained, of secret meetings or of unions sanctioned and approved by the slaves without the benefit of Christian rites. Despite the knowledge that close and durable relationships would be threatened by the cold cruelties of a future day, some men and women welded ties that were vulnerable to nothing except unpredictable policies in the Big House.

In Wes's fourth year on the Blair plantation there were two events that hardened his conviction that he had no choice but to run away. One of those events was what happened to Big Jim. The other was the sale of two slaves to a Mississippi planter. As for Big Jim, though he sang his songs or picked his banjo in the evenings, he became morose and taut. In the fields he would make taunting comments for the ears of the driver, and sometimes without prelude he made stinging remarks to his friends. To Wes he once said angrily, as though Wes were an offensive stranger: "Nigger, keep off my heels!" Big Jim's crisis came one morning when he was goading the driver. Josh stood his ground, whip in hand, telling Big Jim he'd better bend his back and move his hands if he wanted to stay out of trouble. Big Jim moved forward, his eyes red, his arms hanging loosely. Josh jumped backward, the pitch of his voice rising. "Don't lay hands on me!" he shouted. "I'm the head man here!"

At this moment Rousseau came riding out from the barns. Without a change of expression or a word he rode up to Big Jim and lashed at him with his three-tongued whip. The first stroke cut across Big Jim's shoulder, the second across his cheek. Seeing the way things were going, Josh laid his whip also on Big Jim's back. Rousseau's whip was cutting at him from above, and Josh's from behind. Josh was shouting, "Get down on your knees! Pray the Captain to give mercy on you!" Rousseau said nothing at all, his face pale and without expression, as he lashed down on Big Jim's face and neck.

Big Jim lowered his arms and stood listlessly, as though all desire to survive had gone out of him. Rousseau, leaning forward, continued to strike. Then, as the whip came down in a wide arc, Big Jim's hand shot forward, caught it and jerked. His face showing expression for the first time, Rousseau toppled forward out of the saddle, falling heavily on his shoulder on the plowed ground. Big Jim grabbed him, stood him on his feet, and knocked him down. He picked him up again and butted him on the top of his head. Rousseau fell again, half moaning, half calling for help. Big Jim began lashing at Rousseau with the whip, shouting: "Oh, Captain! Oh, Captain! How do it feel, Captain? How many you desire, Captain? How about ten? How about twenty? Tell me when to stop, Captain! This old boy want you satisfy, Captain!"

Josh stood motionless, his eyes bulging in horror. Rousseau's moaning stopped. He lay without moving, his eyes closed. Then Big Jim turned on Josh. Josh began to run, but Big Jim caught him, knocked him down. Josh was instantly on his feet, running toward the plantation buildings. Big Jim snatched up a hoe from the ground and followed him. Before Josh was halfway to his destination the swinging hoe blade caught him on the side of the head, and he fell into a furrow. Big Jim did not bother to strike again, because Josh was obviously dead. He dropped the hoe and stood there, looking first at Josh's crumpled body, then back toward where Rousseau lay.

For the first time, now, he was aware that some of the field hands were shouting at him: "Oh, you poor boy! You done kill the Captain! Now us old niggers goin' to catch it!" But other voices were shouting: "You got to go! Head for the swamp!" Big Jim's eyes turned across the field. He began to walk, and then he was running, dodging where he could into underbrush, toward the meandering Muddy River and the marshes.

Rousseau was not dead. They carried him back to the plantation house, where Old Missus and Jennie took care of him. Within a few hours a posse of planters gathered with dogs and guns and went out in pursuit of Big Jim. Big Jim, of course, crisscrossed the Muddy River several times and swam through Eel Lake to confuse the dogs. But they found his trail eventually. Two days later they trapped him in a tree and killed him.

The overseer was back at work in a week, his battered face showing no emotion of any kind. His voice, when he spoke, was still quiet and disinterested. The large black bruise over his right cheekbone gradually disappeared. There was no driver for quite a while, but the overseer of the Walker plantation came and helped Rousseau sometimes when the slaves were in the field. In time a new driver was purchased from a planter on Sapelo Island.

The other event came a few months later. Jess heard gossip around the plantation house that two young female slaves were being traded by Mr. Blair for a skilled artisan from Mississippi, a slave who was proficient at both carpentry and masonry. For a long while Mr. and Mrs. Blair had been planning to redesign the plantation house and add a new wing to it which would include a ballroom. For the past two years, between the crop seasons, the field hands had spent weeks in the woods cutting down large trees, squaring them, and hauling them back of the barn for stacking and drying. Now the construction work was about to begin. This explained the requisition of an artisan slave. But the rumors that two females were to be sent away in exchange created a tension in the slave quarters greater than had the recent news of a slave insurrection.

Celina immediately sent Jess to the stables to find out if the stableboys knew anything more, and she herself put up her hair in her best headcloth and went to the Big House kitchen to see the cook, Jennie, who had a reputation for knowing everything that was going on. "Evenin', Sister," she said, suppressing her dislike for Jennie. "Down in the camp they is sayin' Old Master sellin' off two field hands to trade for the new artisan."

Jennie, in response, smothered her disdain for field hands in general and her dislike of Celina in particular, for she enjoyed being a source of vital information from the plantation house. "Wipe the mud off your feet if you got to come in the kitchen," she said. "We is all very *clean* up here."

Celina said: "I wipe 'em. Ain't goin' to track up the

floor. Folks is sayin' two women been sold. You hear about it?"

Jennie went on scouring the pots. "Maybe I do," she said. "Hear plenty things around here. But the prophet say, 'Speak no evil.' It don't do no good to run and tell everythin' you hears."

"Course not," Celina said. "That's what I keep tellin' them. They go 'round sayin' this and that, don't know if it's so and don't care, neither. I keep tellin' them Sister Jennie know the truth. So you tell me if it's so or it ain't so, and I go back there and tell 'em hold they tongues."

Jennie put down her pots and placed her hands on her hips. "Now I ain't got lots of time to waste. I work all day and half the night, and all this talk with whoever happen to come in the kitchen door don't do me no good. It's 'Jennie this' and 'Jennie that' from Missus all the time, and 'why you ain't polish the silver like I told you?' How I goin' to please Missus and make all this yakka-yakka with the field hands at the same time?"

Celina shook her head sadly. "Sister," she said, "you got it special hard up here in the Big House."

"Ain't it so," Jennie said. And after a pause: "Well, I do hear Old Master done trade Tessie, for one."

"Tessie? He done trade Tessie? Don't he know she marry up with Simeon Gola last year and is makin' a baby with him?"

"Don't he know? Yes, he know. He know it maybe 'fore she know it. I think Old Master maybe peekin' through the cabin cracks night they was marry. He know it all right. But he think Simeon get too lazy since he been marry."

Celina said: "Both Simeon and Tessie been raised on this land. How come Old Master do a thing like that and not say a word to them?"

"The other one," Jennie said, "is Mary Lou."

Celina's eyes widened. "Mary Lou? What about her four chillen?"

"Don't look at me like that, Sister," Jennie said, "It ain't me that sold 'em. I just cooks and cleans the kitchen."

Celina turned and hurried back to the camp. At six in the morning Simeon was at the barn waiting for Rousseau. When the foreman arrived, Simeon took off his straw hat and held it over his chest. "Captain," he said, "Must have a word with you, if you please, Captain."

"What is it, Simeon?" Rousseau said, yawning and scratching his head.

"It's about Tessie, Captain," Simeon said. "They is folks say Old Master done sell her off."

"Sell her? No, not exactly. Mr. Blair traded her for a carpenter."

"But Captain," Simeon said, trying to control the anxiety in his voice, "Captain, she is my woman, and she is about to born a young one."

"Yes," Rousseau said, "I heard about that. I might have done it different, but Mr. Blair made the arrangements."

"Captain," Simeon said, "this woman is my wife, and she carry my young one. Ain't Old Master think on that?"

Rousseau looked a little surprised. "Simeon," he said, "that woman ain't your wife. You and her never been married."

"Yes, Captain, us is married."

A note of impatience came into Rousseau's voice. "Now look here, Simeon, you ain't *never* been married. You studded her and she's carryin' a pickaninny, but you ain't never been *married*. There been no preacher to this, you and her just went together, and that ain't the same as marriage. You got no rights in it at all, and you better go on back and get to work now."

"Captain," Simeon said, "when two niggers go together like this, it is the same thing as married. We got no preachers and we got no church down here. I am the father of that child of Tessie's, and don't that make me her husband?"

"No, it don't do nothing of the kind," Rousseau said, a

sharp edge to his tone. "You are field hands, and studding a girl don't make you married. Like I told you, I might have done it different, but you are Mr. Blair's property, and what he says goes. Now get on back to work. There's lots of girls around." Simeon didn't move. "Well?" Rousseau said.

Simeon said: "Captain, you can fix it for me. Let me go with Tessie to the new master. I can work for him the same as here. Tell Old Master sell me too."

Rousseau spat in disgust. "It's all arranged. Mr. Anderson don't want no men niggers. What he wants is some women for the ones he's got. Now git."

Later that day when he saw Old Master's carriage coming down the road, Simeon dropped his hoe and raced across the plowed fields to intercept him. He stood in the road waving his arms frantically. Mr. Blair pulled up the horses. "Master, you can give me twenty lashes if you want, but I got to have a word with you, please."

"Well," Mr. Blair said, "what's wrong?"

"Master," Simeon said, "they tells me you sold off my woman Tessie to another master somewhere."

"Yes," Mr. Blair said, "I sold her."

"Master," Simeon said, "before God I ask you sell me too to the same place!"

Mr. Blair looked around him uncomfortably. "Been glad to," he said, "but Mr. Anderson didn't want any men, only women."

"Master," Simeon said, "couldn't you pay cash money for that new man you bought?"

"No," Mr. Blair said, "he wanted two girls. Don't worry, Mr. Anderson treats his slaves well."

"Master," Simeon said, "I was borned on this place, and I work hard for you. I never give you no trouble, and I eat less than some folks around here. You take my woman and child away and you can't count on me no more. You can shoot me down now if you want, because it don't make no difference to me if it's sooner or later."

Mr. Blair removed the buggy whip from its holder and flicked at the horses. They trotted off down the road. The next morning when the slaves reported for work Simeon Gola and Tessie were missing. Four days later they were found hiding out in the swamps and brought back.

As for Mary Lou, when she heard what was in store for her she went wailing to Old Missus and acted so bereft that Old Missus thought, despite a momentary stab of compassion, that the plantation would be a little better off without her. "Oh, Missus, how can you and Old Master sell off this miserable old nigger woman and leave them pretty little chillen behind? Ain't I work my fingers to the raw to make you happy, pretty Missus? Who goin' to care for them young ones of mine?"

Old Missus said: "Why, Mary Lou, is this a way to behave? Don't you know we take care of our laborers . . ." (Old Missus always avoided the words "niggers" and "slaves.")

"Oh, yes, pretty Missus, you takes care of them, but they's only chillen, and what they goin' to do without me?"

Old Missus spoke as to a child: "Now, Mary Lou, I know how you feel, but Mr. Blair knows best about such things. And sometime or another you would be separated anyway. Some day or other Mr. Blair would probably have to . . ." —she found it hard to say "sell"—". . . have to send the children elsewhere to work, some of them anyway. Control yourself, now, Mary Lou."

But Mary Lou could not control herself. She scraped up dust from the courtyard and threw it on her face and shoulders. "If that's the way of it, pretty Missus, you can dig my grave deep and long, 'cause I'll be dead before I gets to the new master's land. I'm a Christian now, I been submerged in the river in the name of Jesus. But where is Jesus at? Don't He live here where the nigger folks need him? What good to be a Christian, pretty Missus, if Jesus don't know it?"

Old Missus was disconcerted by the rising pitch of Mary Lou's voice. "Now, Mary Lou," she said, "Jesus watches all of us. We have to be patient. We all have to suffer. And in time, if we do not lose faith, our sufferings end."

Mary Lou began to scream: "Oh, pretty Missus, yes, there is suffering! You and I know that, cause we are in pain! And pretty Missus, she suffer 'cause the nigger folk suffer! Oh, Jesus, come and save pretty Missus from the pain she feel in her heart! Oh, Jesus, Lord, if you can't help this poor old nigger, leastaways put your hands on pretty Missus here! She need you, Jesus!"

Old Missus was startled by the outburst, and confused by what Mary Lou seemed to be saying. But her mind was relieved when it occurred to her that the woman was out of her senses. After all, why try to make sense out of something that is senseless? "You will make out all right, Mary Lou," she said to end the confrontation. "Be patient, time heals wounds."

As she turned to reenter the house she heard Mary Lou say: "Oh, Missus, and you is so pretty too! How can it be?" When Mrs. Blair was once more safely in the house, Mary Lou returned listlessly to the slave compound, the dust from the courtyard still on her head and face. There, at last, she broke down and cried, hardly ceasing until the day when, red-eyed and broken, she was taken away along with Tessie to be shipped to the Anderson place in Mississippi.

Wes was now seventeen. "Look at that boy," Old Ned's wife Eula said one morning, "he's outgrowed hisself. He's a man now."

Wes hadn't thought of it quite that way. He considered that he had been a man for a long time, dating from the time he went into the fields with his father's work society. But it was evident to him that he was taller and heavier, that Old Ned no longer seemed as large as he once had. It was quite a while since the first time he shaved—with a bit of broken glass.

"I told him that, many a time," Old Ned said. "Either

he's growed up or I growed down." Old Ned surveyed Wes from head to foot. He had a hard time recollecting what Wes had looked like that first day on the plantation. The reluctant, almost shy smile that came now and again was almost the only reminder of Hwesuhunu the young Fon. That and the intent look about his eyes, the way he always seemed to be probing sights and sounds for their hidden meanings. "Son," Old Ned said, "you just about everything but a Christian. I ain't done right by you, that's sure. It's high time to get you baptise." And that next Sunday, at last, Old Ned took Wes to see Mr. Blair.

They waited back of the house until the family returned from church, and when Mr. Blair descended from the carriage Old Ned clutched his hat and bowed. "Master," he said, "hopes you had a fine sermon this mornin'. Need a word with you, Master, most important."

"What is it, Ned?" Mr. Blair said suspiciously.

" 'Taint about the food or the work, Master, it's about this boy here, Wes Hunu. You know he's an African boy, Master, he ain't grow up on this place from scratch like most of us."

"Yes, I know," Mr. Blair said impatiently. "Isn't it something Mr. Rousseau can take care of?"

"Oh, no, Master, it's too important. This boy, now, he's doin' fine all the way around, except only one thing. Ain't been baptise. Guess we all know a Christian field hand is the best kind to have. They do a lot more work and cause a lot less trouble, don't they? What it's about, I'd like to take Wes to the preachin' down in Red Hollow and get him immersed. I know you are goin' to think kindly on it."

Mr. Blair was troubled. "I don't know," he said, "I don't know if it does any good."

Old Ned clutched his hat a little tighter. "Master, this boy ain't got no mamma or daddy here to raise him right. I been doin' the best I know how with him. I like to know I done everything I can to put him on the right path."

Mr. Blair looked at Wes, then at Ned, and smiled. "Ned, this boy don't need his mamma no more. He's almost as big as you."

Old Ned wrinkled his face and looked puzzled for Mr. Blair's benefit. "Master," he said, "you mean a man don't have to be a Christian if he's growed up?"

Mr. Blair turned to go. "I don't know. I don't know if I can allow it. I'll think about it. That doesn't mean yes, it just means I'll think about it. I'll talk to Rousseau."

"Thank you, Master, we sure thank you for it," Old Ned said. "There ain't nothin' like immersion to make a good field hand!"

On the way back to the slave quarters Wes said: "Uncle Ned, you goin' to waste that water on me, 'cause I don't expect I'll ever be a better or worse field hand than now."

Old Ned answered: "You ain't so thick head not to know what I'm talkin' about, boy. You got to tell it so Old Master think he's got a profit in it somehow, else he don't want it. He's got a powerful lot of maybe-yes maybe-no in him, and everything hangs on how much he think he can make on it. One thing, he don't like the niggers to get together in camp meetin'. On the other side, he figure a wild kind of nigger need to get civilized else he make trouble. Yes, Old Master worry plenty 'bout this thing."

There was talk among the old men that day about Mr. Blair and his worry. It started when Old Ned complained about the difficulties Old Master put in the way of baptising, and after a while it developed into a confrontation between Old Ned and Samba. Samba sat there whittling himself a cane with alligators and frogs on it, listening to Old Ned. At last he said: "The way I see it, this Christian thing got plenty of new style to it, but it don't set no one free, now, does it? Seems to me like some folks put faith in it 'cause it's somethin' Old Master and Old Missus got, and if it can make them white folks rich and powerful and make them own slaves, well, then, it's got to be good. Brother Ned, you sure are a Christian from head to feet, but what does it do for you? You tell me Old Master do so-and-so 'cause they's a profit in it. So ain't that why you get yourself baptise, 'cause they's an advantage to it?"

Old Ned was indignant. "Brother Samba, I turn the other cheek like the Good Book say. The question ain't advantage, it's salvation. All them spirits I hear you talk about, they didn't keep you out of slavery, did they? So don't talk down on the Christian way. A Christian knows that God does things his own way, and what counts is what comes later. This life is the ladder, and it don't make any difference if a man is white or black, slave or free, long as you got salvation. All them as has it will be in the same Big House on the day the trumpet blows."

Samba cleared his throat and leaned back against the corner of the cabin. "Now tell me one thing, Brother, just one thing. How come you tell me they is only one spirit, Jesus, when everyone knows they is plenty orisha?"

Old Ned rocked back and forth in his chair. "Never said Jesus was an orisha. Course, some folks don't know the difference. They is only one of Jesus. Only one God, yes, man, only one God, that's all."

Samba sighted along the cane he was working on, pointing it at the horizon. "The way you tell it, Brother Ned, us African people got too many spirits. You say one is better than ten. Now, listen to this. If you got one dollar and I got ten, which is the richest, you or me?"

Old Ned crossed his arms and looked at Samba squarely in the eyes. "What's wrong with that, Brother, is that it ain't what seems better, but what is the *truth*. When you get to know *that*, you got the knowledge. That's all I got to tell you. You still got a little time, but you better get started, 'cause it might take you more time than most."

Samba pushed his lips out pensively. "All I hear from you is a new banjo tune," Samba said. "Man who love one spirit, he's just fine. Man who love ten, he's been left behind."

Old Ned shook his head. "Throw a goose in the air don't make him fly. I tell you and I tell you, but you don't get a grip on it."

Several weeks went by, and Old Ned had to remind Mr. Blair about his request. Mr. Blair said, "I don't know, I haven't made up my mind," and he looked worried again. That was all Old Ned could get out of him. But Sam, the stableboy, overheard Mr. Blair airing his doubts to Rousseau while the two men were sitting together in the carriage house after dinner one evening.

"I don't care much for the whole idea," Mr. Blair said, "and a lot of other planters don't like it either."

Rousseau said: "Well, Mr. Blair, over in Louisiana it don't seem to hurt any. It sort of gives them things to keep on their minds. You take on Sunday, those field hands don't have much work to do except at pickin' time. So they think up complaints and mischief. For my part I don't think a little Christianizing is going to make any difference."

Mr. Blair said: "I've heard that opinion. Maybe it works over in Louisiana, but the worst trouble Tom Walker ever had was with the sanctified ones."

"Well," Rousseau said, "it's up to you, of course. But they're an easy-go lot if you handle them right. You make issues with them on a particular thing, though, and they can act mighty stubborn. Once they get the notion you're taking away something they want, they can do some right mean things to the crops and tools and such, and do it so sly you don't even know what happened.

"One woman cook we had over at Baton Rouge, every time she was criticized she got nervous and cried and dropped two or three plates. In no time at all we figured if there was going to be any plates left we got to handle her different. And those field hands, they do childish things to get at you, like losing wagon burs, or plowing clevises under the sod, or breaking plowpoints on rocks. And the way they do it you can't never prove it ain't an accident, either. Or they get sick. Of course you can gamble they *ain't* sick and are just putting one over on you, but if you lose the bet you might lose a good stretch of work, and maybe an expensive field hand too. I had a lot of experience with these niggers. If a man ain't really sick to begin with, he gets sick to spite you, real sick I mean, with the fever and running nose, and maybe out of his head. I've seen a whole camp of niggers get back at a planter by coming down with the consumption.

"And then there's this mojo business. They won't come right out and start an insurrection, but they start mojoing all the white people. They make these little magic things and plant them around in different places so the Master will walk over it and have bad luck of some kind. Why, there was one place in Louisiana where they got hold of some of the Master's toenail clippings, and they made mojoes out of them and planted them around, and next thing you know that man had a stroke and was paralyzed from the waist down. Course I know mojoes don't mean anything, but it makes you wonder sometimes. The main thing is, it's mischief.

"One thing you can do to stop it is keep 'em at field work seven days a week and don't give 'em time to think up tricks and meanness. Other thing is let 'em do what they want long as it don't interfere with the cropping. If they act up, give them some whip, or cut back on the clothing, or something like that, and if they get real mean give them a day or two in the sweat box. The main consideration is the crops. It don't make any difference to me if they're African style niggers or Christianized niggers long as the crops is taken care of. If a nigger think he's going to just about die if he ain't Christianized, well, I say don't encourage him; but if you let him go ahead he'll probably quiet down."

"It's not just that," Mr. Blair said. "What bothers me is the idea of them being *Christian.* Mrs. Blair says it doesn't seem right to have a *Christian* as a *slave.* Things were a lot better around here before those footloose scalawag preachers started running around stirring things up."

More weeks went by, but still Old Ned got nothing out of Mr. Blair except, "Well, I don't know. I'll think on it." Wes let the whole matter slip from his mind. It seemed more Old Ned's affair than his own.

Then one night after he had fallen into a deep sleep he was wakened by Old Ned shaking him. In the pale light of the oil lamp Wes could see Jess rubbing his eyes and dressing. "Get up," Old Ned said, "I'm takin' you two boys to the immersion." Wes's body ached from twelve hours of hauling logs. He sat up, unwilling to disengage himself from the warm blanket of sleep. "Move there, boy!" Old Ned said. "We ain't got all night, and we got a far way to go. And keep your voice down, not to wake the whole camp." When Wes and Jess were dressed, they followed Old Ned from the cabin, across the fields toward Eel Lake.

"Where we goin', Papa?" Jess said after they had walked in silence for a while.

"We goin' to the camp meetin'," Old Ned said. "Keep your voices low."

They found the woods trail more by instinct than sight. There was no moon, but the air was clear and there was a faint starlight that provided dim silhouettes. Once they were in the woods, Old Ned opened a tin box of fireplace embers, blew them into red coals, and lighted a pinewood torch. They heard dogs barking distantly around the plantation buildings. When they reached the edge of Eel Lake they veered west, Old Ned using the Drinkin' Gourd constellation and the North Star for a guide. They walked for more than two hours, from one patch of darkness into another. Once Old Ned stopped to light a new pine torch. And as they stood there a gentle shift of wind brought the sound of high-pitched female voices and the throb of drums.

"What's that?" Jeff said.

"Camp meetin'," Old Ned said.

"Why we go to the meetin'?" Jess said.

"I tell you right now," Old Ned said, " 'cause when we get there the time goin' to be short. You two boys, I brung you to this meetin' to make Christians of you. I try to give you the right words myself, but it ain't enough. Tonight you goin' to get salvation. And after that you goin' to be baptise."

Wes took it in silently. The sound of the voices and drumming lured him. But Jess said: "How we goin' to get salvation? Who givin' it out?"

Old Ned said sharply: "Don't give me no sass, boy, you know plenty well what is salvation. Listen, now, you go in that meetin' with the other folks, keep your mind on what the preacher say, and *get the spirit!* You hear me talkin' to you, now? Not *some other* time, not just when you got the notion, but *this* time! It's a mighty far distance from home, and it mought be a year or two 'fore they's another meetin' like this one. Otherwise I give you natural time. But they ain't no time. You get the spirit *tonight,* you hear?"

Jess said: "Yes, Papa, I hear what you say."

"Got to be that way," Old Ned said, " 'cause less you get the spirit you can't be baptise!" He turned to Wes: "You got it, son, what I say about this?"

"Yes, Uncle," Wes said.

They went on through a damp meadow and another large grove, forded a stream and entered a low hollow where the meeting was taking place.

There was a large bonfire, and sitting before it were perhaps a hundred slaves. Standing beside the fire preaching to them was a huge man in work clothes, blackskinned and perspiring in the fire's heat. Wes was surprised. Somehow he had expected, though he had not really thought much about it, that the preacher would be white. "There he is," Old Ned said, "the Reverend John Paul Sampson." They found places among the congregation and sat down just as the preacher began to sermonize. His voice was throaty, raspy, and full of inner excitement, and the sounds that came from his mouth were part chant, part song, broken by tension-laden rhythmic pauses. He threw his head back, looked into the starlit sky and closed his eyes. Out of the pages of the Gospel of St. Matthew he tore the words and threw them to the hungry men and women who sat on the ground before him, remolding the shape of the words, in his mouth, giving them new form.

"In those days . . . came John the Baptist . . . preachin' in the . . . wilderness of Judea . . . and sayin' . . . repent ye . . . for the Kingdom of . . . Heaven . . . is nigh. . . . For this is he . . . that was spoken of . . . by the Prophet Esaias. . . . Hay-hay-ay. . . . his voice . . . the one . . . cryin' in the . . . wilderness . . . prepare ye . . . the way . . . of the Lord and make . . . his . . . pathway straight and . . . the same John had his raiment of . . . camel hair . . . and a leather girdle . . . round his loin."

Tension mounted. Hands clapped rhythmically. Voices cried out "Amen!" "Yes, Jesus!" and sometimes the old African call of affirmation, "Ago-é!"

"Jesus came . . . from Nazarene . . . unto . . . Galilee . . . to be . . . baptised . . . of John . . . in Jordan . . . and . . . John said . . . unto him . . . come and talk to me . . . I need . . . to be . . . baptised . . . of Thee and . . . Jesus said . . . unto . . . John . . . suffer it to be so for . . . thus it becomes us . . . to fill all righteousness. . . ."

As John Paul Sampson went on, there were new sounds from the congregation. Cries, moans and sometimes keening melodic notes that wavered in the air, floating up and down and creating a rich polyphony to the sonorous rhythmic text. Wes listened in fascination. It reminded him of Dahomey, and he felt meanings he could not recognize, though they were intimately familiar. When he saw a woman leap to her feet and stagger about uncontrollably, his first thought was that the vodoun Legba had entered her head. But from her own mouth came the words, "O, Jee-eee-sus! O Jesus, ay, ah Jee-eee-sus!" And he knew then that it was not Legba who had entered this place, but the one that Old Ned had so often spoken about.

As the tension spread, other men and women felt the spirit come into them. Old Ned, clapping vigorously, chanting "Amen," sometimes turned his eyes on Jess and Wes to see what was happening to them. Jess was stamping his bare feet on the ground and slapping his hands against his chest, nothing more. But when Wes Hunu sang out some ancient Fon phrases, *"Ago-é, ago-vi, ago-tchi,"* Old Ned's face broke into a smile. And precisely at that moment Jess was upright, bouncing up and down, shouting, "O Jesus! O Jesus!" Old Ned grabbed Wes and Jess by their arms and dragged them forward to the feet of the towering John Paul Sampson, calling out, "Immersion! Thanks to Jesus! Immersion!" Others, too, were being pulled forward.

When at last John Paul Sampson was finished, and an anthem had been sung and a prayer said, the redeemed slaves, those who had felt the hand of God on them, were marched to a swift-flowing river half a mile away, and each one was taken in hand by John Paul Sampson and immersed in the water. "In the name of the Father, the Son, and the Holy Ghost," John Paul Sampson intoned as each one was baptised. As Wes went under he had a moment of fright, remembering his struggle in the sea, but once back on the shore he merely shivered from the cold. He put on his clothes and followed Jess and Old Ned on the long walk back to the plantation.

From Old Ned they heard now about John Paul Sampson. It was Wes who posed the question. "Thought all the preachin' men was white," Wes said. "Where this man John come from?"

Old Ned said: "They is a heap goin' on in this land of Georgia that don't meet the eye. Ain't it so! Old Master, he think he is God A'mighty, and all the black folk has to say to him is 'Yes, Lord.' But the real God is abroad in this country, and you hear it tonight. The planter people don't let no white preacher come down this way to hold meetin' and give baptise, but you can't stop the Lord when he make up his mind. He look around and find his man, John Paul Sampson, 'bout eighteen mile west of this place on the Pratt plantation; just a blacksmith by the name of John, after John the Baptiser; Paul, after the apostle; and Sampson, after the one which kill the lion with his hands and pushed the buildin' down with his arms. And he throw a bolt of lightnin' into this man whilst he makin' horseshoes one mornin', and John turned to preachin'.

"He learned hisself to read and kept his Bible under the straw in the stable, 'cause his Old Master don't like niggers to read. And when he finished with that Bible he learned it by heart, and he can tell you any part of it out of his head. And he don't need the Book no more 'cause he got it inside him, and he passed it on to another man. And when God see John got it all inside him he sent him out to preachin' 'mongst the wild men, just like Jonah was sent to preach over in Nineveh. Only this man John don't run away like Jonah do and hide somewhere."

"How you know 'bout the meetin'?" Wes asked. "How you know where it was?"

"Field hands call it out last week," Old Ned said. "John find out his Old Master goin' away to Biloxi for maybe five-six days. And he send out the word where he goin' to be on such and such a night. Every one of them nights John is preachin' the word somewhere or other."

They walked in silence for a while, fatigue overtaking them at last. After a time Old Ned said, as a kind of afterthought: "Don't need to tell you, got to keep a tight mouth on this thing. If it gets out, Old Master goin' to make a terrible ruckus. And as for that, if they finds out 'bout John, they beat him to death or maybe send him out to Mississippi somewhere."

They were home just before sunrise, their feet cold and

wet with dew from the long grass. It was too late to sleep, so Wes and Jess sat on a log just outside the camp talking.

Jess said: "Guess that preachin' make you happy?"

Wes shrugged. "Don't know if it did. That man John, I don't know what he was sayin', but I like his proudness."

"Must of made you happy, though," Jess said, "You give out with some great whoops."

Wes said: "I said those words many times before, and not for Jesus neither. I still don't know about Jesus. But the spirit sure come into you good."

Jess picked up a stone and threw it. "Oh, never mind that," he said, "I didn't feel nothin' at all. I was just pleasurin' my Papa. I close my eyes and jump around 'cause Papa say I got to do it. Man, that water was sure cold."

Wes pondered long on John Paul Sampson. He saw something in this man that bolstered his spirit. It was not what he had to say about salvation, which to Wes seemed irrelevant. It was something about the man himself, not only his size, which was extraordinary, but his dignity and pride. Wes sensed something in the making that was larger than the camp meeting. He thought, "This man named John has the knowledge." And he remembered a proverb that said, "Knowledge is another name for strength." He resolved to understand, and there came over him a furious desire to know how to read. It burned in him continually. Sometimes when he saw Rousseau in the fields, or Old Master and Missus riding about in their carriage, it seemed to him that their greatest treasure was their ability to tap the knowledge stored in writing. His desire became compulsion. He asked Jess one day, "You know where I can get a book?"

Jess said: "Boy, what you talkin' about? Why you need a book?"

Wes said: "I just needs it."

Jess said: "Ain't no books round here, 'cept in Old Master's house. Not allowed. You get twenty lashes if you caught with a book, and maybe your rations cut back. You want that Bible book Papa talk about?"

"That's the only book I heard of," Wes said. "Is they other ones?"

Jess laughed. "Son, they's plenty books. I looked through the window of Old Master's house one time and seen enough books to build a cabin with, all different, too."

"Can't read, can you?" Wes said.

"No, course I can't read. Ain't hardly no niggers can read."

"Well," Wes said, "how you know all them books was different?"

"Easy," Jess said. "They's big ones and little bitty ones, and all different colors, that's how."

"I got to get one of them books," Wes said.

Jess's mouth opened wide. "How you goin' get one of them books?" he said disapprovingly. It wasn't the idea of getting it that bothered Jess so much as the idea of book.

"Can ask one of the house servants," Wes said.

"You crazy," Jess said. "Ain't no house nigger goin' to thief it for you. Get him in bad trouble."

Wes said: "I knowed some men on St. Lucia who stole guns and bullets for they friends." Jess's eyes opened wide in wonder. Wes told him about Jean Labarbe and the others, and a little about the bitter struggle after the shipwreck.

"Guns!" Jess said in admiration. "Man, that's real thiefin'! Next to guns a book ain't nothin' at all. What you want to do?"

"I want to get one of them books from Old Master's house," Wes said.

Jess thought for a moment. "You can't ask none of them house servants," he said. "They tell each other, and next thing is some nigger want to be in good with Old Missus and splutter it out and leave corn-pone crumbles all over the place."

They sat pondering the matter.

"Could *buy* it," Wes said.

"You got hard cash?" Jess said scornfully. "Old Master don't want a set of drums like you made for Samba."

And after a while Wes said: "All right, then, you show me the room which has the books."

Jess said: "Yeah, I show you. You and me together, we thief one of them books."

And on Saturday night when the slave quarter was busy socializing, Jess and Wes slipped silently out of the camp, circled the plantation buildings and approached from the far side. They lay under Missus Blair's magnolias for a long time, until there seemed to be no movement on the grounds. Then they crawled on their bellies to a particular window which gave off a pale yellow light. Carefully they raised themselves high enough to see through the cracks in the shutters. They looked silently, taking everything in. Wes had never imagined such a room, bigger than a half dozen slave cabins, its polished floor covered with rugs, furnished with finely painted chairs, and pictures on the walls. At the far end Old Master sat at a desk with an oil lamp, busily writing. When he had digested all this, Wes's eyes moved to the shelves where the books were stacked, hundreds and hundreds of them.

"Ain't I tell you?" Jess whispered. "Ain't I tell you 'bout them books?" Wes was transfixed. But the spell was broken when Jess whispered hoarsely: "Come on! The dogs is makin' a big ruckus! We got to get out."

They turned and raced across the lawn, trampling some of Old Missus's flowers in the darkness, and didn't stop until they were back at the camp breathing heavily. "Didn't I done told you 'bout them books?" Jess said. "Didn't I done told you?" Wes clicked his tongue in affirmation. "What you got to say about all that?" Jess said persistently.

"Amen," Wes said. And the two of them fell on the ground laughing at the joke. "Man, you is a real Christian," Jess said.

"Sure is," Wes said, "just like you. I been baptise."

The theft was carried out four nights later. When the camp was asleep, Wes and Jess arose silently and slipped out of the cabin. They followed the same route as before, approaching the Big House from the far side. It was understood that they would have to accomplish the act swiftly, before the dogs in the kennels became aroused. Without crawling this time, they ran quickly to the study window, which was dark and shuttered. Jess poked a broken file through the slats and unhooked the lock. The window sash opened easily. And while Jess stood guard, Wes went through and felt his way to the shelves which held the books. In a moment he had a book in his hand and climbed out. They closed the window and the shutter, which they could not lock from the outside. The dogs were beginning to bark, and the two of them plunged into the bushes just as Duke, the butler, emerged from a side door with a lantern in his hand. He stood there in his nightclothes, shading his eyes from the lamp glare, trying to see into the darkness.

Jess couldn't restrain his giggle. "Look at that black man in that white nightdress, will you?"

Wes said: "Hush up, let's get out of here."

Back at the camp they slipped silently to their pallets, and Wes slept with the book wrapped in a rag under his head. Early in the morning, with the pretext of going to the latrine, he placed the book, still wrapped in the rag, in the hollow of a tree, stuffing dried leaves and twigs in afterward to camouflage it.

Several days later Jess said: "Where's that book? You done read it yet?"

Wes shook his head. "Ain't had no chance."

But Jess didn't seem as interested in the book as in the exploit of extracting it from Old Master's room. "Can still see old Duke standin' there in his nightclothes," he said. "Like to see him prance around front of the white folks like that!"

It was Sunday before Wes had a chance to retrieve the book from the tree. When he did he was upset because squirrels had taken out all the dry leaves and nibbled the edges of the cover to clear their passage in and out of the hollow. But there was no great damage done, and he carried his prize off to an isolated spot and opened it. The cover was black, with gold letters on it. Inside there was page after page of small print, and he looked in vain for something that would give him a clue to the secret. He stared at the pages as though through force of will he could extract something from them. At last, discouraged, he returned the book to its hiding place.

Later in the day Jess noticed his depression and said: "You done read it yet?"

And Wes said: "I don't know what's in it. I read it and I read it, and it don't mean nothing to me. I got to take it over to Preacher John soon one day and ask him."

Jess said: "You got to stay away from Preacher John. Beside that, he live too far. Take you all day to get there if you could find it."

"I got to do it," Wes said, "less I can find someone else."

Jess thought. "Listen," he said, "you never get to John's place. They think you run away and catch you and put you in the sweat box. I been told they's another man not too far north of here can read and write. Seem to me he's on the Radford place. Maybe you can make it in an hour, maybe two. I don't know his name. You can find out."

And that was the way it was left until, three months later, Samba and Wes were assigned to take a wagonload of corn to a new water mill about a mile from the Radford land. Wes put his book under the wagon seat when Samba wasn't looking. On the way he wheedled Samba to take a detour that brought them along the edge of the Radford plantation. And when they saw a work gang near the road, Wes begged Samba to stop the mules so he could have a word with the men. He hopped down, clutching his bundle, and approached one of the workers.

" 'Scuse me, Uncle, I'm Wes Hunu from over at the Blair place. We on the way to the mill. I been told they's a man over here can . . ." He looked around, lowered his voice. ". . . been told they's a man here can do some readin'."

The slave looked blandly at Wes. "Yes, they is, they certainly is. We got a man here can surely read, he surely can."

"Where he at?" Wes said eagerly.

"Well," the slave said, taking off his straw hat to scratch his head, "keep right on this road, and turn off when you get to the main buildin'."

"What's his name?" Wes asked eagerly.

"Why, name of this man is Mister Radford, he's Master here."

Wes's disappointment showed in his face. "He's not the one I lookin' for, Uncle."

The man examined Wes sharply. "Who the one you lookin' for, then?"

"I done hear," Wes said, faltering a little, "done hear it say they's a man, a black man like us, over this way who got the knowledge. I ain't spoke to no one on it. I must talk with this man. Just a few words."

"How come you need a readin' man? You done some writin'?"

"I got a . . . a book," Wes said. "I must ask him 'bout it."

"Where you say you from?" the man asked.

"From the Blair place," Wes said.

"Hmmm. I knowed a man over there. Ain't there no more. Name of Big Jim."

"Big Jim," Wes said, "he was my friend, but he's gone."

"Hear tell they shot him out of a tree," the man said.

"It's so," Wes said, "they kill him after he whup Mr. Rousseau and the driver."

The man leaned on his hoe. "Tell you what," he said, "you keep right on the road to the fork. Go leftwise on that fork. You find him in the field, name of York. Only thing is, keep your mouth tight."

"Thank you, Uncle," Wes said, "I keep my mouth tight to death."

Wes found York there in the field by the left fork. He was a small man, gray and bearded. His eyes were filmed a little. When he looked up at Wes's approach Wes noted that York couldn't straighten up all the way.

"Uncle York, 'scuse me," Wes said. "I must say a word with you."

"Well, say it then, son," the man said, "words is free."

"Uncle, I come a far way, from the Blair plantation. My friend told me you was here. Folks say as you can read. Tell me what this book got in it."

York looked all around to be sure they were alone. Wes unwrapped the book and placed it in his hands. York brought the volume close to his eyes and squinted at the gold lettering. "Where you get this book?" he demanded.

"I get it," Wes said, "I just get it. I got to know what knowledge it got in it."

York opened it and looked inside. He flipped a few pages and handed it back.

"Uncle," Wes said, "what that book have to say?"

"Don't know, son," York said.

"But my friend tell me . . . ," Wes began.

"Son, they is 'bout a million tongues in this world. They is English and French and Italian and lots more. Only tongue I knows is English, that's what folks talk here in Georgia. All I can tell you is I don't know what tongue that writin' is supposed to be. On the cover, now, it look like English. It say . . ." and he took the book from Wes and looked again. "It say H-O-M-E-R. The characters, now, they is English. I understand them. But what it spell, I don't know. And on the inside it's different kind of characters which I never see before or since. You bring me a Good Book and I can spell it out some. I even read the Missus' book 'bout honey bees. But what you bring me, I can't make it out. It ain't Georgia talk at all, that much I knows."

Wes stood looking at Mister Blair's book. York said: "What for you bring it to me?"

"Don't know," Wes said, "Lookin' for knowledge. I can't read, so I find you."

"What your name, boy?"

"Wes Hunu. My real name is Hwesuhunu. They calls me Wes."

"Well, listen here, Wes, what I got to tell you is what you got in mind ain't no way to go about it. First and all you got to study on the *characters*. You got to know 'em each and every one, then you got to study on how they goes together. That makes *words*. Ain't no use cartin' a book around, even in the right tongue, 'less you knows the *characters* and the *words*. You start with that, like I say, and maybe you can read. Then, 'course, maybe you can't. Ain't every man got the knack of it. That's the start and end of the matter."

Wes wrapped the book in the shirt. "Mighty glad you tell me 'bout it, Uncle. Only thing is, who goin' to give me the characters?"

York shook his head. "Can't tell you that, boy. If you was livin' roundabout this place I could give you a little hand in it. The way it is, you got to pick your own cotton. Mighty sorry 'bout that."

Wes said:" Thank you kindly, Uncle." He went back and climbed onto the wagon seat with Samba. In the evening when they were home, he replaced the book once more in the hollow tree, and there it remained a long time, until at last he managed to get it back into Old Master's house.

Wes had almost despaired of finding a way. The fact that he must find a way, and that time was slipping past him, was a relentless, nagging torture. And then one day when men of the north camp and the south camp were working together in the same field, Amos the boatbuilder said to him: "I hear tell you is lookin' for somethin'."

Wes didn't grasp what Amos was saying. "No, sir, Uncle, I ain't lookin'."

"Well it come to me from a friend of mine," Amos said, "that you gone a long way to see what you can find." Wes still didn't understand his meaning. "This friend of mine, we was raise together. Right now he workin' on the Radford place."

At last Wes understood. He said: "Yes, Uncle, it's so. Only just now I don't know which way to turn."

Amos said: "Surprised you never hear it say that before you goes huntin' wild pig, look first in your own 'tato patch."

"What I goin' to do, Uncle?" Wes asked.

"I tell you," Amos said, "but first I got to tell you, this thing got lots of briars in it. You don't watch out and you get plenty scratched."

"I knows it, Uncle, I surely knows it," Wes said, "but I got to have it just the same."

Amos lighted his pipe. "The way it is, I got more boat-buildin' on my hands than I can do. I needs a helper. Reckon you can learn 'bout this boatbuildin' thing and give me aid on it?"

"Yes, Uncle, I surely can do it."

"All right then," Amos said, "I fix it with the Captain. You got to give me all day Sunday to aid me. Every Sunday. Then about four in the evenin' I give you the characters. You study hard on them characters. And when you got 'em all solid, I give you the words, startin' with your name. How you see that proposition?"

"I likes it fine, Uncle, and I surely thanks you for it. I be a good boatbuilder for you, Uncle, I see to that."

"That's fine," Amos said, "but we got to have it clear. You don't get no cash money. You don't get nothin' but the characters and the words."

"That's all I ever want, Uncle Amos," Wes said. "That's

all I truly want, and I proud you goin' to give it to me."

"They's one thing more," Amos said. "You got to keep mighty shut-mouth on this thing. Old Master don't like it at all."

"I'll do it," Wes said, "just like you say do."

"Well, that's all they is to talk on," Amos said. "You be on my place soon in the mornin' next Sunday."

On the next sabbath Wes began the study of letters. He worked with a small hatchet all day making pegs to join boat planks, and in the late afternoon Amos printed out characters for him with charcoal on scraps of wood. Until darkness fell Wes copied and recopied the letters. And before Wes left, Amos gathered the woodscraps and burned them in a fire. "What you takes away you got to take in your head," Amos said. "One scrap of this wood, just one scrap, mind you, wreak vengeance on us all if the Captain find it. You study it in your head, that's all."

"I heed you, Uncle," Wes said.

It was December 24. The plantation bell sounded at noon and the workers came in from the woodcutting and the plowing. It was handout day, when the clothing for the year would be given out. About two in the afternoon the bell sounded again, and the slaves streamed from the north and south camps to converge on the store, an unpainted outbuilding back of the plantation house. Rousseau sat at a table by the door with a list of supplies in front of him. The slaves were full of festive good humor as they fell into line. They joked, exchanged repartee, and laughed. As each one moved in turn to the table he identified himself, though there were few whom Rousseau did not know by name.

"Andrew Gola here, Captain, sir," one man said.

"No family," Rousseau said.

"Yes, sir, Captain, that's right, Andrew Gola, no family. You hit it right on the head, Captain."

Rousseau checked the name off the list and called out

to Shad, the storekeeper: "Pants, two shirts, two kerchiefs, four yards of cotton."

Andrew accepted the supplies as they were laid on the table where Rousseau could check them off. But he stood uncertainly. "Captain," he said, "you forget the shoes."

Rousseau said: "Shoes are in short supply this year. Your shoes will hold up a few months. Come back on March the first."

"Yes, sir, Captain, I see what you mean. But these shoes can't be fix no more. The hide is rotten, can't sew 'em."

"Make do," Rousseau said. "Next man."

"This is Thursday Smith here, Captain, got a woman and four chillen down there in north camp."

Rousseau scratched out some figures on his paper. "Thursday," he said, "where you get that name?"

Thursday grinned accommodatingly. "Why, Captain, 'cause I was borned on Thursday, so my mamma call me that."

"No, I mean your last name. Where you ever get the name of Smith?"

"Oh, it just come on me, Mr. Rousseau. So many folk got the same first name, it just seems natural a man got to have two name. And I hear that name Smith down in Savannah, so I choose it. Now if they is ever another boy whose mamma name him Thursday, ain't no one goin' get him mix with Thursday Smith."

"All right," Rousseau said, his interest suddenly gone, "pants for you, two shirts, two kerchiefs, eight yards of cotton."

"My woman tell me ask you for four spools of thread," Thursday said.

"All right, add four spools," Rousseau said.

"And Captain," Thursday said, "my woman say can she get some of that cotton in blue. She needs blue mighty bad."

Rousseau shook his head. "Got no blue," he said. "Next man."

But Thursday wasn't through yet. "Mr. Rousseau," he said, "you know I been down in the swamp cuttin' wood many days these months. The mud down there mighty hard on shoes. This set I got on is finished. Got no bottoms at all."

"Short on shoes this year," Rousseau said. "Get yourself some hide next week and patch them up."

The rationing went on all afternoon. When Wes's turn came he identified himself, took what was handed to him, and asked for nothing. Rousseau said: "Well, ain't you going to ask for extras?"

"No, sir," Wes said.

"That's a new one on me," Rousseau said, "how come?"

"Well, sir," Wes answered, "it 'pears to me as all them folks ask for extra, all they get is turndown. These things do me fine, Captain."

Rousseau scrutinized Wes's face carefully for a sign of sarcasm, but found none.

"You sure grew into a man fast, Wes Hunu," he said. "I remember the day you arrived here, all scrawny and sickly. I reckon the hard work done you good."

"Oh, yes, Captain, I reckon it do."

Rousseau could detect no irony in Wes's voice, but he felt vaguely uncomfortable. The ones who asked, cajoled, flattered, he understood them and could deal with them. The grinning faces and the sullen faces, he could account for them. But Wes's matter-of-factness disturbed him. "You happy here, Wes?" he asked, knowing that he was talking too much.

"Yes, Captain," Wes answered.

"I mean," said Rousseau, "You getting along?"

"Yes, Captain, gettin' along," Wes said.

"Tell you what," Rousseau said, "set your supplies down over there and give Shad a hand with the stores."

Wes did as he was told. At six in the evening the handout was finished. Rousseau sat at his table adding up figures. When he arose it was already becoming dark. He hardly noticed Wes until he heard him speak.

"Can I go back now, Captain?"

Rousseau looked up in surprise. "Oh, yes, go on back now." But something nagged at him. "On second thought, better carry the table to the barn first."

Wes picked up the table and carried it on his head. In the barn Rousseau lighted a lantern and hung it on a peg. "Where'd you get that name Hunu?" he asked suddenly.

"It's part of my old name," Wes said. "When I was born they call me Hwesuhunu. I was call Wes here 'cause Old Ned say I got to have a new name."

Rousseau probed. "Are you getting along all right here or ain't you?"

Wes understood that it was a confrontation, but he couldn't fathom Rousseau's purpose. "I get plenty to eat, Captain, and like you say, the work do me good."

"You been working with Amos on his boat."

It was a flat statement, with no answer required, but Wes said, "Yes, Captain."

"What you getting out of it, a share?"

"No, Captain. He learn me the trick of it. Some day I goin' to make a boat myself."

"Just the same, you been spending a lot of time over there. You must be getting more out of it than you say."

"Like I said, Mr. Rousseau, I learn plenty things."

"You got no notion to try to buy yourself out, have you? First place, you can't do it without Mr. Blair is willing. Second thing, he don't make no arrangement with young niggers at all. You got a lot of work to do before he'll get his money back, and all the clothes, and those things."

"Yes, Captain, I know it."

Rousseau could not come to grips with his reason for talking to Wes. So at last he sent him home.

After dinner that night Wes and Jess sat talking. "I

learn plenty today," Wes said. "I learn one thing special. Old Master think I *owe him money.* Don't it beat you? Most all the people went over there this evenin' thinkin' Old Master owe *them* something 'cause they work for him so hard in the field. And Rousseau figure it on the paper, and say they can't have this and have that 'cause money is scarce. But all the time he don't owe them nothin' at all, *they owe him!*"

"Well," Jess said, "it's so, all right. That's what he thinks, the niggers owe him money. He figure to make just so much on the crops each year. If he make more, well that's 'cause Jesus is good to him. But if he make less, that ain't Jesus, it's the niggers, and they owe him the money. Reckon my share must be more than five thousand dollars. You owes him more than me 'cause I was born here on this plantation. But Old Master done pay out six-seven hundred dollars for you in cash, plus five thousand from fallin' behind, and that is sure a pile of money."

The next day, Christmas morning, the slaves dressed in their new clothes, or their best old ones. The men wore their new shirts and pants. The women hadn't had time yet to make up dresses out of the cotton cloth, so they tied some of it around them to drape and fall like skirts. Men and women alike tied the red kerchiefs on their heads, and some wore straw hats in addition. Little girls had their hair parted into little "gardens" and tied with bits of ribbon or cloth. Some of the boys had their heads shaved except for a small upright tuft in the front. Those who had shoes put them on.

Two flags sacred to Shango, made of white cotton and covered with appliqué designs, were brought out of Samba's shrine. And at noon, with drums beating, thin lines of people proceeded out of the two camps toward the plantation house. They went forward in a perambulating dance. At the entrance to Old Missus's garden they merged into a single line which passed around the house three times. At the end of the third turn the lines dissolved into a shapeless crowd at the front door. The singing became excited and vigorous.

A dance took shape out of the amorphous pushing and shoving. When at last Old Master and Old Missus came out there was loud cheering and shouting. The drums changed their beat, the flags waved, and the crowd sang the Christmas anthem:

Well didn't you hear what happen that day?
Didn't you hear what happen that day?
King of Babylon stand on the mountain
And throw pennies in the valley.

Old Master goin' pay us share!
Old Master goin' pay us share!
Oh, soon one Christmas mornin',
Wasn't you there? Wasn't you there?

Mr. and Mrs. Blair stood smiling and nodding at the happy throng. After a while Amos the boatbuilder held out a beribboned basket attached to the end of a long pole, and Old Master placed a small packet of coins in it. Again the drums changed their beat and the crowd danced, circling around Amos who held the money basket aloft on the pole. When, finally, Amos moved away rhythmically to the sound of the drumming, flanked by the two Shango flags, the others followed. Back of the storehouse Amos opened the money packet, counted the coins, and paid each man, woman and child his share. It amounted to fifteen cents per head. And now, out of the Master's hearing, they sang:

Well, didn't you hear what happen that day?
Didn't you hear what happen that day?
Bowlegged Master stand in the doorway
And squeeze the pennies till they cry.

Old Master goin' to pay us share!
Old Master goin' to pay us share!
Oh, he gonna do that
When us dead and buried somewhere!

The remodeling of the Big House began, and slaves from both camps were assigned to work under the direction of the artisan Mr. Blair had acquired in exchange for Tessie and Mary Lou. He was known as Turnloose, a name given him forty years before by his mother in the hope that he would be liberated out of slavery. He was a large man, very black, and uncommonly strong. Amos was selected, as an experienced carpenter, to work with him, and on Amos's suggestion Rousseau sent for Wes to join the construction gang. Mr. Blair himself had worked out the design for the new wing, and Turnloose pored over it almost a full day, memorizing it in detail.

Rousseau remarked to Mr. Blair within Turnloose's hearing: "What's he spending all that time at? He been looking at that picture for hours."

Turnloose answered for himself: "Captain, I got to study on it. Too late to take caution when the tiger got you in its mouth. I got to study on which is the best way to make the beams go, how much stone we fetch for the foundation, how many pegs we make for the beams, how much board to saw, how tall is the ceiling, and what is the pitch of the roof. Every one of those things got to be clear, then we start." And after another hour or so of study, Turnloose gave the design back to Old Master, saying, "Now we ready." From that moment onward he never again referred to the picture. Every detail was worked out in his mind, down to the hinges, forged iron bannisters, and other hardware.

Wes worked first with the stone-gathering crew; later he was shifted to sawing and planing under Amos's watchful eyes. Mr. Blair hovered around the construction much of the day, and frequently brought neighbors and friends to see what was happening. As Old Master and Mr. Walker sat together on the veranda one afternoon, talking and sipping cool drinks, Wes overheard them discussing the deathless problem.

Mr. Walker was saying, "They seem to cost more and

do less work every year. I got to get me a new driver. By the looks of it I'm just supporting them and they're eating my bacon. I didn't net more than fifteen thousand last year, and if the crop hadn't been exceptional good I'd of lost money. I'd do better to hire my niggers out to roadwork at fifty cents a day. That way I wouldn't have to feed 'em, either."

Old Master said: "There's plenty of work for mine just now. But I wonder sometimes about the rations. They get a peck of meal and a pound of bacon a week per head. Thought maybe I was cutting it too fine, but you know, some of them are selling it off and when they save enough cash they get themselves a bottle of whisky, I don't know where. Like to get my hands on the one who's smuggling it in. Anyway, I figure if they're selling off surplus I must be giving out plenty. I think next spring I'm going to make them raise stuff on a patch of their own. They've got the time, evenings and Sundays. My overseer thinks they'd be better off with something to take up their slack time anyway. They can raise their own hogs and chickens and I'll provide the ground corn."

"Well, that's one way," Mr. Walker said, "but the thing against it is it might give them ideas. I want my niggers to know where the victuals come from. There's one of them islands down in the Indies, first thing the planters did was to cut down all the coconut trees so the niggers got it understood. If they want to eat they got to work. If a nigger's got his own eggs and pork you ain't got the control over him."

"We get along pretty good over here," Mr. Blair said. "Had only five runaways in the last seven-eight years. I keep thinking about giving them some religious instruction, though, and can't make up my mind if it's good or bad. They're picking it up on their own anyway. Maybe they ought to have regular camp meetings under proper supervision."

"Well, now, Tom," Mr. Walker said, "you assume too

much. Fact is, they ain't got the capability to be real Christians. It's just a big carnival to them. It'd only degrade religion to give them instruction. There's a lot of smart niggers would just pick out places in the Bible to show you they wasn't meant to be slaves, but masters. Like the Israelites. We had one over on our place heard that the seventh day was for rest, and he refused to even harness a team on Sunday till we put him on rice and water for a week and gave him a good thrashing."

"What you say stands to reason," Mr. Blair said, "but just the same I've seen some improvement in these people. Of course you can't keep them clean a lot of the time, but they talk better and act better than they used to, and we have some good workers on this place. I like it said I take care of my black people right."

"Far as that's concerned," Mr. Walker said, "I take good care of my hunting dogs, but I don't have to take them to church. If you got a good nigger around, well that's fine, but don't forget he's an African at heart. Now, I'm no nigger-killer, but the niggers on my place got only one purpose—to do their job. Else what are they here for? If a man don't want niggers on his place, I say to him don't buy niggers. But if you've got them, don't try to make something different out of them."

Mr. Blair caught sight of Wes stacking up boards at the corner of the house. "Look there," he said, "that's a likely looking boy. I've seen plenty of improvement in him since I bought him five or six years ago. When I picked him up in Savannah he didn't look like much, all skin and bones and didn't know a word of English. He's a good worker, and haven't had a speck of trouble from him since the first day. You give them good Christian treatment and they respond."

"Just the same," Walker said, "there's a limit. They haven't got the capability to be civilized. They're property, and whoever heard of civilizing property? They say one thing and mean something else. Just call your likely looking nigger over here a minute and I'll show you what I mean."

Mr. Blair called, and Wes came to where they were sitting and removed his hat. "Wes, Mr. Walker wants to have a few words with you. All right?"

"Yes, Mr. Blair, it's all right with me."

Mr. Walker said: "Wes, you a Christian?"

Wes hesitated. "Not exactly, Mr. Walker. Couldn't say I am exactly."

"You know what it is to be a Christian?"

"Think so, Mr. Walker, but don't know for sure."

"What plantation you come from, boy?"

"Didn't come here from no plantation." He hesitated. "I'm an African, Mr. Walker."

Mr. Walker leaned back. "Knew it without asking," he said to Mr. Blair. "That juju on his neck gave it away. And did you notice he didn't say, 'I was an African.' Said he *is* an African." Speaking again to Wes, he asked: "That juju around your neck, what's it protect you from?"

"It's not a juju, Mr. Walker," Wes said. "That thing was made for me by a friend of mine."

"Come on, boy, admit it. It's to make you attractive to the girls, isn't it?"

"No, sir, it's like I told you."

"Maybe to protect you from the evil spirits?"

"There is such things, Mr. Walker, but not this one. This one is special."

"Well," Mr. Walker said, changing his tack, "don't tell me you don't believe in dead spirits?"

"Don't know what you mean, sir."

"I mean, you pray to the dead, don't you?"

"It's true, sometimes we got to remember the dead."

Walker grinned at Blair and went on: "Don't you reckon it's kind of superstitious, boy? Talking to the dead, I mean?"

"No, Mr. Walker, don't reckon so. White folks pray to Jesus, ain't he dead too?"

"Of course not."

"But they tell me he been killed one time. Don't that make him dead?"

"Yes, he was killed, but he was the son of God, and God brought him back to life again, resurrected him."

"Christian folk around here tell me everybody is child of God."

"Only in a particular sense," Walker said.

"This Jesus," Wes asked innocently, "where's he at now?"

"Everywhere."

"Don't see him," Wes said.

"Just the same, even if you can't see him, he's here."

"Same way with our dead folk," Wes said, "that's why we talk to them sometimes."

Mr. Blair, a little anxious at first about the questioning, now relaxed and drew placidly on his cigar. Mr. Walker's tone had a sharper edge than before. He said: "Now, you told me you're not exactly a Christian. That right?"

"That's right, sir, not exactly a Christian."

"Then tell me why all the ones who aren't exactly Christian think they got to pray twice as hard as white folks that *are* Christian?"

"Don't know, Mr. Walker. Maybe it's 'cause they needs it more."

Mr. Blair nodded. "That's all, Wes. You can get on back to your job."

After Wes had left, Walker said: "You can see what I mean. It's all mixed up in their heads. One thing gets tangled with another."

"Maybe it's true, though," Mr. Blair said.

"What's true?"

"Maybe they need it more than we do."

Walker spat out a piece of tobacco leaf in disgust. "Tom,

if you left it to them to decide what they need, they wouldn't be here in the first place. Your kind of thinking is going to bring your new house down around your ears."

The news came by calls from the fields even before Old Master and Rousseau heard it in the Big House. Preacher John Paul Sampson had been surprised by a posse at one of his camp meetings and had run away into the swamps. They were after him, but he had not yet been caught. News and rumors about John Paul Sampson were transmitted almost every day. It was said that he had been seen down on the coast, that he had crossed into South Carolina, that he was over in Mississippi Territory, that a one hundred dollar reward had been posted for him. For weeks there was nothing definite, until one afternoon they heard the field call:

Ay-hooo!
Hear me callin' you!
Caught John in the jungle!
Treed him in a sycamore!
Brung him back,
Don't run no more!
Ay-hooo!

A few days later the details filtered to the camps from the Big House. John Paul Sampson was caught at the state line and his master notified. He was brought back, whipped, and put in chains until he could be sold further west, where he'd cause no more trouble for the people of Georgia.

When the time for rice planting came, Wes was sent back to the fields. And on the afternoon of that first day, Samba collapsed and was carried back to his cabin unconscious. His oldest daughter, Georgia, ran to find Mr. Rousseau, who came with her to Samba's crude corn-husk bed.

"Looks like he's ailing," Rousseau said. "Go get some vinegar from Celina and wash him off with it. I'll give you a little rum for him too. Then we'll see how he is tomorrow."

In the morning Samba was conscious but too ill to get out of bed. Rousseau ordered him carried to the infirmary, a dilapidated outbuilding back of the storehouse.

Georgia said: "Master, I'll stay here and look to him."

But Rousseau said: "No, there's nothing you can do. You go on about your work. I'll have Celina look after him."

So Georgia went out to the fields and Celina brewed some herb tea for Samba out of roots she had dug the summer before and put away to dry. The sick house, as it was called, was a large shedlike structure without beds or furnishings. Its occupants lay on blankets or rags brought from their own cabins. Two other patients shared the sick house with Samba, one an elderly man with an advanced pulmonary disease, the second a girl with malaria.

At first Samba made an effort to talk, but he soon spent most of his time in heavy sleep. When he was aroused he was briefly alert, only to slip off into sleep again even while his friends remained there to cheer him up. In the evenings his friends came and sat next to him on the floor, conversing about the day's small events, making jokes when they could, and trying their utmost to make him feel engaged in what was going on. For two weeks there was no change. Samba drank herb tea, nodded recognition to familiar faces when they appeared, and dozed.

One morning Rousseau came in to see the patients. He said to Samba: "Now, Samba, I've always been straight with you, and I think you've always been straight with me. I want to know right from your own mouth if you're really that sick or just putting it on."

"Sick for true, Captain. Believe I'm goin' to die," Samba said.

Rousseau nodded. "All right, I take your word for it. You're not going to die, though. I'm going to send for the doctor over in Richville soon as I can."

Later that day Mrs. Blair looked in on the sick house.

The sights and smells inside were too much for her, and she scolded Celina sharply. "Land sakes, doesn't anyone ever clean up in here? I've never seen such filth. You get a broom and sweep that floor immediately."

"Yes, Missus, I'll do it for you. Course I got the cookin' to do, but I'll do the sweepin' first like you say. But tell me how I'm goin' to sweep out *under* those poor folk in there? Missus, it ain't right that sick folk should lay on the boards like that. 'Taint right even for a corpse. Can't you get Mr. Rousseau to fix up some beds in there? The wind comes up right through the cracks."

"Well, I'll speak to him," Mrs. Blair said. "In the meantime, open up some shutters to let the sun in."

"Missus," Celina said, adjusting her apron and looking away, "ain't you notice? They ain't no windows in this place."

Mrs. Blair looked somewhat surprised.

"Missus," Celina went on innocently, "does the white folks' sick house got windows?"

Mrs. Blair ignored the question, looked inside once more and hastened away.

The doctor from Richville came the next day and examined all the patients. "The one with the consumption, I can't do nothin' for him," the doctor said. "He's too far gone. The girl will be all right in a week or two. The other one," nodding toward Samba, "he's got the African disease. I'll leave medicine for him, and I'll be back in a week or so to take another look."

Rousseau said: "Mr. Blair can't afford to lose him. He's a good stout worker."

"Well, there isn't much you can do about the African disease," the doctor said. "They get pretty sick and then they usually come out of it."

Several days later, before the Richville doctor returned, Georgia came out to the field to tell Wes her father wanted to see him. She took over his job, and Wes went to the sick house. Samba was wide awake. His voice seemed stronger than it had for a long while, and when Wes lighted the oil lamp he saw that Samba's eyes were unusually bright. Wes squatted beside him.

"Georgia tell me you need me, Uncle."

"What they doin' now out there?" Samba said.

"Plantin' rice, almost done."

"Seem to me like I done plant my last rice," Samba said.

"You're talkin' foolish, Uncle. They's plenty rice waitin' for you yet."

"Never mind all that. I got business with you."

"Yes, Uncle, what you want me for?"

Samba put his thoughts in order. "It's this way," he said. "I'm the only babalao around here, ain't another one for twenty-five miles or more. When the babalao goes, he's got to turn his knowledge over. I got no boy of my own, 'cept one what die 'fore you get here. Who's goin' take over on this thing?"

"Don't know, Uncle," Wes said, "I'd be proud to take it on if I got the knowledge. But my people is Fon, not Nago."

Samba held Wes by the wrist. "Now listen to me, son. Only goin' to tell it once. First thing is, you ain't a boy at all no more. You made me some fine drums like no one else on this place could do. I hear you sing them old songs the other folks done forget a long time ago. You knows the orisha, and you knows the right beat. Any old fool can bang the drum and make confusion, but it's a big difference 'tween a proper sound for the orisha and a plain ruckus. I pick you to follow up for me, and they ain't no way out of it 'cause you are the only one with the knowledge."

"Uncle," Wes said, "I'm proud to hear what you tell me. But Old Ned, he wish for me to be a Christian, and I been baptise already."

"Never mind Old Ned," Samba said impatiently. "This

country is too full of Old Neds. You let this thing down, and who's goin' to serve the orisha?"

"Sometime I believe the orisha and vodoun never get to this country, all stay in Africa," Wes said.

Samba said: "You know better. They are here, all right. The wind you hear in the trees, that's Loko. The sound Muddy River makes, it's Panchagara. When the storm comes, it's Shango. They're all here. When the spirit comes down at the buryin' ground, that one is Oya. When the rice sprouts, it's Oko. Your Fon vodoun, they the same as the orisha, only they got different names. You say you been baptise. All right, Christians say it's spirit of Jesus. Just the same, that water don't belong to no one but Panchagara.

"Christian preachers say all the folks got to cross over Jerdan when they die. Real name of that river ain't Jerdan, it's Azile. Everything is all messed up here with the black people, they forget everything they know. You take my rattle with the corn seed on it. You take the drums. You take the bell. You take the iron pot for Ogoun. I can't take 'em. When I'm gone below the ground, put my things on my grave proper, my gourd dish, my knife, my lookin' glass, see they is put down on the mound. These things I must take. All the rest belongs to the orisha. You take care of them things."

"Papa," Wes said, "I'll take care like you say. But you're not ready to die. You look fine today."

Samba spoke sharply. "Don't say it, son. A man near dead is close to the orisha. Don't lie to the orisha, don't lie to the near dead. It's disrespect. Day I'm buried you take the rattle. I already tell Georgia to give you all these things. But it won't come easy. You got to study on it. You got to be able to shut your eyes and see what the world is really like. You got to hear what the wind say, not just let it go by. You got to sit with a man in the dark and not say a word and know all about this man. When the feel of the ancestors come on you, stop and take it in. All these goin' ons around you, Tom Blair's plantation and the whole land of Georgia, it's nothin' more than a little piece of the world, the part you see with your eye. For the big part you got to close your eye. I'm tired now. Too much to give you all in one spoonful. The rest you must find out. No more talk now, go on back to the plantin'."

For several days Samba seemed no better, no worse. On the day the doctor was to return, Samba died as the eye of day opened. It was Wes who obtained permission from Rousseau for the dance and who officiated at the death rites. He brought to the ceremony everything he remembered about how an important man should be buried. When the body had been washed and dressed, Wes entered the cabin with a bottle into which Samba's orisha was to be transferred. Speaking in Fon, he called on the orisha to depart from the body and enter the bottle. When the transfer had taken place, he corked the bottle and carried it outside. The drums played a salute to Ogoun, and the bottle was broken against a stone to liberate the spirit in it. Wes called on Ogoun to return to Africa, but not to forget his people in Georgia. There was dancing all night, and many times the orisha and the vodoun came and caused people to fall, stagger, faint or have convulsions.

Old Ned stood and watched from afar, deeply distressed. It was partly Samba's death, and partly the sight of Wes, tall and commanding in the center of the rites, holding Samba's rattle in his hand. When the sun rose, Samba's body was placed on a door and carried to the graveyard behind the live oaks. The grave was filled, and Georgia placed Samba's personal things on the top of the mound: his knife, his gourd dish, his razor, his broken mirror, and the little wooden carvings he had made to decorate his cabin. At the head of the grave, upright in the ground, they placed his walking stick carved with alligator figures. And when the festive return to camp was ended, the workers departed to the fields.

That morning Old Ned looked at Wes frequently, unable to speak what was on his mind. At last, forcing himself, he said: "Wes, I took care of you from the day you come.

You slept in my cabin. I treated you the same as my boys. I took you to the camp meetin' to get you baptise. Then last night you run back to the jungle. You lost, boy, 'less you throw that all away and start over from the beginnin'."

Wes answered: "Uncle Ned, I got no father in this land, I got no mother, no brother. You been a father to me, and I'm mighty glad about that. If you wasn't here, times would of been mighty hard for me. That's why I try for you and give you respect. You say the Christian God on high made everything in this old world. Maybe so, but he made me a Fon. All my people is Fon. The inside of me is Fon. I am too much Fon. I think Jesus is a good spirit. I hear about him all the time, but he never come into me. He's not my spirit, not yet anyhow. Some other time, maybe so. I am Hwesuhunu, all Fon, I can't be nothing else, only Hwesuhunu. I know it makes you sad to hear it. But Samba, he's my friend. He need for me to make the service, so I do it. Maybe little by little I'll get to know this Jesus some day, then I'll be Christian. Maybe so."

Wes paused, then went on: "Uncle, when you met me in the first place you know I was African. So do not be angered with me now."

Old Ned scraped at the ground with his feet. He said: "Boy, I don't care what you are. Just get on out of there and chop some kindlin'."

Quiet though it was, Wes's sense of Fa had never departed from him. It was as the Fon proverb said: "A man searches in the bush, as though Fa did not hold his hand." And because his sense of fate was so immediate, he often saw things around him as external to himself. The conflict between what Samba had regarded as the orderly processes of life and what Old Ned felt to be the only safe course toward human salvation sometimes took on the character of the wrestling spectacles he had witnessed as a child. To the sound of drums and bells a wrestler from the north would come trotting into the village with his musicians. His men would sing out challenges in the marketplace, and if there was anyone in the countryside who chose to compete with him there would be a match. Each of the wrestlers would be supported by a chorus of singers who recited his praises to the accompaniment of excited drums. And the champions would meet and stir up the dust, and one would conquer, and after that each would go his own way and the village would again subside into pastoral quietness, having seen a spectacle that was no part of its inner life.

Thus it was with the conflict between Samba's sense of worldly order and Old Ned's vision of salvation. Wes did not see it as a real conflict at all, but only a struggle over outward forms, for the one was only an extension of the other. If the Fon people had their vodouns to placate, and the Nago their orishas, the Christians had their saints. Were they not the same? Was not the Fon spirit of the crossroads and the gateway, Legba, known to the Nago as Etcho? And did not the Christians call the same gatekeeper by the name of Peter? Indeed, one of the slaves from Louisiana had a Christian name for each of the vodouns, and though he served them as a Christian he endowed them with their Dahomean realities. As for God himself, was he not the same as the ancient Nananbouloucou? If, as Old Ned said, God had three forms, the Father, the Son, and the Holy Ghost, did not each of the vodouns also have many forms? The Christians sometimes called him Yahweh, and as every Dahomean would know, *yehweh* was merely another name for the vodouns.

It was an unreal struggle, because the inner meanings were not in contest. But this thing that had captured Old Ned nevertheless was growing like a jungle vine, moving across the ground into every crack and corner, offering connections and communication between the thousands of captives scattered throughout the country, a network of invisible ties that bound them together. And wasn't this the very thing that troubled Old Master and Mr. Walker and the other planters so deeply? Whereas in another time it was the word Dahomey, with all that it signified, that raised men's spirits and gave them an awareness of common enterprise and achievement, now it was a new word, Jesus. And out of this word there could well come with the passage of time a silent explosion that would change the face of the land. It was a white gunpowder, and it gave special meaning to the proverb: "They who make the powder win the battles."

Old Master and Missus were holding their first gathering in the house since the completion of the new wing with its large ballroom, floored with hardwood that not long before had been standing trees in the nearby woods. Pitch pine torches lighted the drive to the front entrance flanked by large white columns. Carriage after carriage rolled up to discharge its cargo of guests, some coming from as far away as fifteen miles. A hum of conversation, laughter and music enveloped the mansion. The house slaves were supplemented by additional help recruited from among the field hands. Six livery boys took charge of the horses, leading them off to a selected place near the barn. The festive air extended to the slave quarters, where a holiday had been decreed.

Mrs. Blair had passed out lengths of red and blue ribbons to the female slaves to adorn themselves for the festivities. The north camp had its own musicians—drummers, jug blowers and a fiddler. By special permission a banjo player came from the Walker plantation to the south camp, his services for the evening to be paid for by the field hands at a cost of twenty-five cents. The banjo player was a Wolof named Mamadu, after the prophet, but Mr. Walker preferred to call him Marmaduke, and this his friends had shortened to Duke. The dancing in the camps this night had a special character, for the slaves were emulating the reels and mazurkas of the Big House, spicing their interpretations with pantomime, exaggeration, and mincing ridicule. When the sound of their high spirits reached the Big House, it was observed with good-humored patience that the niggers were "carrying on."

It was while the festivities were at their height that a small boy came excitedly to tug at Old Ned's shirt and whisper in his ear. Old Ned followed him to the outskirts of the camp. Wes and Jess sensed the imminence of an event and abandoned the dance to come along. The boy took Old Ned to the edge of a small poplar grove, and there, standing tall in the moonlight, was John Paul Sampson. "I'm on the run," John said simply. "I'm hungry and I'm tired. 'Less I get some food and sleep, I'm goin' to be sick as well. I got to save my strength." Old Ned sent Wes to clear everyone out of the cabin. Then he led John Paul Sampson through the dark shadows and brought him inside. He sent Eula for food, while John sat on the edge of Ned's bed.

"What you doin' out here?" Old Ned said. "We hear tell you was taken and sold."

"They catch me, that's the truth," John said. "I been lashed, and they sweated me in the box also. But the Master believe I'm worth a lot of money to him, and he figure to sell me as soon as he can make the arrangements. Sent a message to a planter over in Mississippi Territory, name of Parson. That planter want me bad when he was in Georgia last year, say he willing to pay one thousand dollars, 'count of I'm a stout man. Master say does he want to pay two thousand dollars he can have me. They dispute the matter. Master send the message now that Parson can have me for one thousand if he like. I choose against it. Not goin' to work for Master no more, Mr. Parson neither. I'm gone this time. Goin' to find that white reverend that came through here two years ago, the one they whup and send north. Live out in Ohio somewhere. Goin' to find that man."

"Brother," Old Ned said, "then why you come this way? They's plenty nigger-killers round here, plenty bounty chasers too. They happy to chase a nigger a hundred miles for fifty dollars. How come you don't go straight north?"

"Goin' north is just what they believe I'm doin'," John said. "They lookin' for me now over toward Carolina."

Eula brought a gourd of rice and pork fat. John gulped it down hungrily. "Ain't had nothin' since yesterday mornin' 'cept some roots and leaves. Saw three-four rabbits and one coon, but couldn't catch 'em." Turning toward Wes and Jess, he said: "Ain't these two young men 'mongst them as was baptise?"

Old Ned nodded his head. "Indeed they was," he said, "but I don't believe it took on either one of them boys."

John smiled. "It don't always take easy," he said. "You got to work at it. If it has to be done, I'll be glad to immerse 'em again. Won't be the first time I had to do it more than once. There's one man I had to baptise four times already, and last time I hear him ask where we keep the soap at."

"I don't know," Old Ned said, " 'pears to me my boys is about lost."

"Depends mightily on the hand," John said.

"What hand?" Old Ned asked.

"Oh, it's a old story they tell 'bout the baptisin'," John said. "They was havin' a big meetin' down by the riverside, but they was two friends sat in the shadders playin' cards, name of Jojo and Billy. Well, then, Billy's daddy came lookin' for him and said, 'You come on! Didn't I bring you here for the immersion?' Billy say, 'Yes, Daddy, it's so.' And he took the cards he was playin' with and put 'em in his shirt. The preacher haul him out in the water, shove him under in the name of Father. One of them cards, ace of hearts, float out. Preacher put him down second time in name of the Son, and another card float out, ace of diamonds. Immerse him the third time in name of the Holy Ghost, and two more cards float out, ace of spades and ace of clubs. When Billy's mamma see that, she say, 'Oh, Lordy, my boy is lost!' Jojo standin' there too, and he say, 'Now how in the world can he be lost with a hand like that?' "

After a while they left John Paul Sampson sleeping on

Old Ned's bed. An hour before sunrise they awakened him and took him to a wooded spot near Eel Lake. They built a lean-to for him, and gave him a blanket and a supply of rice. "We'll come back every so often to see what you need," Old Ned said. "You just hole out here and don't come down to the cabins. If you make a fire, don't let it smoke."

The next night Wes insisted on bringing John's food. While John ate, Wes sat on the ground and waited. Afterward he said: "Uncle John, what you goin' to do now?"

"Been studyin' on it," John said, "waitin' for the good Lord to give me the answer. He won't let me down, 'cause he's got work for me to do."

Wes said: "Down below, 'bout a mile or more, the water from the marsh runs into a little river. It keeps on agoin' till it comes to the Big Branch, and the Big Branch goes on down to the ocean."

"Well, it's good news," John said, "but I ain't no fish."

Wes sat poking at the ground with a stick. Finally he stood up, saying, "Come on. I show you somethin'."

John wiped the remains of the food from his hands with some grass. "Show me, then."

He followed Wes through the heavy undergrowth. A mile or so farther on, Wes led the way into a heavy stand of reeds at the edge of the water. He removed some broken branches that looked as though they had been washed there by the sluggish river. Lying across two rocks was a dugout canoe.

"Look at that," John said, "now ain't that a lifesavin' boat?"

"I made it," Wes said.

John looked it over. "It's a right good old-time boat," John said. "How come you make it?"

"I done a lot of work for a boatbuilder," Wes said, "and it come to me I ought to have a boat of my own. This is the way my people use to do it. I find a good tree, cut it down and holler it out."

"What kind of intentions you got for this thing?" John asked.

"Don't know exactly. Seem to me that some time it might come in handy."

"Indeed it might," John said.

"Uncle," Wes said, "this here boat can carry two men. I can go with you."

John shook his head. "I'm mighty obliged, but two men can't go together."

"Why can't they? Two men is twice as good as one."

"I'll tell you, son, I'll tell you why. 'Cause two men is twice as easy to catch as one. If one get caught the other get caught too. Only way it can be done is by yourself, and they's nothin' certain even about that. They's one more thing. It ain't time for you to go."

"I been ready since the first day I got here," Wes said.

"Maybe you been *mindful,* but that ain't the same thing as *ready*. A man is ready when he get the knowledge that what he's got to do is right now, this minute. That's what ready means. Like when the Lord come to me and say, 'John, you goin' out there to preach for me?' And I say, 'Yes, Lord, tonight.' A man who ain't ready don't have the conviction."

"Uncle, you tellin' me that a man don't move till he just can't stand the pain of it no more? They is plenty folk around here won't never do a thing, 'cause they got the notion it ain't so bad as it might be. 'Pears to me that a man who runs away just 'cause he can't take no more, his head too fuddled to know what he's goin' to do next."

John said: "Taint so. They ain't hardly a man, woman or child 'mongst the black folk ain't considered the matter many a time. A man is ready when he got the knowledge that he goin' to take all the chances and maybe die before he ever turn back. Maybe next month, next year you have that knowledge."

"I got knowledge," Wes said, "I can write characters and I can read most anything now."

"It ain't the knowledge I'm speakin' 'bout," John said.

They made their way back to the lean-to. There Wes said: "You take the boat, I got time to make another one. It ain't got no oars, so you got to pole it."

John said: "I'm proud you give it to me, son. If I don't get to freedom it won't be no fault on your side. And you tell your Uncle Ned for me he been wrong on one thing. If that baptisin' I give you in the river didn't take, you been baptise just the same by *grace*."

Wes thought about it. He said: "It seem to me as grace is given by one man to another, and he got to pass it on."

"Don't catch it, son. Who the one give you grace?"

"Many men give it," Wes said. "I think now on a man name of Jean Labarbe who once give me powder and musket balls. That was grace he give me, and I pass it on the best I can."

John nodded his head. "I'm new in the service of God," he said. "You done learn me something tonight, and I won't forget it."

Four nights later John Paul Sampson was gone.

News of another abortive uprising, this one in Virginia, infiltrated the Georgia slave compounds. A Negro freedman, passing through with a wagonload of pots and pans, brought first word of the story, but there was an absence of factual detail until, one day, a Richmond newspaper, having been carried across the Carolinas, arrived as contraband in the Walker plantation slave quarters, from there it was sent to Mr. Blair's north camp. There its contents were examined and revealed by Amos the boatbuilder, who then passed it on to Wes Hunu. Late that night, all those who could force their way into Old Ned's cabin heard Wes spell out the tale in the flickering fireplace light. Those who couldn't find standing room inside clustered around the door.

The conspiracy, said the paper, had been hatched on a plantation near Richmond, but eight or nine hundred slaves scattered over an area of forty miles had become involved. They had armed themselves with muskets, cutlasses made of scythe blades, pitchforks, and crude pikes. Their plan had been first to destroy the buildings on their own plantations and in the immediate countryside, then to join forces at a prearranged place, from where they were to assault nearby towns and acquire more muskets. Three plantations had, in fact, been burned down, house, barn and crops, and fifteen whites had been killed. But sudden heavy rains had swollen the rivers and prevented the slaves from joining forces at the assigned place, so that the final massive stage of the rebellion never came.

In addition, a house slave, for reasons of loyalty, the paper said, had only a few hours before the outbreak informed his Master of the conspiracy, with the result that planters and townspeople hastily mustered armed forces in time to suppress the separate bands of marauders, some of whom took to the woods while others hastily returned to their plantation quarters to feign innocence. Twenty-four participants had been executed, and twelve whose part in the conspiracy was suspected but not known for sure were locked up in the state armory until they could be deported to Mississippi Territory. The leader of the rebellious enterprise, Gabriel Hornblower, escaped immediate capture and headed toward the sea, but before he reached Norfolk he was caught in a swamp and beaten to death by a party composed of constabulary and planters.

Wes was called on to read the news several times. When every detail was at last clearly understood, there began a discussion of the tactics that had proved wrong, of what should have been done, and of the fate that should properly come to the house slave who had informed. Failure though it was, the insurrection had immediate meaning to everyone. Each person reflected on how this outbreak might have affected his life had it been able to break through its limitations and spread over the countryside. Had sufficient momentum been gathered, Old Master's house and ballroom would exist now only in the form of smoldering charcoal and ashes.

The planters, too, had such thoughts. They watched their slaves with suspicion and anxiety, knowing that the madness that had struck elsewhere could strike in Georgia also. There were meetings in town, where proposals were made for securing the common safety, and it was agreed upon that potential troublemakers should be deported from the state as rapidly as possible. As a matter of good policy it was decided that there should be no imports of West Indian workers, who might be fired with revolutionary spirit as a result of the successful uprising in St. Domingue, where the slaves had made themselves masters.

Because there was deep suspicion that freedmen, few though they were in number, were a bad example to slaves, it was undertaken among the planters that any freedmen who could not prove by the firsthand verbal testimony of their former masters that they had in truth been freed would be seized and put to work in the fields. As for those whose freedom could be established beyond question, they would be compelled by warnings, harrassment and force to leave the state entirely.

Plans were made for a system of couriers who would spread word of conspiracies and outbreaks while there was still time for action to counter them. And there was debate, without resolution, as to the wisdom of prohibiting religious gatherings of the slaves. Some contended that permitting them to gather at all, even for the purpose of worship, was an invitation to disaster. It was asserted that itinerant white preachers were undermining the authority of the plantations, that they were stimulating notions that there existed an authority above not only the plantation but above the state itself. One planter put forward the idea that a careful selection of the Scriptures, censoring all references to violent or heroic actions and all intimations of an authority superior to that of the state, could prove beneficial to the state of mind of slaves. He proposed that a volume to be entitled *Selected Scriptures for the Bondsman* be provided to stress humility and the duties of servants, and that religious services confined to its contents be permitted. But the issue of religious teachings was left unresolved.

Thus there was malaise on both sides, with the slaves disturbed by thoughts of liberation through self-help and the planters anxious lest disturbances elsewhere infect the fieldworkers on their own lands. Mr. Walker was prompt to act. He selected fourteen males from among his slaves and shipped them west, and he hounded Mr. Blair to take similar steps. Mr. Blair came out from time to time to watch the slaves in the fields, trying to single out this one or that one who should be sent away in the interest of security and common sense. But he could not decide. On regarding a particular man whose countenance he did not especially like, he would think: "In case of emergency, would he murder me and my family? Or would he, on the contrary, consider that I have done justice to him and perhaps be the man who would come to tell me that violence was being planned?"

In the end, Mr. Blair left it to Rousseau to decide who and how many were to be weeded out. Rousseau carried out the responsibility with the same distance and noninvolvement that characterized all his routine duties. When he presented the list he had prepared, Mr. Blair again underwent tortures of indecision, in which there was mixed a vague and indefinable element of guilt. But rumors of other small insurrections, one of them in Georgia, moved him to acquiescence. Four men from the north camp and two from the south were called in from the fields one morning and shipped out immediately under the supervision of an armed slave broker, who had guaranteed that they would be sold outside the state.

The act heightened rather than lessened the tensions among the Blair slaves. Several of them remonstrated with Rousseau, pleading that the matter be reconsidered, pointing out that one of the men being sent away had four children, another a sick wife. Rousseau was neither angered nor affected by the pleas. He said merely: "It can't be helped."

Mr. Blair now made preparations for a trip to St. Helena Island off the South Carolina coast to acquire replacements. Old Ned and Wes Hunu, selected to make the trip with him, were to follow Mr. Blair's carriage in the wagon. The evening before the departure, Old Ned checked the mules and went over the wagon carefully to see that it would be fit for the three-day journey. He had a front wheel changed and a new tongue attached, and then instructed Celina to prepare provisions.

Old Ned and Wes were ready at daybreak, waiting for Mr. Blair to finish his breakfast and say goodbye to Old Missus. As the carriage, with the wagon following behind, moved along the curving drive to the road, some of the houseworkers stood by and waved their hands as though Old Master were leaving them forever, but Old Ned and Wes understood the kind of jokes that were being made in the wake of the departure. "There goes Old Master," someone was surely saying, "doin' his lick of work."

They forded the Ogeechee River the first day and spent the night at a farmhouse west of Savannah. It was a small farm compared to the Blair estate, with only ten field hands on the place, and Wes was intrigued by the different atmosphere that surrounded the slave quarters. The people were better clothed and appeared better fed. All of them wore shoes. Their cabins had glass windows, like the main house, and the yards were tidy and stocked with firewood.

"You got an ambitious overseer on this place," Wes said to one of the men. "Ain't everyone goin' to put out ninety cents a pair for shoes for every hand."

"They's no overseer in this place," the man said, "just Master and us. And this Master we got is a workin' Master, a German from up north. Ain't a thing to do here that he don't get in on hisself. No," he said with obvious pride, "this ain't like where you folks come from."

It was a revelation to Wes that a white man would work like that, and be spoken about like that by his slaves. And when they were preparing to leave in the morning, any doubts that lingered in Wes's mind were washed away by the sight of the farmer harnessing up Mr. Blair's horses himself. Mr. Blair kept saying, "I'm deeply obliged, but my niggers will do it," and the farmer kept saying, "No, it's for me, you are my guest. And besides, for a long trip, it must be done right."

Mr. Blair seemed disturbed by it all and said once: "Is it good letting them stand and watch you heist harness like that?"

The farmer laughed. "Ach, these boys, they have fun watching me do things right. But do not worry. Work, they have plenty. You should see these lummoxes when I crack the whip. They jump, they holler. And soon it is done. Is it not so, boys?"

They laughed in good humor at his talk, as did Mr. Blair himself. But when Mr. Blair drove away, his heavy eyebrows were creased and he seemed deep in troubled thought.

They crossed the Savannah River the second day on a log raft poled by two Negroes, who collected a fee of twenty-five cents. In the few minutes it took to get the carriage and the wagon across, Wes learned that these men had constructed the raft themselves and had been given leave by their master to ply their ferry service whenever fieldwork was slack. Early on the third day they reached Beaufort and the tide-water that separated it from St. Helena. The carriage and wagon were left behind, and they crossed in a boat manned by two oarsmen and a tillerman. On the island shore, which resembled marsh rather than sea coast, another carriage and wagon were waiting, and they rode through lush vegetation and swarms of mosquitoes to the main road on higher ground, and thence on to the plantation of Colonel Thomas Hilton, their destination.

It wasn't Colonel Hilton who greeted Mr. Blair, but Rudy Vespey, the plantation overseer. The colonel himself divided his time between Barbados, where he had another plantation holding, and London, coming to St. Helena only for a few weeks' stay each year. The St. Helena estate was twelve hundred acres of fields, marsh, and woodland, with a normal complement of ninety slaves, and Vespey handled both land and slaves as though he were the proprietor.

Colonel Hilton had a fair idea of what his St. Helena establishment should produce, and he left management, accounts, and the handling of money to his overseer. He sometimes had suggestions to make, but as long as the plantation netted a decent return each year, he had no particular interest in where the pennies and dollars came from. It was Vespey who put his stamp on the plantation. In welcoming Mr. Blair, he did not really represent Colonel Hilton so much as himself. His normally ruddy complexion glowed an even warmer color as he shook Mr. Blair's hand at the entrance of the plantation house.

"Grateful for your visit. Hope my niggers didn't splash you with tidewater coming across." He led Mr. Blair up to the veranda, while a house servant showed Wes where to carry the luggage.

That night Wes and Old Ned slept in an empty grain bin in the barn with Julian, the groom. In the morning Wes and Julian rowed back to the mainland to see to the horses and mules, where they had been stabled, and when that was done they took the boat to a small cove and fished. After a while they just lay in the boat and talked.

"I once made me a boat and hid it in the swamp," Wes said. "Figured to take it and get away some day, but I never did. Now I don't have it no more."

"Takes more than a boat to get away from here," Julian said. "The main question ain't gettin' off the island, it's what to do after that. They been pickin' up stray niggers all over the place, even free ones, and puttin' 'em to work. One old man named Silas, he been peddlin' dishes and pots for many a year over there on the other side of Beaufort. 'Bout seventy years old, that old man, and he bought his freedom twenty years ago. Well, now, they caught him and put him back as a field hand. Tell him his freedom paper wasn't no good. I knowed four or five men and one woman that run away from the islands. The woman, well, her husband been sold by Vespey, and she set off to follow him. They caught her forty miles away and brought her back. Vespey have her whupped till she's almost dead. After that she lost her mind, couldn't do no fieldwork no more, and Vespey sell her to some poor white woman for fifty dollars. Then they was two men over on St. Simons Island run off last year, both of 'em Africans. One they catch the first day out, his name was Sayboy. . . ."

"Not Sayboy," Wes said, suddenly alert. "It's Sebo. That man was a Fon."

"Anyway, they caught him," Julian went on. "The Master had that poor boy beat till the skin was gone from his back, and then they put him in the sweat box for a week, and when he come out he didn't know if he was dead or alive, and didn't care neither. Other man, his name was Kana. . . ."

Wes sat up. "Kana? That man's Fon too! He was my friend. We come over here together. You sure about his name?"

"Sure thing, that's his name, Kana. The Master hated that man. Kana gave him great trouble. He told the Master one time, 'You don't own me. You say so, but it can't be true, 'cause I'm a man like you. You hold me, but can't no one own me.' Master don't like that at all. He give Kana the worst he got to give. When he pass out the tasks he take two tasks and put them into one, that's Kana's share for the day.

"They's four tasks to the acre, so sometimes Kana got more than half an acre to do. Them other hands come in at three or four in the evenin', but Kana don't hardly ever get in till dark. After three-four weeks of that, the Master tell this boy: 'What you got to say now? Do I own you or don't I?' Kana say, 'No, sir, you can force me but you don't own me.' The Master try everything on him—sweat him, whupped him, starved him half to death, fettered him in the field with the cows, even put him in Beaufort prison, but he never broke him.

"One night Kana and Sayboy set fire to the barn and the field, then they lit out together. They caught Sayboy 'cause he hurt his foot and couldn't run no more. But Kana kept agoin' for seven weeks. Some hunter over there in South Carolina caught him in the woods, but Kana broke that man's arm and took his gun. After that they put the dogs on him, and when they come up on him in the swamp he killed two dogs. The men went all around him in a circle and he couldn't get out, and he shot hisself dead 'fore they could get they hands on him."

Lying silently in the boat, Wes relived a part of his life that had seemed distant, but which was suddenly alive again. After a while he said: "That man Kana, he was a Fon. He was my friend. It's a sorry thing you tell me."

Julian said: "Vespey, he's a devil like that Master on St. Simons, one part *meat* and nine parts *mean*. He's got the women doin' heavy work like the men. Some women lost they young 'uns 'fore they was born 'cause of heavy work. Even the other Masters 'round here calls Vespey a nigger-killer. He works the niggers off, gets the most he can from them in seven or ten years, and after that he don't care if they's blind, crippled, or crazy.

"When the crops ain't comin' in right, or the rice don't get thrashed fast enough, he cuts back the grits and bacon, and they ain't enough of it at the start. Everyone has to set out rabbit traps and things like that to make it up. Four-five women went to Vespey last year just before Colonel Hilton come and say to him can they get a little more meat and grits 'cause they too weak for fieldwork. You know what Vespey do? Send them women into the woods to cut trees. Made 'em live right there 'mongst the rattlesnakes and moccasins and chop wood three weeks, till the colonel come and gone. After that he tell them do they have any more complaints, and they say, 'Oh, no, God bless you, Captain, just get us out of here, we got no complaints.' Vespey say ain't that nice, it's good for him and the niggers to understand each other.

"He's always tellin' the other white folks 'bout how him and his niggers gets along fine 'cause they understand each other. If them dirty northern rascal preachers would stay away from the niggers, he says, they wouldn't never be no trouble at all, and this would be a mighty fine world, that's what he say."

Wes said: "Our Old Master, he's got one thing with your Master. He don't see a thing. Lives right there, but don't see a thing. If a boy goin' to be whupped, Old Master shakes his head like it was somethin' the Lord put on him, and if Rousseau wants to give fifty lashes, Old Master says, "Oh, no, fifty hurt too much, make it forty-six, then he walks off and lets Rousseau do what he thinks fit. And if he tells Rousseau to give out so much yard cloth on Christmas, Rousseau says, 'No, that's too reckless, better make it less, and never mind the shoes this year, wait till next Christmas for that.' Old Master says, 'Oh, yes, ain't it so,' 'cause he always wants to give too much and better do like Rousseau say do."

"One thing," Julian said, "is that Vespey is always goin' after the women and the girls, any girl as catch his eye. They's one man here now, name of Shad. When Missus Vespey was gone to see her sister in Charleston one time, Vespey tell Shad to send his wife up to the house for the night. Shad say, 'Captain, that woman is my wife,' and Vespey tell him, 'Shad, I make you sorry you was born if you don't do what I say.' Shad say, 'Captain, I got to do anything you tell me, but I can't do that thing.' Well, Vespey beat that man for sassin' him and took the woman too. Seven or eight babies around this place, Vespey's they father."

It was Saturday night, and Vespey had a social gathering in honor of Mr. Blair, so there was a shindig in the slave quarters as well. The slaves danced in a large circle to the music of drums, rattles and a wooden trumpet. They stamped, turned, pirouetted, sang and shouted, while little naked children on the outer edges moved their feet and clapped their hands. Bearded men and old women sometimes joined in for a while, then retired to sit down and watch.

Up at the Big House, Vespey was telling a group of planters over their drinks what they had heard from him a thousand times before, his philosophy of managing a plantation. "It's nothing but bookkeeping," he was saying. "You have to balance the production against the costs. I figure it this way: Out of ninety workers, thirty are young stock that can't earn their keep in the fields. Four or five are in the sick house all the time. Women delivered of babies are away from the fields for three weeks. . . ." ("Longer than that on my place," someone said as though in agreement, but there was a suggestion of criticism in it.) "So you can see," Vespey went on, "that only half of them are working, but you have to feed them all. So you got to get all your work out of 'em in ten to fifteen years, after that you're feedin' 'em for nothing."

In the morning after harnessing the horses and polishing the carriage for Mr. and Mrs. Vespey and Mr. Blair to go to church, Julian said to Wes: "Want to go over and see the white folks' praise meetin'?"

"Like it fine," Wes said. "We allowed to do it?"

"Come on," Julian said, "we'll go the back way."

When the carriage was gone, Julian bridled two mules, and they rode bareback across the fields and through a patch of woods. They tied the mules at the edge of the church graveyard and approached the building from its blind side. Standing outside the partially closed shutters they could see and hear everything. Other slaves in Sunday dress who had driven their Masters to church were also at the windows.

The minister was delivering his sermon. He finished with a prayer, there was a hymn, and then the minister said: "Before we all go home, I want you to hear a few words from a visitor, the Reverend George McAuliff of Philadelphia. We have debated back and forth about what we might do about religious teaching for our bondsmen. There are some, and I belong to their number, who think we ought to have a church for the bondsmen to attend on Sundays. And I am telling you nothing that you don't already know when I say there are some families on the island that are against it, even against religious meetings on the plantation grounds. Reverend McAuliff has given a good deal of thought to this question. Let us give his words reflection."

When Mr. McAuliff stood up there was a rustling of starched dresses as the women shifted expectantly on the benches. "Friends," he began, "Christ has put in my heart, as in yours, the greatest concern for the welfare of these islands and all their people. Although you are separated by water from the mainland, we are all joined in a common purpose. I hope you will hear me not as an interloper from another place, but as a brother in the Faith. Some of you may think I am here to discourse on the rights of bondservants to the detriment of their masters. This is not my intention. The rights of the African are defined by the laws of the various states, and supervised by conscientious men and women like yourselves. If I mention rights at all, it is merely within the framework of these laws.

"I am not one of those who suggest abolition of slavery. I only advocate easing the bondsman's life through some manner of religious teaching, which surely cannot infringe any other man's God-given rights. Is there anyone here who believes the Scriptures are harmful? Or that a person who accepts Christ's teachings is not an asset to his community? I think not. Now, I put it to you: Do we wish these black people, on whom we depend so heavily, to obtain false and apocryphal impressions of the Christian way? Are we willing to leave their education to scalawag preachers who roam in the night? Or to let the slaves educate each other?"

Outside, standing at the window with Julian and Wes, an old gray-bearded slave nodded his head, punctuating McAuliff's statements and questions with exclamations of "Yeah, it's the truth!" and "Ain't it so!" McAuliff went on, urging the planters to provide a Sunday meeting house for the slaves, or if that was not possible, to have Sunday meetings on the estates where the slaves could hear the Scriptures read and explained. There was applause when he finished, particularly by the ladies, followed by a buzz of conversation.

Outside, Julian said: "He's from the north. If he wasn't a preacher friend of the minister here, they'd set the dogs on him."

Inside the church, a tall, gaunt man dressed in a white suit stood up to address the congregation.

"That's John Hale, love money and hate the nigger," Julian said. "Always talkin' about one or the other. White folks don't like him neither."

Mr. Hale nodded to Mr. McAuliff, wiped his forehead with a red pocket-handkerchief and began without any formalities: "It's nice of this reverend to come so far from way up there in Philadelphie to give us some advice on our problems. I'm sure we're all greatly obliged. I don't believe the reverend come here just to interpret the Scriptures, though, 'cause what he's been talking about is business matters. But I don't believe he said whether he ever had any experience managing a plantation or ever produced any cotton.

"I don't intend to get in an argument about the virtues of the nigger. But it's clear enough that when the Good Lord measured things out for the different races, he gave some more and some less. Each thing was made for its purpose. The white man was made with the ability to think, and the black man was made with a strong back and natural servility. Givin' the nigger letters and the Scriptures is against nature. He don't need to sign any papers, and we provide him with his wants, and giving him the Scriptures and such can't but harm him and us too. . . ."

"Come on," Julian said. "I heard it many a time. We got to get back."

As they rode across the fields, Wes said: "Well, now, you black nigger, I guess you know what you are."

The next morning Vespey and Mr. Blair got down to the business of selling and buying slaves. They rode out to the fields, where Vespey pointed his buggy whip at various men. "There's a good one there," he'd say, "less than thirty years old, and been treated well where he come from. A good Barbados nigger with good work habits. Strong as an ox and real compliant. Got him six months ago in a West Indies shipment. He's yours for twelve hundred. And over there on the other side, that boy's not more than twenty-five. Got him from Cuba, but he's African born, solid of bone, good eyesight, stout with an ax, and never made no trouble since he come. Same thing for him, twelve hundred, and a real bargain. If you got enough girls on the place, that nigger will give you a plantation full of first-rate pickaninnies."

The tour lasted several hours. Mr. Blair was becoming fatigued. Vespey pointed out twelve or thirteen slaves with whom he was prepared to part at prices ranging from eight hundred to twelve hundred dollars. Blair had difficulty sorting out in his mind which ones he wanted, and it seemed to him that the prices were high. But he knew enough about Vespey's reputation to consider that the figures that would ultimately appear in the accounts prepared for Colonel Hilton would be somewhat smaller. He wished, now, that he had sent Rousseau to procure the replacements. Rousseau could have dealt better with Vespey. But it was too late, he could wait no longer. Blair finally made his selection by rejecting those prospects who had come from the Indies.

Vespey laughed. "Mr. Blair, I read your mind. There's lots of planters down your way is leery of West Indian niggers. Can't say I blame 'em, of course. But the trick is to know how to get along with 'em. I can get along with just about any kind of niggers, and they get along with me, because I start them right and don't take no nonsense. If they don't do as they're supposed, I give them *reasons,* and after that there's no trouble. There won't never be no insurrections on this island, I guarantee it. Well, never mind, you take the ones you want, and you'll have some workers been properly trained. Just the same, if you want to make the accounts come out in your favor, don't try to run no old folks' home for rheumatic Africans. Get your money's worth out of them before they're forty, then get rid of 'em. I haven't got but three niggers on my place is older than fifty, and they won't be here long."

They worked out the transaction before the midday meal. Blair wrote out a check on his Savannah bank, thinking painfully that the slaves he had sold had netted him quite a bit less. Vespey prepared the transfer of title in a flourishing script with many misspellings. And after they had eaten, Mr. Blair went to his room to sleep.

Julian and Wes were sent across to the mainland again to check Mr. Blair's horses and mules. On the way back they rowed into a wild cove surrounded on three sides by giant trees hung with a heavy curtain of Spanish moss. There they fished for an hour or more with lines dropped from the boat's edge. "Need plenty fish," Julian said, "else my people be powerful hungry. Vespey tell the Colonel he give us this, give us that, but ain't a nigger on the place ever get what Vespey say they get. Sometimes when folks ask him for a little more of something so they don't get all drybone, Vespey say, 'Go catch you a fish or a rabbit.' That's what you been doin' anyhow, but if you get caught doin' it Vespey say why ain't you at work. If a man had a musket and some ball he could catch something to hold him. They's plenty deer around. You can't get nothin' in snares 'cept coon, rabbit and birds."

Wes felt a growing warmth for Julian. He said: "The Blair place sure is a long way from here. But it's good to know I got one friend out here on the island." Then, embarrassed, he said: "Maybe Mr. Blair lookin' for me. Old Ned, he goin' to be mad." They pulled in their lines and rowed to the landing.

Back at the plantation they left the wagon at the edge of a field and turned the mules out to graze. Julian gave his string of fish to a small girl to take home for him. Then they sauntered lazily toward the outbuildings. Julian suddenly stopped talking and put up his hand for silence. His face turned to the barn, he listened intently.

"You hear a call?" he asked Wes.

"Don't know," Wes said, "seem like it."

Julian walked toward the barn, his bare feet noiseless in the grass, Wes following a step behind. They went through the large wagon door and stood on the straw-covered threshing floor. They heard the sound clearly now, from the granary where they had slept. It was a thin, plaintive child's voice saying, "Please, Mr. Vespey, please. . . ." Julian ran across the floor and tore the granary door open with such force its leather hinges came off. Vespey was standing with his back to the door, a small dress clutched in one hand. Cowering naked in the corner was a girl of thirteen or fourteen, her eyes wide with terror. At the sound behind him, Vespey turned. He and Julian stood staring at one another.

"Nigger," Vespey said, "get out of here!"

Julian ran his tongue over his dry lips. He said in a voice so low it sounded like a whisper, "Turn her loose, Mr. Vespey."

Vespey's face flushed, and the veins in his forehead swelled. "Nigger, ain't I told you to get?"

Julian said again, "Mr. Vespey, turn her loose."

Vespey took a wooden grain scoop from the wall and

brandished it. "Nigger, you damned black African nigger. . . !"

Julian's voice was still low. There was a touch of pleading in it. "Mr. Vespey, she's only a little girl."

Vespey came forward, the grain scoop poised to strike. Julian backed up, step for step with Vespey's advance. When he had crossed the raised doorsill Vespey said, "Julian, you no-good African, you giving me orders?"

"No, sir, Mr. Vespey, I only ask you to turn the girl loose."

"What you need," Vespey said, "is a month in the sweat box, but before that I'm goin' to flay the skin off you!"

Julian measured the intent in Vespey's eyes. "Don't do it, Mr. Vespey," he said.

Vespey lunged, swinging the scoop, but Julian stepped out of range. Sweat began to run down Julian's face, and his shirt was suddenly wet. As Vespey swung again, Julian moved away, but his motion was halted by the wall behind him. He dodged again, and this time the grain scoop splintered against a post. Wes stood motionless, calmly aware that he was in the presence of Fa. For him, for Julian, and for Vespey alike there was no going this way or that way, because Fa had revealed itself. When Vespey struck again, the splintered scoop caught Julian across the cheek, opening a jagged cut from which blood began to ooze. Almost without thinking, Wes picked up a hoe that lay in the straw and struck hard at the back of Vespey's neck with it. Vespey staggered, turned, and seemed to see Wes for the first time.

"Blair's nigger!" he roared. "Blair's going to take a dead nigger home with him!"

Julian slid along the wall and picked up a heavy piece of cordwood. Vespey turned and moved after him again, his head thrust forward like a bull's. This time the scoop caught Julian on the shoulder, but before Vespey could move away Julian brought the cordwood down on his head. Vespey sank to one knee and remained there momentarily, swaying as though about to topple. But he arose again, squinting his eyes as though darkness had fallen, and this time he charged wildly at Wes. Wes timed his blow well. It landed just above Vespey's ear. The overseer slipped in the straw and fell. Once more he stood up and struck a blow that was never finished, for Julian's cordwood club came down first. Suddenly everything was quiet and Vespey lay motionless on the threshing floor, blood running from his mouth.

Julian and Wes didn't even notice the cluster of people at the door until one of them, an old woman, ran in, bent over and placed her ear to Vespey's chest. "Do, Jesus!" she said, turning her eyes upward. "Tell Father God this mean old man is on his way!"

Breathing heavily, Julian went to the granary. The girl was still cowering in the corner. He picked up her dress from the floor and slipped it over her, then carried her out. "Aunt Sarah," he said to the old woman, "take her back to the cabin."

He and Wes silently left the barn. The people at the door pressed back to make way for them, murmuring their concern. One voice called out sharply: "Quick, into the canebrake! They's a holler-tree canoe down there!" Julian nodded. He looked toward the plantation house, but there was nothing up there to indicate any awareness of the event. He said to Wes: "Come on, boy, or we're two dead niggers!"

They started across the fields, running as close to the tree lines as possible. At the far side they entered a patch of dense woods webbed with vines and briars. They sought no path, but forced their way through, reckless of the briars that tore their clothes and left ugly scratches on their bodies.

Once when they stopped to catch their breath Wes said: "Which way we goin'?"

Julian said: " 'Less we can cross the water we're done for." And they plunged once more into the wild tangle of vines, underbrush and thorns.

The ground became marshy, and they took wide detours

around places where the tidewater had seeped in to make ponds. Gradually the trees thinned out, and they were in a forest of canebrake from which long-legged water birds arose at the sound of their passage. When they reached the land's edge at last, they turned northward, and half an hour later they found the dugout canoe nesting among the reeds, camouflaged by a cover of hanging moss torn from the trees. The sun stood only at late afternoon. There would still be two more hours of daylight. Julian said: "We got to stay here till dark, 'less the dogs come on us first."

Wes examined the canoe. "No oars," he said.

Julian nodded. "Can paddle with our hands. Main thing is to get across 'fore morning."

They sat on a fallen swamp tree. After a while Julian said: "He was a mean old devil. I thought on doin' it many a time. He give me plenty misery. Glad I done killed him."

"The little girl?" Wes asked.

"My little sister, Julie Anne." He kicked at the ground with his heel. "How come you stepped in like that? Wasn't your trouble."

"Reckon it was mine, all right," Wes said. "Everything about it was mine. This thing was bound to come. I knew it all the time. You're my friend, that's one thing. Another thing, I got to rememberin' Kana, the man you told me about over on the other island. He was my friend too. We was together on the ship. We drank from the same gourd. Fought together on that French island. When Vespey tried to kill you, you looked just like Kana to me. It was mine all right. Over here in this country when a thing happens they say as God meant it so. Ain't that way with my people. It ain't God that do such things as make slaves. Ain't him that makes Vespey and old Rousseau do like they do, beatin' and killin' niggers. It's Fa. Christians say God is good. Fa ain't good, ain't bad. Fa is what happens. Every man got his Fa. When I see Vespey 'bout to kill you, my Fa say, 'Wes, ain't you remember yourself? Your name is Hwesuhunu. You're from the Fon people.' I hear it. I remember. So I pick up the hoe and hit him."

Julian mulled it over. He said: "Just the same, if you done held back you wouldn't be in the canebrake now."

Wes said: "The thing is finished. My people say, 'When trouble comes for one man it belongs to the village.' "

They waited for the sun to go down behind the mainland. Already it was touching the treetops, and the shadows were long. There was a rustling in the cane, and they tensely flattened out on the ground. "Someone's in there," Julian whispered.

Again the sound in the cane, this time followed by a low call. "Julian, you there? Where you at, Julian?"

"Over here," Julian called back in a low voice. "Who's that?" They could see the cane moving now. A shirtless boy pushed his way through, hugging a bundle to his chest. "Sammie," Julian said, "why you follow us?"

"They sent me," Sammie said, "they sent you these things." He handed the bundle, wrapped in an old cloth, to Julian. Julian untied it. There were several pieces of corn bread, some dried beans and goobers, a ball of twine, two knives and a fish hook.

"Who sent it?" Julian asked.

"Don't know. They just give it to me and say to run."

"All right, Sammie. Get on back. Tell them we thank them. You hear anyone comin' after us? You hear any dogs?"

Sammie shook his head. "Ain't hear nothin'."

"Well, we're obliged, but get runnin' now, and go back a different way."

Sammie nodded.

Wes said: "Tell Old Ned for me, tell him I'm sorry I didn't have no chance to say farewell."

Sammie disappeared into the canebrake.

"It's time now," Julian said. They pushed the canoe into the water. Lying on their stomachs, they paddled with their hands. The canoe inched slowly out of the reeds into the open. They kept it moving northward, parallel to the mainland shore. The sun dropped behind the horizon and darkness came. There was only the faint sound of the water, and from the distance the piercing call of the night birds.

The smell of the sea called up memories that had been dimming, and in Wes's mind there came again a vivid picture of the seventh day out of Cotonou, when the captives were brought up out of the hold to cleanse themselves with salt water and fresh sea air. He seemed to feel the blinding glare of the sun, to hear the snapping of sails and the creak of timbers and the babel of voices as the slaves crowded to the washing pails. He saw Old Grandfather trying to throw himself over the side, saw him hanging by his leg chain.

"Hwesuhunu—it is a good name," the old man had said down in the stench of the ship's belly. "You have a strong fetish." And Wes remembered the smells of the stockade in Cotonou, heard his father saying, "Above all, let us live. It is destiny to be alive. There is plenty of time to be among the dead." He pictured his father working in the fields of the village, and then that last sight of him in the Cotonou stockade, approaching his death but speaking only of the virtue of living. The years at the Blair plantation were compressed into a small interlude, and he saw this new voyage as a continuation of the old one.

As his hands dipped into the water he reflected that it was the same sea that lapped at the shores of Africa. The wetness on his skin was his contact with the village of Yabo, where the men went out each day to encourage the earth with their hoes; and with his mother, his brothers, his hunting companions, and the ancient ancestors. He heard an old priest singing:

What is life?
It is the knowledge of things.

What is man?
It is he who gains the knowledge.

But knowledge was great, and a man's life was short. The nearer one approached to the knowledge of things the closer he was to the edge of death. He was forever in the shadow of dying without having had life.

Hwesuhunu tried to sum up the things he knew. They were few. In the dark of the slave ship, Dokumi had given him a wari nut, in which was wrapped the meaning of all that happened between people. And he had given Dokumi an invisible thing in trust, his secret name, Alihonu, He-Who-Is-Born-on-the-Road. The exchange was the force of life. And on St. Lucia, Hwesuhunu had given the same nut to old Jean Labarbe. And Kofi, his friend from St. Lucia, just before he was hanged, he had given Hwesuhunu the brass figure from around his neck, and thus had cheated death.

Each thing was a part of knowledge, but where was the wholeness? It was here, if one could but see. For knowledge, like Fa, was an invisible passenger in the small canoe. The task was to get knowledge to reveal itself, for surely the meaning of life was something more than endless flight before a pursuing evil. It had to be something more than a bridge to the land of the dead. Hwesuhunu wondered if his father's life, and his grandfather's, had also been a kind of flight. Or had it been a confrontation with the forces that sought to drive men from the villages into the dark forest? There had been drouth, wars, migrations, and often death. But there had been victories too. There had been no King Adanzan then, Adanzan the Despoiler.

Adanzan had been sent among men, perhaps by Sagbata, He-Who-Sowed-Smallpox. Who before Adanzan had denied the common soul of the Fon and sold his own people like cattle in the market? Such a thing had never happened in the time of King Agongolo, or Mpengla who came before, or Tegbwesou before that, or the great Agadja, he who had brought the vodouns to Abomey. Adanzan the Despoiler was the spirit of madness. Or was he only the instrument of madness, like Vespey, Walker, Rousseau and that man in the church who cried out that Africans were wild and unclean? Or were all of them, like Hwesuhunu and Julian, merely victims of the disease, blood sacrifice to the madness of Sagbata himself? And how many thousands would be expended through cruelty, suffering, and degradation before the madness burned itself out? Above all, where was the face of the great madness that it might be placated, reasoned with, or confronted? It was nowhere and it was everywhere. As there was a common soul among the Fon until Adanzan had denied it, there was now a common madness that spread across oceans, and there was no use invoking it for mercy, for it was a force without a central personality.

For ages past men had wrought random forces of cosmic whim and accident into positive and useful shapes. There was the ancient man who had brought yams to Dahomey; there was he who had brought sound and distilled music from it; there was he who had fashioned the dance from motion; he who devised the art of speech between men; he who perfected the art of supplication. There were the men who had brought the laws, the proverbs and the sayings, and who recorded in their songs the meaning of thunder, harvest, disease and death. Thus knowledge and purpose had come into the world. But now, if there was knowledge still, it was in hiding, while the great disease ate out the heart of Dahomey.

Julian broke the long silence. "Boy, I'm hungry," he said. "Give me some goobers. And let's get to oarin' this boat."

◎◎◎ PART 3

The Wilderness

For two days there were no signs of human settlement. They pressed away from the sea toward the west, seeking to surround themselves with solitude and wilderness. They forded a half dozen streams and passed through a dense stand of timber. On the third day they crossed a rutted red clay road. Here they paused to consider whether their direction would bring them to settled country or further away from people. To the north and east somewhere lay Charleston, to the south, Savannah. They didn't know whether they were in South Carolina or Georgia. At last they crossed the road and entered a region of rolling hills and pine. And when the road was a full day behind them they built a lean-to among the trees, gathered pine needles to lie on, and rested. The corn bread, goobers and beans were gone. For their evening meal they ate raw bacon.

In the morning Julian took out the twine and made two spring snares to capture game. Wes went in search of a fragment of dry hardwood, and when he returned he fashioned a fire drill from it. They made a fire and sat before it, not talking much, not precisely thinking, but soaking in the silence, relishing their lostness and wondering dimly what was beyond their sanctuary. Neither had given thought to what might lie ahead, to where they would go, or to how they would meet the challenges of their flight. Though there had been stillness on the island, the stillness here was greater. It was not a stillness of sound, for they could hear the wind in the trees and the call of birds, but a stillness of burden. There were no fields to be tilled, no rice to be threshed, no trees to be felled, no roads to be made, no drivers, no overseers. Time stretched out to match the open spaces, and the confrontation with Vespey became a thing of the distant past. Wes and Julian were content merely to absorb the wilderness, receive what it offered, and live according to its rules.

Within hours of the first setting of the snares they caught a muskrat, which they cleaned and roasted immediately. In a small brook nearby, using bacon as bait, they caught fish. Their minds stubbornly turned away from such questions as what the sequence of events would be, and what choices they might have. For the present, life seemed to consist of nothing more than keeping warm in the chill of night, smoking the fire with green wood to drive away mosquitoes and covering their lean-to so that rain would not come through.

In this roofing enterprise, Julian had begun by laying branches and leaves across the top. But Wes shook his head. "The way you doin' it," he said, "they goin' to be more water inside than out." He took Julian to a clearing where the marsh grass grew waist high. They cut grass and bundled it into sheathes, and they laid the sheathes on the lean-to roof like shingles and wove them together, as Wes remembered doing it in his village. They saw deer sometimes, and Wes carved a spearshaft and affixed his knife as a point. All one night he lay in the brush near a place where the deer sometimes came to drink. As the morning dawned he threw his spear at a nervous buck and missed. The buck bounded away, leaving behind nothing but deep imprints in the ground. Wes wondered for a moment whether he should pursue it.

Then there flashed into his conscious mind the name Atogon, surfacing from the deeps where all ancient memories were hidden. As though there were no connection at all, Wes chose not to pursue. He went instead to find some other game, and after he had killed a groundhog he returned to the lean-to. Julian also was out hunting somewhere. Wes lay in the shade with closed eyes, feeling the breeze moving across his moist skin. Atogon came back again. Atogon, the hunter, who had pursued game into the wilderness and never returned.

That night as Wes and Julian sat talking across their fire, Wes asked: "You ever hear about Atogon?"

Julian said: "Never did."

Wes said, after a pause: "That story, I heard it when I was small. Then I didn't remember it any more. Today the Old People sent it back to me. He was in the wilderness like us."

"Well, then, what about this man?" Julian said.

"He was a hunter. His name was Atogon. Lived all by himself near the forest. One time the pickin's turned small. He couldn't find no animals to kill. They was too many leopards around, chase all the animals away. Atogon hunt, hunt, find nothin' to eat. He was mighty hungry. One mornin' he see a deer at a water hole. Too far away to kill, but that night Atogon hid by the water hole and wait. The moon come up almost as bright as day. A deer come to drink, the same deer as before. Well, then, Atogon threw his spear. It only cut the deer's neck, didn't kill him. The deer ran away. Atogon felt pretty bad. Had one chance and lost it. But they was a spot of blood on the ground. Atogon said, 'Maybe that deer is bad hurt, I'm goin' to follow him.' When day came, he followed the blood spots. All day he walked, followin' the tracks. Looked around him and said, 'I never been in this country before. What's the name of this place?'

He kept following the tracks like they was only one thing to do in the world, catch that deer. Walked three days, had nothin' to eat. His belly was empty, he believe he's about to die from hunger. Then he come on a small village in the forest.

"Atogon entered the village. The people looked at him, see he's almost dead. They put out a mat for him, made him sit down. They brought him food to eat. When he's fed up good, they say, 'Cousin, you must be a long way from home. How you come to find this country?' Atogon say, 'I been huntin' deer. I hit him with my spear, cut his neck. Since then I've been trackin' him. The tracks come right to this village. Give me my deer. Glad to share it with you, then I'll go.' People said, 'No, they ain't no deer here.' Atogon got plenty mad, said, 'That deer is mine, I marked him with my spear.' People said, 'Go call the chief.' The chief came. He looked sick, had a bad wound on his neck, wrapped over with cloth, but the cloth was soaked with blood.

"Atogon knew then that the deer he cut with his spear wasn't a deer at all, it was this man. He said, 'Uncle, I'm sorry. I was hungry, didn't know the deer was you.' The chief tell him, 'I know you, Atogon, you almost killed me. But I'm all right now. Done is done. But they's one thing you got to know. I ain't a man *or* deer. This place is Lazile. You never hear of it?' Atogon say, 'Yes, seems like I hear of it. It's the village of the dead.' 'You are plenty right,' the chief say, 'This place is the village of the dead. Sorry to tell you, but you can't go back where you come from.' 'How so?' Atogon say. Chief say, ' 'Cause no man ever return from place of the dead. What you goin' to do I don't rightly know, but you can't go back no more.' Atogon say, 'Maybe you are dead, but not me. I'm goin' home.' Chief shake his head. 'Can't make it,' he say. They give Atogon food and water and he start out.

"Now Atogon been a hunter ever since he was so big. Ain't no one can beat him at trackin' deer, leopard, any kind of game. Can find his way by the sun, stars, or scent. But when he start for home he can't find the trail. He say, 'Where's that rock use to be here?' or 'Seem to me they was a big ant hill in this place.' When he come to a place where they was supposed to be a thicket, he finds a river instead. And instead of a hill they was only flat grass country.

"In no time at all he see he was lost. Followed the sun, but it didn't do him no good. Seem like the sun didn't get up and go down same way like it used to. And one day when he feel real low, 'spect he never see his home no more, he come on another village, and he see lots of people marchin' in a line. They was all laughin' and carryin' a body on they shoulders. He say, 'What's the matter, why everyone laughin'?' They tell him, 'It's a funeral.' He go along with them to the buryin' ground. They don't put the dead man in the grave. They take a girl, one of the mourners, throw her in, cover her up with dirt. The body they been carryin', they throw it away in the bush.

"Atogon feel fear come over him. He ask them where his own village is at, they tell him they never heard of it. 'What's the name of this one?' he say. Headman step up. Got no clothes on, only bells on his ankles. Say to Atogon, 'This place is called No Name.' 'What's the name of the people here?' Atogon want to know. 'People here is called No Name People,' the man say, 'got no tribe, no family.' 'How come?' Atogon ask him. ' 'Cause,' the man say, ' 'cause they got no soul. When the souls was given out, these folks didn't get none. So what good is a name without a soul?' Atogon feel afraid. He say, 'This still the land of the dead I'm in?' The crowd laugh ha-ha-ha! The headman say, 'No, man, we are worse off than the dead. The dead got souls, we got none.' Then they grab one boy and begin to cut him up. 'Why you do that?' Atogon say. 'We plenty hungry,' they tell him. 'We been carryin' that old body 'round five-six days, made our belly empty.'

"Atogon lit out, glad to get hisself lost from them people.

But he didn't find no game, had to eat grass and leaves. And one day he come on a trail, seem like maybe it's a game trail, so he followed it. And he come to a crossroads, but didn't know which way to go. He heard a sound down on the ground, it was a old drybone skull settin' there, talkin' away, loose teeth clatterin' like a gourd rattle. 'Take the thin trail,' the skull say. 'How you know what I want?' Atogon ask. 'Don't make no difference,' the skull tell him, 'take the thin one.'

"So Atogon took the thin trail and it bring him to a market. He had never seen nothin' like that market before. All the people there got pale red skin, like they been turned inside out. And everyone carried a skull in his hand, else had it slung on a string on his shoulder. The big man had a big man skull, the little boy got a little boy skull. One old man without no teeth, he had an old man skull without no teeth. And the skulls done all the talkin' for the people, tell them what to talk about. Two friends meet at the market, they don't know what to say, till one skull says, 'Howdy, cousin.' His man picked that talk up and say, 'Howdy, cousin.' His friend wait for his skull to tell him what to say. That goes on with all the people, skulls talkin' for them and givin' them the words.

"Atogon want to know where he is. And when he start talkin', all the people come down around him, lookin' mean and red-eye. Skulls say, 'Who's that man tryin' to make conversation without a skull speakin' for him?' And the people say the words they was told to say. Whatever Atogon try to tell them, they don't listen. Skulls say, 'He make it up from his own mouth, he ain't got no skull to give him the knowledge. Better kill him.' So all the people say, 'Yeah, better kill him.' Atogon lit out again, back the way he come, and down at the crossroads place the first skull is still there. He fetch it a kick and scatter it in two parts. The jaw is still goin' up and down like it's talkin', but the voice come from the head part. 'Now you done it,' it say to him, 'you done destroy the knowledge of the world.'

"And so it is with this hunter. He go on like that from one place to another, and the sickness and misery in him gets worse all the time, till at last he start lookin' for that first village, name of Lazile, where all the dead is at. 'Look like I'll never get back to my forest,' he say, 'and of all these places I seen, the only fittin' place is 'mongst the dead.' But he never find Lazile again."

"That's all?" Julian said.

"That's all," Wes said.

Julian ruminated on it. "I hear things like it before," he said. "But I 'spect it ain't true."

Wes said: "Every story is true for one man, maybe the man who tell it, or for everybody in the village, or maybe for someone not yet born. I wasn't five years old when I hear this one. I ask my Mamma 'bout it. She laughed, told me it was story to scare the chillen and make 'em behave theyself. I ask my Papa. He tell me this: 'Son, for most folks this story don't mean nothin'. A story is like a feather blowed around by the wind. Some folks see that feather and say, "Oh, there's a feather," that's all. One day a man pick that feather up and weave it into his gbo, the thing that protect his house from bad spirits. The same way with a story. One day a man picks it up and makes it his own. Then it is true.' " Wes paused for a moment. "Today when I went to spear that deer this story came back in my mind. Atogon come under the power of his Fa when he tracked that deer of his into the wilderness. After that, everything was changed with him, nothin' ever come back the way it was, and he had to go through with it, 'mongst the dead, the No Name People and the talkin' skulls. I think this story belongs to me."

Days and nights slipped by in a kind of timeless flow. Wes and Julian fished, tended their traps and made occasional improvements on their lean-to as though there were nowhere to go beyond this place. But one morning a new sound intruded. Though it was distant and faint, they recognized it as the baying of hunting dogs, and thereafter their senses continually probed to isolate this sound and assess its meaning. The first day they were content to attribute it to a hunting party, but they heard it again the second day, and on the third, though it was faint still, it seemed somewhat nearer.

"Could be bounty hunters," Julian said, voicing what up to then had been unspoken, "or maybe a sheriff's posse." That day they made preparations to abandon camp. They stripped their traps of two possums and a muskrat and spent the afternoon smoking the meat so they could carry it with them. That night they slept fitfully. In the morning before the stars had yet faded they left their camp behind and began walking west. At midday they came to a wide sluggish stream, through which they sloshed for several hours so as to leave no scent that a dog might follow. At last they emerged into a wide meadow beyond which they could see only low rolling hills with no mark of human presence. Here they stopped to eat their smoked meat, and afterward they stretched out in the shade to rest.

"If we keep agoin', where you think we goin' to come out?" Wes said.

"Don't know. Mississippi Territory maybe."

"That a good place to be?" Wes asked.

"Not particular, it ain't," Julian said.

"What if we go north?"

"South Carolina, Virginia. It's a big country. Past that I don't know."

"Any of them places any good?"

"They ain't, not from what I hear about it."

After a thoughtful silence, Wes said: "A man once told me Ohio was a good place."

Julian nodded. "I heard that one too, but not 'less you got special friends up there. They catch you on the street or somewhere and they hold you till they find out where you from, then send you back."

"What's the other side of Ohio?" Wes asked.

"Don't know," Julian said, "ain't never heard of it. Thing of it is to keep movin', never mind the direction. North or south, it don't matter, least till they get the notion we ain't worth the trouble no more."

"There's one place I heard some men talk about," Wes said, "call it Liberty Island."

"I hear of it too," Julian said. "It's a big town down in the woods, nothin' there but runaways."

"That's the one," Wes said.

It was evening. The sun was beginning to fall behind the western horizon. Julian's senses became taut. He reached for his knife. "They's somethin' out there in the long grass," he said. "Better get down." They flattened themselves on the ground. They saw the grass move, and a yellow dog trotted into the clearing. He stood hesitantly, knowing exactly where the men were. It made them feel foolish.

"That ain't no huntin' dog," Wes said. "Ain't no white man care to claim a dog like that. Wild, maybe."

" 'Tain't no white man dog, true enough," Julian said. "But he ain't wild neither. Maybe an Indian dog. I seen some Creeks once. They had dogs like that." He raised his head and snapped his fingers. The dog wagged his tail hesitantly, lowered his head in submission.

"Come on, Yella," Julian said.

The dog moved forward a few steps and stopped.

Wes and Julian sat up.

"Here, Yella, here," Wes said.

Yella opened his mouth in a kind of smile.

Julian tossed a bone toward him. The dog turned to run, then nosed his way to the food. He lay on the ground and gnawed. When the bone was gone, they tossed him more scraps. When he was finished, he lay with his chin on the ground, watching.

"What you know?" Julian said. "We got a yella dog."

When they stretched out to sleep, Yella inched closer. In the morning when they had eaten more smoked meat and started walking again, Yella trotted at their heels. After a while he moved to the front, looking back occasionally to see if they were following.

"Look like he made up his mind we belong to him," Wes said.

"We got a sure 'nough yella dog," Julian said. "Only thing that trouble my mind is whose dog we got. Must be lost from some Indian camp."

"Well, he don't bother us none," Wes said. "Maybe he know how to hunt. We can use a dog like that."

"I'll be damned," Julian said, "look at Old Yella."

That night they set snares again. In the morning they were awakened by Old Yella's barking, and found him guarding one of the snares with a rabbit in it. They skinned their catch and cleaned it, wrapping the meat in fresh leaves. That night Wes made fire with his fire bow, and they had a cooked meal. Old Yella sat nearby, waiting for his share. "That dog gettin' too familiar," Julian said. "He think he own us."

They continued to move in a westward direction, unhurried but with a sense of purpose. It wasn't that there was a destination awaiting them, but that somewhere behind were white men and hunting hounds. Whenever they came to a stream they methodically walked for a distance in the water to break the scent. The country was still one of rolling hills, but there was more woodland now and fewer open fields. And in one of the fields they came on the first sign of human presence since they had crossed the red clay road many days ago. It was an old cornfield. Its dried stalks stood among a wild growth of weeds, and nearby were the remains of a half dozen campfires.

"Indian camp," Julian said, "but it look like they ain't been here since last year or year before. Creeks most likely. This country been full of Creeks." Though the camp was an old one, the discovery made them alert. "Don't want to run into none of them Creeks," Julian said. "They ain't friendly."

The next day Yella cornered something in an oak grove. Thinking of fresh meat, they hurried forward with their knives in hand. But Yella's quarry was human, a young Indian boy. He stood with his back to a tree, a stick poised in the air to ward off attack. Julian slapped Yella, and the dog turned away. "Don't mind that crazy old dog," Julian said, "he don't know a boy from a coon." The boy stared at them without commitment, then backed away and slipped off into the underbrush.

"Let's get out of here," Julian said. "He looks like Creek to me."

"I don't know," Wes said, "how come you say he's Creek? He's just a boy, that's all."

"This here is Creek country," Julian said, "and if they's Indians around they's probably Creek. Where they's one they's likely more. Them Creeks got arrangements with the white folks. They get hard money for every runaway they catch. And they got they own nigger slaves too."

But before they had time to retreat from the grove, two Indians armed with muskets emerged silently from the undergrowth. Wes and Julian tried conversing with them, but they did not seem to understand. In reply, they motioned with their guns toward the other side of the grove. "Look like they want us to come along," Wes said.

As they walked, skirting the edge of the trees, Julian said: "You folks Creeks?"

One of the men replied sharply: "Tsoyaha."

"Sound like he don't like to be called Creek," Wes said.

The village was no more than a half mile away. It was set in a broad meadow that sloped gently down to a smooth lake. A dozen or more thatched houses stood in a cluster on the higher ground, and several old women were busy cooking over open fires nearby. On the far side was a field of corn. Other women and girls were there at work cultivating. The two guides—or were they captors?—motioned Wes and Julian to stop, and while one stayed with them as though standing guard, the other went down to the lake and called to someone beyond their range of vision.

"He make a sound like a sure-enough crow, don't he?" Julian said. "They make calls like any bird you ever hear of."

Wes made another effort to talk with their guard, but it was useless. In a little while they saw another Indian coming along the lake shore. There was something about the way he walked that struck Wes as different. His skin was quite dark, too, and his hair was short for an Indian's. It was only when the man was a few paces away that Wes saw the three parallel scars on each cheek. Wes whispered: "He ain't no Indian at all. That man's a Nago countryman of mine."

"What you want in this place?" the man said in familiar English.

"Uncle," Wes said, "we don't want nothin' special. Didn't even know they was a camp here. What kind of place is this?"

"This here is a Tsoyaha town," the man said. "We is all Tsoyaha here."

"Uncle," Wes said, "me and my friend not seekin' anything. We just been walkin' along and our dog found the boy back there in the trees. Then the men come and brought us here." He paused. "Me, I am Fon. I was born in Dahomey. Reckon you done hear of that place."

"Yes, I done hear of it."

"Right next to Nago country."

The man nodded. "I knows it."

"From the marks on your face, Uncle, I think maybe you was born there."

The man answered stiffly: "I am a Tsoyaha. I belong with these people. Look to me like you two is runaways."

They said nothing.

"You boys hungry?"

"Well," Wes said, "we had a little somethin' this mornin'."

"Come on."

They followed him and sat on the ground where he indicated in front of his house. A young girl came and gave them each a gourd of cornmeal mush. Wes guessed she was about sixteen. He saw in her complexion and her features that she was the Nago's daughter. After serving them, she went back to work scraping a deer hide. They ate silently. Wes watched her.

Julian noticed. He said, "Don't go lookin' at the girls. We got plenty trouble already."

Wes said, "It gives me comfort to look at her."

When they were finished eating, the girl came and took the empty gourds, and the Nago returned and sat down with them.

"What you said is so," he said. "These here marks on my face is Yoruba, the same as you call Nago. Nago is part of the Yoruba people. I was born near Whydah. I was brought here like you. I was already a man. I had one wife, two children. I left them behind, never hear of them again. I was put to work on a plantation. I don't like livin' like a slave. I run away, hide in the woods. One day I meet the Tsoyaha people. They fed me, took care of me. I stayed with them. I married with a Tsoyaha girl, have three children. Now I am a Tsoyaha. The marks on my face is only like the scratch marks of a bear. Many years now I have not been a Yoruba. I hunt with the Tsoyaha, fish with the Tsoyaha. My blood is now mixed with the Tsoyaha. They give me my name, Kuba. I been born two times. First time was 'mongst the Yoruba. Second time 'mongst the Tsoyaha."

"Uncle," Wes said, "I see how it is. I won't speak of Nago no more."

In the evening there was a meeting. The men came in from fishing and hunting. They ate their evening meal, then they gathered and sat in a circle around a fire. A woman brought a calabash bowl containing a sweet brown beverage. It was passed around the circle, each man sipping in turn. Wes and Julian sat beside Kuba. When the calabash was empty, a white-haired old man adjusted his blanket on his shoulders and began to speak. ("He's the grandfather of this town," Kuba whispered, "name is Katanay.") His voice rose and fell. Sometimes he leaned forward to gesture with his arm. He spoke a long while. Sometimes he spoke with his eyes closed, as though in a half sleep. From time to time the other men made sounds of assent or disagreement.

"What they talkin' about?" Wes whispered to Kuba.

"They talkin' about you. Can you stay or must you go, or what they goin' to do about you. Katanay tell about different strangers, some good, some bad. He ask all the men to speak they advice."

Another man spoke. Like Kuba, he had scars on his face, but they were the scars of combat with a wild creature of the forest, and Wes suddenly remembered Dosu, the hunter, with the claw marks of a leopard on his cheek. The man did not speak long. His voice was sharp, and he pointed sometimes at Wes and Julian. They understood from his tone that he did not favor them. When he was finished, a third man began. He stood up, moved about, acting out his argument. Others spoke also, and some remained silent, merely listening. Kuba's turn came. He talked rapidly and earnestly. Watching him now and listening to the Tsoyaha words tumbling from his mouth, Wes was astonished that he had ever taken him for an African. Kuba was truly an Indian. At last there was silence around the circle.

Kuba turned to Wes. "Your turn now," he said, "the meetin' wait to hear from you."

"What I goin' to tell them?" Wes asked. "I don't know what they been talkin' about."

"Just speak now, they waitin'," Kuba said.

Wes thought for a moment. Then he began:

"We was slaves back there, and we run away. We been walkin' a long time. We won't never go back to that place. We come on the Indian boy in the woods, and we been brought here, 'mongst you people. We got nothin' to give you. Everything that belong to us, we done leave it behind. I don't know what else to tell you 'bout us. But I can tell you a story about two men in my country."

Kuba translated. The old man Katanay gestured for Wes to continue.

"They was two men one time, goin' to the town of Abomey. These men walked far. They was many days on the road. The heat was killin' them. They was hungry, they need water. They come to a place where a man was tendin' cows at a spring. They tell him, 'Please, cousin, we in need of water. Give us a drink.' But the man ain't in no hurry to give them no water. He say, 'Maybe I do it, maybe I don't. Don't know you two at all. Maybe you good people, maybe you bad people, how do I know? 'Fore I make up my mind, you got to tell me your names.'

"One man speak up. He say, 'Cousin, my name is Where-We-Comin'-From, that's all.' Man who have the cows and the water say, 'All right, that's a good name. Go on, get yourself a drink of water.' So the other man tell him, 'My name is Where-We-Goin'-To.' Owner of the water say, 'What kind of name is that, Where-We-Goin'-To? That name got a bad sound to me, I don't like it. 'Count of it's a wrong name, you must be a bad man. Can't have no water here.' The man complain back to him, but it don't do no good. Where-We-Comin'-From, he get water; Where-We-Goin'-To, he don't get nothin'.

"Whilst they was all there together an old man come along the way. They tell him the argument. They tell him to decide which is right. He listened. He studied on it. And he tell the owner of the spring, 'You got it wrong about this thing. Where-We-Goin'-To is a good name. Where-We-Comin'-From, that's gone now, we can't never again get nothin' more from it. What we goin' to find is the other way, where we goin' to. What we find there we don't know, but all we got left in life is there.' And the man who own the water say, 'Yes, I been wrong 'bout this thing.' So the two men get they water, and both go on they way to Abomey. That's all."

Kuba translated. Though Wes and Julian couldn't understand his words, they recognized eloquence in his voice, and they saw rapt attention on the faces in his audience. And when Kuba was through, there were smiles and nods of approval around the fire. The old man Katanay spoke, and Kuba translated:

"The people say all right, you two stay on here and rest in town till you ready to go. Katanay say, 'Give both men water.' They's a small house down by where the corn is cribbed. You sleep there. The girls will bring you food."

"We thank all the people," Wes said. "We're proud to stay."

Katanay spoke again, this time addressing himself directly to Wes and Julian. "He want to tell you 'bout the Tsoyaha," Kuba said, and he translated, making the story his own as he went along.

"One time long past, the Tsoyaha was a strong people. They was more than fifty towns, and all this country round here, both sides of the big river, belong to them. They was plenty corn, plenty meat, plenty fish. We trade with the other nations, live here in war and peace. Sometimes they was fighting with the Cherokee, the Kusa, the Kawita and the Hitchiti. But the Muskogee was too strong. They take some of Tsoyaha towns. They take some Tsoyaha people for slaves. They take some Tsoyaha women, marry them. Now many Tsoyaha is gone. Some has left they towns and gone to work for the white folks. The Muskogee press us, the white folk press us too. The Tsoyaha isn't great no more like they was. Many sick, many die. But this country, it was give to the Tsoyaha people, and we stay here. If it goin' to be war, it be war. If it goin' to be sickness, it be sickness. If men die, they die. But the Tsoyaha stand here till the last man is gone. This is what Katanay say."

Wes lay that night on a bed of skins and blankets, but he could not sleep. He pondered on Kuba. He had accepted the idea of Kuba's transmutation. But what then about Hwesuhunu the Fon? Was Wes Hunu, who now slept in the Indian house, the same person as Hwesuhunu, the African? For the things he knew most closely seemed to belong to another place and another time. Abomey was a real word, but was the place real? The Fon, where were they? King Adanzan, whose soldiers had captured him, he was an evil idea in the mind, but perhaps Adanzan had died long ago. Hwesuhunu's village, by the name of Yabo, did it really exist? His small brothers, if they lived still, were not children but men. And the ancestors, when had he last heard of them, or spoken of them? If they were truly there, why had they remained silent? "Am I Hwesuhunu the Fon?" Wes asked himself. "Or am I merely Wes Hunu, a half-Christian slave who has learned to read?"

It suddenly seemed ridiculous to cling to the past. For here in this land there was no such thing as Fon, only white men, black men, and brown men. When Kuba said, "I am Tsoyaha," that had a meaning, for all around him were Tsoyaha. You could see them, touch them, hear them. But if Wes said, "I am Fon," and looked around him for verification of this truth, there were no sounds, no faces, no music, no dokpwe, no village of Yabo, no Abomey, nothing to testify that the Fon existed outside his mind. Lying silently in the night he summoned up an old village song and sang it inside his head. But did this prove that Yabo ever existed? It proved nothing more than did an Indian hunter's imitation of the call of a groundhog.

For to live was to communicate, as the drummer did to the dancers, as the Legba priest did to Legba, as the storyteller did to the people, as the dead did, on occasion, to the living. If I speak to the old man Katanay in Fon, does he understand me? If I speak to Julian of the vodouns Mawu and Legba, does he hear? Speech alone is not communication. For did not Julian and Vespey speak together without understanding? Nor could they ever, for they shared no common soul between them. Perhaps Kuba had found such a soul with the Tsoyaha. But what Wes remembered as the soul of the Fon, the thing he clung to that had given him the only certainty he had known, was it real or only a trick of the mind? And while he lay there and thought of these things and sought desperately for his identity, he felt an object like a sharp stone pressing against his chest.

He stirred and reached under him with his hand to brush it away. It was not a stone, but the brass casting made on St. Lucia, which Kofi had given him just before going out to be hanged. He felt its contours with his fingers. It was real. It seemed to bring Kofi alive, and all those others who had fought and died on the island, and the feelings they had shared and comprehended. It brought the slave stockade in Cotonou to life again, and his father, and Adanzan, and the village of Yabo, and the kingdom of Dahomey. This crude brass figure of a man, worn smooth now and discolored, was the testimony and the link. All those things that were suddenly real again after having seemed to die and fade away, they had molded Hwesuhunu. And he understood gratefully that Hwesuhunu and Wes Hunu were one and the same, that he was here in the Tsoyaha town only because Mawu, the parent of all vodouns, had thus written it down. In the writings of Mawu were the magic of creation and the fate of all men. In Mawu's mind Hwesuhunu had been given his life, his character and his Fa. So it was. He slept.

Wes and Julian stayed on. They fell into the pattern of life without effort. Wes hunted with Kuba sometimes, and Yella went along as though he were in charge. Indeed, Kuba found Yella to be a good hunting dog, and he took it on himself to provide him with meat scraps at the evening meal. Wes never spoke of Kuba's origin, and for a long time Kuba forebore from asking questions about Wes's future.

But one day when they were skinning a deer Kuba said, "When the time come, where you go from here?"

Wes shook his head. "I been studyin' on that one. Done hear tell of places up north, also west. But they is right far. I tell myself I goin' to move on somewhere. But I ain't yet made up my mind. One man tell me Boston, that's the place to go. 'Nother man say Ohio. One day I goin' to decide."

Kuba nodded. "Best to take your time. I knowed four men lit out from the plantation I was at. One was brought back half starved, been eat up with fever in the swamp. He was too sick to punish him, he already 'most dead. But he don't die after all. Last time I see him he weren't more'n thirty years old and his head already turned white.

" 'Nother man caught by the militia, but he don't let them carry him off, just fight till they kill him. Two other men, they gone, never hear of them again. Maybe they make it somewhere, I don't know. Maybe they already up there in Ohio. I hear tell of men got clean away. They tell me of a black man over here in Georgia got hisself on a British ship one night. They 'spect the captain of the ship run off with him. One year later that ship come back to Savannah. The Old Master what lose him, he go on board, look around. There sure 'nough is his runaway slave.

"He demand to the Captain, 'Sir, I see you got my runaway.' Captain o' the ship say, 'No, you make a mistake, friend, I got no one's runaway.' 'There he is right over there, workin' on the sail,' the Old Master tell him, 'that's my man Sam, run off 'bout a year ago.' 'That man?' Captain tell him. 'Can't be that man. His name ain't Sam, it's Jeffrey.' 'Well, I don't care what he call hisself now,' Old Master say, 'he belong to me, so turn him loose or I come and get him with the soldiers.' 'Well, now,' the ship Captain tell him, 'you made a bad mistake, because that man is one of my worthy sea hands, he been with me four years, and his name ain't Sam at all.' The Old Master go on shore then and get the soldiers, bring them back, demand for his slave.

" 'You mean that man Jeffrey you been talkin' about?' ask the Captain. 'Yeah, it's what I mean,' Master say. 'Well, there he is paintin' the mast over there, but he ain't your man at all.' The planter turn the man around. 'Hey, you ain't the one I see before, where's that black man call hisself Jeffrey?' 'Jeffrey, that's my name all right,' the man say. 'Oh, no, you ain't the one I seen before.' 'Must be so,' the man say, 'ain't you the one call me Sam last time you was here?' 'Yeah, I call somebody by that name,' Old Master say, 'but not you.' Well he never did find his man Sam, but Sam was on that boat all the time, made safe by the Captain."

"It's another thing I think on," Wes said, "Makin' off by sea. Anywhere. Could catch a boat goin' to Boston."

"Main thing is," Kuba said, "take your time. You all right here."

"It's true," Wes said. "But now I run away after so many years, it press on me that I don't keep on agoin' till I'm gone."

One morning when he awoke Wes saw some newly made Tsoyaha clothes beside his blanket. Julian was already sitting up. "That's your new Indian pants and shirt," he said, "I got some too. Two girls bring them things. The ones you got was brought by Kuba's girl, the one you been pokin' your eyes at."

Wes put them on. He went to Kuba's house. "Your daughter bring me these clothes. It make me feel fine. Them old things I had was pretty raggedy."

Kuba said: "She made them things for you 'cause you help the town find meat."

"If you don't mind," Wes said, "I like to greet her for these things."

"Never mind that," Kuba said, "she make it, but it come from all the town."

"Well, I certainly thank you and all the people," Wes

said. But he couldn't think of it as a mere coincidence that Kuba's daughter, Agagonay, had sewn the garments with her own hands.

Wes tried to talk to her sometimes. Mostly it was just sounds and laughing, because Agagonay understood nothing Wes said. He saw her in the cornfield one day cultivating with her digging stick. "You goin' to break your back with that thing," he said. "What you need is an iron hoe." He spoke to Kuba about it later. "How come the girls work with them little sticks? They could do it faster and easier with a reg'lar hoe."

Kuba said: "We know about hoes too. I used a hoe myself till it seemed like part of my hand. But we don't need hoes in this place. We don't grow corn here to feed no fat white master. We don't sell none. What we grow we eat. We got plenty. What hurt the Tsoyaha ain't lack of corn. It's the white folks' pushing that hurts us, them and the Muskogee. They's only one thing goin' to help us here, and the other Tsoyaha towns too. We got to keep ourself Tsoyaha. First you give the women hoes. All right. Then you change the houses, make them all like slave cabins. All right. Then you make girls wear they hair like the white ladies. All right. After that you don't do the Tsoyaha dances no more, you dance the minuet with a fiddle. Might as well talk English too. Well, what happen to the Tsoyaha then? They gone. They give it all up. 'Cept for one thing. White man say they still damned Indians, just like the African nigger. What the Tsoyaha get from it but the same thing as they get now? They lost everything and gain nothin'. Back where you run away from, the hoe do better than the diggin' stick, but not here."

Kuba looked at Wes silently for a moment. "Maybe 'tain't the hoe on your mind so much as the girl." He began to sharpen his knife on a stone. "Agagonay ain't for no Fon," he said, "she got to marry only with a Tsoyaha man."

"Wasn't thinkin' on such things," Wes said awkwardly.

"What pass in the mind ain't stealin' chickens," Kuba said. "Anyway, you goin' on to Ohio one of these days. So you tell me."

"It's true, Uncle. I like it here, and the people treat me good. All the same, I can't stay."

"So don't pester my daughter, boy."

"I won't," Wes said. "Just greet her, that's all."

And so whenever Wes saw Agagonay he greeted her, but turned his eyes away and pretended to be concerned with other things that required his attention. But now Agagonay seemed to move more slowly when she passed, or to be involved in things nearby rather than far away. Kuba noticed without seeming to, and he said no more to Wes about it. Wes's avoidance of Agagonay accomplished nothing for him. He began to dream of her at night, and sometimes he awoke with a feeling of guilt that in his sleep he had somehow violated his pledge to Kuba. Often he slept only fitfully. One morning Julian said, "Boy, you throw yourself around like you thrashin' rice last night."

Several weeks later the Muskogee came. A Tsoyaha hunter reported that a band looking like a war party was heading toward the lake. There was a council in the village. Some men advised one thing, some another. When it was over, the women and small children were sent into hiding in the woods, and the men prepared to fight. Several half-grown boys remained with the men.

Wes approached Katanay and said, "Give me a gun."

Kuba translated. The men discussed it. Kuba said: "Ain't got enough guns for all. Take a club or a bow."

Wes accepted a club that was offered him, made from a hardwood root with a ball of stone lashed to the end. Julian said he guessed he'd try a bow. They went out to a place near the lake and concealed themselves behind an outcropping of rock. There were twenty-eight in the party, counting the boys. Only Katanay and three other men had horses. All the others were on foot. "If we had horses for all," Kuba said, "we could drive them Muskogee off easy." When the Muskogee came in sight it was evident that they also were short of horses. All but ten were on foot.

Katanay and the other mounted Tsoyaha rode into the open and took possession of the high ground in the path of the Muskogee advance. Four abreast, they waited. There were about thirty-five men in the Muskogee party. They halted, and six riders came forward to talk with Katanay. Katanay sat straight and impassive, his white hair reflecting in the sun. The talk was accompanied with many gestures because the speech of the Muskogee and the Tsoyaha was not the same.

There seemed to be an understanding. The Muskogee began to move again, past the four mounted Tsoyaha and toward the far end of the lake. Katanay and his escort remained where they were, but turned their horses around to watch the Muskogee party go leisurely across the field. The strangers were at the other end of the open field now, about to disappear into the trees. Suddenly their mounted men wheeled and galloped back, making piercing war cries as they came. The four Tsoyaha remained motionless until the Muskogee fired their first shots. Then they too were in motion, riding off at an angle to draw the attackers toward where the main Tsoyaha force was hidden. The Muskogee were met with a fusillade of musket balls and arrows. Three of them fell, and the others wheeled once more and rode back to the end of the field to regroup. Several Tsoyaha moved swiftly to retrieve the Muskogee muskets, and they brought back two horses as well. The odds had changed. There were now six mounted Tsoyaha and seven mounted Muskogee. They came together once more in the center of the field. Unmounted Muskogee and Tsoyaha joined the battle.

Wes heard sharp battle cries all around him. He balanced his clumsy weapon in his hand. When a Muskogee rider came galloping toward him, Wes threw his club. It struck the rider in the shoulder, causing him to drop his musket. Wes picked up the gun and fired it. Both parties fell back to reload their weapons. The firing continued at long range, until the Muskogee suddenly desisted and moved into the shelter of the woods, leaving five dead behind. Three of the Tsoyaha also were dead. Another had a leg wound, and Julian's arm was bleeding from an arrow. The dead and injured were carried back to the village on horses. The Tsoyaha had begun with four ponies. They now had six, and they were richer by four muskets.

"How come them Muskogee passed by so peaceable and then come back like they did?" Wes asked.

Kuba said: "They don't know if they can whup us. They think maybe they's more of us around. They's tired. They been fightin' somewhere already. All they after is the horses. They talk it over after they pass, think maybe they get the horses quick and go away before more Tsoyaha people come. Now they lost two horses of they own. They not come back till they get more men."

Tsoyaha scouts were stationed at the outposts that night while the funeral orations were given. The bodies of the dead men were laid out, each in his own house, and washed and dressed in their best leggings and moccasins. Their breast pendants were placed around their necks, and their tobacco pouches fastened to their waistbands. Outside, in the large circle around the fire, the praises were given. The story of each of the dead men was told, his bravery and accomplishments in battle recounted. Then the orations went on to describe the actions of the other men and boys. The narrators crouched, gestured, and moved about the fire as they acted out details of the fight. One of the orators danced around the circle, pausing to point his ceremonial stick, decorated with feathers, at Wes and Julian. ("He speak of you," Kuba whispered. "He say today you make yourself true brother to the Tsoyaha. He say we lost three men but gain two.") When the speaker was finished, Wes was presented with the musket he had taken in the battle, and Julian was given a bow.

Katanay, in his turn, spoke solemnly, looking backward in time, of the greatness of the Tsoyaha people, their ancient victories and their ordeals. The Muskogee, he said, remained a tribulation, for they gave the Tsoyaha only the choice of fighting and dying or becoming vassals and slaves. But though the Muskogee were many compared to the Tsoyaha, they were being split and scattered. Some had gone out of the villages and become servants of the white men. Other villages had broken away from the nation and become the Seminole. But the Tsoyaha, though they were diminished, lived on. Pressed though they were, they still held to the land where they were born. When we die and are seen no more, Katanay said, still this land will be known as the country of the Tsoyaha.

In the morning, graves were dug in the earthen floors of the houses were the dead men had lived, and their bodies were buried there.

That the Muskogee would come again was taken for granted, perhaps next time in overwhelming numbers. For they had left their dead behind and lost horses and guns, and they must return to regain their honor. Perhaps next week, or next year, or the year after. Some time or other they would come.

Wes said to Kuba: "Me and my friend come a long way. We see plenty fields, plenty woods, plenty rivers. How come you people don't move on, so the Muskogee don't find you? They's too many. My people say when a man is alive, he got no right to throw it away."

Kuba said simply: "This country belong to the Tsoyaha."

Only once in the next few weeks were the quiet routines again disturbed. Four white men came riding from the east, and they stopped to ask directions. Wes and Julian were instructed to remain out of sight, but Kuba stood at Katanay's side to translate. The white men looked at Kuba curiously, but made no comment about him. They were searching for a slave coffle that was supposed to be coming from Tennessee, destined for the Mississippi Territory. When they were gone, the life of the town went on.

Wes began to be troubled about thoughts of Kuba's daughter. And one day when he stood watching her from a distance Kuba came up silently behind him and spoke. "I tell you before, she's not for no man but a Tsoyaha. But you runaways ain't runaways no more. You belong to the Tsoyaha town now."

"Uncle," Wes said, "I don't know how to tell you about it. I don't keep company with her, I don't talk with her. But she's on my mind, Uncle."

"Like I told you," Kuba said, "the town accept you. You are a Tsoyaha now."

That evening Wes met Agagonay coming from the lake with a pot of water. They both stopped on the trail. Agagonay said something he couldn't understand. "You been talkin' and talkin'," Wes said, "and you ain't said a word of English. But I 'spect I can carry water as good as you." He took the pot, which she gave up reluctantly. It seemed to Wes she was scolding. "Believe I got to teach you English," he said. "I ain't heard a word a man can understand."

She went on talking. He listened, watching her face and seeing her lips form sounds, as though some old secret had suddenly been revealed to him. She reached for the pot and tried to take it. He laughed and set it on his head. It came to him that never before had a pot of water had so much meaning. They tussled for its possession and the water spilled. Agagonay began to scold again, but seeing the water dripping down Wes's nose she began to laugh.

"Now you done it, girl," Wes said. He was overcome with a contentment he had never felt before. "Well," he said looking away and gesturing toward the lake, " 'spect we got to go fill it up again."

They walked slowly, holding the pot between them, swinging it as though it were a game. When they passed through the cornfield they sometimes became entangled in the stalks, provoking them to laugh again. At the edge of the lake, Agagonay refilled the pot and set it down on a flat rock. She waded into the water without removing her moccasins and stood watching the swallows dart and curve overhead. Wes looked on silently, noticing every move she made. It was as though all the paths in the world had led him to this place. He waded into the lake after her. Agagonay retreated into deeper water, then began to run through the shallows. Wes followed. He caught her by the skirt and they both fell. They lay for a moment, laughing, quietly sensing the water lapping against their bodies. Wes arose, lifted Agagonay and carried her to the shore, surprised at how light she was. He put her in the dry grass and sat down. They removed their wet moccasins, both talking, neither trying to fathom the other's words, both acutely aware of each other.

Wes reached for Agagonay without any thoughts in his mind at all, as though the volition belonged to the grove of trees where they were hidden. They were enveloped in the fading light of evening, while overhead the swallows continued to dart and swoop over the shore of the lake. They remained there until long after darkness had fallen, and when they returned at last, without the water jar, the Tsoyaha town was asleep.

Often after that they were together in the evenings. In the daytime when he was hunting or fishing with the men, Wes frequently looked toward the sun, measuring how much time remained before nightfall. When he slept it was almost without dreams, and when he awoke in the morning it was as though, like Kuba, he had been born a second time. Somehow the Tsoyaha town and all the wilderness around it belonged to Wes now in a way that his native village in Dahomey never had. As the weeks slipped by, only the little events distinguished one day from another. Kuba watched, seemed to see nothing, but was aware of everything.

Then, one night, Wes dreamed of something that was outside the Tsoyaha town, and he awoke with a feeling of heaviness in his breast. It seemed that he had heard the voices of men who were no longer among the living. The heaviness ebbed a little during the day, but that night when he was with Agagonay it seemed to her that Wes was listening for sounds in the distance. Even when he smiled his eyes betrayed a fever within him. When he went hunting he no longer measured the height of the sun. Though his companions saw it, they said nothing.

A morning came when Wes awoke flooded with the knowledge that he could not stay here with the dying Tsoyaha. Though they had given him everything, it was not his. If it was true that every man owned a share of the world, Wes's share was not here. Whereas before he had been only quiet and troubled, now he was morose.

One day Kuba said to him: "The winter has come on you. This is your town, these are your people. Stay and make your own house. The Tsoyaha will give you a new name."

Wes struggled to find the words. "Uncle," he said, "the Tsoyaha are my people forever. But I can't do it, Uncle. I hear from the Old People in my dreams. My Fa, it drives me."

Kuba did not answer immediately. He gave all his attention to greasing and cleaning his musket. After a while he looked up, not at Wes, but at a high tree across the lake. "My daughter, Agagonay, she is a Tsoyaha. She must stay here," Kuba said.

Wes said: "Your daughter, I love this girl. But I must go with my Fa."

"Agagonay is Tsoyaha," Kuba said again, "she must stay."

Later Wes went to find Julian. "Old Yella, is he my dog or your dog?" he asked.

Julian said: " 'Spect we got to cut him down the middle."

"Make you a bet," Wes said. "First one to kill game gets the whole dog."

"That's fine, just fine," Julian said. They took muskets and went hunting.

"What kind of meat it got to be?" Julian said.

"Any kind on four feet," Wes said, "no birds."

"Son," Julian said, "you must be endeared to that crazy dog."

They separated, Julian crossing to the north side of the meadow, Wes moving along the south side. Wes stalked silently, his senses tense. Once there was a rustling in the leaves, and he brought his gun up, but it was only a big partridge which took to the air with thundering wings. For a time he saw nothing more, until he spied a buck grazing on a distant knoll. He moved around in a wide arc to get downwind, then crept forward. When he arrived, there was no buck to be seen. He moved stealthily around the hill. On the far side his buck was lying under a tree. As it sprang up, Wes went down on one knee and fired. The buck staggered, tried to run. But he ran crazily and awkwardly. Wes dropped his musket and raced forward, caught the animal around the neck with one arm and killed it with his knife. He heard Julian coming.

"Looks to me," Julian said, "as if you just won yourself a no-good yella dog. How come you laughin' now, when just before you was almost cryin'? How come you need Old Yella all to yourself anyway?"

"Hush up," Wes said. "Put this meat on my back."

On the way back they stopped to rest near the edge of the lake.

Julian said: "You got somethin' botherin' your mind. It ain't the yella dog. Since you win that dog from me, it should make you happy. But it don't. You act poor and miserable."

"They was a man one time, walkin' in the night," Wes

said. "He fall into a deep pit dug for game. And when daylight come he see a buffalo done fall in that pit the day before and kill itself on the spears. The man was happy. If he crawl up on the buffalo he can get out. But he get to thinkin' about it. He cut off some of the buffalo meat and ate it. He think maybe he could stay there a while till he's hungry again. Later he ate more meat. Never had so much meat to hisself. He stayed on. Every day he ate more, till the buffalo was all gone. Time to go now. But it's too late. He's got no dead buffalo to stand on, and besides that he's got hisself too fat to climb. So he's finished. He stayed there till he died, and his bones was mix with those of the buffalo."

"Sure a fool, ain't he?" Julian said. "But how come it makes you so miserable?"

"We done fall into the pit with the game," Wes said. "The buffalo is half gone. We got to leave this place."

Julian thought about it. "I don't know," he said. "When I run off with you I don't never figure to meet up with a place like this. I done killed a white man. Where can I go? In this place it don't matter. No one seeks me here. The people is friendly. Don't know as I care to leave. Why you so anxious?"

"It ain't the place I started for," Wes said. "I ain't been cared for so good since I can remember, but it ain't my place here. What happened back on the island ain't what made up my mind to go. It just give me the signal. I can read and write characters. But they ain't no characters here. These people don't want such things. I don't know where I'm goin', but I got to go."

Julian reflected on Wes's thoughts. He said: "They's plenty fishin' to be done here. I got nowhere to go. Nobody is waitin' for me. This poor boy better stay on a while and see what happen."

Wes said: "Julian, these people is dyin' out. One day this town goin' to be only a graveyard, and all the people will be gone."

"Ain't you see old Katanay face down them Muskogee?" Julian said. "They was proudness in him. These people goin' to make it. I ain't afeared for them."

"They is proudness in all of them," Wes said, "but it's the proudness of death. I cannot stay no more, 'cause I got the proudness of life."

He picked up the buck and wrestled it onto his shoulder. They returned to the camp. Wes left his kill in front of Katanay's house. Then he found Old Yella and brought him to Kuba.

"Uncle," he said, "when I meet up with you I got only one thing belong to me, part of a yella dog. Other part belong to my friend Julian. Today I fix it with him. Old Yella belong to me now. I wonder many times why this dog find us out there in the wilderness. Last night I came to understand. I want to leave you somethin'. I leave you Old Yella. He will hunt for you. Old Yella now belong to you."

"I accept him," Kuba said. "You must follow your spirit."

In the evening Wes sought out Agagonay where she pounded grain in her mortar. He stood near but did not speak, and she did not break the silence. After a while he took the cord with the brass figure from around his neck and slipped it over Agagonay's head. Still he was unable to say anything, and after a while he went away.

That night sleep would not come. He left his blanket and went out into the open. He heard the night birds, the frogs along the lake and the wind in the distant pine trees. He smelled the dew-laden air and the ashes of the dead fires. He accused himself. Everything was here. Here were friends. Here was a common soul. Here was Agagonay. Here they would give him a new name. All that was required was that he arise in the morning as usual and go hunting with Kuba. Yet when he finally went back to his blanket he knew that he had hunted with Kuba for the last time.

He was alone now, following the setting sun, drifting a little to the north as the big river flowed. He carried the gun, the shot and the powder that the Tsoyaha had given him. For his daily food he caught small game in snares or fish from the river. Several times he saw Indians in dugout canoes, and once he had to detour in a wide circle through dense woods to avoid white men camped on the river bank. At night he slept in high dry places where the mosquitoes did not plague him. On the fourth or fifth day (he was beginning to lose track of time) he crossed a rutted wagon trail that led to a wooden shed at the river's edge.

Then, unexpectedly, he was in inhabited country with cleared fields, houses and barns. From a distance he could hear human voices and crowing roosters, and from time to time he could see the silhouette of a man and a mule plowing on a hilltop. He rested there on the edge of civilization, as the white people called it, contemplating his next move. The shadows were beginning to grow long. At last Wes made his way up the hill. He stopped at the plowed furrows and waited for the plowman to return.

He heard him before he saw him again; the voice was sharpened in the open air, with faint echoes from the wall of trees behind. "Come on, you overgrowed jackass, 'fore I belt you one! Eeee-ah! Move, son, move! Else take over the plow and I'll draw for you! Eeee-ah! Straighten out, keep you mouth off'n them greens! Don't you hear me talkin' to you? Lean into it, move!" The mule's head appeared first over the horizon, then the body, unconcerned with the urgings and flickings from behind. The man was tall and dark, his face and chest glistening with sweat. He saw Wes from afar, but gave no sign of recognition until he came abreast, when he shouted, "Whoa, you four-footed overgrowed jackass, whoa when I tell you!" Looking at Wes, he said: "This is the orneriest she-devil mule in forty miles, got no mind for nothin' but grass. She plow the crookedest furrow I ever see, must have short legs on one side."

"Look like mighty straight furrows to me," Wes said.

"That's cause I keep her strained straight. Leave her alone and she go in zigzags and circles." His eyes took in Wes's buckskin clothes and his gun. "Catch any deer out there?"

"Ain't huntin' exactly," Wes said.

"Thought maybe you was one of Crawford's men. But I guess you must of come further than that. Folks don't wear clothes like that around here."

"Who's Crawford?" Wes said.

"He's a planter over west of here. He send his men out for deer and bear sometimes. Too fat to go hisself. Anyway, it ain't huntin' he like so much as bear steak. Seen any bear out there?"

Wes shook his head.

"Where you bound for?" the man said suddenly.

Wes motioned vaguely toward the west. The man busied himself adjusting the harness, and from somewhere under the mule he said: "Who you belong to?"

"Belong to nobody," Wes said firmly.

"No? Then I expect you are a free nigger."

"That's what I am," Wes replied.

"You been livin' with the Creek?"

"Tsoyaha."

"Never hear they name before."

"Some folks calls them Yuchi."

"If you free, what you doin' round here?"

"I'm on my way," Wes said.

"Runaway?"

Wes was silent.

"Well, you worse off than me. I'm Jim Harris's man, cause he bought me in Charleston, but I reckon I'm more free than you."

"How come?"

"I tell you how come. I can walk down this road twenty miles, north or south, and no one bother me. They say,

'That's Jeb, Jim Harris's nigger.' You, man, you can't walk down the road either way."

"Don't plan to tarry around here," Wes said.

"You hungry?"

"Not too bad. I fished some."

"Go on back down by the trees till dark. I'll send you somethin' to chew on."

"Mighty obliged to you," Wes said.

"Come on, you overgrowed jackass," the man shouted, "why you standin' there?"

Wes retraced his steps to the edge of the field. He found a protected place among the trees and fell asleep in a bed of leaves.

That night the plowman and his son came with some bacon and corn bread. While Wes ate, the man talked. "You got to take a wide turn here less you want trouble. The way you headed is lots of people that's suspicious of strange niggers. Go on south till you meet the river, then swing again. 'Nother thing, you better shuck them Indian clothes and the musket. If you caught with the musket you're a dead man. Don't say I ain't warn you."

Long before sunup Wes was on his way again. For two days he skirted the plantations, then he was in the wilderness once more, charting his direction by the sun and the north star.

He traveled steadily, stopping only to camp for the night or to catch game. Once he found no small game for two days, and in his hunger he killed a bear with his musket. He carried some of the meat with him, and discarded it at last when it became spoiled. Though the country was wild, he came every so often on signs of human settlement. From time to time there were wagon trails, and several times he sighted rafts or boats on the river. Once there was a flotilla of eight Indian canoes. At the possibility of confrontation with men, Indian or white, Wes retreated into the underbrush.

He came to think of himself as a man of the forest, like Ota, of whom he had heard tales when he was a child. Ota-with-the-Matted-Beard, he was called. For some old and forgotten sin against the vodouns, Ota had been exiled from the village to the forest. There he lived, unkempt and naked, trapping and digging roots. At the sound of hunters, Ota fled into the darkest shadows of the forest, unable to bear the shame of being seen living like an animal. Wes felt a kinship for Ota now, for the unfortunate man had been caught in the grip of a Fa too great and too terrible to understand.

As for his own Fa, Wes believed he understood it, or at least he accepted its reality. The task was to recognize it for what it was, to comprehend its meaning. His mind went back continually to the story he had told Julian about the hunter who had pursued a deer to the land of the dead, never to return. In this story Fa was revealing itself to Wes. Yet, being bound to the wilderness, he nevertheless felt the need to be aware. For a destiny without awareness was only a meaningless waste of life.

Thus he often asked himself, "Who am I?" And he answered silently, "I am Hwesuhunu the Fon. I remember my father and mother and brothers. I remember my village. I have kept faith with the vodouns and the ancestors. I am he who lives out his Fa, all that has been written down by Mawu." But to the question, "Where am I going?" he had no ready answer. And he wondered why he was pressing westward, when in this direction there lay hundreds of miles of wilderness interspersed with plantations. Where there were plantations there was slavery. The free country lay elsewhere, far to the north. Why, then, this way?

The answer came to him unexpectedly one night when he was roasting a fish in the coals of his fire: Liberty Island. It lay out there somewhere on the river. But was it real, or only a legend? Or was it like the ancient city of Wagadou which lived and disappeared, only to reappear again centuries later? Of Wagadou it was said that it lived every hundred years, and in the years between it lived only in men's minds. Yet Wes was confident that Liberty Island was out there somewhere. It was the place where slaves took refuge when their insurrections failed, a place where men came in the pride of living free, far in the wilderness where the bounty hunters, the militia and the dogs did not follow.

It was on the northern bank of the river that he met Jaeger. Wes stood in a screen of cane and saw the cabin, smoke spiraling from its crude chimney. For the first time the urge to remain invisible was equaled by a need to hear a human voice. He was afflicted by a sense of lostness and loneliness, and he stood there at the water's edge, careless of his safety, assessing the cabin and its unseen occupant. When he heard the voice he yearned to hear it came from behind. Wes spun around. There stood the man, short and bearded, appraising him. He spoke with the heavy accent of one born in a distant land.

"Ya," he said, "so what is it? You are looking for the master of the house?"

Wes nodded, uncertain of how he must act in the presence of this white man, though the man seemed somehow to be a race apart. "Go in, go in!" the man said impatiently. "Do not stand there like a stubborn mule!" Wes approached the cabin, the man behind him. "Well, so it is, you have arrived," the man said. "I am Jaeger, the renegade. And you?" Wes was considering what he might say. "You are an Indian on the outside, but you do not fool me. You are a *neger,* no? So we are even. On the outside I am a Christian, on the inside a pagan. I believe in spirits. Like this butterfly." He held up a yellow winged butterfly and examined it critically. "This one I found in the woods. What is its color, its size? It doesn't matter. What I look for is the spirit. Also, the spirit of the trees. Even the rocks, who knows? Ya, I am an animist. And what are you, a damned black Christian here to convert me?"

Wes found the words at last. "Uncle, I am Wes Hunu."

Jaeger spoke sharply: "Uncle, am I? Well, thank you, but do not call me uncle. I have turned my back on the human race. I don't want it. They don't want me. Together we are both miserable. Apart we are happier. Two kinds of craziness do not go together. Yes, I am a little bit crazy. But the rest of the human race is mad. You are a runaway?"

Wes nodded.

"Good, then we are both runaways. Maybe you are a little crazy too. If so we are friends. If you are not willing to be a little crazy, go about your business. What is your name again?"

"Wes Hunu."

"Ya, that is a crazy name. Come and sit. But turn that damned musket the other way. You will not make bear grease out of me."

Wes sat on a tree stump while Jaeger went inside with his butterfly. In a few minutes Jaeger came out with a piece of crude corn bread which he handed to Wes. "Eat some. How stupid it is, how we eat. Eat, eat, all the time. But it don't feed the spirit. Do you know there are some insects that eat nothing at all? And what is eating for? It is a prison, this eating. All your life you must grub and grub for something to eat. Why are you looking at me that way? Because I am out of my senses or because you think I am a damned *neger* owner in disguise?"

"No, Uncle, I do not think so. I only listen."

"Well, I will tell you something. I was a *neger* owner. I had a farm. I could not stand the farming or the *negers* either. I was a slave myself to the farm and the *negers*. They tell me what to do. They drive me like a mule. I do not like this slavery, so I run away. One damned *neger* of mine, he follow me for fifty miles and try to make me come home. But I slip away in the night and I'm rid of him. Farming is all right, but only to stuff yourself with food all the time. So I am here. I catch a fish now and then and I am pleased with myself. I do not talk so much only because you are here. I talk all the time. I do not need people to make talk. Where are you going?"

"Out there somewhere, to Liberty Island."

"Ach, dumbhead. There's no Liberty Island. How can there be liberty where there are people? The place you are going to, they will eat each other up like cannibals. The damned *negers* that were slaves, they want to be masters. They will chew each other like the mantis. You, maybe you are a mantis also. Did you kill an Indian for the buckskin you were wearing?"

"No, Uncle, I lived with them. The clothes and the gun, they gave them to me." Wes was aware of a great heaviness inside him. He was homesick for the Tsoyaha. And in his mind he saw the face of Agagonay. He wondered why he pressed day by day farther and farther away from the village.

"Well," Jaeger said, "so you are a savage. That is fine. I too am a savage. You can sleep in the cabin if you want. Me, I must hunt in the woods for wild tea and tobacco. You do not think so, you damned Christian? Well, if you have eyes I will show you when I come back."

Wes went inside the cabin, put his musket in the corner and slept on the earthen floor.

When he awoke, Jaeger was at the fireplace cooking. Scooping food from the pot onto a metal plate which he passed to Wes, Jaeger said: "Here, fill your savage belly, and then I give you forest tea, yes?" Wes ate what he took for rabbit stew, though he could identify nothing on the plate. Jaeger was silent, his brows furrowed, his thoughts far away. He seemed to forget that Wes was there. Suddenly he blurted out: "The double diurnal oscillation of the barometer! Ya!" And turning to Wes excitedly, he exclaimed: "The world turns, no? Like a top! And moves around the sun? Twice each damned day the speed of any spot on the earth changes —faster, slower, faster, slower! So the barometer does a dance each time! Is it not so?"

He looked demandingly at Wes, but Wes could think of nothing to say.

Jaeger shook his head. "What can an Indian *neger* know of such things as a barometer? Eat, eat, that's all he knows." He poured a steaming hot liquid from an iron pot into a broken china cup. "Drink it."

Wes drank. It was bitter at first, then pleasant.

"Forest tea," Jaeger said with contempt. "All the damned planters know is cotton. Can you drink it? No. But do they look around to see what is growing in nature's cotton patch? The forest is a Garden of Eden. Forest tea, waiting to be picked from the bushes." He showed Wes the leaves from which the tea was brewed, and told him where they were to be found.

The next morning Jaeger looked critically at Wes. "You know how to catch rabbit? Good. You catch rabbit for me, I go out to nature." Wes set snares that morning. In the afternoon he went out with his musket and killed a buck deer, which he carried back to the cabin over his shoulders. Jaeger stood there angrily waiting for him.

"You damned *neger* scoundrel! I said rabbit, not deer! The deer, I do not touch them, they are my people in the forest! And that shot will be heard across the river. Next thing you know all the damned dumbheads will be coming and snooping around."

But Wes skinned and quartered the deer and hung the meat over a greenwood fire to smoke.

By the time two days had elapsed Jaeger had forgotten his outrage and absentmindedly ate the smoked venison. Wes's traps yielded abundantly, and there was more food in storage than required. He looked around for chores, but after he had laid up a large supply of cut wood for the fireplace there was little else to do. He took to following Jaeger on his daily jaunts through the countryside, observing and listening to the man talk to himself. Most of the time Jaeger was only half aware, or not aware at all, of Wes's presence. But occasionally he lectured Wes on some of his theories or discoveries.

"Habit," he said on one occasion. "Some of these damned trees don't think, they just do things from habit. Dumbheads. Look at that one. All the leaves gone, and the other trees are full. Maybe it's just stubborn, ya? I fix it some time. I will dig it up and freeze it for six months, only for that I have to have ice. Then I plant it again and the leaves will all come out the wrong time and go away the wrong time. Some of those damned trees are just as confused as people."

It was on one of these daily jaunts that they encountered bounty hunters. They were prowling along the edge of the river when two canoes appeared around a bend. The canoes swung and moved toward the shore. Jaeger looked angry. In one of the canoes were two white men, in the second a white man and an Indian. They stepped out on the bank and stretched their legs. One of the white men nodded cordially to Jaeger. "Howdy," he said, "is there a settlement below here on the river?"

"Why should there be a settlement?" Jaeger said testily. "There are enough people already. Some there are should go home."

"You live around here?"

"I am alive, ya? What are you looking for?"

"Well, we been hired to catch some runaway niggers. We heard there were a few along the river."

"Runaway *negers?* You are *neger* catchers? Go away, there is nothing to catch but rabbits here, and damned if I ever see any black ones, only white."

The man glanced at Wes. "This one belong to you?"

"Belong to me? Yes, this no good one belongs to me. I would trade him for a good horse. He is lazy and sassy. But just the same he belongs to me. You want him? Eight hundred dollars cash."

"We ain't buyin' niggers, we just huntin' down runaways."

"Oh, you want *negers* for nothing, ya? There are no *negers* for nothing around here."

"You got a plantation down the river?"

"Plantation? That is for the crazy ones on the other side. I have a place, ya, but it's too small for you. It's not for people, only room for me and my *neger.* Go to the other side."

The man looked again at Wes, his unsatisfied curiosity showing in his face.

"What's your name, boy?"

"Boy?" Jaeger said. "Does this no good lazy *neger* look like a boy to you? He's a man, except he's a dumbhead. He's no good, but he's the only one I got."

The man examined Wes's buckskin clothes slowly, then turned to speak to the Indian. Wes could not understand what was said, but he heard the word Tsoyaha. "Where'd the nigger get them Indian clothes?" the man asked.

"Ach, he got them from the savages," Jaeger said. "This ungrateful *neger* run off and make at home with the redskins, I have to chase him two weeks. So ungrateful he was. When I catch him I beat him, ya. I make him cry. Now he don't want to run away no more." Turning to Wes angrily, Jaeger said: "Ach, do not stand there like a tree! Get back to the garden and start hoeing the cotton! Don't leave no damned weeds this time, or I take the stick to you! And when you finish with that, haul some water to the big kettle and wash the clothes! *Raus,* you lazy bones!"

Wes left the men standing on the shore and went back to the cabin.

"You make him wash clothes too?" the bounty hunter said. "Ain't you got no females?"

"Females?" Jaeger said. "Who wants the damned females hanging around?"

The man seemed to lose interest in Wes once he was

gone. "You ain't seen no runaways around here, have you?"

"No runaways," Jaeger said. "Why you chase so much the runaways? Let them be. There are too many *negers* anyway."

"Price on runaways is up," the man said. "Planters having trouble getting new African niggers these days. They cost too much. Have to pay up to twelve or fifteen hundred dollars for a prime slave sometimes. Catching the runaways is cheaper. They paying fifty dollars all the way to two hundred for a runaway. Sometimes we can sell 'em off for new."

"Well, no damned runaways around here," Jaeger said.

The men got back into the canoes and shoved off. After they were out of sight Jaeger resumed his prowling among the trees. When he returned to the cabin he found Wes sitting at the door.

"Didn't see no cotton patch, Uncle. No iron pot, neither."

"Ach," Jaeger said, "what a lazy dumbhead *neger.*"

A few days later Wes prepared to leave. Jaeger insisted that he take some of the smoked venison with him. "You are a stubborn savage," he said. "You should go north, instead you go west. North is the place for the black dumbheads, not Mississippi."

"I got a reason, Uncle. I'm mighty obliged for all you done for me."

"I haven't done nothing for you. I try to civilize you, that's all. But what can you do with a savage? So now you're going I will have peace and quiet again."

"I goin' to remember you, Uncle."

Jaeger had nothing more to say. He busied himself examining a grasshopper, refusing to look up as Wes disappeared among the trees.

A few days later Wes ran into the four bounty hunters again, camped along the river's edge. It was the Indian who spotted him and alerted the others.

"Let's get him," one of the men shouted. "He's prime stock and worth a thousand to anybody!"

Wes veered into the tangled underbrush and struggled to higher ground among the hardwood trees. He ran then, dodging from side to side where the cover was heaviest. He heard the voices behind him, muffled in the foliage but not far off. He reached an open stretch and sprinted across. On the far side he dropped panting to the ground and loaded his musket with powder and ball. He waited. The first of his pursuers he saw was the Indian. Before the Indian was halfway across the open, Wes fired. The Indian turned and ran back the way he had come. Wes could see the others standing hesitantly among the trees. He abandoned his river course altogether and struck out northward. It was slow going, but it was clear that the river was not safe.

In the week that followed he detoured around two large plantations. He was so close that he could hear the bell summoning the slaves to the compound, and a few times he even heard the voices of women calling and laughing in the fields. But during these days it was hard to find enough to eat. For some reason no game entered his snares. He ate wild onions and berries. And he was already thinking of returning to the river where he could catch fish when he came upon a rocky creek that flowed toward the west. Here he caught a small trout and roasted it at midday. He had not followed along the creek more than an hour when he reached a small clearing, at the other side of which stood a rickety cabin made of logs and mud, surrounded by small patches of garden. From behind a woodpile a dark face emerged.

"Hey, there," the man said, "where you goin' and what you want in this place?"

" 'Scuse me," Wes said, "didn't see you there, Uncle."

"Not s'posed to see me. I'm s'posed to see you. You a Creek nigger?"

"No, I ain't no Creek. Some Indian friends give me these things."

The man came out from behind his woodpile, ax in hand. He was small and bent, and walked with a limp. His clothes were ragged and grotesque. The shirt was nothing but a tattered memory, and more skin showed than cloth. The trousers were blue with white polka dots, and appeared to have been adapted crudely from a woman's skirt. He wore one shoe, and the foot on which he limped was bare.

"This way take me to Liberty Island?" Wes asked.

"How come you goin' to a place like that?"

"I hear of it, and I make up my mind."

"What you hear, that it's the land of milk and honey?"

"What's wrong with Liberty Island? I hear of this place a hundred miles away."

"That show you what's wrong with the world," the man said, shaking his head. "People go by *words.* Pick the right word and you got 'em eatin' out of your hand like chickens. Turn back, son, turn back! Go find yourself a mean old white master somewhere and do yourself a favor."

"What you know about Liberty Island?" Wes insisted.

"I seen 'em go in and I seen 'em come out. They goes in like babes to a christenin', comes back like they runnin' from all the devils in hell."

"You ever been there yourself?"

"No, never been there. Ain't never see it myself."

"Well, I got to find out then," Wes said.

"Go on, go on. I don't bar the path. On to the devil's ball. Foller the creek to the river, turn east till you hit the cedar swamp, and you is almost all the way to hell. From there you can see it out in the river. Make your way across on the driftwood. See you here again next July, maybe, goin' the other way."

"You livin' here alone?" Wes asked. "You a free man?"

"Free as I'll ever be," the man said, honing his ax on a smooth stone.

"You got any papers?"

"Papers? Don't mean a thing. I was slave to old Joe

Barnes, the only slave he got. Joe Barnes couldn't write no papers if he wanted, didn't know the characters. He was cuttin' wood one day and a big swamp oak fall on him. I bury him, say the words over his grave. Ain't nobody but me know old Joe Barnes was ever alive. I come down here and make my cabin. I traps and grows my corn. And when I got nothin' much to do I watches the parade to and fro from the island. Papers? Why I knowed of one man got papers, signed by the sign of the white master who freed him. They catch this nigger one day whilst he was on the road, said they got another runaway. So he brought out the paper from his pocket. They tell him, 'Nigger, you can read this thing?' He say no, he ain't had time to learn the characters. They say, 'Well, this old paper ain't nothin' but a worn-out old list for the general store.' And they take him back. That's all. So don't speak of no papers. And don't tell me no more about Liberty Island, just get on to it."

Wes continued along the creek. Before nightfall he reached the river, and he bedded down among the trees. But he slept badly because of the torment of mosquitoes that swarmed around him. He arose at dawn covered with bites and went along the vegetation-choked bank until he came to the cedar swamp. While he stood there contemplating the half-submerged tree trunks and the litter of driftwood, he saw a woman paddling a dugout canoe through the open water. He waved, and she turned and guided her craft toward the shore.

"You want across?" she said.

Wes nodded.

"Cost you ten cents."

"Ain't got no hard money."

"Well, you can cross by foot over there. You a new one?"

"I come to look it over."

"Got any folks here?"

"No mam."

"Got anything to trade?"

Wes shook his head.

"Want to trade the musket?"

"What for?"

"Well, for victuals, somethin' like that."

"Don't need no victuals."

"You better off to trade it if you comin' in."

"'Spect I better keep it," Wes said.

The woman swung her canoe around and moved away. Wes walked out cautiously on the nearest tree lying among the cane, stepped from there to a tangle of logs and old roots embedded in mud and worked his way toward the low-lying line of pines that marked the edge of Liberty Island. Sometimes there was a stretch of open water between the accumulations of driftwood, and he had to wade. Clouds of mosquitoes rose out of the dampness, attacking with fury. The last stretch of forty or fifty yards was relatively easy, and at last he stood on the mucky shore, which was a desolate tangle of broken and upended trees, vines and brambles. By the time he reached higher ground his skin was scratched and bleeding.

He paused there, waiting for the sensation of freedom to come, the fragment of a moment that arrives on the heels of victory in battle. But it did not come. He felt only a heightening of his senses, like those of the hunter in the forest when he closes in upon his leopard. Or was it the heightening tension of the leopard that he felt? "Well," he said aloud, "so this is Liberty Island." But in his mind he heard another voice saying, "Devil's ball."

In the distance he heard village sounds—the ring of an ax, the high-pitched call of a girl, a shout, a laugh, and behind these sounds the shapeless hum of human life. He followed a muddy trail through the trees, and as he entered the village—camp was a better description, for there was a haphazard and temporary quality about it—he was challenged by two armed men who stood directly in his path. One was naked above the waist except for iron armbands and a red ribbon holding a charm around his neck. The other wore a much patched blue shirt, tied tightly around his waist by a red calico sash.

" 'Dentify you'self!" the man with the armbands said.

"Name is Wes Hunu. I'm just comin' in, just arrive."

"What you want here?"

"Goin' to stay here a spell."

"Who told you so?"

"I hear about Liberty Island. They say a man can come if he need to."

"Who them they you talkin' about?"

"Just folks, nobody in particular."

"Somebody send you?"

"Ain't no one send me. Just like to stay here."

"Listen to that black boy, will you?" the man with the sash said. "He just figure to stay! We don't let just any old people in this place. No, man, not just any old nigger can't come in here. You got to face down the General on that proposition."

"Oh," Wes said, "I thought you two was the generals."

The one with the armbands said: "We're the colonels. I'm Big Tom, colonel of the militia. And this here is 'nother colonel name of Joe Sharp. We in charge of the General's business when he ain't around." He looked at Wes's clothes and his gun with interest. "You got any hard money on you?"

"No, ain't hardly ever had no hard money on me."

"You could turn it over now, be real easy on you. General don't like folk comin' in with hard money all over them."

"Don't have none."

"Might as well give it over as have it took from you," Joe Sharp said.

Wes shook his head.

"Well," Big Tom said, "guess we better take him to the General. He'll take care of everything."

"Sure," Joe Sharp said, "he fix him."

They marched Wes through the camp like a prisoner of war, Big Tom snapping out orders such as "Haw, gee, forward double time! Straightaway now! Circle the fire! Look handy, man, don't dawdle the march!" They zigzagged among open fires and crude shelters that were clearly incapable of keeping out rain. Most were simple lean-to's, others nothing more than grass roofs held aloft by forked sticks. People who moved about among the shelters seemed intent on small invisible purposes. They were raggedly clothed, or hardly clothed at all. Some of the men wore tattered shirts, but most were bare chested, and even some of the women had no cover above their waists. The children who ran about the camp were naked except for the dirt encrusted on their skin. Here and there women sat by merchandise they hoped to sell—scraps of used cloth, bottles, fish already too dry in the sun, rabbit pelts. Two men were arguing loudly over some coonskins. The odors of boiling fish, wood smoke and human excrement blended heavily in the air.

"Walk smart, now!" Big Tom ordered. "Make it look dandy! Haw, now, up there to the Big House, quarters of General Descamps! Whoa, boy, hold it where you are and don't graze off!" He went to the door and called out: "General, Colonel Big Tom talkin'. Just picked up a new man. You want to see him?"

From inside the log cabin that Big Tom called the Big House came a hoarse, gravelly voice. "What he got on him?"

"Don't altogether know," Big Tom said, "but he totin' a musket."

General Descamps appeared instantly, his huge body filling the doorway. He was at least six and a half feet tall, and had rounded muscular shoulders. The lids of his bloodshot eyes drooped as though he were on the edge of sleep. An earthen jug hung from the crook of his little finger. With his other hand he tugged at a scraggly, disheveled beard. He tilted his head back to look down at Wes.

"What's he want here?" Descamps said, distrust and hostility showing in his face.

"Don't know," Big Tom said. "He just came floatin' into camp like he takin' a cool drink of water."

Descamps's eyes fastened on Wes's musket. "Where you get that gun, boy?"

"Took it in an Indian fight," Wes said. "It belongs to me."

"Well, I don't allow folks to carry guns round here 'less they on gov'ment service," Descamps said. "Reach it here."

Wes made no movement to comply. "This gun," he said, "I need it to hunt my meat."

The General's eyes opened wide for the first time. He looked full into Wes's face for a moment, then his lids drooped again. "Boy, 'count of you is new here, reckon I got to tell you 'bout this place. First thing you got to know is this place named Liberty Island. Second thing, now, is the law. I'm the General, and I pass out the law. See what I mean? Now the first thing about the law is ain't no nigger can run around with muskets here. I keeps count of all the muskets inside, in the arsenal. See what I mean? When they's a raid I pass 'em out to the militia. All the other times, I keep 'em inside. So pass over your musket. We make a note of it. What you say your name is?"

"Wes Hunu."

"All right then, Wes Hunu, reach it here and I keep it in charge."

Wes considered for a moment, then he handed the musket to Descamps.

"Also the powder and ball," Descamps said.

Wes gave him the powder horn and the little packet of balls.

"All right," Descamps said, a little sharper tone to his voice now, "we get around to the permissions. You got any hard money?"

Wes shook his head. "Got no money at all, hard or soft."

"Let's see the pockets," Descamps said.

"They's no pockets in these clothes," Wes said. "Indian clothes got no pockets."

"Well, then, what you figure to do 'bout the permissions?"

"What's the permissions?" Wes asked.

"That's second thing in the law," Descamps said. "Law say when a new man come to the Island he got to pay the permissions. That let him in. If he don't pay he got to get out."

"What's the permissions for?" Wes wanted to know.

"What the permissions for?" Descamps echoed, anger showing in his face. "The permissions is for the permissions, that's what!"

"How much it cost?"

"Well, ten dollars can do it."

"Already told you I got no hard money."

Descamps's eyes fixed on Wes's buckskin clothes. "Where you get that shirt?"

"Give to me by friends," Wes said.

"All right, I'll take the shirt for the permissions."

"General," Wes said, "I can't part with this shirt."

The General glared. "I say I'll take the shirt." He raised the jug and took a long drink from it. "I take one more sample of this jug," he said, "and when I finish with it I want the permissions in my hand." He tilted his head and let the liquid gurgle into his mouth. Wes stood motionless. Descamps let the jug down again. "Take the shirt."

Wes felt a blow on the back of his head and found himself on the ground. Big Tom and Joe Sharp were stripping the shirt from him. In a few moments Descamps had the shirt in his hand. Wes arose, his head throbbing. "Now," Descamps said, "get out of my yard and don't give me no more trouble."

Wes walked back through the camp. He felt unsteady and lay down under a tree to rest. Fatigue overcame him. He slept. When he awoke, it was late afternoon. Slowly he became aware of hunger pains. His eyes took in the ground and the litter of fishbones and other refuse. He raised his head slowly, reluctant to see what he already knew was there. It was something like that old slave compound at Abomey, but decayed and devoid of a life force. He sensed listlessness in the air, as though this was the village of the damned in which dwelt all the dead who were denied permission to cross the Azile River in their voyage to the final destination. It was a place in which there was neither hope nor expectation, in which death offered no final solutions and life was lived only from habit. Wes watched an old woman tending a boiling pot. She stirred it without interest, and seemed unaware of the comings and goings around her.

From a nearby lean-to came loud voices. A girl ran out followed by a man. He caught her by the arm and dragged her back. His words were rough, disagreeable. "Where you think you goin', you black gal? Ain't I give you two yards of calico? You tryin' to thief me? Get down 'fore I knock you down." Wes arose and moved away, pausing in the shade of a half dead pine tree. A bearded man sat there whittling. In front of him was a pile of shavings. He was not carving anything at all, merely whittling a stick into nothingness.

"Evenin', Uncle," Wes said. "Is they anything a man can do about somethin' to eat and a place to sleep?"

The whittler looked up in surprise, as though the sound of good evening was strange in his ears. "Evenin'," he said. He cleared his throat and repeated it. "Evenin'." He kept on whittling, as though he did not want to break the continuity of his purpose, slicing his stick into fragments that would never again go together. Wes repeated his question.

"Is they any food around here? And where can I sleep for the night?"

The man motioned vaguely with his knife.

"Sleep? Anywhere you like, don't matter. You can get some catfish in the river."

Finally he put his knife down.

"Guess you new here, ain't you?"

Wes nodded.

"Look to me like you already got your feathers picked. What the Rooster get off you?"

"You mean the General?"

"General? Yeah, Descamps. We calls him the Rooster."

"Took my musket and my shirt."

"Boy, you get off easy."

"He really in charge here?"

"*Make* hisself in charge. Ain't nobody 'lect that man king. He just 'point hisself. Had to whup quite a few stout men to do it. Now he's the Rooster, all right. Killed two men since I been here, throw they corpses in the river. Course, he got them bully boys, call 'em his militia."

"Told me it was the law he had to take my musket."

"Law? He got only one law, pick the chickens and skim the cream."

"I got to find me a place," Wes said.

The man turned his attention once more to his whittling. "Go on out to the edge somewhere. You find something out there."

Wes moved among the trees that encircled the camp. But he found that others were ahead of him. The lean-tos were scattered about everywhere, as dense and as haphazard as on the open ground. He walked on, certain that if he went far enough he would find a little space. But where the shelters ended the oozing marsh began. As Wes turned to try another direction, he observed that he was being followed by a small naked boy.

"Boy," he said, "is they some good dry ground out that way?"

The boy stopped and stared, but said nothing. Wes continued along the edge of the marsh. The human sounds faded behind him, shut off by the trees, and at last he found an uninhabited knoll. Although his body ached from weariness and hunger, he went to work with his knife. He cut down slim saplings which he braced against a gnarled water oak and tied in place with vines. Then he began covering the frame with twigs and leaves. He noticed the boy again, standing in the undergrowth watching him.

"Boy," he said, "where can a man get something to eat around here?"

The boy disappeared into the brush. By now the light was fading rapidly, and Wes resigned himself to turning in without an evening meal. But before he had finished covering his shelter, the boy reappeared with a bundle wrapped in leaves, which he put on the ground. Wes opened it and found four river crabs.

"Son," he said, "you sure saved me. Now all I need is fire."

Again the boy disappeared and when he returned he carried a burning stick. Wes gathered some dry wood and made a fire. He roasted the crabs in the coals and shared them with the boy. They sat on the ground and ate. Wes spoke now and then, but the boy only watched Wes's face in the glow from the fire.

"Where you from, son, where's your mamma and daddy? 'Spects you got a mamma, ain't you?"

The boy stared at the fire.

"Well, then, who you got?"

The boy looked at Wes without expression, and Wes stopped asking. He accepted that the boy had no one. Another thought came to him.

"Son," he said, "can't you talk?"

The boy turned his head, as though he were listening to sounds in the distance.

Total exhaustion came suddenly to Wes. His eyes closed heavily. He crawled into the lean-to and fell instantly into a deep sleep. The boy sat by the fire until it burned itself out, then he crawled into the lean-to and slept on the ground next to Wes.

Wes awakened slowly in the morning. Somewhere nearby a turtle dove made its mournful call, and farther off there were sounds of catbirds, red birds, and crows. Wes lay in pleasant warm comfort, contemplating the beams of early morning light that poked through the leaves overhead. It was only when he moved that he felt the ground under him and the small stones pressing into his back. For a long moment he could not remember where he was. In Yabo? On the Blair plantation? Or should he be up and hunting this morning with Kuba? He thought of Agagonay, and a surge of well-being flooded through him. Then he sat up. Next to him the boy was still sleeping, his thin cheek pressed against the hard ground. Wes remembered now, and there was a pang of regret. So, this was the Liberty Island he had heard so much about. He shook the boy by the shoulder. "Come on, you lazy no good roustabout, we got to fetch somethin' to eat." The boy sat up, rubbed his eyes. "Let's go out and find somethin' to put in our bellies. You reckon it got to be catfish?"

The boy sprang up and ran toward the center of the camp. In a little while he was back, clutching a crude fishhook and a line.

"Where you get that?" Wes said.

The boy only stared back at him.

"You steal it?"

The boy nodded.

"Ain't you know stealin' is a sin?"

The boy shook his head.

"Well, come on," Wes said, "them catfish don't know the difference."

They went down to the river, stopping only to turn over stones to find grubs for bait. They caught a catfish and a small eel and returned to their shelter. The boy again brought a burning stick from someone's fire. Wes cleaned the fish, wrapped them in green leaves and roasted them. As they ate, Wes looked the boy over silently. The boy's belly was rounded, but his legs were thin and his face gaunt.

"You sure you ain't got no folks?" Wes said at last.

The boy shook his head.

"Where you come from, then?"

The boy gestured toward the east. "Well, I reckon you got a name, anyway. How I goin' to know it? Is it John? Joe? Daniel? 'Zekiel?" He tried all the names he could think of. "Seem like I never goin' to get it thisaway. Believe I got to give you a new name. How it be if I call you Ransom? 'Cause you ransom me from hunger with them crabs last night."

The boy stared at Wes and nodded.

"All right, then, Ransom, we christen you with a bath in the river, get all that mud off you. Next thing after that, we got to find you some clothes. You naked as the day you was born."

There were nearly three hundred people on the island, more than two hundred of them men. They spent their days fishing, trapping, bartering skins, meat and scraps of cloth; arguing, boasting, idling, sleeping in the shade, complaining, and looking off into the distance as though there were something out there that couldn't be forgotten. There were only a half dozen or so corn patches on the island, all of them ill-kept. "What the use of plantin' corn or beans, even if you got the seed for it?" one man told Wes. "'Fore it's ripe somebody get in there and strip the stalks, steal everything you got. Better off if you eat the seed, then you have least one good meal out of it. One man build his shelter right in the middle of his patch to guard it. But they come in the middle of the night and nearly whup the life out of that man, take everything fit to eat and tromp the stalks to the ground."

"Who the folk do this thing?" Wes asked.

"Why, just about anybody do it when they's hungry enough. But the whuppin', that come from the Rooster's bully boys. They's two-three men put they gardens on the other side of the river in secret places, but the Rooster root some of 'em out just the same."

A foraging party, led by the General's militia, went out one morning at dawn. They returned two days later with flour, a side of pork, a small calf and two girls about fifteen years old. There was a commotion in front of the General's cabin when the loot was displayed. Descamps commandeered the pork, half the flour, and one of the girls. The argument over the remaining flour and the calf was soon settled. But several of the men claimed the second girl, and their shouts and curses were heard throughout the camp. In the end, two men fought for the prize, and when one lay battered and senseless on the ground the other took the girl to his shelter.

Wes could not get the scene from his mind. It was not so much the battle for the booty as the girl standing terrified against the cabin wall, and Descamps sitting there heavy-eyed with his jug, a look of ultimate authority and pleasure on his face. It was hardly different, Wes thought, from that day with Vespey and Julian's sister. Back on St. Helena a white man had been killed in consequence of such an act. But here it was taken for granted.

"Why they bring new people down here?" Wes later asked the bearded whittler, who still spent his days alternately honing his knife and shredding sticks. "They ain't enough food for what they is."

"Seem plain to me," the man said. "It's the liberation. Make the nigger free. Old Rooster, he the savior of all them people."

"Them two girls, they was took just like prisoners. No one give them no choices."

The man looked sharply at Wes. "You ain't fixin' to straighten things out with the Rooster?"

"Never cross my mind," Wes said. "Take more than one man to do it. Don't 'pear to me as anyone else care 'bout the way things is, though."

"Maybe they do," the man said. "But they ain't talkin' on it, not much anyway. You seen that black man with the ears cut off? He lost four teeth too, all from sayin' he don't care for the way Descamps do things. Already told you two men been killed. And three-four men just disappear, folks don't know if they run away or the Rooster throwed they corpses in the swamp somewhere."

By now Ransom had become a fixture in Wes's household. He went out to set snares with Wes, and patrolled them twice each day. If there was game he brought it back. Wes taught him how to skin rabbits, and how to scrape the skins and peg them out to dry. One morning Ransom came back from the snares in agitation and motioned Wes to come with him. Four snares had been sprung and the game taken from them.

"You see who done it?" Wes asked.

Ransom nodded vigorously. He motioned toward the camp, and started off, Wes following. Ransom went directly to the shelter of Colonel Big Tom.

"This it? You sure?" Wes asked.

Ransom nodded.

Wes stood uncertainly for a moment, then called out: "Big Tom, you there?"

"Yeah, I'm here. Who's that?"

"Wes Hunu."

"What you want?"

"Like to pass a word with you."

Big Tom came out.

"What you got on your mind?"

"Reckon you make a mistake about the snares," Wes said. " 'Spect you figure they don't belong to nobody."

"What snares you talkin' about, boy?"

"The ones you took the game out of this mornin'."

"Who tell you I thief the snares?"

"Ain't say you thief them, say you made a mistake, and I come for the game."

A crowd began to gather around Big Tom's house. Big Tom glanced up toward Descamps's cabin, but neither the General nor any of his other militiamen was in sight.

"You say I thief the snares?"

"Ain't what I say. 'Course you believe them snares don't belong to no one, that's why you take the game. But I the one who set them out. So give me the meat now, and thank you for the trouble." It occurred to Wes that if Big Tom hadn't shared the game with Descamps he wouldn't care to make a big thing out of it. "You want the General to judge the case?"

Big Tom wore an angry face, but he was sweating.

"Well, you take it back that I thief the snares?"

"No," Wes said, "you didn't do that, you only think they don't belong to no one."

Big Tom again glanced nervously toward the General's cabin. "You right on that one," he said. "I find a rabbit and a racoon." He went inside and brought out a rabbit and a racoon, and threw them on the ground at Wes's feet.

" 'Cordin' to the snares as was sprung, they was four," Wes said.

Big Tom looked grimly at Wes. "Look to me as you is after double trouble."

Wes spoke softly. "No, if you say they was only two, I takes your word. And thank you kindly." He picked up the game and started back, Ransom at his heels.

The whittler said softly as they passed by: "Better sleep 'cross the river tonight. They goin' to fix you."

"The game was mine," Wes said. "He took four, he still got two. Ain't that satisfy him?"

"The game, that's only part of it. You callin' him a thief, that's the other part."

"I ain't call him that."

"That's so, you don't, but you do. He don't mind bein' a thief, he mind bein' told so. Better cross the river till a day or two."

Wes was watching the man's knife slicing rhythmically at the stick. And he remembered something from his boyhood in Yabo. "Believe I'll stay," he said. "But I can use you, if you give me the favor of it."

The man shook his head. "I been out there in the wilderness 'most a year. I got nothin' here but a place to sit down. But I ain't ready to leave, and I ain't goin' to fight no bully boys neither."

"All I want from you is stakes," Wes said, "just about one hand long and sharp points on both ends."

The whittler looked into Wes's face solemnly. "Reckon I can whittle a few," he said. "How many you want?"

"Many as you can make," Wes said. " 'Bout a hundred or more."

"Show me how you want 'em," the man said.

Wes took out his knife and cut a model.

"All right, then. Tell the boy there to bring me the sticks, I make the points."

All that day the whittler carved under his tree. Inside his shelter Wes also carved. And that evening as the light was beginning to fade he set the stakes in the ground on the trail and all around the lean-to. He saved some for planting inside the shelter itself. After they had eaten their evening meal, Wes and Ransom crept into the undergrowth a hundred yards away and waited.

The moon shone intermittently in an overcast sky. They could not see the lean-to from where they were lying, but their ears were alert to all the night sounds. Ransom fell asleep, and just as Wes's eyes were beginning to close he was alerted by a sudden silence. The night birds had stopped their calling. He heard a faint rustling and a cough in the darkness, and sensed that four or five men were approaching. There was a sudden muted exclamation and a groan. Voices were audible for an instant, followed by silence again. A moment later, another cry of pain, less muted than the first. Then a voice: "Get in there and get him!" There was a rustle of movement, more cries. "Wye! My foot been stabbed to the bone! Can't walk on it!" "The place got a greegree on it! I'm goin'!" another voice said. After that there were only the faint sounds of the raiders retreating down the trail.

In the gray light before dawn, Wes and Ransom returned and pulled out all the stakes. While Ransom went to check the snares, Wes sauntered through the center of the camp. He saw Big Tom limping heavily, a dirty rag tied around his left foot. Joe Sharp had no bandage, but he was walking on his heel. Two other men were limping. No one spoke of the event, but there was an air of subdued humor and satisfaction in the camp. A toothless old woman grinned at Wes as he passed.

Later that day Wes brought eight coon and rabbit skins and put them on the ground in the place reserved for trading. He was offered various things in exchange—freshly caught fish, half of a small 'gator skin, and dried corn—but he held out for cloth. At last someone offered a worn and patched skirt, which he accepted. He took it to a woman who owned a needle, and she agreed to make pants for Ransom in exchange for fresh meat or fish every day for a week. And when the week was up, Ransom was wearing his first clothes.

In the days that followed, using charred sticks and scratching them on a flat rock, Wes began teaching Ransom his characters, starting with R and the other letters of his name. But Ransom wasn't satisfied with only one name, and Wes gave him the family name of Rivers, because it was on an island in the river where they had met. Ransom learned hungrily. The knowledge of characters gave him a voice. And one day Wes found written on a stone in the shelter: "Gon to snars."

For five months Wes and Ransom lived on small game, fish and dried corn that was sometimes available for trade in the camp. On one of his trips across the river Wes saw deer tracks, and he determined to get his musket back from Descamps. He approached the General directly. He went to the cabin and said: "General, I need my musket back now. Seen deer tracks out there. Want to get some fresh meat."

Descamps said: "*Your* musket? Ain't got no *your* musket here."

Wes said patiently: "General, when I come here you took the musket off me, said 'cause of the law I had to leave it. I reckon you used the gun, but I ain't had no good out of it since I come. Now I goin' huntin' cross the river and I need it."

Descamps opened his bloodshot eyes wide. "Who's this black man tell me give him the musket?"

"I'm Wes Hunu, I live here."

"Don't recollect you, nigger. You paid the permissions?"

"I paid it," Wes said. "You're wearin' it."

"Sound to me," Descamps said, "that you're sassin' the law."

"I been here a long time, General, and I ain't bothered no one. All I want is the musket."

"Hmm," Descamps said, "you fixin' to steal from the arsenal?"

"Don't know nothin' 'bout the arsenal, General. All I know is the food is poorly 'round this place, and I want fresh meat, so I need the musket."

"All the muskets in the arsenal belong to the gov'ment," Descamps said. "We ain't got no private muskets."

"You say when you took it that you put the mark of my name on it," Wes said.

The General took a drink from his jug.

"What's the name on it?"

"Wes Hunu."

The General shook his head sadly.

"Got no musket here with that name on it."

"Let me come in, then, I show you the one."

Descamps stood up in a rage. "Nobody cross this threshold, else the law fall on him! Go on, get off my yard fast as you can!"

Wes left. He considered ways to get his musket back.

Steal it, perhaps? It was too risky. Bargain for it? He had nothing to bargain.

That night, on the trail to his lean-to, Wes was ambushed and beaten senseless. Ransom found him, got help, and they carried Wes home. They put a mud poultice on his head where the scalp was torn, and wrapped it with leaves and vines. But it was not till he regained consciousness and tried to sit up that they realized his arm was broken. Then they sent for Entoto, the Congo herb doctor. Entoto came with all the instruments of his profession. With a cow's horn that had been pierced at the end he sucked out the evil forces causing the arm to pain. Then he shook red powder from the horn into the fire. Afterward he tied Wes's arm tightly with leaves and vines and plastered the bandage with clay. Ransom paid him with two fish taken from the river only a few hours before.

While Wes was recovering, Ransom took over the task of bringing in the daily food. He sometimes brought dried corn or a piece of pork, and Wes was never certain whether these things were procured through trade or theft. The whittler came sometimes to see Wes, and always when he left the lean-to floor was covered with shavings.

There were no more confrontations with Descamps or his militia until some days later, when Joe Sharp arrived with a message from the General. "He want to see you," Joe Sharp said, "tell you to come to the Big House."

"I'll study on it," Wes said.

"Man, don't you study a thing like that. When the General want you, better shuffle along."

"Don't the General know where I live? If he want me he can pay me a call."

Joe Sharp looked surprised.

"Seem like you bound to make trouble, ain't you?" he said at last.

"I ain't seek no trouble," Wes said. "But I got nothin'

right now to tell Descamps. If he got somethin' to tell me, he can find me."

Descamps eventually came, his two colonels tagging at his heels. He stood at the lean-to opening looking down at Wes through his half-closed eyes. He spoke slowly, sweetening his hostility with friendly words. "I been watchin' you some, Hunu. I reckon you the man I need."

"Need for what?" Wes said.

"For the supply raid tomorrow. We goin' to load up at a plantation 'bout thirty mile down the river. Got seven men for the expedition already, and I like for you to get in this thing."

"Don't know as it please me," Wes said. "What part is for me in it?"

"You just go on with the rest. Big Tom in charge. He tell you what to do."

"What Big Tom got to tell me don't interest me none," Wes said.

"Well, you can fuss around here till you die and you get nothin' but catfish and rabbit."

"If I go," Wes said thoughtfully, "what share I get?"

"Hard to say," Descamps said, controlling his anger at the cross-examination. "Depend on what we turn up. But you get somethin', be sure of that."

"Who get the lion share?"

"Why, surprised you questioned that one. First part goes to the gov'ment. That's natural, ain't it? Sides that, it's the law, gov'ment get the first pick. But the rest is for the men."

"Who I got to fight to get my part?"

Descamps laughed, but he was annoyed. "Why, the fightin' is only for the girls. You want to get one of them and you got to claw for it. But I passes out the rest."

"Think I'll go on this one just to see," Wes said.

"Well, that's fine then," Descamps said. "You be down to the Big House at sunup."

When the General had left, Wes said to Ransom: "Why he want me, you think?"

Ransom motioned with his finger across his throat.

"I don't know if I don't think you hit it right," Wes said.

But in the morning he was at the Big House with the militia, standing in front of the door. Descamps came out, disheveled from the night. "Now, you men get out there and get the provisions," he said. "The gov'ment just about run out of supply. Two days down and two days back, and I want a boatload of bacon and meal and corn in the liquid form. And get your hands on some powder and ball, too, and don't spare no one, white or black, to get it. This is war, and they hang you if they catch you, so shoot 'fore they does. One thing more, I need a lookin' glass for the Big House. Catch on to one of them. Won't never hold off the planters from this place 'less we got the provisions. That's all. Colonel Big Tom tell you the rest."

"All right, then, watch it!" Big Tom ordered. "Marchin' formation! Gee around there in the back!"

"They's only one thing," Wes said to Descamps. "I need the musket."

"Musket? You don't need no musket. Can't every man in the army have a musket. You just go along and do what Colonel Big Tom say. Got enough musket in the bunch."

"Long as I'm goin' I need a musket," Wes said. "I'll take the one I left in your arsenal."

"Well, never mind that," Descamps said. "You go on with the militia and they take care of everything."

"Ain't goin' without the musket," Wes said.

Descamps stopped trying to persuade him. He called Big Tom inside, where they conversed in low tones. When he came out he said: "All right, you can carry the musket. Which one belong to you?" Wes pointed it out in the hands of one of the militia.

"Give the man his musket," Descamps said. "Now get on the march!"

"Musket ain't no good without powder and ball," Wes said.

"Never mind that, Colonel Big Tom in charge of the powder and ball."

"Just the same, I left powder and twelve ball with you when I come. I take them now."

A look of fury passed over Descamps's face, and the veins in his forehead swelled.

"All right, then," he said, trying to disguise his anger. "Give it to him."

The militia moved raggedly down to the water's edge to the accompaniment of Big Tom's staccato marching orders. "Step proper! Long steps, not baby steps! This is the army! Gee around in the front! Get on with it!"

"That the way they call it out in the army?" Wes said.

"Move it, boys, move it!" Big Tom shouted. "And don't no one give me no sass!"

They boarded two crude log rafts and pushed out into the open water, floating with the current. Two men poled to steer. Big Tom kept on with his orders, but no one paid much attention.

"Big Tom," Wes said after a while, "why you think the General want so bad for me to come?"

Big Tom looked away. "Reckon he need to fill out the ranks."

"Maybe want me out of camp?"

"Now look here," Big Tom said, "don't start no trouble, you hear me? I don't ask the General no questions. He say what he want, and the army take care of it. That's the way it is."

Wes calculated the probable time when Big Tom would try to dispose of him. The most logical moment would be when the attack on the plantation was launched. That would be the instant when he would have to be alert about what was behind him as well as in front. A bullet in his back would complete that part of the mission given to the militia. For the time being, at least, there was security. When he was not taking his turn at poling the raft Wes lay and dozed, his musket tucked under his body. The current was slow but steady. Once they spotted a small boat on the river and hurriedly maneuvered the rafts to shore under heavy foliage that hung out over the water. Later they passed an Indian encampment. They did not go ashore when night came, but stayed aboard the rafts, sleeping in shifts. There was a full moon, which provided enough light for navigating the turns and twists of the river.

They were just poling the rafts toward shore for a landing a short distance above the plantation when the attack on Wes came. One of the dripping poles, lifted out of the water, struck him across the back and knocked him down. Waiting hands quickly seized the musket, powder horn, and the sack of lead balls. A musket butt struck the side of his face, and he was shoved into the river. He did not remember swimming, but he somehow remained afloat.

When he became fully conscious he was clinging to a tree root that stuck up out of the water on the shore opposite to the place where the landing was scheduled to take place. He hung on weakly until some of his strength returned, and then pulled himself to land. Sharp pains reminded him that he had been injured. His hand wandered over the left side of his face, which was swollen and bleeding. His left eye was closed. There was nothing across the river that gave him any clue as to whether he had floated beyond the plantation or whether he was still above it. He stood up to move to a place that would give him a better view of the shore, became ill instantly and retched out swallowed blood and river water. He lay on the ground to recover, and it was only then that he realized that three teeth were missing from his mouth.

Twice he had survived the water, once in the ocean on the voyage across, and now again in the river. How truly he had been named Thing-of-the-Sea. And how true was the saying in his village that a man destined to die by the spear would never drown. Without intending to, he slept. When he awoke he felt stronger, even though the pain in his head was acute.

He ate from the little supply of smoked rabbit meat that he carried tied to his waist, and then began the long walk home. When the meat was gone he ate wild berries. It was three days before he caught sight of the Island, and he waited till dark to cross over. He avoided the center of the camp and reached his shelter by a route along the edge of the swamp. Ransom was excited by his appearance. He futilely tried to convey some information, then ran to get the whittler. When the two of them arrived, Wes was sitting before the fire eating some of Ransom's roasted fish.

"Well if it ain't Wes Hunu, come back from the dead!" the whittler said in genuine surprise. "We hear you was killed by the white folks out there!"

"You hear all that 'bout me?"

"That's what we hear from Big Tom, all right. He say you was shot down in your tracks when they assail the plantation."

"I never got to cast eyes on that plantation," Wes said. "They beat me and throw me in the river, figure the water carry me off. Old Rooster get what he want from the raid?"

"Well, he got that lookin' glass, that's the truth. It's hangin' there in the Big House right now. He's probably standin' there admirin' his ugly face. They fetch two pigs, some smoked meat, and a barrel of corn liquor. 'Sides that they got some clothes includin' three-four pair of boots, couple of axes, some tobacco, some yard cloth, salt, and all kind of notions like that. Also some money. Reckon they cleaned out whatever they could carry from the plantation house, also the cook woman. Rooster got her up there cookin' for him right now. From the look of her I reckon she ain't want to come in the first place. She ain't said a word to no one since she come. Big Tom say they killed a parcel of white folks, but one of the other men say they wasn't no one at home at the time 'cept the niggers. They found two boats and come back on the water with the provisions, and they consume a powerful lot of liquid corn on the way. Old Rooster share out a little of the stuff and store the rest away for the gov'ment."

"Listen, Uncle," Wes said, but the whittler cut him off.

"Now lookee here, you been callin' me Uncle too long since you been here. Call me Coffee, that's my name."

"All right, Uncle Coffee. What I want is you don't let it out that I'm back, not till I say so."

"Well, I'm goin' to do it, boy, just like you say. I'd like to be there when Rooster find out."

At dawn the next morning Wes was sitting on the stump in front of Descamps's cabin. He threw small pebbles at the door until Descamps called out hoarsely. "What you want?" He opened the door half asleep, and saw Wes sitting there.

"Mornin', General," Wes said.

Descamps just looked, said nothing.

Wes got up leisurely and walked away, leaving Descamps standing at the cabin door. He went to find Entoto, the Congo doctor, on the far side of the camp.

"How many Africans on the Island and 'cross the river?" Wes asked.

"Not too many. Some Ewe, some Ibo, three Congo. Also five-six Yoruba and maybe one Fiote. Maybe twelve, fifteen all together."

"You forget me," Wes said.

"You? Man, I thought you was born and bred in Georgia."

"They ever have a yam service or prayer for the dead here?" Wes asked.

"No, never did. Almost had one once, but Rooster 'spect they try to fix him with a spell, and he don't let 'em do it."

" 'Bout time for a service for the dead."

"Yeah, it's plenty time. They's some Africans been

killed here ain't even had funerals. Need a meetin' for them men."

"You help me," Wes said. "I'm goin' to make a service for the dead."

Entoto was reluctant. "Rooster make trouble for that thing. 'Sides, I'm a doctor, not a gangan."

"I'll take the burden of it," Wes said. "You can help me. Maybe the whole camp will join this thing."

"Oh, no, too many Georgia niggers for that, too many Christian."

"Where all the Christians hidin'?" Wes said. "Ain't hear of no camp meetin's, no christenin's neither. Anyway, you goin' to help me?"

Entoto finally agreed.

That day Wes began to hollow out a section of log to make a drum. When it was finished he covered it with a double thickness of coonskin from which the hair had been removed. One evening when the drumhead was dry and taut he beat out some Fon rhythms on it. Within a few minutes, two of the camp's Africans appeared, both Ewe men. Delight on their faces, their arms upraised, they went into a shuffling dance step and cavorted around the drum. When Wes's rhythm faltered, one of the men stopped indignantly, saying, "Gimme that drum! I goin' to make it talk!" He laid it on the ground and sat astride, playing the drumhead between his legs. The other Ewe kneeled behind and beat sticks against the body of the drum. The sound rose up among the trees and throbbed across the camp, and more people drifted to the scene. Soon fifty or sixty men and women were crowded around Wes's shelter. There was little room, but they danced nevertheless. The Ewe drummer tired, and a Yoruba took his place. When darkness fell, they held burning sticks aloft to light the dance area.

Eventually General Descamps arrived with four of his militia. He glowered and raised his hand for silence. The dancing stopped. "What's goin' on here?" he said.

"Just a good-time dance, General. Join the fun," someone called out.

"Ain't you know you got to have permissions for the dance?" the General said.

"Well, General," someone said, "this ain't no *real* dance, it's just *practice.*"

"Who the man start this thing?" Descamps demanded.

"Matter of fact," another man called out, "ain't no one start it, rightly speakin'. Started by itself."

Descamps didn't like the tone of ridicule he heard in some of the voices. And when the drummer rubbed his fingertips over the drumhead to make an insulting sound, Descamps grew furious. "Goin' to tan the hide off some of these niggers!" he shouted. "Go and get me that drummer!" Suddenly the burning torches were extinguished. There were shouts, milling and shoving. The drum disappeared with the drummer, and the crowd melted into the woods and underbrush, Wes and Ransom with them. Descamps picked up a dying torch, blew it into a flame, and set Wes's shelter ablaze. In a few minutes the lean-to was gone.

But Wes had found out something he wanted to know. During the days that followed he sought out the Africans individually, and he even found some on the other side of the river that Entoto didn't know about. There were twenty-two men in all, and a half dozen women. He spoke about forming a dokpwe. They were intrigued. Wes then approached others. He talked to Coffee about it.

"The men is goin' to have a dokpwe. You want to come in?"

"Sure I want to come in. But what is it?"

"They call it that in the place I come from. The men get together, they work together. They got a chief. Some do one thing, some another. They divide the fish. Divide the game. And divide the work too. Some sets the snares, some go for fish, some hunt for meat. When a house got to be built, all share the work. Same with the corn patches."

"Well, now," Coffee said, stripping the bark from a twig with his knife, "all that sound mighty fine. But what old Rooster goin' to say about this thing?"

"Reckon he not goin' to like it at all. But the dokpwe, they takes care of they own."

"How you mean?"

"They guards the snares and the corn. And if a man is in trouble with the militia or the General, they stand by him."

Coffee sat up straight, and forgot to whittle.

"Whoo! Man, that sound like war to me! Only trouble is, Rooster got the musket and powder."

"The dokpwe can take care of that."

Coffee whittled rapidly. "Yeah," he said, "think I'd like to get in this thing. What you call it again?"

The dokpwe held its first meeting across the river. Forty-two men gathered around the fire. They discussed the matter. They argued almost through the night. A half dozen times they had to scout in the dark for wood to keep the fire alive. They appointed teams for the various tasks, including dugout canoe building. Ten men were assigned to work as scouts and guards. Before they finished for the night, a man stood up to say: "One thing more. We got to have a deacon." Everyone laughed.

"Boy, where you think you are at," someone called out, "in church?"

They elected a chief. At Wes's insistence, they chose the eldest African among them, Entoto the Congo. Wes was placed in charge of the guards and scouts.

The next day they went to work in groups to gather food, to start the building of dugout canoes, and to set out new snares on the far side of the river. The canoes, when finished, were used for fishing. After several weeks, food for the dokpwe was more plentiful than it had been. More important, a new spirit took hold of the men. There was less sitting around, loitering and sleeping the day away. A sense of purpose, or at least an illusion of purpose, came into being. Occasionally outsiders came to Entoto or Wes to say they wanted to join the dokpwe. But they had to wait, they were told, until the next meeting when their requests would be considered. Because only men could be members, the African women formed a group of their own, and within a few weeks it had grown to more than twenty.

During the first days, Descamps seemed unaware of the things that were happening. Then he became alert. His militia, carrying their muskets, were here, there, everywhere, watching and asking questions and running back to report. Descamps himself took to patrolling the camp and prowling around its outskirts. But he found nothing to bite on. All he saw was people at work in groups rather than alone. One thing that bothered him was the singing. Every song seemed to hide a conspiracy or an insult. Indeed, some songs seemed to refer directly to the General and the militia. One song in particular enraged him:

Rooster crow at mornin',
Rooster crow at night,
Rooster crow till his face get red,
Never mind that, he soon be dead,
So that's all right.

"You go out there," he told his colonels, "take four-five men, and you bring back any man you hear say that thing! I goin' to whup him myself and hang up his skin on my wall! Go on, get him, and be quick on it!"

The militia came down on the work party, their muskets at ready. "You, there, with the hatchet, the General want you," Big Tom said loudly. But the man didn't move. Big Tom was about to speak again when he heard the leaves rustle behind him. He turned. Standing there with their workknives out, directly behind the militia, was the dokpwe's guard and scout force, reinforced by half a dozen fishermen.

"What you want?" Big Tom said. " 'Tain't none of your business. Go on, pick your cotton."

"These men belong to the dokpwe," Wes said, "and everythin' 'bout the dokpwe is they business. What you want with the dokpwe?"

"What's the dokpwe?" Big Tom said, his voice faltering.

"It's this here *thing*," someone answered. "Reckon you like to join? Only problem is, you got to *work* for it."

Big Tom said: "Well, just want to tell you the message from the General. He say let they be no trouble."

"Oh, they's no trouble, Tom. Relieve your mind of that. Ain't gonna be no trouble, either."

Big Tom looked once more at the wall of men behind him. He called out in a blustery voice: "All the militia, rear march!" The militia straggled off silently.

The next meeting of the dokpwe was held on the Island, in the very center of the camp. It began with a discussion of how the work had been going, and after that they took in fifteen new members and initiated them. One of the Ibo men had made a grass skirt and a grass mask. He was the major-domo. To the beat of the drums—there were two drums now—he danced out of the firelight into the shadows, returning each time with a new initiate who was brought before Entoto.

"You want to belong this thing?" Entoto asked.

"Yeah."

"You ready to share the tasks, do what is told you?"

"Yeah."

"You keep you mouth tight 'bout these things?"

"Yeah."

"You share what you gain with the dokpwe?"

"Yeah."

That was all. And after the swearing-in ceremony was over, the dance began. By now the crowd had swelled. Most of the camp was there. Many danced, many just stood around the edge of the festivities and watched. Before long, Descamps was there also, with eight armed men. He pushed to the front of the spectators.

A Yoruba named Okwana St. Joseph was convulsed by his protective deity. His eyes became glazed, he staggered as though carrying a great invisible weight, and he began to speak African words. He moved around, stopping to gaze into the face of one person after another. After a while Okwana stopped speaking Yoruba. He would look into a man's face and say, in a resonant voice that was not his own, "Not the one!"

At last he stopped in front of Descamps, peering into his eyes. Descamps stood a head taller and had to look down at Okwana, but the sweat came out on his forehead. Suddenly Okwana was talking Yoruba again, the words pouring from his mouth. Descamps stood glaring, and when he couldn't stand the tension any longer, he shouted: "You black African nigger, don't you put no greegree on me! Else I have you quartered! You hear me?" Some of the other dancers came and took Okwana away. The dance went on. Descamps and his militia disappeared. The festivities ended long after midnight. Late the next morning, when Okwana failed to join his work group, they found him butchered in his lean-to.

The leaders of the dokpwe met at once across the river. There was general agreement that something had to be done at once about the General.

Entoto said: "We turn it over to the scouts."

Wes said: "The scouts is ready. But we goin' to need extra help."

Entoto said: "We give it. What you want?"

Wes thought for a moment. "First thing, we hold a service for Okwana. We do that tonight. Tomorrow we bury him. After that, we fix the other thing."

The dokpwe organized the service that night. Wes Hunu invoked the vodouns and the ancestors to see that Okwana's spirit was guided safely across the three rivers, the Azile, the Gudu, and the Selu. He placed a fragment of tobacco in the hand of the corpse to pay the first boatman; he added a penny to pay the second boatman; and a piece of cloth to pay the third boatman. Because Okwana was a Yoruba, one of his countrymen invoked the orishas. And still another man came forward to ask Jesus to extend his mercy.

Then the orishas, the vodouns, the ancestors, and Jesus were supplicated in honor of all the others who had died on Liberty Island without a funeral service. Afterward, there were drumming and dancing. And at sunrise they took Okwana, wrapped in cloth procured in some way by the dokpwe, to a wooded place north of the camp, and there they buried him. They placed his drinking gourd on top of the grave.

The scouts then met in a secluded spot. They sent for extra men from the working teams, a few from each group. The rest went out to fish or trap as usual.

The plan was simple. The scouts were to scatter in pairs or threes. They were to capture the militia one by one, as quietly as possible, and bring them to a small swampy cove on the north side of the Island. Wes and two others went after Big Tom. He was still sleeping. They approached his shelter. In the full light of day their movements were observed by all Big Tom's neighbors. Some of them, sensing a crucial event, retired into their lean-tos. A few, squatting nearby, merely turned their heads away. Big Tom's wrists were tied behind him before he was fully awake. Wes picked up the musket from the ground and pointed it at him.

"Where's the powder and ball?" Wes asked.

The look of surprise was still on Big Tom's face. "It's all in the musket," he said, "the General give us only one ball, that's all he allow."

They marched their prisoner swiftly to the cove. One other prisoner was already there. They tied the two of them securely and bound their mouths with cloth. Later, another party arrived with Joe Sharp. His face was cut and bleeding, and the skin was rubbed off his back from dragging him over the ground. Two more prisoners were brought in, and after that no more.

"Can't wait no longer," Wes said, "else Descamps get wind of it. Better go for him now."

The thought of going for Descamps was too much for some of the men. "Wes," one of them said, "why don't we leave the Rooster be? He got nothin' much left now without the bully boys, anyway."

"We ain't got all the militia," Wes said. "If you let Descamps be, it goin' to start all over again, and it be worse next time."

"Just the same," another man said, "why don't we just tell him to pull out? Tell him to go without no more trouble, that's all. Just light out."

"Goin' for Descamps now," Wes said, ignoring the suggestion. "Two men can stay here and keep an eye on the militia. Don't let 'em go. We'll take the muskets."

There were five men in the party, two of them armed with the captured muskets and a single ball for each. Descamps's cabin was closed up tight when they arrived. There was an unnatural silence over the entire camp. "Believe they's in there," Wes said. He picked up a stone and threw it at the door. "Descamps, come on out!"

Descamps's voice came back hoarse and muffled from inside. "You black devils, you turn on the gov'ment? I goin' to have your skins! Got my militia in here, goin' to feed you all to the 'gators! 'Less you get off the Island you goin' to be dead 'fore sundown!"

A shot was fired from a crack in the cabin wall, but the aim was erratic. Wes and his men drew back toward the trees.

"Can't have more'n three muskets in there," Wes said. "Maybe got two men with him. One man with the musket go around back and watch the window shutter. Other one stay in front. We goin' to smoke 'em out."

He sent men to gather rags, leaves and kindling, which he tied into a bundle. With a smoldering torch in one hand

and the bundle in the other, he approached the cabin from the chimney side and climbed to the roof, where he nested his fuel next to the chimney and set it afire. The first wisps of smoke seemed to be coming from the chimney, but as the roof itself became ignited the smoke spread and hung heavily along the shingles.

"Descamps," Wes called, "if you ain't comin' out now you goin' to be smoked out, and if you ain't smoked out you goin' to be roasted out."

There were sounds of commotion inside, but the door remained shut. "Hunu!" Descamps roared, "I goin' to strip the hide off'n you! You goin' to wish you never been here! Burn down the gov'ment, will you, you black nigger? Tomorrow this time you be hangin' by your ugly feet from the swamp oak front of my house! Alive or dead you be hangin' there! Put out that fire, it's your last chance!"

"Come on out, Descamps, can't no one stop the fire now."

The roof was aflame in a widening circle. The door opened a little, and Descamps's voice came through the more clearly now. "We can talk. What you want with the gov'ment?"

"Don't want no talk, Descamps. Just want you and your men to come out. Talk is for later."

After a pause Descamps called out: "All right, then. The gov'ment comin' out."

"Throw the musket first," Wes answered.

There was another pause, and the sound of coughing inside. Then Descamps threw a musket through the partially opened door. "There she is."

"Throw the rest, too," Wes said.

"That's all," Descamps answered. "Ain't no more."

"Don't come out till you put the other muskets out here on the ground, else you get shot acomin'."

Two more muskets were tossed through the door opening.

"All right, that's all, we comin' now," Descamps said. He came out coughing and red-eyed, his two militiamen behind him.

"All right," he said docilely, "we here now. You done burn down the gov'ment, you goin' to catch plenty for that trick. What you want?" He approached Wes almost meekly. But when he was only a few steps off he bounded forward and caught the man with the musket, raised him over his head and threw him toward Wes. He seized a tree branch from the ground and thrashed around wildly with it. He kicked out with his feet, and a blow from his fist knocked Wes down. But the scouts closed in, fearful though they were. Someone swung his musket like a club, striking Descamps across the back. He turned and lunged at his tormentor. Another musket butt landed on Descamps's neck. His legs sagged for a moment, then he struck out again savagely with his crude weapon. Blows were falling on him from all sides, but he refused to go down. He caught one man by the throat, butted him with his forehead and let the limp body fall. Descamps himself never fell. He merely sagged, until at last he lay stretched out on his face, eyes closed, blood trickling from his nose and mouth.

"Well, there he is," someone said breathing heavily, "there's the gov'ment for you!"

The scout who had been butted lay on the ground without moving, and someone went for Entoto to take care of him. They trussed Descamps to a long pole and carried him like game killed in the forest.

The camp was in ferment. People pushed and shoved to get a view of the Rooster, or to get close enough to insult him.

The two militiamen who had been in the cabin with Descamps had disappeared during the fight, but they were rounded up and brought back. There was a widespread air of wonder, as though a miraculous thing had happened. "Saved by Jesus!" a woman shouted hysterically. Thus, so simply, it had been accomplished, and some began to wonder silently why the thing had not been done long ago.

The trial was held the next day in the center of the camp, with Entoto, as chief of the dokpwe, presiding. The testimony was long. Several women and girls told of how they were taken and abused by the Rooster or his men. Various men told of beatings. The man whose ears had been cut off displayed the scars. There were charges of murder, and of disposing of the bodies without proper burial. The accusations were sometimes quiet and soft-spoken, sometimes excited and dramatic.

One man said: "I run away from my Old Master. I couldn't stay no more in that place. I live six months in the woods. I hear of this place and I come. Didn't have no permissions for the Rooster, so he make me catch fish for him. Everything I catch, he take it, 'less I hide a little somewhere. Rooster get fat 'till the butter come out on his skin, all I get is drybone. One time I find a buck deer caught in the woods by his horns 'cross the river. Well, I kill that deer, hang it up and cut off a quarter for myself. Then militia catch me eatin' of it. They whup me and carry me to the Rooster. He tell them whup me again. Then I got to take them cross the river where the deer was. They take it. After that they whup me again. They take all the meat and the hide too. My Old Master done better than that for me."

Another man testified: "When I come here I got no one. I find a woman. I bring the fish, she cook 'em. We get along all right. I got no complaints with her, she got no complaints of me. She take care of the corn patch other side of the river sometimes. One night Rooster come down on her, tell her come to his place. She say no, she's my woman. Rooster take her just the same. She fight and claw, scratch up his face. He beat her, make her stay. I hear of it, went to the Big House and told Rooster I come for my woman. Them militia boys knock me down, kick me, break my nose bone. The woman gone now. Run off, couldn't stand this place no more."

A Congo man jumped up in turn. Clapping his hands rhythmically, he sang out proverbs to be applied to the judgment:

"You know the thiefin' dog 'cause he seek out the other thiefin' dogs! True! Stick that beat the small dog beat the big dog too! True! Lion eat the hunter's baby, too late to tell the hunter he sorry! True! Thing that live in the ant hill and crawl like ant, well, that must be the ant! True! Leopard don't listen when goat cry for mercy. When the hunter catch him he want mercy twice as loud! True! Big tree tell the forest he see 'cross the world, but when he fall he make the biggest noise! True!"

Sometimes Entoto questioned the testimony. When a man seemed to be carried away by his moment in public, when his story seemed extravagant, Entoto would stop him, saying, "All that true? You swear it on your father's grave?" And if the witness toned down his story in consequence of the admonition, Entoto would say, "When everybody go to the praise meetin', devil think he go too."

But the unquestionable evidence was overwhelming, and it had to be cut short. At last Descamps was brought forward to the center of the court, his arms tied behind him.

"You, Rooster," Entoto said, "you got any words?"

Descamps was sullen, but there was panic in his face too. He looked around. "You all goin' 'gainst the law," he said.

"Who make the law?" someone called out.

"Gov'ment make the law. You done knock down the gov'ment. That make you fit to hang."

"Who goin' to pull the rope?" another man said.

"Now lookee here," Descamps said, his voice changing from accusation to supplication, "ain't no call for this thing. What you want, I give it."

Entoto said: "Court ain't talk about tomorrow, talk about yesterday. You do all them things the people say?"

"I ain't do such things, no sir, them folks just lyin' people, that's all! 'Course, if the gov'ment don't meet satisfaction we can talk on it. . . ."

"Till now they ain't been no gov'ment here," Wes said.

"Any you militia got words?" Entoto asked.

"We in the army," Big Tom said. "We got to do what the General tell us. We bring plenty supply for the camp. We keep the peace here."

"Well, that's all," Entoto said. " 'Pear like these men got to go. Anything they got that belong to someone else, take it away. Send 'em cross the river to find someplace else where they can run with the thiefs on the other side. We put a greegree on them. Any man of them thiefin' niggers come back to the Island, he's dead on the spot." Entoto arose from the stump where he sat, and with a fern in his hand he danced in front of the convicted men. Touching each one with the fern, he recited a formula in Bantu. They paled and drew back in fear. Big Tom licked his lips and said plaintively, "Don't have to do this, Entoto, we goin' in peace!" Entoto ignored the plea, and went on with his ceremony to the end. "Finish," he said. "Send 'em out."

The trial turned into a festival as the crowd swarmed around Descamps and his militia. The convicted men were tugged and shoved toward the river, the whole camp pressing on their heels. Two or three of the militia, knocked down by the disorderly crowd, were almost trampled. Descamps himself walked rapidly to stay ahead of the milling bodies. He was first in the water, first to reach the dead trees and driftwood which formed a bridge to the mainland, and first to reach the shore. There, diminished in size by distance, he was seen to turn and strike one of the militiamen. After that they were all soon lost to sight.

Three nights later there was another service for the dead. The vodouns and the orishas were invoked by the Africans, and those who had been baptised paid their homage to Jesus.

In the days that followed, Liberty Island settled down again. The dokpwe made food more plentiful and became a central social element in the camp. Several other work groups were formed also, but many men preferred to come and go by themselves as they always had. A few new refugees from the plantations appeared, while some of the inhabitants of the Island crossed to the mainland and did not return. With the disappearance of the General and his army there was a lessening of anxiety and resentment, even a greater sense of liberty. But depredations went on.

Gardens were raided sometimes, and traps were stripped of their catch in the night. There were fights over women and thefts of clothing, knives and cooking pots. As time passed the Islanders again seemed to be waiting for something to happen that would bring some kind of a solution to their situation. For, though they were unmolested by the planters and the bounty hunters, there was a pervading awareness of the Island as a prison. Some, indeed, remembering friends and family with whom they had grown up, became nostalgic for the slave quarters from which they had escaped.

Once it was reported that four mounted and armed white men had captured two of the Islanders, a man and a woman, over on the mainland. There was a flurry of activity then. A sense of urgency was on them, and a strategy for defense was worked out instantly. Snipers were placed at the water's edge wherever a crossing from the mainland could be made, and other defenders with hand weapons were stationed to deal with any crossing that might be accomplished in the face of fire. But time went by and no white men appeared. As the emergency faded, the sense of purpose diminished with it, and gradually the camp reverted to the little routines of hunting, fishing, eating and waiting for something—a bolt of lightning, perhaps, or an earthquake, or some other revelation—to signal a way of escape from this place suspended between worlds.

There was another event that brought them out of the

slough for a while, the arrival of a white preacher. He came riding on a donkey, and when he reached the river he was surrounded and detained until his purposes were understood. At last he was brought across, and the next three days were given over to camp meetings, christenings and baptisms. The sound of singing and hoarse shouting reverberated among the trees.

The preacher called himself Joseph, and his theme whenever he preached was the Revelation of John. He recalled John's visions as though he himself, Joseph, also had stood there near the throne, and he described the scene so vividly that the escaped slaves sitting on the ground before him saw it clearly. They saw a great city sparkling with jewels, and in the center a magnificent throne with a halo surrounding it, and in the hand of him who sat there a book of writings sealed with seven seals. And later, when the sixth seal had been broken, the earth shook, the sun turned black, the moon turned to blood, the sky was torn apart, and the stars rained down. Then an angel of the east arose and commanded: "Do not harm the earth or the sea, until we mark the slaves of God on their foreheads." And so they were marked, the slaves of God, those who had been saved from great destruction.

"Yeah, it's true! Slaves of God! It's so!" came back to Joseph from the congregation. And he went on to describe the woman clothed in the sun, the moon under her feet and a crown of stars on her head. And from among those people who shared the vision with John and Joseph there came a keening sound and a musical cry. Someone shouted out, "Wonder in the heaven!" Another voice sang back, "Yeah, mighty wonder in the heaven!" The words turned somehow into music, and soon they were singing:

Wasn't that a wonder in the heaven?
Wasn't that a wonder in the heaven?
Yeah, wonder in the heaven?

Woman clothed in the sun,
Moon underneath her feet,
Crown on her head,
And the wind tied 'round her waist!

Here in John's vision was the message they sought, the knowledge that though they had reached the Island at the end of the earth and could not go safely north, east, south or west, there was a city of golden trumpets that awaited them, where they would wear white clothes over their bodies and reflect stars in their hair.

When it was all over and Preacher John rode away on his donkey, Wes pondered on it with a heavy heart. For they had grasped at the preachments like drowning people, as though each of them knew that freedom now lay only in a thin threadlike road that stretched into the sky. Liberty Island, Wes thought, was the pointed end of the antelope horn. As one entered the horn there was room to turn or return, to make choices. But when one had followed the spiraling course to the point of the horn there were no choices left, and one could escape only in visions.

Yet for himself Wes was moved by the certainty that his Fa had not yet been acted out, and he sought to discover what it would be. This poised moment in the point of the horn, perhaps it was merely a place where Mawu had paused to rest in the writing of the story, which remained unfinished.

One night he dreamed he was back among the Tsoyaha, hunting with Kuba, then lying again with Agagonay in the open fields. He awoke with the knowledge that he had not left Agagonay behind after all. His distress was turbulent. He could not eat the roasted fish that Ransom provided. The pain left him slowly as he worked with the fishing crew, and by evening he had almost forgotten it. But that night he dreamed of Agagonay again. They were sitting quietly somewhere together, and he saw her face clearly and without the distortions that dreams sometimes bring. It was as though they had just awakened together for the thousandth time, and she was preparing to soften buckskin to make leggings for him, and he was making ready to join the hunters in the forest.

The dream of Agagonay and the Tsoyaha came back again and again, and sometimes he sought sleep eagerly with the knowledge of what it would bring him. There were some dreams that disappeared from the mind almost instantly when the eyes were open to the light of day, but these dreams of Agagonay persisted even while he was at work under the hot sun. There came a question in his mind sometimes whether what seemed to be real all around him, Liberty Island and all it contained, was not in fact the dream that came in the night, while the village of the Tsoyaha was the reality. It was as though Mawu had relented what had been written and was now recasting the Fa of Hwesuhunu the Fon.

He awoke one morning remembering that in his sleep he had seen Agagonay crowned with stars and girdled with the winds. Thus had the vision of St. John touched him. He felt as though the vodoun Mawu had sat by his side in the darkness of night to reveal something. He knew now what he would do—return to the village of the Tsoyaha to claim Agagonay. He contemplated on what had to be finished here on Liberty Island. He could think of nothing yet to be done, for the Island was only a way station, where each person had in his mind thoughts of where he might go and how it might be accomplished, or perhaps the thought of merely resting until death resolved what had no other solutions.

This was what the preacher had brought, a vision of a road that led not into the wilderness again or back to the slave quarters, but to a place where there would be no more unequal struggle, where faith and good behavior provided invulnerable armor against the predatory evils of the world. They would wait here, fishing for catfish and eels, until the seventh trumpet was blown and the lightning rent the sky and the stars fell like hot coals. The road would open then, and they would follow it, and at the end their shoulders would be draped with white cotton cloth and they would stand in diffused light reflecting from a golden throne. This single hope remained, to have their names written on the gateposts of the city.

On Liberty Island there was nothing to finish. Wes could leave tomorrow, the next day, or instantly, for it would change nothing. But his eyes fell on Ransom poking up the fire, and he saw one thing that had to be done. He arose and went to Entoto to ask the dokpwe for clothing for Ransom and himself. A meeting was called, and a few hours after that some tattered but clean clothes were provided for the two of them. That night there was a torchlight dance in the camp. When dawn came, Wes and Ransom crossed over to the mainland, and in a few hours the Island had fallen away into the past.

Wes's eyes searched out familiar landmarks, and he sought to retrace the route he had taken when he came to Liberty Island. But the landmarks that had seemed so evident then were elusive, and he guided himself mostly by the sun and by instinct. He felt relieved when, on the second morning, he spotted the mud-chinked cabin of the old man who had described Liberty Island as a devil's ball. As they reached the edge of the little clearing, Wes paused, waiting to see the old man emerge with his ax from behind the woodpile. But there was no sign of life, and they approached the cabin and entered. A squirrel scampered across the floor and went out through the chimney. The leather hinges of the door had been gnawed away, and nut shells littered the fireplace. Daylight came through the walls where the mud chinking had fallen from the logs.

"He's gone," Wes said. "Ain't been here for a long time from the looks of it."

They made their way along the creek. Wes paused to examine the fresh marks of horses' hooves where the ground was soft.

"Most likely more of them bounty hunters," Wes said to Ransom. "We got to be on the lookout for them."

Three days later they reached the clearing where Wes had last seen Jaeger. He felt a pang of alarm, for there was no smoke coming from the cabin chimney, no sign that the place had been inhabited in recent days. A warped shutter blew listlessly in one of the windows. Ransom sensed Wes's concern and watched his face closely for a clue to its meaning. Then there was a sound of breaking brush near the river and Jaeger appeared with a sack of booty from the forest. They went forward to meet him.

Jaeger stopped, his eyes going from Wes to Ransom and back again. "Ach!" he said at last. "So here is the *neger* again! And now you go the other way? So much coming and going, you tramp down the grass and make a damned highway past my house. And a little *neger* too. Is he yours? Maybe you make him? No, you do not have enough time. Now I have two savages. You think I have an inn here? I am not a damned innkeeper. And do not shoot any more of my deer."

"Uncle," Wes said, "I won't shoot no more deer."

"But you think to sleep in my cabin, all the same."

"We can sleep on the ground," Wes said. "I ain't stayin' for long. Got a ways to go."

"Why do you talk so much?" Jaeger said. "The little one does not make so much talk."

"He call himself Ransom," Wes said. "He can hear, but he can't talk. Couldn't leave him behind on the Island, he got no folks."

Jaeger looked at Ransom more closely. "So," he said impatiently, "if he can't talk maybe he can eat. You want to starve him? A boy can't live on grasshoppers."

Wes sent Ransom to gather firewood, and he himself carried Jaeger's sack to the cabin. Then he went out with his musket for meat, Jaeger calling after him: "No deer, you hear? Do not shoot the deer!"

Near a fallen tree under which he found a burrow Wes killed a large groundhog. He brought it back and skinned it. When Jaeger saw what it was he exclaimed: "Ach! My marmot! Now you are killing my marmots!"

"He's a groundhog," Wes said.

"You dumbhead, a groundhog is a marmot."

"Well," Wes said, "he taste like a groundhog. Indians eat them all the time."

"Never mind the damned Indians!" Jaeger shouted. "I do not care what they eat!"

But when the groundhog was roasted over the hot coals in the fireplace Jaeger ate his share of it.

Exhausted by the long journey, Ransom fell asleep among a litter of bags and rags on the cabin floor.

"So now you have had enough of rooting in the woods," Jaeger said. "You are going back to the plantation?"

"No, Uncle, I must go back to the Tsoyaha camp."

"Come and go, come and go! So busy! Why can't you stay in one place?"

"Ain't never find the place," Wes said.

"So you go to the Indians, then you go somewhere else, then you come back and eat my marmots some more. Who is chasing you then?"

"They was men chasing me, but I have lost them. They ain't chasing me no more out here."

"Maybe they are not chasing you, maybe you are chasing them. You, with all the coming and going, they just sit, yes? And wait for you. Ach, the damned *neger* with the running feet."

"I am goin' 'cause I must find the Tsoyaha again. Uncle, if you please, I got to leave Ransom with you till I come back. He'll chop kindlin' for you, set traps for rabbit, skin them, make the fire, do everythin' you need. He won't be no burden. Got no one else to ask for this thing."

"What!" Jaeger roared. "*Verdammt!* You're not going to leave me with your pickaninny! Everywhere the *negers* are making babies, so I have to have one yet? Take him and get out of my place! I am no black mammy! I am not a damned Christian, either, so do not come to me with stories to break my heart like a dumbhead! With the stupid people there is always talk, talk, and not a word of sense in it, only cotton and money and ladies. Of this I have had enough in my life. If I want babies I would stay on the plantation."

"Uncle," Wes said, "Ransom won't never bother you with talk."

Jaeger was silent then, and Wes continued: "This boy got no one. Never found out what happen to his folks, he ain't had the way to tell me. But I swear on the Good Book. . . ."

"Oh, now you are giving me the Good Book! Can't you swear on the grave of your father or the virtue of your damned sister? What good is swearing on the Good Book for a *neger* who jumps around like a bouncing ball?"

"Uncle, I can't take the boy, 'cause the distance is too far. When I find Agagonay I will surely come back for him."

"What is this Agagonay, then? You are looking for Inca gold?"

"She is a girl belong to the Tsoyaha people."

"Ha! While you chase through the woods like a satyr, Jaeger nurses a baby!"

"Ransom goin' to look after you good, Uncle."

"If he cries I give him something to cry for."

"He don't cry. Ain't never once cry about anything."

"My marmots they kill, then they give me babies," Jaeger said. And now his mind turned to other things.

Wes left the cabin long before morning without waking Jaeger or Ransom. There was a bright moon, and it was almost like day. He followed the river as far as a bend, then struck out through unfamiliar fields, sensing his way like a forest creature. In his mind he could already see the Tsoyaha village.

But an undefinable uneasiness came upon him, a vague

awareness that all was not well. Once he loitered on a high rise of ground to survey the landscape, though he saw nothing that should not have been there. His malaise faded, but it came again that night while he camped at the edge of a brook, a feeling that something was amiss. He slept fitfully. For reasons he did not altogether understand, he set out earlier than usual the next morning, before the sky was light, and he walked rapidly. Later he detoured to the crest of a hill and climbed into the upper branches of a pine. In the distance there was the misty silhouette of a low mountain range, and to the south a thin column of smoke rose into the air from a plantation, but there was nothing to account for his discomfiture. Nevertheless, the feeling did not leave him.

He stopped to fish whenever he found a likely brook or stream, though usually he did not eat until he camped for the night. Once while moving along the river bank he saw a party of woodcutters on the far side. He paused to listen to them sing and to hear their axes biting into the wood. They were comforting sounds that reminded him of his distant home in Yabo, but he suppressed an impulse to make his presence known and quickly slipped back into the cover of the trees. Another time he thought he heard the neigh of a horse behind him, but the sound did not come again and he was not sure.

Sometimes he saw deer, but the thought of shooting them was put aside even though he was hungry. Who might hear the shot and what it would mean to them he didn't know, but he remained certain that something hostile shared the wilderness with him, as though a leopard lurked among the trees, watching his movements and waiting. Lying in his bed of pine needles one night, Wes decided that he must establish the nature of the unknown thing that intruded on the wilderness.

In the morning, instead of continuing on his way, he retraced his course. His mind sought out each sound he heard, identified it, and classified it. One by one the sounds of a croaking frog, a crow's cawing, and the wind in the trees were registered and put aside. There was a disturbance in the underbrush that he translated into partridge taking to the air. But later there was a sound behind a sound that caused Wes to stop and listen instantly. This time he was certain—a neighing horse, somewhere along the river bank.

He did not press his way directly to the river, but circled around a sprawling marsh. He approached slowly, stepping carefully to avoid dry leaves and twigs. When he reached the open ground overlooking the river bank he saw them, five men fording from the other side, four of them on horses, the fifth walking behind. They stopped when they reached the near bank, and the horsemen dismounted. There was something familiar about them, but they were too far away. Wes maneuvered closer behind his screen of briars and vines.

He looked again just as one of the men turned his way. He recognized them now—the bounty hunters, the same party that had once questioned Jaeger about runaways. Three white men and an Indian tracker. The fifth man, the one without a horse, sat partially obscured by a fallen tree. Wes had to shift his position again to see him. Even before he had a view of the man's face, Wes recognized him by his size and the shape of his head. Descamps, the Rooster, sat with his shoulders thrust forward, his arms tied behind. So it had happened. He had been exiled from Liberty Island to be pursued and caught, and the sentence was being carried out. For his crimes against his own kind Descamps would now be sold at bargain rates, and perhaps be carted off to Mississippi Territory.

But Wes's satisfaction was diluted by the sight of the men whom fate had made an instrument of justice. He remembered King Adanzan, who had sold his own people into slavery, and felt a pang of guilt. Perhaps what had been done to Descamps on the Island was not justice after all, merely revenge, for one does not give to an enemy who does not understand justice the power to exact it. Could have shot him down ourselves, Wes thought, maybe that would have been better.

He brushed away thoughts of Descamps as unimportant and pondered on whether it was mere accident that the hunters followed him. Perhaps they were merely on their way to a slave market with their prize. Yet if this were so, why had he been so aware of their presence? No, his awareness had meaning, it was the Old People speaking to him. They would not have come to disturb his thoughts without good reason. The Indian moved out of sight, and when he returned he spoke earnestly, pointing to the ground and gesturing toward the east. They were discussing signs of Wes Hunu's passage. There was no doubt that he was the quarry. But they appeared to be unhurried in their pursuit.

Wes retreated into the underbrush and fled for several hours without rest. He reflected on his alternatives. He could go on to the Tsoyaha village. There he would be safe. Or he could return to Jaeger's place. Or he could seek out such desolate parts of the wilderness that they would not follow. The decision to go on to where Agagonay was waiting came easily. He did not stop to catch fish that day, eating only wild berries that he found along the way. The next day he shot a groundhog, unmindful of the signal he was giving to the hunters. Thereafter when he approached a human settlement he did not skirt it as widely as before. There was not time enough. Sometimes he went along man-made paths or logging trails.

He worried sometimes that he might have drifted too far to the north and that he might miss the Tsoyaha village by a good many miles. And so when he came unexpectedly on the camp of an Indian family, he did not avoid it but approached to ask questions. The Indians, one old man, one young, two women and several naked children, aware of his coming even before he emerged into the clearing, were grouped near their temporary shelter waiting for him. The young man stood holding a musket across his chest. The old one sat before the shelter, a ragged blanket around his shoulders.

Wes wondered nervously whether they were Creek. He addressed the old man, first in English, then with the few words of Tsoyaha that he knew, but the old man seemed to understand nothing. At last Wes said simply the word Tsoyaha over and over again. The Indians spoke together, then the old man said the word Yuchi. "Yes, Uncle," Wes said, "Yuchi, some folks call them so." The old man motioned vaguely toward the east. Wes went on, still not certain about his route, but relieved that they had shown no special interest in him.

In time he came to the river again. Fording at a shallow place, he followed the opposite bank for half a day, then crossed back again. That night as he camped he was certain that he heard the voices of the hunters upriver, and in the morning he heard a muffled musket sound. The bounty men were getting their breakfast.

That day he sought to confound his pursuers by leaving a meandering trail with large gaps in it. Clinging to driftwood he floated slowly downriver for several hours, and did not come back to the land until he became snagged in a wild tangle of half-submerged tree roots and debris at a sluggish bend. His arms ached from holding his powder up to keep it dry. He left the river bank and its clouds of mosquitoes and found his way to a meadow on higher ground. When night came he lay down to sleep in a field of tall grass, aware that once his trail was found again the Indian stalker would inevitably make his way to this very spot. But his body ached, and he slept heavily without moving.

When he opened his eyes the sun was already above the treetops. He did not wake naturally, of his own accord. A faint though threatening sound had penetrated into his slumbering mind, and he reached for his musket and loaded it. His eyes searched for the slightest movement in the tall grass. There was no movement, but the sound came again, the brushing of a moving body against undergrowth. He pointed his musket and fired, then bent low and raced to the shelter of a clump of trees. There he reloaded, took a last look behind him, and went on, first running, then walking, then running again. He never considered that the sound had been made by a deer or a groundhog. What it was he knew too well. He struggled through virgin thickets unmindful of the tearing of thorns against his skin, resolved to leave his trail, if he must, through places where a man could not follow on horseback.

In the late afternoon he emerged once again into open fields that sloped gently up the side of a partially wooded hill. At the crest he climbed a tree and looked back at the terrain he had crossed. Beyond the fields, and beyond the low-lying underbrush behind them, Wes saw the hunters, tiny in the distance, hardly seeming to move. Even as he watched, the sun moved closer to the horizon and the horsemen were lost to sight in the lengthening shadows.

Wes accepted now that they would follow him as certainly as death follows life. Whatever twists and turns he might take, they would come, patient, unhurried, stalking their prey. He likened them to the messengers of Fa, relentless, without passion or anger, acting out the text of what Mawu had written down before Hwesuhunu the Fon was born. Yet balancing this certainty, Wes now understood that Agagonay, too, was a part of his Fa. Therefore the pursuit could not be the end. He slept on the ground again that night, his loaded musket clutched in his hand. In the dawn he awoke to the sight of a young rabbit nibbling the dewed grass only an arm's length away, and he struck it down before it was even aware of him. He cleaned it and ate the flesh raw, gratified by the omen that his flight was not to be the final act of Mawu's drama.

Henceforth Wes hardly deviated from his course except

to skirt impossible terrain. His feeling of panic disappeared. Once at the Tsoyaha village he would be safe. He had several musket balls left, and he resolved to use no more than one of them for game. He no longer worried about leaving marks of his passage behind him. Whether they lost his tracks or not didn't matter. He stopped frequently to refresh himself at the river. And when he saw a doe one afternoon he killed it with the single shot he had allowed himself. He built a fire that night and smoked part of the meat. For several days thereafter he lived on smoked venison and wild berries.

A time came when he felt the nearness of his destination. A certain hill seemed familiar. He remembered crossing a stream at a particular place. He recognized the turns and twists of a faint game trail. And suddenly he was in the wide field where the battle with the Muskogee had occurred. He stopped and remained motionless, taking it all in, remembering the old man Katanay sitting like a king on his horse waiting for the Muskogee attack. He loitered with the memory even after it faded, anticipating what was yet to come. His heart quickened, knowing that Agagonay, her digging stick in hand, would be the first to greet him. She would stand up in the field and shade her eyes from the sun with her arm, and she would wait for him to approach. Wes felt his body tremble as though he had the swamp fever. He moved on across the battlefield, passed through the familiar grove, and came to the high ground overlooking the village.

His eyes moved across the meadow, from the wall of trees behind to the lake's edge. At first his mind refused to acknowledge what he saw. Perhaps he was mistaken, perhaps he must go on to the meadow beyond. But there were the cottonwoods. There was the small stream from which the drinking water came. And on the ground where he stood was the trail that led to the fishing cove. But where the houses had been there was nothing.

He crossed through knee-high grass and came to the place where the nearest house should have stood. From there he could see everything that remained to be seen, a flat stretch marked by patterns of charred wood, nothing more. He walked as though in a dream. Here where Katanay's house had stood there was only a rectangle of hard packed earth through which new seedlings were pressing up among blackened wood that had once been roof poles. He moved on to the next place, now only an empty square of ground over which wild morning glory vines climbed among patches of ashes. He entered where the door would have been. There was nothing to be seen there except a half-burned moccasin. The nature of the disaster was slowly forming into pictures in his mind, but he rejected them. He went slowly to the place where Kuba's house had stood and looked long at the bits of charcoal that littered the ground.

It seemed like a dream from which he must certainly awake, but there was no awakening. He saw the circle of stones where the food had been cooked and a broken pestle nearby. The emptiness was absolute. Here where men and women had lived the gift of life there was nothing, only markings on the earth which would soon be obliterated by other life reclaiming what it considered its own. As Wes looked at the vanishing lodge sites, he was struck by the thought that not all of the Tsoyaha had departed. For there were the bodies of those who had been buried beneath the earthen floors. And here he stood among them, his only link to those Tsoyaha who had given him a place in their village, among whom he had fished, hunted, and loved. Or were there perhaps other links, still unburied?

The scene that he had not wanted to see broke upon him then, the Muskogee edging through the trees silently in the night, and in the faint gray light of the false dawn falling on the village with lances, muskets, battle-axes and fire. If the Tsoyaha had merely moved to a new hunting site they would not have burned the village down, but left it for a return some other day. Wes was taken by an unbearable agony. Had

Agagonay been carried away as a prize of war, or was she among the dead? And Kuba and all the others?

He wandered down to the lake, his thoughts in turmoil. He saw the prow of a broken canoe thrusting out of the water, a silent eddy around it. Among the reeds nearby lay what remained of a Tsoyaha, as could be told from the buckskin leggings.

Wes wanted to see no more. He tried to empty his mind, to think of nothing at all, and he went back into the shelter of the trees with no purpose except to flee and no conscious awareness of where he was going. The trembling came on him again. He lay down by a great oak, and even while the evening light still lingered in the sky he found escape in sleep from a hurt that was too great.

When Wes awoke his muscles trembled involuntarily, and he knew that he had the swamp fever. He ate what was left of his smoked venison and returned to the site of the village. Almost listlessly he prowled among the ruins searching for something that might contradict what he already knew. He found a string of stone beads hanging on a tree where a Tsoyaha man had placed it. A battle-ax whose handle had been burned away, a digging stick lying in the long grass, broken pots, a clay pipe with tobacco that had never been lighted, charred buckskin clothing. There was no reprieve in any of them. Each discovery only filled out the picture of the massacre, as did the bodies Wes found in the surrounding meadow. There were fourteen of them, all anonymous now. Wes sought to recall who each of them was, but they had given up their identity. From the clothing he could tell only that women as well as men had died, nothing more.

With his knife and a digging stick he scooped out the ground and buried the dead where he found them, marking their shallow graves with stones. He had to stop frequently because of the fever attacks that shook his body, and it was nearly night when he was finished. His inner hurt left no room in his mind for concern about the bounty hunters, though he knew they could not be far away. He returned among the trees and lay on a carpet of pine needles. He did not really sleep, but rather slipped downward into darkness and hovered between dreams and the night sounds that surrounded him. Once it seemed that he was laboriously writing a letter which said: *Dear Jaeger, I am very sorry I can't come back for Ransom. When I entered the horn of the world it was large, but now I have come to the pointed end, and it is small and dark and there is no room left.*

He wondered if the earth would ever again turn light. But eventually the eye of day opened, and Wes lay watching a beam of sun that came through the leaves overhead and fell upon his body. There was no need to go anywhere, and he had no desire to eat or drink. Here the bounty hunters would find him, and here he would come face to face with Fa. It occurred to him that Sosu, his father, would want to know everything that had happened, and that he would have to tell the story so that the parts came together, so that his name, Thing-of-the-Sea, would be finally explained and understood. He tried to recall all of the things that had fallen on him since he left Yabo, but each thing remained separate to itself, refusing to merge.

The fever in his body and his acceptance of fate blurred one into the other. He had no will to run any further, or even to arise from where he lay. His mind was slipping down into darkness again when he heard the voices of the hunters somewhere out beyond the dead cornfields. He calculated the route they would take into the ghostly village, and he thought of going out to meet them.

Then without reason the fluid of life began to flow again, and his mind cleared. He stood up and began to move cautiously, but soon he was running. At the edge of the lake he found a broken tree limb and pushed it into deep water. Kicking his feet, he floated his blind away from the shore, keeping his head just high enough to breathe. He stopped and allowed the eddies to become still almost at the moment the horsemen came riding into the meadow. As before, Descamps followed on foot, attached by a long leash to the saddle of the last rider. The Indian dismounted and examined the ground, walking first one way and then another trying to make a story out of the crisscross of tracks Wes had left there. He pointed to the east, then set about making a fire. The other hunters also dismounted and lounged in the shade. Descamps sat against a tree, his chin resting on his chest, his shoulders thrust forward awkwardly.

The shaking came on Wes again and his teeth chattered. The water felt like winter on his skin. He prayed that they would go on quickly, but they loitered and made no move to depart until they had cooked some bacon and eaten it. Two of the men came to the edge of the lake and stood looking out on the water. Their eyes rested for a moment on Wes's float, then turned elsewhere. Finally two of the hunters and the Indian mounted and rode away slowly. The other man remained behind with Descamps who, his arms now freed, began to construct a lean-to. The scene signaled to Wes that the two men, captor and captive, would camp there for the night while the others closed in on the quarry.

He began to move his blind toward the shore below the camp. It seemed an endless time before he felt the ground under his feet. He could not control his shivering, and he lay motionless on the shore allowing the sun to warm him. Suddenly he remembered the musket that he had left behind among the trees, and he lurched weakly to his feet and made his way back to where he had slept in the night. The musket was there, but he realized that his powder was sodden with lake water. Further on he found a rocky sun-warmed outcropping, and there he removed his clothes to let them dry. He clung naked to the warm rocks until the shivering passed, and then his mind drifted back again to the Tsoyaha disaster.

When he thought of Agagonay it was without the hurt

he had felt at first. The original pain had become dull and heavy deep inside him. He sensed that he would feel it again at another time, but for the moment it was contained, like the shaking that came with the swamp fever. He was able to wonder almost without emotion whether it was fate or fear of fate that had caused him to leave Agagonay. He remembered saying to Julian that the Tsoyaha had the proudness of death. Thus the proudness of death was their fate. Or was it, rather, their choice? If so, were not his own actions also chosen? But the choices a man made were always consistent with his character, and there, finally, was the ingredient of Fa.

Then, against his will, he was thinking again of Descamps. The picture he saw was not the drunken tyrant of Liberty Island, but the dark-skinned man sitting awkwardly on the ground with bound arms, or plodding wearily behind the horses. Knowing Descamps's crimes, Wes was impatient with himself. *Serves you right,* he said to Descamps. *What them bounty chasers do to you don't bother me at all. You done earn all of it.* But the picture of the arm-bound captive would not leave him.

When his clothes were dry Wes put them on, thinking now about the strategy of escape, and beyond that, about where he would go. Ever since leaving Liberty Island, the Tsoyaha village had been the ultimate destination. There had been the certainty that once among his Tsoyaha friends the need for critical decisions would no longer exist. He would have been content to stay with the Tsoyaha, to fight by their side, if necessary, against the Creek or any other predators, to merge his life with theirs. And he could have had pride, too, for the proudness of death was only the willingness to face death in exchange for the gift of life. But now the Tsoyaha were gone, and he could not follow. They had left no message for him, no word from Agagonay, or Kuba, or Katanay, or Julian, nothing more than a string of beads hanging in a tree. He took the beads from his pocket and hung them around his neck.

He saw the sun declining in the west. Back there, somewhere, was Liberty Island and, beyond it, Mississippi Territory. In that direction there was no escape. Toward the east there was only densely settled plantation country, the cities and towns, and eventually the ocean, and should he go that way he would one day surely hang. And there was the Spanish territory to the south where a dark skin was a certain sentence to a slow death in the fields. He wondered where John Paul Sampson had gone. Was he, too, still roaming the wilderness, or had they caught him at last, or had he somehow broken through the circle and found his way to his friend in Ohio?

Ohio. It was somewhere to the north, how far he had no notion, and what lay between was mystery. His thoughts strayed, but they came spiraling back around the word as though it were a solid form like a stone. Like the word Dahomey, Ohio had an essence all its own. It was more than a place, it was a thing with profound inner meanings. He could not picture its shape or hear its voice, but he knew it to be there in the same way he knew the vodouns and the ancestors were there. Like Old Ned's salvation, it was something that could not be experienced except by revelation.

No more than a mile away was the camp of the pursuers, so close that if the wind were right Wes could call out and be heard. Yet he felt no panic. He sat without moving from the rocks, searching for the meaning of his presence in this place, and formulating, without being aware of it, a course of action. He knew that soon, perhaps the next day, or even during the night, the absent hunters would return with the certainty that he had not continued in that direction.

It was time now to move again. He glanced once more at the setting sun, and turned his face toward the north. He calculated the advantages the bounty hunters would have. Horses, supplies, greed for money and, like the overseer Rousseau, whom he remembered now only dimly, relentless-ness without passion. He calculated his own disadvantages. He must stay in the wilds. He must stop to forage for food. He must keep forever moving. He could not walk openly down the carriage drive of any plantation, nor through the streets of any town. His color alone would sound an alarm. And should he be detained anywhere there was not a single fragment of law that would protect him, for he had violated almost everything that the Masters deemed sacred. It would be another long journey of Atogon, the hunter, searching for release from the land of the No Name People and the talking skulls. And what did he have on his side? One thing only. He was Hwesuhunu the Fon.

Down in the camp there was still Descamps. What was his part in all of this, and what was the inner meaning of his name? What had Mawu written down in his book for this man? He was a random element of evil, like smallpox and death by lightning. And the burden he carried inside him was not his slavery but his malevolent character. But wasn't his character really a decree of Fa? For no man endows himself with character.

Wes sensed the direction of his thoughts and tried to divert them. But his mind was now seized of Descamps, and he could not relinquish him. *What part do I have in the Fa of Descamps? We have crossed paths like wild game in the forest, nothing more. I have nothing to do with him and he has nothing to do with me.* But he knew it was not so, for everything a man saw or touched became united. Every stone a man walked on, every dream he dreamed, every word spoken and heard, all were tied together for all time. Good did not exist alone in the world, neither among men nor among vodouns. Descamps was an expression of wild and untamed forces, an extension of the vodoun Legba who cheated, tricked and raped. Descamps was compounded of whim and readiness to destroy what other men valued. But it was said by the Old Ones that good and evil must feed upon each other as long as the world exists.

Wes understood now. The sun was already setting. He arose to go down to the camp, and he stopped only to pick a few blackberries to quiet his hunger. When he arrived at last at the edge of the Tsoyaha meadow it was already night, but the full moon was high and the details of the camp were clearly visible. A small fire burned in front of the lean-to, in which, presumably, the hunter was already sleeping. It was a little time before he spotted Descamps half-reclining against a tree to which he was trussed. He did not see the horse until it snorted and rolled over on its back from one side to the other. It was part way between the lean-to and the trees, and there was no difficulty in reaching it. At the sight of Wes, the horse came to its knees and stood up, but it couldn't move away because it was tethered. Wes led it slowly to the tree line and tied it there. Crawling on his belly now, he went for Descamps across the flat and naked ground. Until Wes was no more than an arm's length away, Descamps heard nothing, but then he stiffened, craning his neck around in alarm.

"Hush up," Wes warned. "Don't make no noise. I'm cuttin' you loose."

"Who's that?" Descamps whispered hoarsely.

"Keep down," Wes said. He took his knife from his belt and cut the rope that held Descamps's wrists behind him. "Come on," Wes whispered, "don't kick the ground and don't make no shadows."

They began to creep across the moonlit field. Descamps said: "Where we goin' to?"

"Down in the jungle," Wes said. "Stop talkin'. You can talk later."

"Hold on," Descamps said, "got to fetch somethin'." He began to crawl toward the lean-to.

"Come on, we got no time!" Wes said urgently. But Descamps was already on his way. When he returned he had something clutched in both hands. "What you got?" Wes whispered.

"Got that boy's bacon and his corn liquor," Descamps said gleefully.

They reached the horse and mounted, Wes in front and Descamps behind, and rode in the shadow of the trees till they reached the cornfields. Once out of the meadow they headed north, guided by the north star that was only faintly visible because of the moon's brightness. Descamps wasted no time in uncorking the bottle and drinking.

"I'll have some of that," Wes said. Descamps handed him the bottle. Wes felt warmth and strength flowing into him as he drank. He returned the bottle. Descamps didn't cork it again but drained it and threw it into the brush. Only then did he begin to think about Wes. "Seem like I knows you," he said, "but I just can't place the name."

"Wes Hunu."

"What's that again?"

"Wes Hunu."

"Oh, yeah, now I place it," Descamps said, not really placing it, though there was something about it that troubled him. It was only when they dismounted for the night on the edge of a natural clearing that Descamps saw Wes's face clearly for the first time.

"You the boy that burnt down the gov'ment, ain't you?" There was open hostility in his voice. Wes felt a heavy weariness coming over him. He nodded.

"And run me and my colonels off like dogs?"

"They was quite a few men wanted to kill you," Wes said.

"Knocked down the whole gov'ment! Should of turned you out the first day you come." He pondered on it, then was struck by a new thought. He spoke sharply. "What you want with me?"

"Just turned you loose, that's all."

"Turned me loose? Ain't nobody goin' to do that without he's got somethin' in mind. What you do it for?"

Wes was too tired to argue it. "Just wanted to get you out."

Descamps peered around suspiciously.

"Believe I catch on to you, Hunu. Believe you is out to get the bounty money yourself!" Triumphant to have fathomed the riddle, he went on: "Well, now, how you like what I got in mind for you? Maybe I get the bounty on you instead? How you like that one?"

"I don't want nothin' from you, Descamps."

"Then how come you fetch me out?" Descamps's mind was churning. He recalled the way Wes had been dressed that first day on Liberty Island. He remembered the Indian shirt. And it came to him that Hunu was a black Creek. "Well, I'm on to you, nigger! You fixin' to turn me over to the Creeks, ain't you?" He looked around him again, peering into the shadows nervously. " 'Fore I let you do that, black boy, believe I goin' to break you in two."

Wes cocked the musket, aware that it was unloaded and that his powder was wet. But Descamps moved back.

"Toss over the bacon," Wes said.

"Bacon? What bacon you talkin' about?" Descamps said almost plaintively.

"The bacon you thief down there."

"You say I thief somethin'?"

"Don't come close, just toss it," Wes said.

Descamps tossed it on the ground at Wes's feet. "You ain't goin' to take it all? You got to give me some, Hunu."

Wes cut it into two pieces and threw one back to Descamps. He knew now he could not risk camping the night with Descamps. He went back to the horse and mounted again.

Descamps protested. "Hey, where you goin' with my horse?"

"Your horse?"

"Yeah, been thiefed from my place, ain't it?"

"Descamps, I cut you loose, you got to hoe your own row

now. Where you go I don't care, but you got to make it on your own."

"They goin' to hang you for thiefin' that horse! You take off on it and I'll go back there an' tell those men where you're at! That finish you off good, Hunu!"

Wes wheeled the horse around.

Descamps's tone was wheedling again. "You goin' to leave me here for the Creeks, Hunu? Why you do a thing like that?"

"Ain't no Creeks out here," Wes said.

"Then why you fetch me? Answer me that one."

"Don't know as I can tell you, Descamps. You ain't no good to me or no one else. I'd like it a whole lot better if you'd been John Paul Sampson 'stead of who you are. But you cross my path, and you're black like me. Maybe your folks come from Abomey for all I know, or maybe they was Nago. Anyway you and me is the only black men around here, and that makes you my cousin. That's all they is to it. You find your way out of the wilderness, and I'll find mine."

He kicked the horse, and it started to walk.

"I'll see they gets you!" Descamps called after him. "They goin' to catch you for thiefin' that horse!"

Wes observed the moonlight shadow of a horse and rider on the ground beside him. He acknowledged it silently, as though it were a companion. He noted that the dark rider's back was bent, sharing his own exhaustion. The horse stumbled once, and Wes clutched blindly at its mane to keep from sliding off.

Then there was Descamps again: "Where you think you goin' to?"

"Ohio," Wes said, his voice echoing in his ears as though it belonged to another, perhaps his shadowy companion. He heard no conviction in it.

"You're crazy, black boy!" Descamps shouted. "You ain't never goin' to make it at all!"

Then, Wes thought, let it be this way. Atogon also had

to see the face of Fa. Does a man ever return from the land of the dead?

He heard Descamps's voice once more, faintly this time, sensing the hate without comprehending the words. He rode across the field, his head down, letting the horse find its own way in the night.

About the Author

HAROLD COURLANDER is a novelist, folklorist, and specialist in the oral traditions of African and Caribbean cultures. He has written more than thirty-five books, including the best-selling *The Cow-Tail Switch and Other West African Stories* and *The Drum and the Hoe: Life and Lore of the Haitian People*. He is a Guggenheim Fellow and has done much of his work with the assistance of academic research grants from various foundations. He is a former editor for the United Nations and a former political analyst for the Voice of America. He lives in Bethesda, Maryland.